Nigerians in Space

A *novel by*
Deji Bryce Olukotun

Unnamed Press
Los Angeles, CA

Unnamed Press
Los Angeles
www.unnamedpress.com

Cover art © Paul Wadell
Cover design by Ben Lutz
Unnamed Press logo by Eric Gardner

International Standard Book Number: 978-1-9394190-1-9

For Laate and Bayo

Table of Contents

Do you know where home is?

Do you want to go there?

Book I

The Moon Rock Thief

1993
Houston, Texas

Wale was in the locker room, dripping, after he'd just missed the final shot as point guard for his team in the West Houston, 30 and over, co-ed spring 1993 basketball C-league.

And he was opening his locker, hearing the clang, seeing the ball spinning out of bounds, over and over, with his head between his knees.

"Shake it off, Wale," Bill Dalton said. "You win some, you lose some."

Wale agreed with his teammate. But he didn't move.

"I was right under it, Wale, boxing out Perez just like we practiced. Another second on the clock and I would have had the rebound. Did you see me get him with my cross? I owned him."

Dalton began stripping down. He was a melonfaced ex-linebacker whose cheeks flushed crimson at the end of the first quarter, and held the color for a full two hours after a game. He ran a TGI Fridays restaurant franchise and a used car lot. Wale was stoutly muscular and could jump higher than anyone his size.

"We've got to peak, Wale. We want to take 'em in the playoffs. This was a size-up game to see what they're made of. Linda had six points, three blocks, four steals. That's half-way to a triple double." He patted Wale on the back. "Come on, pick your head up. We're going for a drink."

Wale managed to grab at the towel in his locker, and a tiny slip of paper spilled out from its folds. It looked like a receipt.

"I can't make it, Bill. I'm on the night shift."

"Tonight? It's Friday. You can't go to work sulking over a shot like that. It's bad luck. Just one beer."

Dalton believed in buying rounds, so it was never just a beer. He bought a drink for everyone present and then you had to buy the next round, so it made it worth your while to stick around until the rounds evened out. Then you were drunk.

"No, Bill, I'm almost late. I should be there already." Wale showered and dressed, spraying on liberal amounts of Old Spice. He shouted good-bye into the shower room, where Dalton was now jiggling his pot belly while singing the Beach Boys.

"You're the nightmare, Wale! The Nigerian Nightmare."

It was while Wale was fishing for his car keys that he felt the slip of paper again. Under the weak yellow halo of the cabin light of his Corolla, he read it: Call. N.B. 512-212-3235.

The shower had done nothing to clean him up and he was already sweating again under a low-hanging sky, the clouds brown and withering like late-autumn leaves. He stopped at a 7-Eleven and picked up a payphone. There was a clutch of Latino teens chattering in Spanish and they eyed him suspiciously. He dialed the telephone number, which forwarded the call to another number that he wasn't permitted to know. A voice picked up on the first ring.

"Wale Olufunmi?"

"Yes."

"This is Nurudeen Bello, Special Adjunct to the Minister of the Environment."

"I know who you are. I told your man to stop following me and there was a note in my locker."

"I've arranged everything," Bello said, ignoring him. "Get on the red-eye to Washington. The drop is at 11:26 tomorrow."

"There isn't a storm. Why do it now?"

"The situation has changed. Go to the Contingency Plan."

"Listen, Bello, I don't like any of this."

"Any of what?"

"I don't like this pressure. Let's let things settle down a bit, then I'll come."

"I told you we will deposit double, Dr. Olufunmi."

"It's not about the money. I'm not in this for the money."

Bello could be heard sighing on the other end of the line, exasperated. "We need you," he began, "because it's time to end the brain drain and move to brain gain. It's time for a great mind of Nigeria to return home. You're the mind we need, Doctor. The marsh can't pretend that it isn't fed by the river. You're a part of Nigeria, too."

A low-rider Honda pulled up in front of the 7-Eleven and the Latino teens began passing around a bottle in a paper bag. Bello continued on, quoting Winston Churchill and people getting the governments they deserved, complimenting Wale on his professional success. How Wale had rocketed to the top of the academic world as a lunar geologist, only to slam into a glass ceiling while Americans soared through to upper level positions and he rotted away in a lab. Wale wanted to keep up his guard, but Bello had a way of buttering things; Wale was a scientist and Bello a public relations man. In a battle of words Bello would win every time.

"Alright, Bello, tell me the details again. I want it clear."

"Everything is arranged," Bello said, infusing optimism into his voice. "I'll meet you in Washington. If anything goes wrong go to the fallback position in Cape Town. Until then, stick to the Contingency Plan."

"You mean the Contingency Sample. Why don't you just call it that?"

"Stick to the protocol, Doctor. This is for your own safety. The tickets are under your floor mat."

Wale looked back at his Corolla. Its mustard yellow coat took on a violated look under the arc lamps. Bello's insistence on code language had at first charmed him but now it was an annoyance, a blurring of meaning. He did not like the fact that someone had been in his locker or his car, and tried to convey this to Bello. They discussed the nitty-gritty of the drop.

"You'll be in Nigeria in forty-eight hours, Doctor," Bello said. "Take heart—you're going home!"

Wale dialed his wife Tinuke and told her to pack some essentials and retrieve a suitcase he'd stashed in the garage. In the background he heard his boy crying—tired, sick, or hungry.

"Our tickets aren't for two weeks," she protested.

"There's been a change of plans, Tinuke."

"I'll have to call Uncle Sheyi to let him know."

"No need. They're picking us up at the airport."

"You weren't fired, were you?"

"No, it's a good thing. A promotion. I'll explain everything later."

Tinuke told him the boy missed his Daddy, and this meant she missed him. Nowadays all their emotions were mediated through the child. He sulked back to the car. He knew that the basketball game had boded poorly; his feet had felt sluggish the whole first quarter and the rim shrank down to a thimble when he spotted it from the three-point line. He should have known: the operation would be tonight.

The highway was still smeared with mud from the flood, from the hurricane that had pulverized Galveston, from the tussling fronts of the Gulf. The sycamores reflected on the pavement's sheen with their sharp-fingered leaves. Somehow there was, at nine in the evening, still traffic. But driving by the stadium, he realized it was because there was a baseball game. Either the Astros were winning big or losing big, as it was too early for the game to be over and for so many people to be leaving. He tuned into the radio to prepare some office talk for the evening. Baseball had a wonderful way of whiling away the time, even after the game ended. Good stuff for a night shift.

The guard waved down his car at the second boom gate. He was a pimply guy fresh out of training college who chatted it up with the enthusiasm of a man who thought that guarding a boom gate at NASA's Johnson Space Laboratory was the first in a serendipitous series of steps to becoming Congressman. If he had known that what Wale was about to do would get him fired, he would have wiped the smug expression from his face. They exchanged some words about the baseball game and Wale followed the black mamba of a road to Building 31-A. He went to park in the unnumbered employee lot, and then decided it was his last day, so he parked in his boss' spot. A final thumb-on-the-nose.

The chickweed and nightshade and dewberries and all the love-making plants had sent out their pollen in droves and he sneezed, cursing the spring. He'd never had allergies in Nigeria, his nose had been stuffed by America and so was his thinking. Maybe Bello was right that he should return to the clear-minded motherland.

He swiped in his security card and made his way through the cubicles to his small, windowless office. His colleague Onur Unkwu wasn't in yet. But Onur was usually prompt, and would arrive within the next few minutes with a pastry in hand. Wale decided to beat it to the lab to avoid chatting with him. He was beginning to feel nervous, and thought he'd give himself away.

"Remember," Bello had said on the phone, "Brain gain."

"Can't we forget the contingency sample? Isn't it me you want?"

"Commitment. We believe in commitment. We are offering you a lot of money—more than you'll ever see in that play pen. We need a sign that you are on our side, Doctor, and haven't become one of those baseball-tossing coconuts. Brown on the outside and white on the inside, if you catch my meaning."

"I hate baseball," Wale said quickly. "Basketball is my game."

"That is what I'm afraid of. Our sport is soccer. You've been away too long, Doctor. Get me that sample and I'll see you in Nigeria. It's high time you came home!"

Wale hated the Contingency Plan and had fought Bello on it since they first started talking. The only plan that would leave him with any chance of backing out involved a hurricane. Then regular procedure demanded that all rocks would have to be moved above the water line and transferred to the double-wall vault. Taking a specimen in those conditions would be difficult, but possible. There was even a chance that he could get away with it and remain on the staff. But not the Contingency Plan. The Contingency Plan meant the end. He couldn't say good-bye to his colleagues or his basketball team or anyone.

The lunar lab was a sterile jumble of stainless steel, blinking LED lights, hard-backed aluminum chairs, magnetically shielded electronics, analog scopes, and full-spectrum overhead indirect lighting. It was—although few people had ever heard of it—America's repository for the hundreds of pounds of rocks that had been painstakingly transported back from the moon missions, and the largest and most sophisticated such repository in the world. Every rock that had been collected by the astronauts on the Apollo missions; every speck of dust that had swirled onto their spacesuits; every mite that had gathered in the lunar module; these had been rigorously preserved for decades.

Two doors opened at either end of the lab, one leading to a scanning electron microscope and the other to the double airlock, which in turn led to the Lunar Sample Collection. There was no lead in the paint or sheetrock and no organic matter. The plastic Christmas tree perched in the corner had never been removed because it was the closest thing to life that snuck in. But Wale was a scientist, hard-trained, and like the rest of the lab geeks all the life he needed was contained in the Lunar Sample Collection. Under the microscopes, the moonrocks teemed with the cosmos.

When he could get to them. Even as a senior staffer he could not access the collection himself. There had to be a Second during the day, and a guard to monitor the gas levels in the chambers. At night one person could access the collection while the other monitored. Usually it was Onur that went into the collection and Wale kept his eye on the dials. If you were alone, you had to occupy yourself with studying a low-priority specimen in the glass glovebox, a sealed aquarium with two rubber gloves welded into the glass. This Wale did, sticking his hands into the glovebox and nervously scratching off a layer of plagioclase feldspar from a fifty gram specimen that had been gathered by Apollo 16. The specimen had already been photodocumented on the moon, with the down-sun ratio, color chart, and stratigraphy inputted into the LSDB long ago.

There were three hours before Wale had to get on the plane. Panic flashed through him as he began to consider that he would never see the lab again. With panic came tachycardia; with palpitations, the memory that his father had died from an unidentified heart condition; with his father, a photo of his sister leaning precariously over the coffin, as if about to dive in; then his sister's family of step-this and half-that and her current invalid husband. And there was the matter that he hadn't sent anyone money in six years. And what of his mother? In the face of this Texan largesse, this first-world life?

Patience, Wale, patience. Where you begin your climb, the proverb went, there you will descend. He would deal with those problems when they came. He was returning his mind to Nigeria, he was going home. Wale would have his chance, finally, to go up in space. This was not a sacrifice. This was a dream being realized.

Patience becoming him, briefly, he honed away at the glassy black agglutinate of the specimen in the glovebox until Onur arrived.

"Say, Wale."

"Hey, Onur."

Onur was a barrel-chested man, a historical bulk descended from olive oil wrestlers and the legion of warriors called the Slappers, sent out by the Ottomans to absorb bullets and thump in the crania of the enemy. He also had, despite this, delicate fingers with plated rings on four of them and a stud in his lobeless ear. Onur was perhaps the most considerate man Wale had ever met, except when it came to the Kurds. The Kurds could never do anything right. The wounded look on Onur's face meant that something had happened between him and his beautiful Armenian wife.

"I am there until the seventh inning stretch," Onur whimpered. "It is a blowout. The Astros are losing by eight. I try to leave it early. But so does everyone else. And Lousine says she is hungry so we are eating. Then I am late."

Despite his numerous degrees Onur had managed to avoid learning to speak in anything other than the present tense. He was already taking off his rings and putting on the mask to go into the vault, but Wale stopped him.

"There's a specimen I'd like to check out, Onur."

"Oh?" Onur looked mildly interested.

"A four-three. There's some correlation with this agglute."

"You are running it under the SET?"

"No. The new directive said we can only access the microscope on Tuesdays. It's in the latest memo."

Onur shook his head. "Memos, schmemos."

"The h2o is set at four. There's some K.R.E.E.P. that I want to move in the seven-eighths."

"We are moving it last year."

"No, Tugwell was tasked with moving them. He never finished. Please sustain the levels for seven minutes."

Thank god for Tugwell, Wale thought, thank god for bureaucracy. Tugwell had provided any number of excuses since he'd been fired for corrupting a core sample of K.R.E.E.P.—a kind of sawdust from the surface of the moon—with a glob of milk chocolate. If anyone cared, a whole comic strip could have been written about Tugwell's antics in the moonrock business. Watery coffee, milky tea, dusty files and magnetic tapes, the old granules of cigarettes, must, egg-sandwiches melted into the cafeteria walls, the dull-aching bones of the people who swept up after him—thank god for bureaucracy. How much easier to steal from it.

And then Wale was in the hiss of the air shower and disappearing behind the mist into the vault with his mask. He had four minutes. Anything longer and Onur would become suspicious. Inside, the filtration system sputtered as it sucked up his terrestrial emissions. A row of stainless vaults squatted above a white linoleum floor, with blue LED lights on the front. All blue, all uncompromised. Any change in weight or chemical composition and the alarm would blow. He paced straight to the seven-eight vault and opened the thick-walled cabinet. With the h2o levels up the cabinet emitted a fine cloud of vapor. He reached into his lab coat and removed three glassine bags with coin-sized valves in them. 78-5329-23 was a small sample encased in a glass Petri dish, looking no more important than the rest. The 23 meant that it had already been contaminated, but that was the Contingency Sample, that was what Bello was paying him for. The 23: his commitment.

Wale emptied the contents of 23 into a glassine bag and removed a false Petri dish from his other pocket. After switching the Petri dish, he took the bag and walked quickly to the nitrogen tank. Attaching the hose to the valve, he vacuumed the air out of the bag and flushed in some nitrogen. He did the same for two more bags so that the specimen was protected, and kept these in his pocket. Next, he opened the

46 vault and removed a dimpled, ashen breccia rock that looked like a mangled barbecue briquette. He stepped back through the airlock trying to look innocent with the breccia extended before him, and set it in the glass glovebox.

"I am not seeing you on the monitor," Onur said. "You alright, Wale?"

"It was the h2o levels. You can take them down now."

Onur had produced a bag of Dunkin' Donuts from somewhere. A donut was gone but for a dollop of cream on his chin. Wale pointed at the dollop and tossed Onur a napkin.

"Thanks. No, I mean, you are tense. Is your wife okay?"

"By the grace of God, she is in good health."

"Oh, I am thinking you look tense. People are talking about you and the boss. You forget about him. He is a wonk. When he is going you will be promoted."

"I don't want a promotion."

"You are too modest, Wale. You deserve one—you are the best in the lab. Next to me," he laughed.

But Wale was speaking sincerely. He had long ago resigned himself to bureaucratic routine, joined a Rotary club and churned out journal articles to cut onto the academic circuit one day, an honorable change of career. But after Bello found him with Brain Gain that was all over. A dream had been reborn. He was going home.

Obliviously Onur wanted to talk about his wife. He swallowed a can of Mr. PiBB in one go, and suddenly burst into tears. "She is crushing me!" and he went on about her spending, the way she flirted with other men, the way she wouldn't give him a child, the way she threatened to move to Florida to live with her sister, "where at least they are having a beach with the heat. Lousine is too beautiful for any man to leave. As lovely as—as an agglutinated highland roid. She must leave me first, oh my brother."

Wale consoled him, pretending to cut away at the breccia rock he had extracted from the vault. And they went on comparing notes, Onur telling him how envious he was about Wale's little son Dayo, Wale peppering the conversation with astute observations about the clasts and melt of the breccia rock. Everything was going off fine.

Then the small B-tone of the alarm went off. Onur snapped to attention and rapidly toggled through some screens on the computer.

"It is the seven-eight. Are you closing up in there?"

Wale glanced at the screen. "Yes, I sealed it fine."

Onur typed away on his computer. "What's the number of the sample you moved?"

"Thirty-seven."

"It is twenty-three."

"Must have been the h2o."

"No, it is the weight. Off by a microgram."

They watched as the indicator light moved between blue and red. Onur tapped the screen.

"It appears to be vacillating," Wale observed. "Could be the scale."

"Yeah."

The indicator went back to blue for about thirty seconds, then dipped into red again.

"Hell, we are going to be worrying all night. I am taking a look."

"I'll do it."

"No, Daddy Wale, I am sitting on my ass all evening with donuts. You are staying here."

"I'll raise the h2o levels."

"No, I am a lightning flash."

Onur pulled off his rings and his chain and the stud in his nose and threw on his lab coat. No one could have guessed that he'd been crying a moment before, or that he'd likely do it again. Wale tried to protest but Onur was adamant and outranked him.

Nervously, Wale switched on the closed circuit camera to see Onur come onscreen in the airshower. Maybe Onur wouldn't notice, he thought. Maybe he would think it was just a hitch. Even if Onur did notice, though, he had no understanding of the sample or its true value.

No one besides Wale understood the significance of the twenty-three—but that didn't mean Onur couldn't suspect something. Suspicion could ruin him. Tampering with lunar samples could get you fired. Stealing— well, stealing was much, much more.

Onur strode to the seven-eight vault and keyed it open. He bent over and examined the sample on the shelf without budging it. He picked it up briefly and shook it around, then put it back on its shelf and watched. The scale LED held steady blue for a second, before dropping into red.

Dammit, Wale thought.

Onur picked the sample back up and took out a small flashlight, illuminating the sample. His actions began speeding up. He quickly turned and held the sample at the camera with an inquisitive look, and his lips were moving. Wale activated the sound monitor.

"Wale, what is this? It looks like it is from the mare."

Wale turned on his microphone. "You must be mistaken, Onur. Compare it with the—" and then suddenly he remembered that all microphone conversations were recorded. The tape room was in a different building entirely. He tried to sound reasonable. "Please repeat."

But Onur was starting to look suspicious. "Wale, what did you do here? Where is the twenty-three? Why are you—"

Wale flicked off the sound monitor. It wouldn't make a difference— the tape would still go through. He just couldn't bring himself to hear it anymore as Onur went through the inductions through his head, piecing it together.

"I stole," Wale whispered.

And his hands were moving fast. He manually bolted the airlock. He went to the dials. He pushed up the h2o and lowered the o2, pumped in n2. The gas could be seen hissing into the collection onscreen, and Onur immediately clutched at the mask, pressing it closer onto his face. He wouldn't be hurt but he would fall asleep.

Seal up the damn vault, he thought, seal it, Onur. Otherwise all the specimens in the seven-eight would be compromised. But Onur was already ahead of him and had pushed it shut. He was waving his arms in front of the camera lens and pointing at the gas hissing into the chamber.

Wale flicked on the sound monitor for a second: "There appears to be a malfunction, Onur. Stay calm."

"No, Wale! What is going on here? Get the levels! The levels are off!"

"Stay calm, Onur. Keep your mask on."

Onur couldn't pull the emergency lever because all oxygen would be sucked from the collection room to put out any fire. The air would in theory be immediately filtered back in and he would be able to breathe normally, but that required total faith in the system to reset. They both knew that the lever had not been pulled in eight years. So it was a last resort.

Realizing this, Wale decided to do something that was very clever and cruel. He soothed Onur on the audio monitor and adjusted the levels back. Then he made up an excuse about the airlock being broken. He told him to hang tight and he would call security for help. He left Onur standing there, cursing, his dark Anatolian eyes wide and questioning, with his lips fluttering in the magnetic wobble of the closed-circuit screen.

"Keep your mask on, Onur."

Wale did not call security. Instead, he swiped out and made his way to his office, clearing a few personal items: photos of his family (immediate, not extended), the ticket stub from a Rockets playoff game, after which he had had drinks with Hakeem Olajuwon, trying to fathom the man making love to his wife three feet shorter than him, a signed form letter of congratulations from former Vice-President Dan Quayle on his only promotion. He fingered two half-empty Tupperware containers of ogbono stew and changed his mind and left them on the desk. Finally, he reached into a drawer and took out a snowglobe that he had drained and replaced with distilled water. A figurine of a black cat rested in the middle. He unscrewed the base and there was a valve. Pulling out the glassine bags with the sample from the vault, he attached them to the valve and squeezed the contents gradually until the regolith salted the water. The dust settled onto the cat, getting caught between its ears, on the curve of its haunches. Then he rescrewed the base. Now it looked like any old snowglobe. But the moon was inside.

The front steps of the building were drenched in a dark, brownish mist of smog and tallow pollen, the sidewalk criss-crossed by snail slime. He was half-way down the walk when emergency lights went on.

Impossible, he thought, that Onur had tripped the alarm so quickly.

His hand reached for the briefcase until he realized that the lights were on top of a tow-truck that was about to slide its lifts under the wheels of his Corolla.

"Hey!" he shouted. "That's my car!"

The driver cranked down his window, a white man with a look of apathy and disaffection so ingrained into him that it had creased his cheeks.

"It's too late. I put your plates in the system already."

Wale began to protest when he saw that there was another car idling behind the tow-truck. A brand new cherry-apple red Dodge Intrepid. It was his boss Tom Rilker.

Rilker was trying hard to avoid eye contact under the arc lamps, but Wale stomped right up and rapped on the window. Rilker was sporting a tuxedo, with cufflinks of miniature violins.

"Dr. Olufunmi," Rilker said. "Can I help you?"

Wale tried to keep the tone casual. "There appears to be some mistake, Mr. Rilker. That's my car that he's towing."

Rilker looked at the tow truck as if he was noticing it for the first time.

"That's yours, is it? Still got your Corolla. Great car. I just got one for my daughter. Well, you see, you were parked in my spot."

"I thought you were in Washington, Mr. Rilker."

Rilker considered this as if it was a novel idea. "Washington? Well, that's true, yes, I was. Very nearly got Senator Palimpsest to put the Moonrock Bill in too. There's some very lucrative language in there. You hang on tight and we'll get you tankards of rocks." He coughed. "Didn't you get the memo about the reserved bays? It's not just about my spot. I could give a damn about my spot. It's about security."

"Yes, Mr. Rilker. I understand. I only intended to park for a moment and I was delayed inside. Please tell the driver that the vehicle is mine. My child is sick and I need to take my wife with him to the hospital." Thinking quickly: "I will be back before my break is finished."

Rilker watched the Corolla as it was towed up onto the bed of the tow truck. He seemed reluctant to move. But he turned off his car and walked over to the driver. They exchanged a few words and the driver was backing out, car on top, and heading away. Rilker returned looking sheepish.

"Damn it. I'm sorry, Doctor. Man was as tight as a tick. We'll get it back tomorrow. We can pay it out of Travel."

Wale reminded him about his sick boy. Rilker snapped his fingers. "That's right. Hell. I suppose it'll be too expensive to get a cab here"— Wale nodded—"but you're not far out of the way. I just came in to pick up a file and then I can drop you at home with Tinuke. Can you take a cab from out there? Good. Get in. I'll be right back."

Rilker always grinned after he remembered the names of his employees' spouses, as if he had done them a service.

"Thank you, Mr. Rilker, that's kind of you."

Wale watched as Rilker heeled towards the building, his patent shoes looking oily under the lamps of the parking lot. He had a stiff-armed gait that could at any moment have transformed into a full-fledged march. His office was located on the other end of 31-A, and there was no reason for him to go anywhere near Onur. Still, if Onur tripped the alarm then it was over.

I'm already in too far, Wale thought. Much too far.

The lies he had told Rilker would never add up with what he'd told Onur. He opened up his briefcase and looked at the snowglobe. There was no way to hide what he had done. His only chance was to hope that Rilker didn't notice anything out of the ordinary. If Onur kept his mask on and didn't act rashly there was the slightest chance of getting away with it.

Wale got into the car and was inundated by the smell of the polystyrene coat on the new leather. There was music on the stereo, a voice he normally associated with Christmas: Nat King Cole singing selections from Porgy and Bess. Cole's voice was incredibly crisp and the instruments sounded livelier than the real thing. Nice car, he thought, the Intrepid. And then he saw the keys, right in the ignition. Waiting for him. There wasn't much choice.

Now. He got out of the car and went around to the driver's seat. The vehicle jerked forward as he pressed the pedal down, but when he adjusted to its power the going was smooth. Now.

The guard waved him through as he approached the boom gate and he was on the highway and merging with the rest of them, an anonymous speck in the city of cement and water and gravel and veins of cars.

His wife Tinuke fought him the whole way to the airport. She never asked about his decisions—by unspoken agreement—but he was expected to volunteer, and she could sense how much he was holding back. He tried to be stern with her, promising to explain in due course. His schedule had been moved up, he said, at the last minute. Why hadn't he told her? He'd only just found out.

He nearly forgot his boy in his baby cradle in the rear of the taxi. His heart climbed into his neck through security. But Onur hadn't tripped the alarm yet, or at least had not brought it up to any sort of level involving an airport. Security seemed normal and the guards didn't search anyone more than usual.

They made their way to the domestic airline counter, with a very dark--skinned, full-lipped attendant offering Wale a toothy smile. Passports. He brought out their passports. Tickets. He searched his pockets. He looked at his wife, who frowned. He went through his briefcase and, in a fit of confusion, actually turned over the snowglobe in its bag. But the tickets did not reveal themselves.

The Corolla, he thought.

His mind went through the calculations. He was remarkably fast, remarkably quick at the thought processes required of a thief. When the police—or the FBI, more likely—searched his car for the stolen sample, the tickets would be found under the floor mat. And with the tickets, their destination. With their destination, arrest, jail. Either a life of hiding or outright turnover to the American authorities. There was no going back after stealing a state treasure from NASA. He added up the time and distance it would take to return home, but it was too risky. The tickets were merely a connecting flight to Washington, anyway. They were supposed to meet Bello there.

"Give me your credit card," he said to Tinuke. They bought three economy seats to Washington, leaving forty-five minutes after the flight Bello had booked for him. It would put them there a full hour before the drop. He'd give Bello the snowglobe, Bello would hand him the international tickets, and they'd be shepherded onto Nigerian Airways, first-class to Abuja. Everything would turn out fine, he said.

There was a dark gloam on the horizon that snuffed out the jet-streams and coiling engines and airport vehicles flat like baking pans. Wale tried to ignore the smears of water on the viewing window, the thick raincoats the baton-men and baggage handlers pulled over their heads as the drops coated the runways with rain. The storm came on hard and fast for a full thirty minutes. He waited on the plane, tapping his foot.

To console himself and quiet his boy Dayo, he removed the snow-globe and shook it. The boy stabbed at it with the rice-paper nails of his little fingers, trying to run his hands over the cat in the snow under the glass. Bright-eyed and giggling, Dayo looked at his Daddy and Wale felt a surge of pride. This was all, after all, not just about going into space but about the boy. He'd always imagined raising his family in Nigeria, and now he was returning to make the country a better place.

Brain gain. Returning the minds, giving back what had been sto-len. Going home, and, after he got the lunar program running, walking on the moon with his countrymen. He wouldn't hit golf balls like the American astronauts. He would squeeze out rhythms from a talking drum into the blackness between the stars. These were the drums of war and of death, of celebration, the drums that had bonded the towns of his homeland over centuries in tonal communication. He didn't actually know how to play one but he figured he could take lessons. He would bind the stars with the drums. There would be dancing.

The plane flight was not turbulent, the cashmere clouds above the storm limpid and frictionless. A gibbous moon hung in the air, coating the sky in a soft royal light. In the moonlight the snowglobe tingled at his boy's fingertip with the charged energy of a plasma lamp. Dayo giggled.

"Where you'll go one day, Dayo," Wale whispered, "the Earth will rise and set. Not the moon. Just you see."

Somehow the captain turned their thirty minute delay into a fifteen minute delay by the time they touched down in Washington. The captain did not explain why captains didn't do the same thing when flights were on time and arrive early. But Wale didn't complain.

"On time," he said. "We've made it on time."

Tinuke was growing increasingly furious with his secrecy and flatly ignored him.

They had arrived at 10:45 and the drop was at 11:26. The boy seemed fascinated by the baggage carousel and stared at its scaly conveyor belt until he hiccupped from nausea. The bags spat out interminably: black bags, ruffled bags, those new ones with wheels on them, hard-backed old-leather, garment bags, Samsonites, then a cardboard box wrapped all up in tape, a guitar, a double-bass the size of a coffin, a surfboard and two sets of golf clubs, and finally, at 11:15, Tinuke's duck-taped duffle.

They rushed up the stairs, Wale carrying all three bags and not feeling their weight, Tinuke with the boy. Bello was to meet them at the Nigerian Airways counter. He had no idea where it was, not having been home in twenty years. Find someone who knows. I don't know, I work for American. Do you know? It is over by Air France. Where is that? Terminal D. What terminal are we at? Terminal B. You gotta take the shuttle, sir.

The shuttle, oh the shuttle, waiting for the squat people-mover bus with walls of windows as it whinnied up with its subway straps and excess baggage space. The driver had the nerve to dismount and smoke a cigarette. Two minutes. The shuttle ran counterclockwise. It puttered to Terminal A first, loaded on some parched looking stewardesses and a chippy co-pilot who pinned some wings on a little school girl's lapel. Then to C, which was apparently the terminal for geriatrics. Walkers, canes, and the weathered arguments of golden anniversary couples. ("I told you not to leave it open." "Yup.")

And then they were at D, and he could practically smell the pepper soup, could heft the yellow saran-wrapped gari in his hand. Home. The counter was right there. 11:26 and 59 terrestrial seconds. Home. As calmly as he could, he scanned the passengers with their bulk luggage full of designer dresses, university memorabilia, jewelry, Nintendos, CD players, NBA jerseys.

Bello wasn't there. He watched the line for a full ten minutes and didn't see Bello anywhere, or anyone looking remotely official. There were police a few counters away, flirting with an attendant. Not looking for him, which was good. Not looking for him yet. A flash of insight and he realized the handover might be arranged at the counter. He recalled the agreed upon language.

"Welcome to Nigerian Airways. Passport."

"I am going to Taro."

"Pardon me?"

He drew out the R and sounded the O, throwing in his best imitation of a Hausa accent. "I said, I am going to Taro." He waited for the agreed upon response.

"Pardon me?" Shaking his head, he beckoned the other attendant over. "I am going to Taro."

She blinked her eyes. "This flight is to Abuja. You can take a bus to Taro from there."

"Get me your manager."

The manager was equally puzzled. So Wale drew aside the security guard, a Yoruba man. He tried the password in his mother tongue. The man started laughing: "You've been away too long. Ta-ro. Listen to how this man says Ta-ro. It is time you went home to your country mister—"

"Doctor. Dr. Wale Olufunmi."

The guard stiffened at hearing the appellation. "Dr. Olufunmi. It is time you went home."

"That's what I am trying to do!"

Wale asked anyone he could find and eventually gave up the password and asked for Bello directly. An agreeable black American told him he knew Bello and led him to the taxi stand. "That's not Bello."

"Damn sure it is. Bello's his name."

His name was revealed to be Bellevue, from Port-au-Prince, and it was a nickname.

"Sorry, Doctor."

Before long the plane began boarding. Then the gate was closed. The women at the desk were eating brown-bag lunches and chatting in a lively way that could only be about men. His wife Tinuke was tired and livid. He normally shared things with her, even, when he could stomach it, emotions. But the twitch in her right eye, the quiver of her arrow-head nose, told him that he was in the process of shattering something that would require months to glue back together. Perhaps years.

Okay, the fallback position. The fallback to Cape Town. Cape Town! He hadn't even realized how absurd that was—as if a Nigerian could just saunter into South Africa. The country was reeling towards civil war, for chrissake. President De Klerk was breaking his promises and people were already killing each other by the thousands.

He dragged his family to the South African Airways counter. Tinuke spoke her first words in hours when she saw the destination. "I am not going to South Africa, Wale."

"We have to go."

"Why?"

Because I stole a state treasure from NASA, he thought.

"Can I ask you to trust me?"

"I'm not taking our child to South Africa," Tinuke said. "There is a war coming there. There is apartheid."

"I'll make an inquiry, that's all. Cape Town's a very European city."

He advanced forward in the line, where the white receptionist scanned his family up and down. She did not ask him for his passport—

she asked him, shortly, for his visa. It would take ninety days, she said, for the police background checks to go through, a police background check that he knew was out of the question.

A white woman edged him aside to be greeted with smiles and laughter. She was offered cupcakes, courtesy of the airline.

His boy was crying. People were waving good-bye at the gates and hugging and getting plastered at the bars. A crowd of Hindu men and their wives in gold and scarlet saris and their licorice-haired ginger-bread children rushed by in a commotion. On a sports bar TV there was a highlight of Dominique Wilkins missing a dunk so hard the ball slammed off the rim all the way to the top of the opposite key, where another dunk was missed by the opposing team.

At least, Wale thought, I am not the only one.

He opened his duffle bag and took out the snowglobe. Tinuke began whimpering next to an escalator. He shook up the snowglobe and held it above his head.

Come, Bello, come.

Bathing with Perlemoen

Present Day
South Africa

Thursday Malaysius had worked at Abalone Silver for two years. It was the largest abalone farm in the Southern Hemisphere, covering ten hectares, with kilometers of epoxy tanks teeming with the mollusk. The long administrative buildings were made from prefabricated aluminum siding. When Thursday clocked in at eight, a fog layer nursed Hermanus Bay, and whales could be heard snorting and breaching in the distant waves in the spring time.

Thursday used to work as a clam shucker in one of the government fish factories, but got fired after negotiations with the employee union went south. So he simply walked down the street to Abalone Silver and they hired him as an abalone cleaner. The main difference between the creatures was that a clam had two sides to its shell and an abalone only had one, and was more of a glorified snail that fetched hundreds of dollars in East Asia. When the abalone were happy, they slid along on tiny eggplant colored tentacles, which they would retract when afraid. He sometimes imagined a battle between the abalone and clams of the world; the clams might be better at slicing the abalone with their shells, but the abalone were faster and could suck out the clam with their large feet and then cut it up with their teeth.

He thought about this battle more than you might think. Although he tried to remain objective, he would play favorites and manipulate the battle conditions in his mind so that the abalone, surviving in a narrow latitude around the world (compared to clams, which flourished in rivers and streams), could come out victorious. Abalone functioned better in the darkness, so he gave them that, and abalone liked fresh kelp, so he put that there, too, in the battles of his imagination.

The work at the abalone farm was more stressful than at the fish factory. The bosses were looking to turn a profit rather than provide a government service to society, so the lunch breaks were short and no one brought any brandy. And the job was messier. The sea water got piped in and the mollusks lived for years, so the tanks had to be regularly cleaned and scrubbed, whereas the clams at the fish factory had been killed on the spot. Thursday was charged with trimming the slimy green foot from the seventy millimeter adult abalone for export to China. He was good with a knife and could get through about four in a minute. But when the sea water grew too warm or the pumps clogged, worms would wiggle in and eat the shells, and they were a nuisance because the abalone would outgrow the half-eaten shells and taste acidic. For two months every year, baby anemones would squeeze through the filters and then mature in the tank. They would squirt their seeds into his eyes and cause them to swell up, making it hard for him to get a date. He didn't cut his fingers much because of his clamming skills.

Thursday was a steady, reliable worker. He didn't put in overtime but he punched in on time and didn't sneak off early. He acknowledged his mistakes and was amenable to criticism. After eighteen months at Abalone Silver, he'd been promoted twice with a two rand per hour increase each time. He also managed to pocket a few shells and buff them into an opalescent polish for the whale watching season to sell to tourists, but he was discreet about it. Discreet that was, until Brother Leon showed up while Thursday was counting the big adults on an abacus.

"Aweh howsit, Thursday?" Brother Leon asked.

Leon was good looking and cinnamon-skinned, affable, persuasive, skilled at domineering, and wore a hat all day, not a sailor's snoek cap like his father, but a red brimmed baseball cap that covered a beautiful head of dark-curled locks. Thursday was balding and wiry and the squat Malay nose had never been bred out of him. His deep brown eyes were lozenge shaped, with the left one half-closed in a squint. Brother Leon considered fish factories and abalone farms beneath him. Being a mate, Leon liked to remind him of all of these things. Leon also had a bigger penis.

"How'd you get in here?" Thursday asked.

"I snuck in through the gate."

"Get out of here or you'll get me in trouble."

Brother Leon had a way of completely ignoring what you said and making you think you were having a conversation. "Give me a few of those perlies, will you, Thursday?"

Thursday declined.

"I just need ten. No, say, a few tens. Seventy."

"No ways, my bru. We count in every day. I've got a promotion coming."

Leon raised his red cap off his head and his locks spilled onto his forehead. This was a trick he used with the women: get 'em drunk, and then razzle-dazzle with the locks. "What's that promotion going to bring you? An extra rand, my broer. That's donkies. You can make a lot more than an extra rand."

"I told you a hundred times that I won't. I'm not a poacher. They've got that dog. Snoopy. The paper said her nose can smell perlemoen through the water." Feeling righteous, Thursday added: "I'm an honest man."

Leon looked hurt. "Ten is all I need."

"You that broke?"

"It's terrible."

Thursday would not give in to Leon's pleading that easily, not until Leon gave his word to pay it back. Brother Leon was never really down and out. He had a half-dozen girlfriends who would have given him the PIN numbers to their credit cards just to catch a glimpse of his pretty face. Three of them, Jackie, Fadanaz, and Thembisa, left their windows unlocked at night in the hope that he would sneak in, he said. Thursday decided to bring Brother Leon a bag full of some polished shells over the weekend and even bought him some chips, but didn't listen to his pleas. Then he returned to work at the abalone farm thinking he was as right as rain. Trimming and counting, cleaning and slicing, Thursday enjoyed the gentle way of the abalone.

Thursday's boss Mr. Pretorius, a jolly biologist from Kwazulu-Natal, called him into his office one day. It seemed unrealistic to receive another promotion, but Thursday wasn't going to complain.

"Thursday, have a seat," Pretorius said.

Mr. Pretorius's mauve sweater stretched over his beer belly in a way that made him look like a butternut. He had a round, lumpy nose and eyes that must have been bright blue as a child, but had faded. He moved in a big way, an assured family man with two kids that played rugby and enjoyed the library, and he maneuvered the steering wheel of his bakkie with the butt of his palm, easy and smooth. Pretorius liked to buy Thursday bags of crisps and loose cigarettes and enjoyed handling the abalone in the tank. He was fantastic at the kind of small talk that can only be perfected by businessmen, and could say entirely original things if he passed Thursday ten times in a day.

Pretorius's office had a few posters of the Orient on the walls. Black sample cans of their Abalone Silver export product lined the shelves in eight different languages.

"You've been great here, Thursday, so I—" Pretorius avoided looking Thursday in the eye. "—I think the easiest thing is to look at this yourself."

Bashfully Pretorius left the room, returning with a television stand with a video player. He juggled his belly around, wheezing, and plugged in the unit.

Maybe a training video, Thursday thought. For the promotion.

Pretorius turned on the television and took the remote with him to his desk. He sat heavily in his neoprene office chair. The screen flashed on with a digital date, then there were some rows of something stretching into the distance. Everything was greenish.

"This is a surveillance camera, Thursday. We had them installed before you got here."

Onscreen a man walked by with a night-stick.

"That's Ronald," Pretorius said.

Ronald was a security guard from Gabon. In the video Ronald sat down and had a smoke.

"Going to have to talk to him about that," Pretorius muttered.

He fast forwarded the video and the screen turned greener. He pressed Play.

"Night time now. Watch over there, by the generator. Look, where the fence is. There!"

On screen a black form could be seen behind the wire fence. The form raised some clippers and then you could see the fence wobbling. Thursday leaned in. The fence peeled up and the figure stepped through, walking straight in the direction of the camera for a few paces. Wearing a cap. Then the figure turned and disappeared off screen.

"We didn't get him on the next camera," Pretorius said. He hit the Pause button and swiveled his office chair towards Thursday. "Do you know who that is?"

He was looking at Thursday with a discerning eye. Pretorius was a business man who had grown Abalone Silver from a few tanks to a 10 million rand enterprise in five years. He talked straight. If he was asking, he had a good reason.

"Can I see it again?"

Pretorius obliged him, rewinding the tape. There was the form in the green darkness. The fence wobbled and then the athletic, confident swagger of the intruder. Then the hat, the turn and the form disappeared off screen. No doubt now: Brother Leon.

"We lost forty of our oldest females over this, Thursday. A few of them have been around since I started this business." He leaned forward. "Those will fetch about thirty thousand rand on the streets and they're worth much more to us for breeding. I'd be grateful if you could tell me who might have done such a thing."

Thursday swallowed. Leon! He knew that Brother Leon had a bad thing coming to him. It was plain to see. And any self-respecting man would have turned Leon in, returned to the tanks to shuck, clocked-out, gone home. Come back and worked again the next day as the market forces adjusted to the loss of the stolen abalone. This was what Pretorius wanted him to do, though he was giving Thursday his poker face, and trying to act neutral about it. But Pretorius didn't see some things.

When they were ten Leon told Thursday that the first feeling he could remember was jealousy. He didn't say what he was jealous of. That was the same year that Leon had changed for the worse, the year that the new green ping-pong table had become a prime attraction at Chief Albert Luthuli Elementary School.

Leon and Thursday played together as a team. Leon painted the corners with his wristy forehand and Thursday could block smashes with his good reflexes. They'd made it to the semifinals of the school tournament and been eliminated by a pair they should have beaten. The other kids cheered for the teams in the finals while Leon and Thursday commiserated. The prize of a set of fishing lures, they thought, was going to the wrong people.

"John can't even serve, my broer," Leon said.

"He's got no backhand," Thursday agreed.

"I didn't want the lures anyway. Line fish is for voetsaks."

"Ja."

Thursday didn't care much for fishing himself, or for competition. As they stood and brooded, a kid named Diego decided to play a trick on Thursday. Diego was the class clown. He shuffled next to Thursday while his eyes were following the game. Thursday was in the perfect position, with his knees locked tight and his back already straight, for the take-down to work.

Thursday fell back and banged his head hard against the ping-pong table. Diego went to help him straight away, but one of the kids began egging Thursday on to fight. Thursday just laughed it off.

"Good one, Diego," he said. "You got me with that one, bru."

Then Thursday saw Leon's face. He was scowling at Diego in anger. Thursday smiled sheepishly at Leon and he smiled back, but with his lips curled full of venom. Just as soon the look was gone.

Leon leapt on Diego in a fury. Diego scuffled and tried to use Leon's weight against him but Leon had this deadly headlock, where he'd clamp his arm around you and then needle his little bicep into your neck. The cheering and the shouting fanned Leon's rage and he wrapped Diego in that headlock so fast he didn't know what hit him. Diego's face grew bright red and he scrambled to take a breath, but Leon held him firm and used his free hand to slap him. There was laughter.

The teacher came and broke it up. Diego ran home to his mother's house. The finals were rescheduled and never played because a storm blew in. But something about Leon's eyes told Thursday that he never would have let go. That whatever rage was buried in him had just been awoken.

Over the years he watched Leon beat men senseless for the most ridiculous affronts. Sometimes it would be slights against Thursday for his squinty eye—calling him an ugly badprop maybe—other times Leon would be insulted if someone looked at his girl, at his clothes, or just looked him in the eye. Leon would be calm for weeks, months, maybe, before he'd erupt. For anyone besides Thursday it was hard to perceive any sort of pattern.

And Thursday had to admit that Leon stuck up for him. Leon would track down the bullies and knock their teeth out, with Thursday on the side wondering if he should intervene. Leon would smile, kiss his lacerated knuckles, and spit down into his victim's face. It was his signature. Even thugs with guns would bow down before Leon, pocketing their pistols as if the bullets would only bounce off him. And Thursday knew that Leon's fury was of the unstoppable kind. Practical things defrayed it—witnesses, evidence, tourists, whites, police sirens—and they were mere happenstance. If those little obstacles hadn't been in the way, Leon would have left a string of bashed-in dead men around Hermanus. And this fact, that he was being stopped from carrying out his will, fueled his rage even more.

It's not that Leon's home life was all that bad, either. Thursday had been over to Leon's house any number of times. His family had a neat, well-swept home that they kept free of roaches, with a good gas range and a wide stoep. There were always poinsettias and creepers blooming with bright flowers in the garden and seven kinds of pepper plants. His father wasn't good with money, but he loved his children, and his mother made the sweetest koeksister pastries in the whole town. They were generous people.

So maybe Leon's anger had nothing to do with that school yard. Maybe that was just the first time that Thursday had seen it, and it had been there simmering beneath the surface all along. Maybe Leon was a man who'd been taking names from the day he was born, furious at the dirty friction of the world.

All Thursday knew was that it was that day in the school yard that he stopped thinking all men were created equal. He'd really been expecting something else.

That was what Thursday was thinking as Pretorius sat back and blue-eyed him, not the family, not the ping-pong, but Leon's rage. A prison cell couldn't keep in that rage. Leon was too strong for it, too smart. Pretorius, with his straight-talking bottom line ethics, would never understand that rage, and one day somebody like Leon would come along and crush his rugby-winger boys and their Herman Charles Bosman bedtime stories.

Brother Leon had a bad thing coming to him, plain as day. But Leon was tough and smart, and he'd stuck up for Thursday so many times that he'd lost count. If Thursday turned him in, Leon would call up one of his girls and make bail, and then he'd shoot out of the prison looking for names. He'd know. Somehow he'd know.

The green video screen was fluttering over him. Thursday could hear the digital hiss and the whir of the motor of the video player.

"I don't know who that is, Mr. Pretorius. I count in every day. You can check my logs."

"Don't get me wrong," Pretorius said. "You're in the clear. I know you wouldn't do that kind of thing. I just want to know if you have an idea. Perhaps a name or a face."

Thursday was happy to hear he was in the clear. But he felt Leon was right there in the office with them, lifting his hat and spilling out his locks, listening. Leon went everywhere with Thursday. He was a part of him. The difference was that Leon knew what to do in situations like this.

"I—"

"Yes, Thursday?"

Mr. Pretorius the butternut stared at him with those faded blue eyes. The eyes: quick, compassionate, of a family man. Leon hated families. He never would have kissed a fat white family man's ass in an office full of white folks. That was what Leon would do, go on the attack. The best defense is a good offense.

"Why do you think I would know, Mr. Pretorius? Because I'm coloured?"

Pretorius took a long, slow gaze at him and sighed. He averted his eyes and fished out a cigarette. It was the look of a disappointed father. He offered the cigarette to Thursday, gave a weak smile.

"Thursday, I'll ignore that. I think you and I both know that I'm not a racist. And I think you're above that, too."

But Thursday was committed to his statement now. To Leon's statement. "That's what all white men say! You think I don't know how it works? Us coloureds do the heavy work while you drive your bakkies. That's the business."

"What about Paul? He's out there with you. And Stefan. They're white and you're all friends."

Thursday felt that he was rehearsing a speech that he'd seen on TV somewhere, the lines came out so easily: "No, we can never be friends. They go home to their wives and gardens and I go home to my shack."

"I don't think you mean that."

Thursday wasn't sure if he meant it. "I do."

"I'm sorry then. I didn't have you pegged that way." Pretorius offered up the pack of cigarettes again. "I know it wasn't you, Thursday."

What wasn't me, Thursday thought, the theft or the TV speech? Could he still blame it all on Leon and save face? Could he get down on his knees and beg?

But Pretorius was done with him. "That's all."

Thursday took a cigarette and left.

Mr. Pretorius told Thursday a few days later that he knew Leon had stolen the abalone, but he didn't intend to press charges. He also said that he couldn't keep a liar on his staff so Thursday had to leave. Thursday bummed around for a while, going to his mother's, who didn't mind the attention, but she soon grew tired of him.

"Thursday, you only come here to feed, you lazy hollang. Go out and get yourself a job!"

There weren't many to be found. Hermanus was a small town that thrived on whale watching tourism. There were a few little shopping centres, some bed and breakfasts, and upscale restaurants that the locals could not afford. A chain of mountains filled with pinpoints of purple frutencen blossoms overlooked the town, and you could run on the beach for kilometers. Most of the young men wanted to quit Hermanus and get to Cape Town as soon as possible. Thursday, on the other hand, thought Hermanus offered him what he needed and saw no reason to leave it.

He applied at a new internet café but he didn't have any web design experience, and he had neither the charisma nor the acting ability to serve the tourists at the cafés lining Old Hermanus Bay. It was the low season anyway and the managers told him no one would be hired for a few weeks. He borrowed his brother-in-law Angus's fishing rod but wasn't able to catch anything, and Angus began to lord it over him, asking him to do the dishes, weed the garden, and so on. Thursday drew the line when his sister tried to set him up with an ugly friend of hers, and stopped visiting them.

So he was happy to see Leon when he drove up the street in an iridescent champagne painted Merc and rolled down the window.

"Bemandge car, Leon."

"Yeah, it's cool. Come on, I brought it for you, my bru. Get in."

They drove around, popping in to see Fadanaz, and then Luluma—his latest acquisition—and Leon dropped hundred rand bills here and there with no explanation. Thursday could sense that Leon wanted him to ask where he'd found the money, but managed to hold off, hoping

Leon might confess about the theft. Then he started realizing that the perlies he'd stolen from Abalone Silver would never cover the cost of a Merc, and his curiosity got the better of him.

"You're rich, Leon!"

"No," Leon said. "This is donkies. This is just the beginning, bru."

"But, how Leon? I can't get a job as a dishwasher."

They were sitting at the corner table at The Anchor. Leon slapped a coin down on the bar and the bartender brought over another quart. The Anchor had a policy of leaving all the empties the customers ordered in front of them so that they couldn't stiff on the bill. Leon looked at the row of receptacles that had once held the liquids sloshing inside him. "We've only had eight quarts, Thursday. Last night I had fourteen, and Thabisa had six. The positions that put her in—like a gymnast. So flexible. Listen to me, brother, six quarts and a girl will do anything. Six quarts and a pair of earrings." Thursday reminded him about his question. "I don't want to talk about money right now. I was hoping you wouldn't bring it up. You come with me tomorrow and I'll explain everything."

It took four nights of heavy drinking, cajoling, and a wet kiss from Leon's girl Fadanaz for Thursday to say he would consider going into the water. Even then he never thought it would come to pass. But soon they were sitting in the Merc next to a row of strelitzia palms that wound along a dirt road to the beach in the dusk, their fronds spreading out like press-on fingernails. He would have been able to hear the pounding surf if Leon wasn't thumping his Kwaito music, and they'd both grown up near the sea so he didn't smell the seaweed any more. Thursday had resolved that this time he would be firm with Leon—he was not going in the water, there was no way he was going in.

"I can't do it, my broer," Thursday declared. "I don't know how."

"Come on, Thursday," Leon said. "I started with nothing. I was out there in the rocks all alone with the police, pulling myself on the kelp." Leon laughed, in awe of himself, reminiscing. "Should have been on the news. I can barely even swim. You've got the breather and my lank equipment. The breather is easier than a tank." He began pumping his head to the syncopated rhythms of the Kwaito.

"Can't you give me your mask?"

"I gave you my old mask, voetsak. My new one cost a thousand bucks. It's not my fault you've got a conch for a nose."

"You must be mad," Thursday said. "I'm not going out there. There's a storm coming. There's sharks."

"There hasn't been an attack in months."

Thursday was skeptical. Attacks on poachers were never reported anyway. Another diver would deliver the news to the family, and if he was polite, give over whatever money he'd made from selling his catch. That was how it worked in Hermanus.

"You sure?" Thursday asked.

Leon assured him that no poacher had been attacked in months and reminded Thursday of his victories on the swim team in Standard Eight. "You need a lookout, Thursday. That's the first rule. I would have let you be the lookout, but I'm sick." He shivered for emphasis. "I set everything up yesterday. If you don't take the perlies someone else will. Just go for the blue plastic eggs. I'm the only one who uses them. There's hundreds. Maybe five hundred. That's like two hundred thousand rand. But I'm not selfish: you just take as many as you can and bring them back." He showed him a pistol stashed beneath his seat. "Don't worry. We're protected."

You've got to be firm, Thursday thought. He reached over and turned off the stereo. "Don't listen to your music. I don't want any cops."

"Stop being such a poes. You said you need the money, right? I'm doing you a favor. The cops stop at four and it's seven o'clock. You've got the cell phone, né?"

Thursday adjusted the condom-wrapped cell phone he'd shoved next to his crotch. "You'll call if they come?"

"Of course."

"No music."

"Ja, no music."

They went over it one more time. He was to look for the plastic eggs, the blue ones with sand in them. Three buzzes on the cell phone or six flashes on the light meant get out of the water. Thursday took the dry suit and the fins and the surface breather. The condom was lubricated so the cell phone slipped down to his calf by the time he walked along the crescent beach and waded into the surf.

Thursday swam around for half an hour in the bay, kicking his fins quickly from fear in the darkness, and the only thing of interest he found was an old warped field hockey stick. Leon had made it sound like the visibility would be just like the television show Baywatch, and once he was underwater he'd see everything as clear as a bathtub. The blue plastic eggs would be sparkling like jewelry, and he would be able to kick leisurely down and scoop up the abalone. But fog kept covering his mask and he had to blow out hard with his nostrils to get the steam out, then there was the problem of the umbilical line of the surface breather, which must have had a leak in it, because the air had a wet taste to it that made him wheeze. He could see about a meter in front of him. In the blackness there could be anything: fish, abalone, a whale, a rock, a chest of gold doubloons.

Moonlight streaked down and he realized he was near a kelp bed; then the shafts retracted behind a cloud bank. He kicked towards the edge of the kelp bed and turned on the flashlight attached to the tip of his speargun. An octopus scowled at him from a cragged rock, but when he reached in to grab it, it disappeared in a splotch of ink. There was nothing else in the water but kelp and tiny green diatoms, things he could not eat or sell, not even a crab. He could not believe it—Leon said he'd been here only yesterday, and marked the area with a blue plastic egg. He'd said five hundred. Thursday had expected fifty.

But now everything had been picked clean and canned, or picked clean and dried, bound on a ship to the Orient. Perhaps another diver had already found the plastic eggs. There was no point in shivering in the water.

His head surfaced in a white rush of foam. In the distance, he could see the stacks of dark-churning clouds being flash-bulbed by the heavens above Old Hermanus. The storm's advance was not fast—Leon had been right about that. On shore, the soft curl of the beach spread blue in the moonlight, and dim stars shined through the mozzie net of salt spray. Leon had parked the car behind the tallest tree. Thursday lifted the flashlight from the water and beamed out a simple signal, telling him that he would be coming back on shore.

He waited for Leon's response, and it came. Four flashes, nothing else. This had no meaning other than the fact that he was there waiting and not, hopefully, listening to music.

But then there was another flashlight: moving, bobbing. A light that had come from the beach. No, two of them. Moving quickly.

He could see them bouncing up and down the sand and out towards the forest, then disappear into the dark foliage behind the beach. Then, a flash of red and blue lights from far on the other side of the beach streaking towards the foliage, right where Leon was waiting.

A raid.

Treading, he saw Leon's headlights go on and then start out through the forest, and then just as soon stop. The red lights and flashlights surrounded the car. Two more sets of red and blue lights approached on the beach and he could hear the warble of a megaphone. Some muffled dog barks. There was no way around it: Leon was caught.

"Yissus!" Thursday breathed.

He sank and rose in the rhythm of the night swells. Leon had not prepared him for this situation. Other than the flash signals, they had not developed any kind of plan for arrest. He had no idea what to do as he de-fogged his mask.

Suddenly, a wide beam of light swathed through the waves around him. He rose up in a swell and turned to see another wave about to crash, but he ducked his head under the wave with the respirator clumsily in his mouth. Shouting voices could be heard:

"—one hundred meters… ident—"

Then more barks, more megaphone.

The swell rose up and the beam of light came closer, and when he sank with it, the light silhouetted him briefly in his lycra-capped skull onto the approaching swell, then moved off him. But in a few seconds the beam had swung back around and steadied onto his head. They'd spotted him.

A rogue wave dropped down on Thursday hard and pushed his head below, tumbling him about. He swallowed water and surfaced and began to cough, but the umbilical line was sucked into the next swell and before he could take his lips off the respirator it pulled his whole body forward as it got caught into the surf and advanced towards the beach. His mouth exploded in pain. He cut himself free with the tip of his spear gun, then finned down hard and held his breath, listening to the steady chug of the boat. The breather rumbled and gasped as the brine seeped into the battery, sending up green alkaline tufts of cloud.

Under the flotsam he could hear the engine of the police boat as it coordinated the arrest with the officers on the shore. They would be watching for air bubbles. Maybe for his flashlight, too. He could make out the boat's clothes-iron silhouette against the moonlit surface. When it passed over, he kicked up, taking a few more breaths. The police spotlight was fixed on the surface breather and already he could see a long hook being extended down into the water to pick it up. He dove down again, finning hard, until he was clear of the wave break. The police boat continued scanning the waves in the surf with its spotlight.

"This is the police!" the megaphone blared. "We know you are here! Come to the surface and identify yourself or we will shoot!"

That didn't sound like the police. The Hermanus police were soft and never shot anyone, much less put any poachers in jail. That was why half the town poached: easy money with low probability of capture. A few months of steady abalone picking and you could buy yourself a Merc. That's what Brother Leon had told him tonight, anyway, in his Merc.

Crack!

Crack!

Two sharp cracks rang out and Thursday could see the water splash up in the circle of the spotlight in the surf.

But he could see from the spotlight that the boat was headed in the wrong direction, towards a cove popular with the poachers. Maybe there were other divers out tonight. Hopefully there were. He caught another breath and sank down again in the black wash of the sea.

The storm clouds slowly swallowed up the moon, and he found himself in total darkness, with no sense of up or down. His imagination went wild and he started to panic: sharks, hostile poachers, police bullets, all of them could be hurtling towards him in the water. He fumbled to hit the button on his flashlight, expecting to see a jaw full of jagged teeth about to gulp him whole, or a bullet streaking towards his brain.

But there, in the midst of the shooting and the raid and the approaching storm, he didn't see any sharks. No bullets, either. What Thursday saw instilled in him the deepest relief he'd had since he'd left Abalone Silver: the beacon of the blue plastic egg. He'd descended right into Leon's abalone patch.

The mollusks were healthy and active in the night, sliming along the rock in a little garden of red gracilaria. There were urchins, a couple of crayfish, and a rock lobster. He found a largish looking abalone covered with seaweed and pried it off. The abalone slid its foot onto his hand and nursed at it like a babe.

He couldn't believe its weight: enormous, much bigger than the oldest abalone at the farm. It was so big that the shell covered both his hands. Maybe thirty years old, maybe forty, and worth a few thousand bucks by itself. The flat kelp noodled up harmless to the surface, and nothing dangerous was in sight.

Above him the boat chugged off towards the cove, expecting the divers to flee onto the beach. Any other novice would have swum into the hands of the cops by now. But Thursday was beginning to feel comfortable without the tangled line of the surface breather. And amongst the abalone, with their patient ways, he felt to be amongst friends. He could hold his breath longer than most people and his ears didn't bother him when he dove down deep. He just had to be careful about the spotlight.

It would be some time before the police boat stopped searching, and he might as well make the best of it. It would take maybe ten trips. He took out his pry bar and went to work.

Hermanus's biggest industry was whale watching and the tourism that went with it: stuffed animals, shipwreck maps, shell jewelry, whale carvings, fynbos guides, hiking books, whale videos, whale song audio recordings, whale novels, kites, ships-in-a-bottle, chocolate dolphins; then handicrafts made from carded lambswool, wicker, stinkwood, pine, and tie-dyed cotton. These trades did not give rise to a lot of crime, so the police station was simple. The most frequent users were residents needing certified copies of ID books.

The station was shaped like an L. The gray holding cells stretched out the back and were located right next to the courtroom, which had a door that opened into the magistrate's chambers and, on the other side, the prosecutor's office. It was a one-stop shop for justice.

The guard told Thursday they had ten minutes. Leon wearily approached the window, looking haggard and grumpy in an orange jumpsuit, but upon spotting Thursday he assumed a dignified expression. He didn't smile.

"Howzit, Leon?" Thursday asked.

Leon tensed his muscles. "How do you think it is, bru? It's kak. I've been in here four days. And you come to me now all smiling and cute. They're transferring me to Pollsmoor in a week."

Thursday hadn't smiled, and he wasn't sure if he had been acting cute. He let it slide. "I didn't want any trouble."

"Trouble? Trouble? Now you're in a shitload of trouble, you poes."

"Me?"

Leon leaned in and whispered. "Yeah, you, voetsak. You ratted me out."

Thursday got confused. Leon was the one who was supposed to warn him if the police were coming, by calling him on the condom-wrapped cell phone.

"They came from the ocean," Leon explained. "Didn't you hear the boat? You flashed like a hundred times, broer. They saw you. You gave me away."

"But you flashed back, Leon."

"Shhh. Keep your voice down, broer. Keep it down. I'm in enough shit as it is. That wasn't me. That was them. I was supposed to flash six times, remember? Six times. That was the cops."

Thursday thought over it. "What were you doing, then?"

"I was listening to my klop Kwaito, broer. And if I'd kept on listening I would have been fine. Then you bloody gave me away, you poes. When I get out of here, I'm—"

"When do you get out?" Thursday asked nervously. He knew what would happen when Leon got out and didn't want to hear the grisly threats.

"I don't know. But I'll get out a lot quicker if I give them something."

"Like what?"

"A name."

There was something sinister about the way Leon said 'name'.

"Whose?"

"Who do you think?" Leon grinned.

"Me? But I didn't do anything, Leon. I'm an honest—" He wanted to say that he was an honest man, but that excuse no longer seemed appropriate. "What about bail? Can't you call up Thembisa? She's got to have some money. Or Fadanaz."

"It's a hundred thousand rand. Fadanaz has a thousand."

Thursday frowned. Thembisa had a good job as an assistant manager at a bank, but she certainly didn't make a hundred thousand rand in a year. All of Leon's girls put together probably couldn't muster up more than ten thousand, and Thursday had been fired from Abalone Silver with five hundred bucks to his name. Rent was four hundred.

"What about the Merc?"

"Impounded."

"A hundred thousand rand? But you didn't have anything on you, Leon. How can they charge that?"

Leon looked away. He hesitated and said, softly: "Racists, bru."

Thursday barely heard him. He was scared already and distracted, thinking about how Leon would chop him up, or crush his head in a vice—Leon was capable of all of these things. And Thursday would never survive Pollsmoor prison. He knew he wasn't tough enough, not like Leon.

"I got the work, Leon."

"What?"

"I said I got the work, my broer."

Leon's eyes widened. He relaxed his shoulders a bit, and Thursday could see him thinking out a strategy already. Leon was quick.

"How many?"

"Two hundred. Big. Thirty years old."

"Where are they?"

"I've got them in the bath."

Leon was calculating.

"Two minutes!" the guard shouted in.

"Alright," Leon said eventually. "That's enough. That's enough, but you're going to have to go straight to Ip."

Everyone in Hermanus had heard of Ip, but few had ever seen him. First you went to a dry-house and shriveled up the abalone. Then a runner stuffed the dried perlies in rooibos tea boxes and took them to Ip. Thursday was under the impression that Ip lived in another universe, in China maybe, and didn't want anything to do with him.

"Don't you know a runner?" Thursday asked.

"No, no. Two hundred in the dryer won't make it. If they're as good as you say, they've got to get there alive. He'll pay twice as much. And it should do." Leon explained how to contact Ip, tousling his own dark locks with relief. "You've done good, Thursday. I always knew I could trust you."

The guard escorted Leon away, and Leon looked over his shoulder and winked. A moment ago, Thursday remembered, Leon was about to tell him how he was going to kill him.

Of all the poachers in Hermanus, Thursday was the best suited to take care of live abalone because of his time at the factory. He'd already gone down to the rocks to pick up some fresh kelp, but the abalone were having a hard time digesting the seaweed with all the stress. He walked straight out of the police station to the pet shop in Old Hermanus. The large black-winged gulls were nibbling muffin bits and crisps from the sidewalk, awaiting the arrival of the whale-watching children who would stuff their gullets full of sweets. The sun rippled off the bay through the shop awnings at the end of the street.

He picked up a couple of cans of low-protein fish meal and took them to the counter. The two tellers were busy poring over the Times.

"I can't believe it," one said. "She was so young."

"It's awful," the other agreed.

"What happened?" Thursday asked, to move things along.

He was so new to the smuggling business that he felt guilty buying fish meal, as if the cans were attached to a hotline and the police would come arrest him on suspicion of feeding perlemoen in the bathtub. As if fish meal was an indicator of criminal activity.

"You haven't heard?" the teller asked. She was a plump white girl with hairy dreadlocks.

"No." Thursday never heard anything.

She showed him the front page. There was a healthy black and white Border collie nobly posing over a mound of abalone. The fishnet sacks had been arranged so that it looked as if the police had just dumped the shells onto the floor. He could practically hear them clattering against the tiles. It was the dog that the police had trained to track down abalone in drying facilities.

"It's Sassy," the teller said.

"Can I take a look?" Thursday asked.

She handed him the paper. The headline was clear enough: "Sassy Killed by Poacher". He scanned the story:

New Hermanus Bay — Sassy, the police dog that became the pride of Hermanus, died of complications at Protea Veterinary on Wednesday.

"We tried everything," veterinarian Linda Sussex explained. "She fought hard but the bullet had crushed her left ventricle. It's a miracle she lasted as long as she did."

The police said that Sassy, a Border Collie, was shot with a nine millimeter pistol. A local Hermanus man is being held on charges.

Sassy left in glory, on the eve of the successful launch of "Operation Trident." Trident represents new coordination between South African Police Services (SAPS), the border patrol, and the South African Navy, with increased powers of search and seizure and lower evidentiary standards for abalone poachers.

It is hoped that these efforts will curb the illicit trade that is plagued by local thugs, Chinese triads, and international drug smugglers. The threatened Haliotis midae is considered second in quality only to Mexican abalone.

On Friday, ten poachers were arrested in four hours and a catch valued at R730,000 was confiscated. The success of the operation was credited to Sassy.

"We owe the entire catch to her," presiding officer Van Zyl Smit explained. "She's a hero."

Thursday looked up to find the tellers staring at him, expecting a reaction. He just shook his head and paid for the fish meal. This seemed to be enough for them.

Sassy's demise actually made him relieved because she wouldn't be sniffing him into prison. The new powers of search and seizure were what worried him. All he had was a padlock on his front door.

Casually, he went through the procedures required to contact Ip the smuggler. He sent an SMS to the name Telemann. Ip sent a return SMS within moments. Efficient. Thursday went to a pay phone and dialed the number. It picked up after the first ring.

"Leon?" Ip asked.

Thursday didn't know whether to say he was Leon or not. If Ip didn't know him, then he might get scared and hang up.

"Yeah," Thursday said.

There was a pause. "You don't sound like Leon."

"I've got the flu. Two hundred fresh adults," he said. "Thirty years old."

The phone hung up.

Shit, Thursday thought, as he continued home. That was evidently the wrong answer. He must have been too aggressive. Now what would he do? He had no contacts and Leon would kill him if he found out he'd blown the phone call.

The abalone had all receded into their shells and were unmoving in the bathtub, unhappy with their new claw-footed home. Poor dears. He dropped in a few scoops of fish meal. His tiny, lime-washed house only had two rooms, and in those two rooms there was one couch, a rickety pinewood table, and a mattress on the floor, so he spent as much time as he could smoking outside, listening to the far off hoots of the ships navigating the bay. He left and lit a cigarette.

The phone call was a fuck-up, but Thursday was a cautious optimist. He played with the idea that maybe he could take the perlies to Abalone Silver. There were some prime females in the bathtub. Maybe Mr. Pretorius would offer him some money for them and give him his job back. If that didn't work, he could give some to Leon's mom. She made a nice abalone stew and it would make her happy, which she might tell Leon about. Also some to Leon's stepsister, who had a beer batter recipe she liked to cook perlies with. That might be the difference between death and survival, by a hair. But a hair was enough. He returned to the tub and saw that a few of the more adventurous abalone had already begun extending their radulae to nibble on the fish meal.

There was a hard knock on the door. He carefully drew the shower curtain around the tub, shutting the bathroom door behind him. He peered out from his bedroom to find Leon's girl Fadanaz.

He opened the door and found her looking pouty in a red shawl, with one foot stomping in front. He smiled and leaned in for a kiss, but she held him back.

"How could you do it?" she asked.

He stopped smiling. So she knew he'd been involved. Play it cool, he thought. She doesn't know you have the perlies in your tub. All that's in there are shampoos and soaps. "How could I do what?"

"What do you mean, 'do what'? You know what you did. You are a pig. You don't deserve him, you poes. But I won't let him go to jail for you. Not my Leon. I'm turning you in, Thursday!"

Fadanaz's breasts pushed out when she was angry, and their presence made it hard for him to register her words. "Leon was supposed to warn me."

"So you go and shoot a dog, Thursday! A dog! You are a pig." She turned on her heel, but Thursday grabbed her by the elbow.

"What did you say, Fadanaz?"

"Leave me alone, you killer. A helpless dog. You pig! I'm not going to let Leon go to Pollsmoor for you. No one, and I mean no one, will take away my Leon!"

"Fadanaz, I didn't shoot Snoopy."

"Sassy!"

"I was in the water. I don't know who shot Sassy."

"You lie. Leon told me everything. I can't pay for bail! I can't help him!" She began wacking him with her purse. "And I'm not going to let your ass go free!"

Thursday covered his head with his hands as she battered him. He considered showing her the bathtub, but she ran off when he took his hands away. He fished out a cigarette.

What had Leon been talking about, saying that he shot Sassy? Why would Leon make that up? Thursday had promised to help him at the police station, and Leon was dependent on him now. Why would he lie about that?

The only thing he could come up with was that Fadanaz had gotten to Leon first, and he'd said some nonsense to get Fadanaz to help him. Leon always talked a lot of kak, and Thursday couldn't blame him for wanting to get out of jail. If he got transferred to Pollsmoor there were 60,000 prisoners ahead of him who hadn't even had a trial yet. But now Thursday had a bathtub full of poached perlemoen and Fadanaz was on her way to turn him in.

He had to move, and he had to move fast. If she informed the police that he'd shot the dog, they'd be there in minutes, with photographers in tow. He ran inside and picked up the fishnet bag, and began stuffing the abalone in, handfuls at a time, recklessly.

"Hang in there," he cooed, "I'm taking you home."

Their tentacles retracted into their shells in abject fear. He put the fishnet sack in a garbage bag, gathered up all the money he had, and deadbolted the door. Circling around the building, he weaved behind some houses through a paddy of wild lilies towards the bay.

Why, Leon?

He crunched along the small pebbles of the beach and scrambled over boulders until the waves were crashing just in front of him, his face wet with salt spray. Teetering, he held the bag up over the water and began to toss the abalone towards a kelp bed one by one. They were strong enough, he hoped, to slime out to safety.

Then he felt the cell phone vibrating, and dug it out of his pocket with his free hand. One new message. He opened it:

78A, L. Main. Obz. C.T. 10am. Ip.

Cape Town was two hours away by minibus taxi. Half of the perlemoen had already been plunked into the water. The other half, still in the sack. Beyond he could see the reflection of an ocean tanker on the water, and far away on the beach, the mahogany sheen of a child running along the sand in the spume.

Evil Knows Where Evil Sleeps

1993
Stockholm, Sweden

Wale was the first on the tram, the fifth to descend from it, and one of many walking through the balmy Stockholm streets. Somehow, at four in the morning, it was already light. The low lying boats on the canals were beginning to slide from their moorings as the sun dappled through the water. Wale was wearing a Western suit, a fresh shirt, the polysaccharides of four greasy inflight meals, and a five-at-night shadow, left in place to disguise his face.

People were still expected to work in these conditions, Wale thought. Just pretend that they'd had a restful night of sleep with the sun prying open their eyelids and start all over again. In the winter it would be worse. Yet so many Africans on the continent thought that Scandinavia was the answer to all their problems.

The tram driver told him to turn left along Oxenstiersgaten and Wale did so, pushing past bakeries, a butcher, and a few electronics shops with astronomical prices. The bakers were up. The bouncers were up. And there, strolling past him in fishnets and white paint, a pair of—punks, was it? Or goths? Wale had never followed the trends but the kids seemed to be returning from a party.

He turned left onto Vallhallavagen. The red bricked buildings of the Royal Technology Institute lined both rows of the street, the laboratories softly aglow with safety lights. Soon, rosy-cheeked graduate students would fill the halls with the promise of fellowships and grant monies in pursuit of a bright future of innovation.

If only they knew, Wale thought, the life of a dead-end lab. Bureaucrats peering down at you through the glass ceiling like you were an exotic fish.

Bello had never arrived at the airport. Wale had stood holding the snow globe with its swirling contraband for some twenty minutes until his shoulders screamed from the pain, and then clutched it close to his chest like a baby. This alone had drawn the attention of airport security, but more out of curiosity, and he'd dragged his family through terminal after terminal until he could decide on a plan. He couldn't go to Nigeria without Bello's escort and he couldn't get to Cape Town, the fallback point, without a visa. He was angry with Bello and more than that afraid of what would happen if he were caught for stealing the moon dust. What would happen to his family? His career, his American life of fifteen grueling years? Learning the names of baseball stars and, worse, their stats, batting averages, slugging percentages, stolen bases, ERAs, all to fit in, all just to make it through the slog?

Hoping that Bello had made a mistake, Wale had pestered the numerous airline counters for secret messages or dropped codes, anything that indicated what Bello wanted him to do or where he should go. Instead, he learned the names of countries that he'd never heard of, Tonga, Slovenia, Kyrgyzstan.

The problem was that Bello had kept his secrets when assembling his team for its triumphant return to Nigeria. He hadn't once revealed the names of Wale's fellow scientists in Operation Brain Gain, although he'd spoken glowingly of them.

"We've got people from America, Canada, the UK, Holland, Switzerland and France. The absolute best, the absolute brightest all returning home to feed the river." By river he meant Nigeria. "It will pay well," he'd added. "Winsomely."

Wale had never been interested in the money, feeling that a bigger home or a faster car wouldn't move him any closer to where he'd wanted to go, which was Up. Not in the air but in the silky atmosphere of Earth's great satellite, the Moon. Even with that vision, Wale was pragmatic.

"I don't care about those things, Bello. I want to know that this will work. I don't want to get to Taro and find out that we don't have any power. We can't have our computers reset in the middle of a data set. You can't have blackouts in the middle of a launch." The last time that Wale had visited Nigeria he'd left with the smell of agusi and diesel gasoline burning in his nostrils from the power generators. The country was plagued by rolling blackouts; he'd been at a wedding once, and the bride and groom had stopped their first dance as the power supply winked out. When the music changes, the best man had laughed, so does the dance.

"We'll have it ready," Bello insisted. "We've identified a launch site and we have people who know how to clear it. We've got a construction engineer who worked on the platforms in French Guiane for the Ariane rockets. Half the world's payloads launch from French Guiane, Wale. Our team knows how to clear a jungle and pave it into a world class hub of technology. We have twice the funds and three times the land area. It might take a while, but the palm wine tapper will climb down from the palm tree. Be patient."

"I don't want any palm wine. I want electricity."

Bello had then disappeared for a few weeks. At the time, Wale had felt some relief and resumed his duties at the Lunar Lab, even resurrecting a belief that he might be promoted or that his boss, Tom Rilker, would increase his acquisition budget. He felt like he'd avoided a catastrophe but the thought nagged him that he had missed something grand, something wonderful, a dream that would be scratched apart under the lunar microscopes.

Eventually, Bello had called him again. "I've found someone for your electricity," he declared happily.

"Who?"

"You know I can't tell you that."

"Why is that? Wouldn't it be better if we knew who we were working with?"

"Look, Wale. This is a revolutionary program. We're returning the best minds to Nigeria. Connecting the marsh to the river. The country has been ruled by the fist for years, not by the mind. Evil knows where evil sleeps. We don't want Brain Gain to get mired in corruption, handouts, or nepotism. We want transparency that's free of the extended family. We want Brain Gain to be functioning before the politicians can slap their grubby slogans all over it. Nothing scares autocrats like sunlight. We have to fly above them—straight to the moon."

By now Wale had learned to sift through Bello's public relations hyperbole. "That's all well and good, Bello, but it's not enough for me to uproot my family. How do I know you found the right person? You can't just pull electricity out of thin air."

At this Bello had laughed. "This one can. You'll see soon enough. All I can tell you that he's a mechanical engineer in Scandinavia. Tenured."

It had been Bello's first, and perhaps only, slip. Until that conversation, he'd only hinted that Wale would be working with top-class expatriates, all scientists who had established themselves abroad in the hinterland: computer scientists, civil engineers, geologists, and microbiologists. Bello himself had a science background—he was Special Adjunct to the Minister of the Environment after all—and could speak their technical languages fluently, or at least well enough to be understood. Except Bello didn't know how few Nigerian mechanical engineers had become tenured professors in Scandinavia. There was only one, and his name was Dr. Obafemi Ferguson.

With his baby boy crying in Dulles Airport and his wife Tinuke questioning him—how could you do this to us?—Wale bought tickets to Stockholm on that knowledge alone. He checked the family into a small airport hotel and took a shuttle to the city's downtown.

He hadn't seen Dr. Obafemi Ferguson since graduate school at Birmingham. He'd corresponded with him once, inquiring about his family—good health—and his publication record—four peer reviewed articles at the time—more as a measuring stick than out of friendship. Ferguson was a mechanical engineer who disliked idle conversation and disdained basketball and soccer. They'd tolerated each other in Birmingham in England as two Nigerians in a class of Indians, Irish, Egyptians, and even a few English, as reminders of life at home rather than friends. Ferguson had laid out his career in deliberate, carefully ordered steps, with articles, fellowships, and lectures patiently guided into place like a suspension bridge. Everything in Ferguson's career hedged against surprises, Acts of God. Wale was shocked that Bello had successfully recruited him.

Wale peered through bleary eyes as the sun illuminated the endless rows of brick buildings: industrial engineering, civil engineering, electrical engineering, computer engineering, some sort of nuclear lab, and then, finally, at the end, mechanical engineering. He found a bench outside and sat down. By now it was four forty-five in the morning. The professors wouldn't arrive until eight. He would wait.

Ferguson never came to his lab, so Wale tracked him down in his office in an administrative building. He no longer wore the geeky spectacles that he'd sported as a graduate student and he'd whipped his hair into a gray-brown afro. Although he had a Yoruba name, Ferguson was raised Muslim and he had extended family that was Hausa in the north. The room smelled of a fruity potpourri, the kind that Tinuke liked to place over the toilet seat. Ferguson was anxiously flipping through a scholarly book.

"Dr. Ferguson," Wale said politely.

"I'm not holding office hours today," he said, not bothering to look up.

"Good," Wale said. "Because then you couldn't speak with me, Femi, could you?"

Ferguson placed a finger to mark his page and then his head snapped up. Wale, feeling impatient and reckless, circled around the desk. He seized the book from Ferguson's hand. It was entitled Photovoltaics Under Carter: A Promise of Policy. "When did you get into photovoltaics?"

"Ten years ago. It's my specialty. I'm assistant director of the PV lab here at the Institute." He leaned back in his chair, extending his hand. Wale clasped his palm and they snapped their fingers together and touched their hearts. Neither had used the greeting in Nigeria but the two had shared it while at Birmingham. "Wale," Ferguson smiled, "I haven't seen you in years! Please, please, have a seat."

Wale shut the door to the office.

"We have an open door policy—"

"—you'll have to excuse me, Femi, but this is a pressing matter. I'm sorry but I don't have time for chit-chat."

Ferguson nodded, evidently glad to be able to avoid it.

Wale went on: "Is there anyone who might be listening?"

"No. We should be fine here. The old nuclear lab is bugged but we don't have anything worth monitoring."

"Good. I'm going to say one word and I want you to tell me what it means to you."

"Ah, an old Yoruba riddle. I haven't heard one of those in a while," he smiled. "Go ahead."

"Bello."

Ferguson instantly sat up straight. He looked more closely at Wale now. It was enough to know that Bello had spoken the truth. Bello had spoken to Ferguson, maybe even met him.

"Have you heard from him?" Ferguson asked.

"Not since yesterday."

"He told you to come here?"

"No, Femi. Look at my eyes. I haven't slept. I was supposed to be in Abuja right now. For a few days. And then off to Taro."

Wale told him briefly what had happened. How Bello had arranged the flights and left him and his family at Dulles begging for visas like table scraps. How he'd flown to Sweden on a hunch. He left out the snow globe.

"Better a beggar than a thief," Ferguson intoned. Wale tried not to react to the proverb, and anyway he didn't know the proper retort. It was a Hausa expression. "But how did you know about me? Did he tell you? He wouldn't tell me about the other scientists."

"I recruited you," Wale said, "in a way. I told him that we needed electricity and he said he'd found an expert. Now that I see you're into photovoltaics, I understood what he meant. You can pull electricity from the sun, right? He must want solar power in Taro."

Wale took the time now to look around the room. It was surprisingly spacious and decorated with streamlined modern furniture, a mixture of wood and leather. Dolls from Ife and Oyo state were sprinkled about the office along with a hanging scroll decorated with Arabic characters in flowing Diwani script. Papers were amassed on Ferguson's desk and an Ascot hat hung on a coat rack. Another day at the office.

"You don't look like you were traveling anytime soon," he observed.

Ferguson grabbed his hat and placed it neatly over his afro. "I think it's best we take a walk, Wale."

They left the building and headed towards the canal. The sun pressed into Wale's eyes and coated everything in a patina of primary colors. "I don't understand how you do it," Wale squinted. "It's bright as the devil."

"Ah, the midnight sun? We use blackout shades. The problem isn't sleeping, but waking up again when the room is dark. I'm working on something like that, on the side. An alarm clock that wakes you by light instead of sound."

Same old Femi, Wale thought. He'd always admired Ferguson's inventiveness, as if a solution to every problem was around the corner. Bello had chosen well. It would be invigorating to work with an optimist for a change. Ferguson had heard of Bello, he'd known something about the program and, in Ferguson's quite manner, he seemed excited about it. Wale started to feel better. He found himself drawn to the scent of fresh pastries, also the smell of coffee.

"Come," Ferguson said, "I'll buy you a kanelbulle."

They ate the doughy cinnamon pastries in silence over a bar height table.

"He asked you to steal something, didn't he?" Ferguson asked, sipping on his coffee. He said it so casually that Wale found himself nodding before he meant it, then quickly shook his head vigorously like a madman. "It's alright. He wanted me to take something too. He called it my commitment."

"It's collateral so we don't back out. Did you take it?"

Ferguson smiled, tipping his Ascot. "I'm wearing it right now."

"A hat!" Wale's coffee spilled down his shirt. He quickly wiped it up. "That's it?"

"Quiet down, Wale. Quiet down. It's not the hat. It's what is in the hat. My latest PV cell. It works like a roof tile. You can hammer through it and still link it to a simple base unit. We'll line all the roofs of Taro with these when Bello's project money arrives and channel it right back to the grid."

"You developed this?"

Ferguson adjusted the hat, but didn't take it off. He explained that he'd developed the PV cells with university funds, so he'd been forced to assign all the patents back to the university. The government was subsidizing wind energy and not solar, and SIDA, the Swedish development agency, was pushing an experimental water filtration system so didn't consider PV a priority. His Nigerian birth prevented him from becoming director of the lab under the Institute's bylaws so he had no power to appropriate the needed funds. He also wasn't a citizen because he hadn't married a Swede, but a Malian.

"I refuse to let my work rot," he said, "when cities like Jos have two hundred fifty days of bright sun a year."

The story felt eerily familiar, Wale thought. The dead-end lab. Bello had chosen his team wisely. "What about Bello? I haven't heard from him. I'm afraid he backed out."

"The money's in my account, Wale. Quite a lot of it. Have you checked yours?"

Wale hadn't checked. He'd been too busy fleeing the country as quickly as possible. You couldn't just check a numbered Swiss bank account at a Western Union. Bello had promised double. If he'd truly backed out, Ferguson said, he would have taken the money too.

"There's a branch in Basel. It's a two hour flight from here. Why don't you stop there on the way to Abuja? I'm sure something pressing came up, Wale. Besides, if there was any trouble Bello would have at least warned us. Why don't we give him a call when we return to my office? I'm sure everything is arranged as planned."

"You have his phone number?" Wale couldn't believe it. Bello would always contact him or leave beeper numbers. He'd never enjoyed direct access.

"Of course! How do you think I speak with him? He left the number with the tickets along with the address in Cape Town. It's not his direct

line, though. Bello uses a go-between. He's the one that's been organiz-
ing everything, the tickets and so forth. I dial up the go-between and he
puts me through to Bello."

The tickets, Wale thought, the tickets! He'd forgotten them in the
Corolla in Houston and had been forced to buy his own tickets to DC.
From there, Bello's go-between was supposed to send him on to Nigeria.
There might have been instructions along with the tickets, and anyway
Ferguson had his number and they could simply call him. If Wale could
swallow his pride, then Bello's slip was forgivable, even understandable.

They finished their coffee and walked along Strandvagen by the port.
Now that he'd had a cup of coffee, the primary colors had begun to
develop nuance, intensities coming into focus. The boats bobbed in the
waves in a measured harmony. He couldn't call the waterfront buildings charming, but they had a ship-shape, mercantile appeal to them
with the occasional balustrade.

I made the right choice coming here, Wale thought.

"Wale, you still haven't told me," Ferguson said.

"What's that, now?"

"What you took."

They paused to let a tram thunder past. On the tram, Wale caught a
glimpse of a few Africans watching them curiously, almost as if he was
intruding on their space. He'd had that feeling before, arriving at a party
in Houston and thinking he was the only Nigerian in the room, feeling
unique, when another walked in wearing a flowing agbada. He'd have
to revisit his image of Sweden, he thought. He'd thought they were all
buxom and leggy blondes who either sang opera or wore swimsuits.

"It's the Contingency Sample," Wale said, "from the first Apollo
moon landing."

"What do you mean by 'contingency'?"

Wale was so accustomed to working with lunar geologists that he
assumed that all scientists thought in the code language of the lunar
lab. "During each Apollo moon mission, there was the risk that the astronauts would not be able to complete their experiments. They might
be low on air, say, or the landing craft may have been damaged during

the flight and need to be repaired. There was any number of possibilities that would prevent a full moon walk. NASA wanted the astronauts to leave with something no matter what in order to justify the expense. This was called the Contingency Sample."

Another tram passed by. No Africans on this one, just Swedes packed in like rosy-cheeked sardines.

"Go on," Ferguson said.

"During the first mission, the task fell to Neil Armstrong. Right after he took his first steps on the moon and said his words, he used a rake to scoop a sample into a bag and return it to the landing craft. Of course, nothing else did go wrong in the next few hours. Armstrong had sealed the bag improperly and the contents mixed with dust in the landing craft, so it didn't have any scientific value. I was one of the only people who knew where the sample was located. Bello asked me to take it. He said it didn't belong to America but all humanity. He said we would return it to the moon when we landed our first mission as a symbol of 'the colonized returning the cultural patrimony of all mankind.' He wants us to plant a Nigerian flag."

Ferguson allowed himself a smile. "That sounds like Bello."

Ferguson's flight wasn't for a few more days and he said that the missing PV cells wouldn't be discovered for some time, perhaps even years. He'd replaced the cell with a mock-up in the lab and would retain his title as an emeritus professor. He was so patient and calm about the situation that Wale felt childish. Wale hadn't sold the house in Houston or negotiated any sort of honorable release from NASA; no, he'd locked his lab partner in a vault and stolen his boss's car. It was unlikely he'd ever be able to return to Texas.

"Don't be so hard on yourself, Wale. As we say, Allah preserve us from 'If only I'd known.'"

They boarded a tram to Ferguson's apartment. Wale wanted to call Tinuke in the hotel and assure her that everything was alright. He also wanted to contact Bello. Ferguson pointed out cultural landmarks as the tram narrowly avoided crushing tourists on rented bicycles. After they stepped off, they walked to an old four-story building with a placard:

1843. Ferguson used a skeleton key to enter the door and they stepped through a portico into a small courtyard lined with ivy. A half-dozen bicycles were parked in a rack and marble steps led into three different entrances to the left, right, and center of them.

"Do you own?" Wale asked.

"Rent." Ferguson jingled another key to enter the doorway on the left, but when he inserted the key the door budged open. He paused. "Strange. I'll have to let the tenants know. It's sort of a cooperative."

A narrow marble staircase twisted up before them, the steps worn from years of use. There was a dank, musty smell that reminded Wale, not unpleasantly, of basements. They climbed the steps until Ferguson stopped abruptly on the third floor.

"What is it?"

Ferguson shushed him quiet. Before them, a dark green apartment door was partially open.

"Wife?" Wale whispered.

"She's in Bamako."

"Maybe it's Bello."

They crept forward. Ferguson grabbed a fire extinguisher from the wall. They could hear papers being tossed and pots banging in the apartment. Whoever it was didn't seem worried about making noise.

"We should call the police," Wale said.

Ferguson pointed at his hat and shook his head. Wale got it, they couldn't call. He was a thief and Wale was too. Better a beggar than a thief.

A large object crashed to the floor. Wale tensed. He began stepping slowly back down the stairs. "Let's leave, Femi. Wait to see who comes out. No need to play the hero."

But it was too late. Ferguson kicked the door open with a yell, screaming maniacally. "This is my apartment! Get the hell out of here!"

Wale stayed glued to the steps.

"Who are you?" Ferguson shouted. "What are you doing here?"

Then, a husky voice, eerily calm: "It's no concern of yours."

"Wait, wait, wait!" Ferguson said, suddenly sounding scared. "It's fine! Put that down! Take what you want. I'll leave."

"No you won't," the burglar said. "You know whatahm looking for, o."

Wale tried to place the accent. West African? He didn't see anything he could use as a weapon. He inched back up the steps, hoping to get a glimpse. Once he knew what the burglar looked like, he could wait for him in the courtyard or follow him, get the jump on him somehow.

"I'm afraid I don't know what you're talking about," Ferguson said.

"The PV cell. Give it to me, o."

So he knew about it, Wale thought. How many people had Femi told? He moved to the doorway.

"You'll leave, then," Ferguson said. "You promise that?"

"Dat depends." There was a pause. "No, hands down! No tricks, o."

"It's not a trick. The cell is on my head. In the lining."

"Get down on your knees."

Wale held his breath. Then he peered around the corner. Before him, he could see Ferguson on his knees on an Oriental rug. The burglar's back was turned to the door and his chocolate-skinned arm was holding a small pistol. Ferguson spied Wale as he crept forward and looked over Wale's shoulder, pointing with his eyes. Wale turned to see a light summer jacket hanging from a hook. Ferguson nodded, just slightly.

"Who are you?" Ferguson said, trying to distract the burglar. "Who are you working for?"

"Not your concern."

Wale fished in the pockets of the summer jacket and found a short thick white envelope. He tucked it into his belt. He searched for something he could use to attack, but could only find a pillow. He picked it up. Put it down again.

"I have money," Ferguson went on. "I can give you a dash."

"Not anymore. We froze your accounts. Toss me de hat."

Ferguson removed the hat from his head and threw it to the burglar. He tore the fabric open.

Wale drew closer now, ready to leap. I can do this, he thought, I can jump on him before he turns.

"You were telling de truth," the burglar said. "You shouldn't have."

And it was all too swift. He snapped the pistol up and fired at Ferguson. Blood sprayed out from his jaw onto a white couch behind him. He let out a whimper. Then he stepped forward a pace and took aim between Ferguson's eyes.

"No!" Wale shouted.

Wale leapt for him as he fired. The bullet thumped into the couch as Wale tackled him in the waist, and the gun flew across the floor. Ferguson fell to the carpet with blood dripping from his jaw. The gun was still close to the burglar and Wale scrambled for it on the floor. He whipped at Wale with a knife, tearing his shirt sleeve until he withdrew his arm. It was all the time the burglar needed. The gun was closer to him now, within reach, and Wale had nothing but his fists. He squinted at Wale with yellowed, watery eyes.

Wale dived headlong into the stairwell as the shot exploded into the door frame. He rolled down a few steps before righting himself with his forearm. Then he leapt the entire distance onto the next landing.

He plunged into the courtyard, expecting to find the burglar barreling after him. But he didn't come. He halted for a moment and held his breath. Then he heard another thump, like a cricket bat slamming into a pillow. He looked for the burglar in the window but he didn't appear. He would have to come down eventually, he thought. But there was nothing to attack him with, only a few flower pots lining the courtyard, which could hardly threaten his gun. He was too quick with it. Wale ran.

Wale hopped on the nearest tram and switched lines three times until he found himself near a park lined with baby strollers. Young mothers pushed their children beneath weeping cherry trees, casting sidelong glances at the nervous, sweaty man. Then he picked up a payphone and called the police, giving a false name.

"Ah, Mr. Smith, you mean he is a Negro?" the dispatcher said in lumbering English, sweetly.

"Yes, a Negro. An African." He went into detail about the burglar's rich chocolate skin and his yellowed eyes, feeling stupid that he had nothing else to give.

"Thank you. A Negro."

"He has a gun! Armed and dangerous! Get there now!"

"But you must be mistaken. Guns are not legal in Stockholm," the dispatcher argued.

Wale hung up. The police might just catch the burglar if they were quick enough. At least that would be something. He hoped they didn't arrive with Billie clubs.

He frightened away a young mother on a bench and stared into space, replaying the incident again and again as the children in the park screamed and giggled and climbed over things. It had all happened so fast. Here they were preparing to call Bello, set things right, and the burglar had appeared. For all his years in Texas, Wale had never seen a gun fired before. His basketball teammate Bill Dalton had once dragged him to a game of paintball and that was enough for him. He remembered the balls whizzing by his ear as he hid behind rocky outcroppings that felt much too small, the sting of a direct hit, and catching Dalton in the act of rubbing off a splash of blue from his trousers, to which he'd replied: "It doesn't count if you can rub it off."

The real thing was much worse. He'd felt paralyzed by the force of the shot that had torn clean through Ferguson's jaw, and then the knife as it had almost sliced him. Somehow the burglar had known about the PV cell. That meant he probably knew about Bello and Brain Gain in general, and he was willing to kill for it. Why? And the dispassion with which the burglar had spoken to Femi when he'd known all along that he would shoot him, as if he'd been toying with him. If Femi had only lied about the PV cell he might not have been shot. If Femi had listened to Wale and stayed out of the apartment in the first place, none of this would have happened.

Allah preserve us, Femi had said, from 'If only I'd known'.

"We froze your accounts," the burglar had said in his husky, almost lazily effeminate voice. Which accounts? Was he talking about the Swiss account? No one knew about it, presumably, other than Bello. Who did he mean by 'we'? Who was powerful enough to freeze someone's bank account? Was it Interpol? The CIA? The Russians? Femi hadn't truly stolen anything yet, unlike Wale. And why did he care about the photovoltaic cell? Even the Swedes didn't care about it—Femi had said so himself.

He tore open Ferguson's envelope. Inside, he found a ticket from Stockholm to Basel and a ticket from Basel to Abuja, both departing in two days' time. There was also a ticket from Bamako to Abuja, stopping in Dakar, departing the following week. The Bamako ticket was presumably for Ferguson's wife in Mali. To his dismay, Wale saw that Ferguson's name was clearly printed on the tickets. They were useless to him. Behind the tickets, he found several small decals on wax paper, the kind you might find in a cereal box, meant to be ironed onto a teeshirt. There were four. Two green and two yellow. Entry visas. Those he could use.

He found a much smaller sheet of paper, a note typical of the ones Bello liked to leave, with this scribbled on it:

Photovoltaic Formula

$$\begin{pmatrix} Cu \\ Ag \\ Au \end{pmatrix} \begin{pmatrix} Al \\ Ga \\ In \end{pmatrix} \begin{pmatrix} S \\ Se \\ Te \end{pmatrix}_2$$

It was an older formula, widely available in scientific journals, and Wale could think of no practical use for it. It was hardly revolutionary or worth hiding. On the reverse side, he found a hand-written address: 251 Upper Tree Road, Cape Town: 41421. Finally, he felt some relief. It was the address to the fallback point in Cape Town.

Laundering

1993
Stockholm, Sweden

Lights were flashing in front of the airport hotel when Wale arrived. Two police cars, one with an officer in it, were parked along the circular drive. He grew frightened. He'd given a false name to the dispatch, but maybe they'd had a tip-off or wanted to question him. Had that burglar called it in? He was capable of such devilry; he was capable of anything. He also had the chilling realization that the description he'd given of the attacker would fit him as well. Ah Mr. Smith, the dispatcher had said, you mean he is a Negro? Wale was a Negro. Ferguson was a Negro. It had been stupid to call the police at all.

His wife Tinuke would be inside the hotel, no doubt calling her relatives to complain about her husband. His son Dayo would be with her, wobbling in his three-year-old shuffle. Wife and son. His charges.

At the nearest payphone he called the hotel lobby and asked to be patched through to their room.

"Tinuke."

"Wale! Why didn't you call? I was worried."

"I didn't want any trouble."

"Where have you been? No, wait, here is Dayo. He wants to say hello."

He heard the receiver being passed to his son. "Papa! Papa!"

"Good, Dayo. Please put your mother on the phone."

"Are you coming back to the hotel?" Tinuke asked.

"I'm right outside."

He looked up at the airport hotel and saw curtains being drawn aside on the third floor. Tinuke stepped into view wearing tight-fitting stretch jeans, a garment Wale found distasteful. She was frowning. "What are you doing, Wale? Come inside."

"It's the police. Have they bothered you?"

"No."

71

"I'll come up."

It was a small, utilitarian hotel room. Every wall was white and sterile and so thin you could hear the programs line by line as the guest next door watched television. There was a high pinewood desk and a stiff contemporary arm chair. The room had a view of the street and, through two identical hotels, the planes on the tarmac of the airport beyond.

Tinuke was washing something in the bathroom sink when he opened the door. His son came tottering up in tiny Hawaiian print Jams shorts with a light blue beanie. Wale scooped him into his arms and Dayo said a lot of gibberish, punctuated by 'Papa, Papa', and the odd logical sentence or two. Tinuke squeezed his arm and for a moment they were a happy family.

"Dayo's been sick. He threw up in your suitcase."

Wale noticed the empty suitcases and the clothes strewn about the room.

"The police didn't come?"

"No."

Dayo began pattering around the room, yelling "Boats! Boats! Boats!" He sped into the bathroom and right back out again. "Boats! Boats! Boats!"

"I told you to keep our suitcases packed."

"Don't start, Wale. Please."

He stuffed his clothes back into his suitcase, ignoring the smell: "You're sure the police didn't come."

"Don't pack them, Wale. Put them in the sink. I have wash to them."

"Did a man named Bello call?"

Tinuke looked at him with sudden concern. "No one called."

He put his thumb on his chin and paced back and forth. They had to leave immediately. It was too dangerous to be here. At any moment the killer could be tracking him down.

"We're going. Pack your things." Tinuke slowed for an instant before continuing to drop clothes in the sink. "I said pack your bags."

"Wale, you just returned. You need to sleep. You were up all night."

"I'll help you pack."

He pulled aside the curtain. No sign of the killer. Tinuke began massaging her temple. He fished around her suitcase for her passport and pulled the clothes iron from the tiny closet. He carefully peeled off the entry visas and ironed them into her passport, one for South Africa, the next for Nigeria. Then he began working on his own. South Africa, yes. Nigeria—and Dayo careened into him.

"Dayo! Stop your running!"

"Boats!"

The Nigeria visa had smudged beyond recognition. It looked like a green insect had been smashed on the page.

No problem, he thought, trying to remain calm. I'll get Bello's man to give me another one in Cape Town.

Tinuke arrived behind him, shaking and tearful. "Wale, I haven't asked. I haven't. So I would like you to answer for me. Where have you been?"

"Meeting a friend."

"You expect me to pack up and leave? When you won't tell me anything? When was the last time you told me the truth?"

"It's not just anywhere. We'll go to Basel—that's only a two hour flight—and pick up a few things. Then we'll go to Cape Town to meet Bello."

"If you want to go to Nigeria so badly, let's go. Let's go to Nigeria. We have family there. In Cape Town I don't know anyone. There's apartheid."

Wale went on about how Mandela had been freed and how there were opportunities for an election. "You've seen the news. Apartheid's over. Bello will be there. We have to meet him at the fallback point."

She began crying on the edge of the bed, but when he tried to comfort her, she shrugged him off. And he thought to himself, what would he tell Ferguson's wife? She was in Mali, according to Ferguson, but how could he tell her that he'd just watched a man shoot her husband in the jaw? And that he'd fled for his life like a coward?

"Come on, Tinuke, this is no time for dramatics. We have to go!"

"Why?"

"To meet him! He's the one that arranged everything."

"You've lost it, Wale! Wake up! It's Nigeria! You're a lunar geologist! What does Nigeria have to do with you, or us, anymore?"

Tinuke had abandoned a career in nutritional science to raise their family, and he remembered this at moments like these, her sacrifices filling the silences. She was smaller than him by a few inches, but broader in the womanly places, with soft, dark brown eyes. He had married a beauty and been plagued by her mind, which probed into his bold assertions with the slipperiness of a microbe.

"Bello will be there," he said coldly.

"Yet you won't introduce me to him or call him. What are we doing here? What did you do, Wale? Why are you so afraid of the police?"

He peered out again from behind the curtains. Still only one police car, but more might be on the way.

"Not now, Tinuke! We don't have the time."

"Are you a criminal?"

"Pack your things. Dayo, come on, Dayo, would you like to get in an airplane?"

"Boats!"

Tears, crying, more dramatics.

"Are you a criminal? I can accept that, Wale. I'm your wife. Just tell me what you did so I know you're okay. We can get through it together."

"Don't be silly! Let's go."

Dayo was playing with a toy rubber vampire. The toy had at first terrified the boy, but he'd conquered his fear somehow and it now became his companion whenever his parents were shouting. Wale picked him up, dragging his suitcase with his free hand.

"Papa!"

"Come, Tinuke!"

She grabbed something from Wale's suitcase. "What is this, Wale?"

It was the snowglobe, still full of the moondust from the Apollo mission. It felt inconsequential after what Wale had seen, and dangerous.

The killer might come for it if he knew that Wale had it. He considered smashing it, then gave up the thought on principle. He couldn't defile a piece of the moon. He removed Dayo's pajamas and wrapped the globe, stuffing it into the child's backpack as Tinuke picked him up and planted a kiss on his forehead. Dayo giggled.

"Snow! Snow!"

"What is that toy?"

"It's nothing, Tinuke."

"If it's nothing, then I am not going with you. Because I will not leave over 'nothing'. Not again."

She returned to the bathroom and began sloshing the laundry in the sink, suds spilling over the sides of the basin.

"It is Brain Gain," he muttered.

"Brain Drain?"

"No, Brain Gain. Bello is the director. I'd hoped that it would be a surprise to you but it has become—well, it has become this."

She rinsed the clothes and pulled a drying string across the bathtub. She began draping the soggy clothing, and Wale groaned, thinking they would never dry in time. "What did Bello promise you?"

"He promised to take me back to the country to steer it to a better future. I am going to head the Lunar Department."

"Nigeria wants to go to the moon?"

How would Ferguson have told his wife? Everything had been so simple for him, even planned, yet Wale felt like he was groping blindly.

"It's not the moon that's important: it's what that trip to the moon will produce. We'll have communications satellites, improved crop yields, accurate population censuses. Nigeria doesn't need weapons. We need innovation." He was growing excited now, triumphant. "And it will all trickle down to help the impoverished! I always intended to return home and Bello is my passage back. All I have to do is share the knowledge that I gained abroad."

"Abroad?" Tinuke said. "Abroad is our home. We weren't living abroad, Wale. We were living in America. We've been citizens for years. Dayo was born there! There was never any work for you in Nigeria—

no job. You left because Nigeria has no meteorites. You followed your dream and I am proud of you for that."

An image flashed before his eyes of Ferguson's bloodied jaw. He had allowed himself to be drawn into an argument, when action was required. Tinuke was now emptying Wale's suitcase again and pulling out more of his soiled clothes.

"You hate going back to Nigeria, Wale. I beg you to go all the time and you complain about the graft."

"That's right," Wale admitted. "I do find certain aspects of my homeland to be distasteful. That's what Brain Gain is for! Brain Gain will change that. America would never send an immigrant like me to the moon. You remember Rilker. He was an asshole! He wore cufflinks to McDonald's."

"Language!"

"Nigeria needs me. I wanted to tell you everything but Bello made me swear secrecy. He wanted a last minute surprise. He called it the 'Unveiling'—he's Muslim, you see, and likes to play with words. He's very good with words, actually."

"I see that he is," Tinuke said, pointing to the suitcases on the floor, "because he has done this to us. He has made my husband believe he is going to save Nigeria all by himself. And you still want to find him, this Bello. This man I have never met."

"Don't you see, Tinuke? It's real. Bello is real!"

"Contact him. Tell him what happened to us."

"I can't. Ferguson has been—incapacitated. I don't have his number."

She began frowning at him. "Who's Ferguson?"

"Ferguson is an old friend."

"You never mentioned him before."

"It doesn't matter anymore. Someone shot him."

"Shot?"

Tinuke looked him straight in the eye this time, and it wasn't fear, but anger that he saw there. She immediately called out for Dayo and hugged him close until he squirmed and ran away.

"I need you to trust me, Tinuke. Just this once. Can I ask you to trust me?"

"Did you put us in danger?" she whispered. "Did you put my child in danger?"

"No—not me. I didn't shoot Ferguson. It was someone else. Someone I've never seen before."

"Is it because of what is in that glass toy?"

He ran to the balcony. There were still only two police cars outside the hotel, but a third car had joined it, a Volvo. It could be unmarked.

"I will tell you in Basel," Wale said. "For your own protection."

Tinuke turned suddenly from the sink. She scooped Dayo in her arms, her face full of tears. "Dayo, do you want to stay with me or go with Papa?"

Dayo had gotten the globe now from his backpack. More than the rubber vampire, the snowglobe was enough to keep him mesmerized for hours. "Dayo, look at me," Tinuke repeated. "Would you like to stay with Mama or Papa?"

Dayo kept on grasping at the globe as Wale tried to understand what his wife was doing. "Come on, Tinuke, don't be silly! We're going together!"

"Dayo, Mama or Papa?"

"Papa!" the boy said. "Papa!"

Good answer, Dayo, he thought, good answer. He knew Tinuke would never leave the child.

The bell of the elevator began ringing. The police might be there in seconds. Wale could practically see the bulbous jackboots already, feel the scrape of the handcuffs. "Come, Tinuke!" he hissed, pushing open the door to the stairwell. A blast of summer air tunneled up to meet him. But she was shaking her head. "Come, Tinuke! Meet us outside! We'll go to Basel. I'll tell you about the toy there. I'll tell you everything—I promise. We'll all go together."

Georgie

Through the pine boughs, a whitewashed midliner with a blue under-belly could be seen chugging towards the docks of New Hermanus. Piet Cilliers stood behind the helm, guiding the ship through the gunmetal waters with a rolled cigarette dangling from his lips and a turtleneck sweater. He'd once let Thursday steer that same ship, years before, as a child, when Cilliers had pulled in catch after catch of yellowfin as the pilchards were running, when captaining a ship meant a large home and a stable income. Like most of the captains in Hermanus, Cilliers never bought a trawler because of the cost and because he loved the artfulness of line fishing: the rush from seeing the pole bend on its staunchions; reading the currents and following the seafowl. He'd once had a full crew of eager seamen and now he had just one lazy deckhand and a Humminbird fishfinder. Thursday knew it had been a poor catch as the deckhand threw the ropes onto the moorings. No one on the docks scrambled to offload their fish; only the Angolans would stoop low enough to scrape together a living as a stevedore, but they knew when to conserve their energy.

Thursday had been sitting on the cooler of abalone for over an hour, hitchhiking on the main thoroughfare of Hermanus, with the morning sun burning his neck through a pine grove. Old Hermanus was just a ten minute walk away. The police station was five, but no one had come to arrest him yet.

After a stream of mistrustful glares from tourists in rental cars, a red hatchback pulled over to the shoulder. Thursday made his way towards the car as a curvy young black girl stepped out. It was Leon's girl Thembisa and the look on her face told him she wasn't about to offer him a ride.

"I didn't shoot the dog," he said.

She scrunched up her nose. "What dog?"

"I meant I didn't do anything."

Thembisa ignored him. "Thursday, you tell Leon that I'm not waiting around for him any more. Monday night is our night. I look the other way most of the time, but not on Mondays. I'm finished with his disrespect!" She headed back to the car, also finished, it seemed, with her speech, putting one foot in the car before turning around again: "For Fadanaz! I waited all night for him and he went to that bitch. Monday is our night."

Thursday didn't say that Leon had been in jail on Monday night because he thought it wouldn't help the situation. "Can you lift me to Cape Town?"

"Tell him he'd better be there next time, Thursday!" She slammed the door, gunning the engine so pebbles spat in his direction, and drove off.

Thursday felt obligated to take the next car that stopped, a beat up Opel Rekord, thinking he should at least get moving, even if he had to transfer somewhere along the way. There were two Rastafarians inside, one with a dreadlock so fat that he mistook it for a ferret slithering up his shoulder, and the other man short and brooding. In the back seat a fawn-colored shar pei panted lazily.

"You going to Cape Town?" Thursday asked.

"Salt River."

"That in Cape Town?"

"Ja. Next to Observatory."

Thursday couldn't believe his luck—his meeting with Ip was in Observatory. The short Rasta walked around to the boot and popped the trunk. Inside were two garbage bags the exact same size as Thursday's. Thursday smelled dagga and tried to pretend he hadn't noticed.

"Are you Nigerians?" he asked, nervously.

The driver laughed. "No mon, we don't deal with them lekwerekwere fucks. What's in your bag?"

"I can't show you."

"You show or you walk. What's your name? We don't want no cops."

"Hampton," Thursday lied.

Thursday opened the bag and, after the Rasta insisted, the cooler, where the live abalone were stacked high in the sea water. He had placed them with their shells facing down, but some of the mollusks had flipped themselves over. One had glued its foot onto the bottom of the lid.

"Look at that! I'n'I gon have us a mighty clam suppa!"

"They're not clams, they're mollusks."

"Mollux? Give I'n'I a couple for the ride."

"Maybe when we get there."

The Rasta shut the boot, nodding and smiling. "A mighty clam suppa!"

They were driving now, with the radio set to an oldies station. It was eight thirty. Ip had said ten o'clock, and if they kept up a good pace Thursday should arrive with time to make the delivery. If things went really well, he could get the cash from the sale to Ip, take a cab home, and bail Leon out of jail by dinner time. He spent the ride figuring out how he could avoid giving the Rasta any abalone which were worth a hundred times the cost of a taxi. The shar pei kept poking its maize-colored nose into his arm so he petted its oddly sticky fur.

"Nigerians, mon, we won't touch 'em. We picked up a Nigerian once, drove 'im all the way to Bloemfontein. We get there, 'ee says, let's go get mah friend. So we're good Rastamen, we go and take 'em to his friend. He got a cooler just like yours. Small, like for fish. I ask to look inside. He like you, he don' want to show me. I say we won' go nowhere unless he show me. He open it up and what's inside?"

"A liver," the driver chimed in.

"A liver, mon. A human liver. We 'ont touch 'em no more."

"Never, mon."

"Never."

He saw Thursday caressing the small dog. "Careful touchin' Georgie, Hampton. He cute but he get you full o' lanolin."

Thursday expected them to take the N2 highway into town, but they followed the mountains by the sea, taking their time on the slow curves. After forty-five minutes, they rounded a corner onto False Bay and there was a long strip of white sand below them on the left side, with Table Mountain visible across the water, the thin clouds above it slightly askance like a toupé. The driver pulled off onto a small dirt driveway that led down to the beach, motoring along low concrete buildings until they reached a cord of wire strung across the road. A white kid with a deep tan, about eight maybe, untied the wire, and they drove behind a long building. The two Rastafarians got out of the car and popped the boot. Thursday stepped out as well.

"How long will you be?"

"Five minutes, brotha. Then I'n'I have our clam suppa."

"I'd like to take my bag," Thursday said, pulling the cooler from the boot.

"Watch Georgie for us, Hampton. Don't let him get into the water or he stink."

The Rastas followed the kid with their garbage bags into the long building. Thursday grabbed Georgie by the collar, but he was a strong dog and dragged Thursday through the sand to some driftwood. He wagged his curled tail with the stick in his jaws. Georgie didn't watch the driftwood when Thursday threw it, relying on his hearing, so before long the dog was rooting in the dunes for another stick. Thursday decided to make the best of his time. Carrying his load to the water, he unwrapped the plastic, opened the cooler, and rinsed the abalone in the sea. The fresh cold water would do them good.

After cleaning the abalone, he found another stick for Georgie and the dog didn't watch the trajectory again and for some reason got riled up and charged into the water. He trotted back to Thursday smelling like sheep dung.

All this time the Rastafarians hadn't come out of the long building. He heard them arguing with someone inside the building, not the kid, but an older man from the sound of it. He knocked on the door.

"Who is it?"

"Hampton."

"Who the hell are you?"

"I want to go to Cape Town."

A white man with a beard and long hair opened the door a few inches, maybe the little kid's father. Thursday could smell chlorine and realized that the building held an indoor pool. Behind the man, one of the Rastas was wearing a swim cap and frog-kicking towards the far end. "Come back later."

"Could you tell them I have to go to Cape Town? They said five minutes."

The man pulled a knife from his swim trunks. "I said come back later."

"Okay, my broer. Calm down. I'll come back later."

He knew Leon would never have let a man shut a door in his face like that, but Thursday had a fear of blades, and he didn't want to get mixed up with their dagga smuggling. It was nine thirty already. Ip had said ten o'clock and Thursday was still forty minutes from Cape Town. If he didn't make the sale, Leon would never make bail. He climbed back to the road and stuck out his thumb again. Some surfers were paddling into the water now, invigorated by the rhythm of the waves, and Georgie was running to them, a wet orange mop with a stick in his mouth and a wagging tail.

Tea with Bello

1993
Bulawayo, Zimbabwe

Six months before Wale arrived in Stockholm, Melissa Tebogo turned over a honey-colored, horse-sized pill in her fingers and decided that her two doctors were secretly trying to kill her. A mug steamed on the kitchen table with a concoction that smelled of bucha and wild African garlic, a root a hundred times the strength of the European variety. Her herb doctor had placed a sprig of pelargonium on the rim of the mug like a garnish and left the room uttering mouthfuls of prayers. She was supposed to drink this foul potion and swallow the pill, just wash it down like a bottle of Fanta. All for the cure.

"You've spent too much time beneath your niqab," her doctor had said, the Western one. "You're not receiving enough Vitamin D from the sun. If you keep this up, your legs will buckle with rickets." He had handed her a bottle full of pills. "Take one of these each morning."

"But they're so big," Melissa had protested.

"I can prescribe smaller doses, but you'll have to take more of them."

She reluctantly held out her hand.

"Your father tells me that your family isn't religious," her doctor went on. "You could take it off, you know. The sun is better for you than a supplement."

"No ways."

"Hiding your skin won't help, young lady. It makes you stand out here in Bulawayo. Sooner or later you'll have to embrace who you are."

"You mean what I have."

"If you like."

Her herb doctor hadn't bothered to convince Melissa of the logic of taking his concoction; she was just fifteen years old, the doctor's expertise was assumed, and her father would make her drink the potion in front of him so she wouldn't empty it down the drain, which she had done several times before. But why should she drink it? What had the potions ever done, anyway, other than make her gag? Her skin was still as marbled as a slice of beef, her body covered in a grotesque swirl of sienna and a ghostly white, in a city of beautiful dark skin, of shea butter, oils, and lotions designed for maximum shine.

But tonight her father was unusually nervous, agitated, and merely ushered the herb doctor out the door as quickly as possible.

"Melissa, tonight is an important night," he said.

"You told me already, Daddy. The raid will be at two. I'm packed and ready to go."

"No, not for the raid, for Mr. Bello. He can help us."

"You mean he's a doctor."

"No, he can make things happen. He's a powerful man."

Her stomach already swirled in the cool evening, the moon perched high and full in the sky, and she knew she wouldn't be able to keep the potion down. As soon as her father left the room, she dumped it into the sink and washed away the evidence. She found him in the living room giving orders to his bodyguards.

She peered through the window curtains, wondering if she could catch a glimpse of the man before he arrived. The street lamps winked in and out, drained by illegal tapping from the grid, their sepia light mingling with the curdled moonbeams between the shanties. But she saw nothing. She sat down at her desk in her room and ambled through some math problems her tutor had left her to while away the time. Her father's personal guard, Rufus, knocked on her door once to ask if she was ready, and she could hear him pacing around the house, opening doors, closets, and eventually clinking about in the kitchen.

The Tebogo home was simply arranged and dimly lit. Her father covered the furniture with clear vinyl plastic and hung a few pictures of soccer stars and famous singers on the wall, the kind of wall furnishings you might find at a corner shop. There was a large screen television with a rabbit ear antenna and a VCR blinking twelve a.m., again and again and again, which her father had never learned how to program. But it was a sizeable home, large enough for Melissa to sequester herself in one of the bedrooms as her father entertained guests or attended to the

Freedom Fighters, who would arrive unannounced in the middle of the night with blood weeping from their wounds, begging for refuge. The plastic, as ugly as it was, kept the stains off the couches and made it easy to wipe away prints before the SADF raided the place. This had happened less often now that the ANC was holding talks with the Nats in South Africa, and her father would sometimes go weeks without visitors.

Around eight-thirty, Melissa heard one of her father's guards shout at a visitor at the front gate, and she ran to the window. She saw a small, bespectacled black man in a three-piece suit with his arms raised as the guard patted him down. He was escorted to the front door and made a few nervous jokes. Then Rufus searched the man again and asked him: "Who is the tough old man left behind after a fire has burnt the forest?"

"Ah, an old Yoruba riddle," the man smiled. "The rock."

Rufus nodded and opened the door to the house, escorting the man into the living room. Melissa skirted away into the kitchen and waited for her father to call for her.

"Mr. Bello," her father said, "I'm Mlungisi Tebogo." Her father had smooth, tawny skin and a constellation of freckles on his high cheekbones.

"Melissa!" her father called. "Come meet our guest."

Melissa slowly approached them. If Bello was surprised by her niqab, he didn't show it. He extended his hand but Melissa curtsied instead.

"The pleasure is all mine," Bello said. "A beautiful home you have, and a lovely daughter."

Her father wouldn't like that, Melissa thought. He had never liked bootlickers, even when they could help him. He pointed to a couch and Bello sat down, slipping forward on the plastic cushion. He righted himself with a grunt. Melissa sat beside her father.

"Please excuse the precautions," her father said. "There are rumors of an SADF raid."

"If your men had been any friskier," Bello joked, "I'd be pregnant."

Her father didn't laugh. Rufus drew his pistol and peered out the window onto the street.

"We are short on time," her father said. "I expect the raid at two. You will need an hour to escape the dragnet."

"Perhaps it's best if I tell you a little about myself," Bello began.

"There's no need."

"But aren't you interested?"

"My sources told me what I needed to know. You have been Special Adjunct to the Minister of the Environment in Nigeria for the past ten years. You come from a family of praise singers. Your father had a reputation as one of the best praise singers at coronations, and mastered a number of instruments."

"The dundun drums," Bello said, "bless his soul."

"You gained fame with The Grand Poobahs, a Muslim pop band that played Fuji music. At some point you wooed the Minister of the Environment into accepting you into his Cabinet. How this came to be I am not sure. You have gained a reputation for thriftiness in a department that is notorious for its graft."

"I'm impressed," Bello smiled. "Your reputation is merited, Mr. Tebogo, as a gatherer of information. May I ask how you learned all this?"

"I have contacts throughout the continent."

"A result of the struggle in South Africa, no doubt. But if you must know, I gained the Minister's favor through his own speech. You see, I memorized his words as he was addressing his audience—we were the opening band—and sang his speech back to him. This is a gift that my family taught me, the use of our memories, the praising of hard choices. And I closed the song with this proverb: 'the sugar cane stalk / already came sweet from heaven.' Do you know what the proverb means?"

"He was already great when he came into office."

"Remarkable—I see that you also know our lore. And our riddles." Bello sounded unsettled and glanced back and forth between Melissa and her father. "You'll have to excuse me. Under a full moon, I never quite feel myself. Where I was raised, a full moon was a time for transformations, when things did not quite appear as they seemed. But it can't be helped." He cleared his throat and composed himself. "You were highly recommended to me, Mr. Tebogo, as someone who can move things in and out of a place, based, to be sure, on your experience helping South Africa in its glorious struggle for freedom from the oppressor. Do you work with the PAC? The ANC?"

"Drink, Mr. Bello? Beer? Wine?"

"Tea is fine."

"Melissa," her father said, "bring us some tea. Five Roses."

Even though her father had asked her to be on her best behavior, she couldn't help but groan. "Yes, Daddy."

She moped to the kitchen and filled the electric kettle with water. Her father had asked her to bring Five Roses, as if Bello had a choice. They only had one kind of tea. Her father liked for Melissa to greet her guests because he valued her impressions of them, but he didn't want her to know the details, he said, for her own safety. She should always tell the truth and it was best if she had no truth to tell.

After a few moments, the kettle began whistling. Melissa carried the tray of tea with a tumbler of milk and a bowl of packets of sugar. She could feel Bello's eyes searching her niqab.

"Thank you," he said.

"Pleasure."

Then he knocked the sugar bowl onto the floor. Melissa bent to pick it up and for a moment she knew that he could see the skin of her wrist beneath her sleeve, a pale band of white that ringed her dark arm like a panda. She could sense him recoil, even if he apologized profusely.

"A lovely daughter you have," he said.

Her father nodded. "She is the apple of my eye."

"I didn't realize that you were Muslim."

"We're not."

"But she wears a niqab."

"Ah, no. It's a skin condition. Thank you, Melissa," her father said. "You can go now."

After returning the dishes, this time Melissa crept back into the hall-way to listen. Rufus spied her from across the room, and frowned, but she pressed her fingers to her lips.

"Is it albinism?"

"No, she's not albino. She has a form of vitiligo, a lack of melanin in the skin cells. We've found that she is troubled," her father added, "by certain types of light."

"Don't you have good hospitals here? Private ones?"

"Our hospitals are shit. I've taken her to Tanzania, Kenya, Egypt. The doctors say that it's untreatable." He spat onto the floor. "The cowards."

"That's unfortunate. She seems like a dutiful daughter. Don't think a girl has grown up to be beautiful purely and simply, the saying goes. Her parents have brought her up. Where is her mother?"

"Dead."

Melissa thought that, of all the people in the world, Bello was the last one who should hear this from her father. There was something slippery about his words and his gestures.

"Mr. Tebogo," Bello was saying, "I need a man who can keep a secret, secrecy that I am not, in my naturally effusive way, capable of maintaining. I am moved by banter, chatter, you see. The windpipes of my fellow man are what fluff my sails. There is an election coming in Nigeria. The powers that be are the ones that concern me, with their utter disregard for human rights, and that's what brings me to you: impunity. Actions without consequences. The consequences cannot be helped; the actions may be, if we act with haste, avoidable."

"Speak plainly!" her father snapped.

Rufus gripped his pistol in response, but kept his eye on the street. Melissa craned her neck to listen.

"Yes, yes, yes, of course," Bello stammered. "Of course. Do you know that I'm the only one in my Ministry who does not use a helicopter to travel to the airport, Mr. Tebogo? The Minister owns homes on four continents and a fleet of Mercedes Benzes. My colleagues have apartments on Kensington Square, the Bois de Boulogne, Central Park."

Melissa had never heard of these places, but—a helicopter! A helicopter used like a car! She had never before dreamed such a thing was possible. Her father was right. Bello must indeed be a powerful man.

"I've been saving money for my program for almost a decade. It's a significant amount of money—for a revolutionary idea. A revolution of the mind. No one has ever reinvested in our human capital in this way. I need your services, Mr. Tebogo."

"Why me?"

"Because you are beyond suspicion. I need a go-between who can keep my name in the clear, someone who is absolutely trustworthy and professional. I asked my sources in Accra, Lusaka, Maputo, and they all recommended you."

"I already told you that I'll never return to Nigeria. I have been cheated by your people too many times."

"You are mistaking the few for the plenty. We have over two hundred fifty ethnic groups, Mr. Tebogo, and millions of eager young minds, waiting to be tapped. Besides, you don't need to go to Nigeria. I need your services elsewhere."

"How much are you offering?"

Bello waved his hand around the room. "Enough for you to stop all this hide-and-go-seek. Inshallah."

"That's not a number."

"No, it's a dream, Mr. Tebogo. A dream that I can realize. I've followed the news in your homeland. Mandela is free and elections are coming soon in South Africa as well. The ANC has been unbanned. The Frontline States are no longer of any importance. Your smuggling business has dried up here in Bulawayo, the lion has lain with the lamb."

Her father grew furious. If there was one thing he despised, it was strangers telling him how to run his business. He shouted: "Don't tell me how to run my affairs! Take him out!"

Rufus immediately turned and seized Bello painfully by his upper arm. He began dragging him towards the front door.

"No," Bello said, "please! I can help her. Please, listen! I can help your daughter!"

Her father signaled for Rufus to stop, but he still kept a firm grip on Bello's arm.

"I can pay your fee," Bello said, "and I can do better." He shook himself free of Rufus, who seemed amused. "I have a home in the suburbs of Paris that I rarely use. I purchased it for a rainy day, so to speak, and it has never rained. The area is a medical hub for hospitals and pharmaceutical companies. Send your daughter there for treatment. She can stay at my expense for as long as you'd like. I'll pay her medical bills."

She could sense her father pause, considering the offer. Melissa desperately wanted it to be true, a place where the doctors could treat her. Anything was better than Zimbabwe!

"What's the catch?" her father said.

"No catch, Mr. Tebogo. I can send you the keys immediately."

"And you'll pay my fee."

"Your fee and your daughter's medical bills. No strings attached, all expenses paid. Think of it as a vacation—for a job well done."

"I'll have to talk to my daughter about it first."

"In my country," Bello said, "children do not speak unless spoken to. But I'm a champion of cultural relativism, and if you need to consult your daughter, I am not going to be a traditionalist."

But there was no need, as Bello cajoled her father with his artful hyperbole, for him to ask her. Bello had already convinced Melissa. If he had asked, she was ready to leave that very night. She didn't need much, only a small suitcase, and she would be as pleased as punch to live in France with her father and leave Zimbabwe forever.

After Bello had left, her father visited her room to make sure that she had packed everything for the raid.

"It's time for us to go, Melissa."

"I want to go to France!" she blurted.

Her father sighed and took her hand. "I was afraid you'd heard that. That man couldn't keep his voice down. What else did you hear?"

"He's rich. He could fly in a helicopter but he doesn't because he's honest."

"That's what he said, yes. That's what he said. But he's very good with words, isn't he? They speak French in France, Melissa. It might be difficult for you. You've never studied the language."

"He said they could treat me."

"They might."

"He promised."

"He's not a doctor, Melissa."

"But he's rich."

"It would be a very big change for us. Let's talk about it tomorrow, when you've had some more time to think about it."

But there was no need, and before long she couldn't remember if there had ever been a decision to make at all. They traveled together across town to stay with one of her father's friends. By the time the SADF kicked down their door, she was dreaming of walking the streets of Paris.

The Fallback

Wale watched the bank teller return from the vault, searching her face for anything, a smile, a nod, even a sneer. It seemed to him that the Swiss had genetically molded themselves to swallow their emotions and pass this onto their employees, for this one was, according to her name-tag, Turkish. He needed to know if he should flee or if she'd triggered some kind of alarm. He'd scanned the waiting room for an escape route already. In the airy atrium, an enormous fake palm tree stood next to the bench. If he was quick enough, he could topple it, wedging enough space for him to crawl under the security gate when it crashed down. He still felt a spring in his step from the basketball season and was probably quicker than the armed guard, who was yawning at him like a camel.

"Dr. Olufunmi," the teller said, "the transaction is still pending."

"What does that mean?"

She slid him a printout. He could see his account number and, beside it, the word 'Pending'. It didn't help.

"For an amount this large," the teller droned, "the bank runs extra security checks. The process can take up to ten days for an international transfer."

Wale brightened. The amount was large, meaning that Bello had been true to his word. "Everything's normal, then."

"Yes," the teller said. "It is a normal procedure."

"And then the money will be there."

"If it passes security, yes."

"How often would you say that happens?"

The teller smiled, revealing pointed uneven teeth. Maybe that was the reason she kept a poker face. "Please, Doctor. If you'd like, you can leave your telephone number and we'll contact you when the transaction is complete."

He considered it but remembered the attacker in Stockholm. He didn't want to leave a paper trail. He pocketed the printout and left.

Wale had fled Houston three days earlier. Since then, he'd watched his old classmate, Dr. Obafemi Ferguson, get shot in the face by a cold killer and he'd fled again to Basel, dragging his family with him. Just when he'd been reassured he wasn't the only one involved in Brain Gain, that the thing was really happening, he'd lost the second true ally he'd found. The first one, his wife, was on the verge of leaving him, too. At least he still had his son Dayo, who hovered in Wale's mind above it all, weightless and full of limitless potential. He'd thought about returning to Texas, 'fessing up to his theft and doing his time. But then what would happen to his family? To his dream? He would never work as a scientist again and he'd be abandoning his homeland in the process.

He dredged his memory for a proverb that would suit Bello, almost as if he could entrap Bello in his own flowery language, lure him back somehow. But none came to mind.

Tinuke and Dayo were gone when he returned to the airport hotel. He feared that she'd made good on her threat to leave him until he saw her suitcase stacked in the corner of the room with Dayo's backpack. Maybe they went for a walk. She wouldn't be happy that they would have to wait a few more days in Basel, ducking into shadows like fugitives, and it would be risky. Each day they'd have to wait, Ferguson's attacker could be drawing closer.

Wale had promised Tinuke a large home, a driver, and an au pair so she could resume her studies in Nigeria, or, he had to admit, she had demanded these things in lieu of a divorce.

He decided to use his free time in the room to book refundable tickets from Basel to Cape Town for the entire family. The price was absurd, but he needed to be able to change the dates at the last minute when the money transfer went through. He flipped on the television and was surprised to find a basketball game. Something was strange about it: the key, which spread out in a trapezoid, and the players, who were all white and skinnier than their NBA counterparts. Their footwork was good, though, and their passing wasn't bad. Still, he felt he was faster by virtue of his American pedigree. He thought about his co-ed team back in Houston, which would be in the playoffs next week and useless without him at point.

Maybe he could make a go of it here in Europe, he thought, if his other plans fell through.

He leafed through their materials again to make sure that they were in the proper order. The passports were in good shape—except for his botched visa to Nigeria—and Tinuke had thankfully left her bag packed and ready to go. His eyes rested again on Ferguson's PV formula, trying to make sense of it:

$$\begin{pmatrix} Cu \\ Ag \\ Au \end{pmatrix} \begin{pmatrix} Al \\ Ga \\ In \end{pmatrix} \begin{pmatrix} S \\ Se \\ Te \end{pmatrix}_2$$

Perhaps it was just Ferguson's agreed-upon code with Bello's go-between. A way to authenticate their communications. The thought brought back Femi's face again after it had been ravaged by the bullet, and then Femi's optimism about Brain Gain. He, too, shared the same belief that the project could work, even after he'd climbed his way to the top of one of Sweden's most distinguished institutes of learning. He seemed to have grown more amiable over the years and wasn't the old fusspot that Wale remembered. With his expertise in photovoltaics, he would have been a valuable addition to the team. But now he was dead.

Tinuke returned with Dayo asleep on her shoulder. Behind her, a porter carried four shopping bags. Wale passed the porter a tip and quickly shut the door.

Hardly the time for a spending spree, Wale thought.

She didn't greet him. She set Dayo gently down upon the bed and began opening the shopping bags. She spread a new men's suit, three fresh collared shirts, a pair of black pumps, and a few new dresses upon the bed.

"We should get rid of your old clothes," Tinuke said.

After he had promised her luxuries in Nigeria, she had taken the news about the theft rather well. He still felt edgy around her, as if it might set off an argument at any time. She had never mentioned Ferguson's death again.

From another shopping bag, Tinuke dropped several newspapers upon the bed, Frankfurter Allgemeine Zeitung, Berliner Zeitung, Dagens Nyheter, and the International Herald Tribune.

"Look at The Tribune," she said.

The Tribune featured an article about unrest in Somalia and a possible peacekeeping operation by the UN. Newly elected Bill Clinton was prattling on again about homosexuals in the military. In the NBA, Michael Jordan was contemplating his retirement from the game after three successive championships, which Wale thought would be good for the league, or at least for the Rockets. And then, in the briefings section, Wale saw this:

NASA Puzzled by Moon Rock Theft

Houston—NASA reported a theft from the Johnson Space Laboratory's Lunar Sample Collection late Wednesday night. No one was harmed and no suspects have been arrested. Officials explained that the sample, one of thousands taken from the Apollo moon missions, was not scientifically significant and would not fetch a high value on the illicit meteorite market, questioning the motive of the theft. Although a leading suspect has been

*identified, NASA is withholding the name in or-
der to conduct joint investigations with the FBI.*

Wale tore the article from the newspaper and flushed it down the drain, as if this was the only copy in the world, as if flushing it would mean flushing away the past few days. Still, he felt better. So NASA had withheld his name. The investigators also didn't seem to understand the worth of the sample. Wale had switched the sample so many times over the past few months that it would be difficult, but not impossible, for the lab to discover its true origins. Then the really good news, that no one had been harmed. It meant that his lab partner Onur hadn't done anything stupid and had survived the emergency procedures safely.

"This is good news," he said.

"They haven't printed your name," Tinuke agreed.

"It's probably Rilker. He's always trying to raise funds in Washington. If Congress learned that one of his own employees stole from his lab, he might lose his funding."

He chuckled to himself, remembering how he stole Rilker's fancy new car right out from under him. The fool.

"This is hardly a laughing matter," Tinuke said. "We should get rid of your old clothes. They might give you away. Did you get the money?"

"The transaction is pending."

"What does that mean?"

"It's normal for this type of transaction because of the amount."

"It could mean you're under investigation."

"I doubt it," he said. "It's a numbered account. I'll check again tomorrow." He didn't tell her about the security procedures, not wanting to be drawn into an argument.

Wale couldn't read German or Swedish so he scanned the other papers for Ferguson's name, not finding anything other than a mention of the Manchester United soccer coach, Alex Ferguson.

Now Tinuke was leafing through the passports and Ferguson's materials. That had also been part of their agreement: full access to everything Wale knew.

She held up a slip of paper. "And this?"

"It's a photovoltaic formula. Ferguson was an expert on solar energy. I think it was a communication code for Bello's go-between."

"That man does not deserve to be named. He shot an arrow into the sky and covered his head with a mortar bowl."

That was it, Wale thought, the proverb that could encapsulate Bello. He'd caused all these problems and disappeared into hiding.

Tinuke was now puzzling out the formula. She hadn't been top of her class in her nutrition studies but she wasn't the bottom, either.

"Why aren't there any numbers? In school, our formulas always had numbers. Except for the alcohols."

He felt suddenly grateful to her, tearfully grateful. He hugged her shoulder, gently, and she didn't shrug him off. Beside him, Dayo curled over on the bed onto his stomach, deep asleep. There was no need to talk. He stripped down to his underpants and she rubbed him beneath the cotton. She peeled off the straps of her bra and unbuttoned her jeans. He didn't try to kiss her, knowing not to expect the intimacy. He licked her breasts and her stomach and fell to his knees on the floor between her legs, working his tongue until his jaw burned. Then she pushed him onto his back. He pressed himself into her and they moved together slowly, then roughly, rubbing away the horror of the midnight sun, the nightmare that had beset them.

Afterwards, he felt comforted by his family laying next to him in the tiny hotel room. What had happened to them? Things had grown too large over the past few years, their apartment had swollen into a house, and his ambition had surged into a burning American beast that had ravaged his boyhood dream of touching the stars. The Texan expanse had divided the family from itself. Now, he thought, they were together again. He drifted off to sleep.

It felt like a few moments later when Tinuke woke him, waving Ferguson's note in front of his face. "Does this mean anything to you?"

"Eh? How long was I asleep?"

"Three hours."

He knew not to ask for Bello, although it was the first thought on his mind. He looked at the paper. "It's a formula for solar energy conversion, Tinuke, I told you that."

"No, Wale, look."

Next to each element, she'd written a number.

Cu=29 Ag=47 Au=79 Al=13 Ga=31 In=49 Sulfur=16 Selenium=34 Te=52.

"These are the elements?"

"From the periodic table."

"They might be isotopes," he mumbled.

The numbers looked familiar, almost as if they were on the tip of his tongue. Then he got it: the printout. 29-47 were the first two digits of his own account number at the bank.

"Femi said the money was already in the account," Wale said, leaping from the bed. "This is the number! We can access it."

"Wouldn't that be stealing?"

"No, no, no. Nothing of the sort. We'll give it to his wife as soon as our money comes through. We're not stealing anything. Femi would have wanted us to use it."

"Are you going to walk back into the bank? Don't you think they'll know who you are?"

He remembered the Turkish bank teller and her quiet, robotic gaze. If he hadn't engaged her in conversation, he might have been able to do it. But she would surely recognize him now. He slumped back onto the bed.

"You're right. I can't do anything about it. We'll have to wait."

But Tinuke was already changing into her new dress, primping her hair.

"No," she said, "we won't."

The first thing Tinuke did was upgrade their tickets to Cape Town to First Class. On the plane, she bossed the flight attendants about and drank several glasses of Gewurztraminer, while Wale administered to Dayo, keeping him happy, which meant, for most of the flight, pushing in cassette after cassette on the personal video player: Aladdin, The Best of Bert and Ernie, serial episodes of Teenage Mutant Ninja Turtles, which he found himself enjoying despite the oriental themes, and then, when Dayo fell asleep, the director's cut of 2001: A Space Odyssey. He remembered when he and Onur used to recite the lines back in the lab, Onur playing the part of the ship's computer Hal:

WALE: Hello, HAL. Do you read me, HAL?
ONUR: Affirmative, Wale. I read you.
WALE: Open the LSC bay doors, HAL.
ONUR: I'm sorry, Wale. I'm afraid I can't do that.
WALE: What's the problem?
ONUR: I think you know what the problem is just as
well as I do.
WALE: What are you talking about, HAL?
ONUR: There aren't enough donuts for the both of us.

Onur would vary the last line. The point was to stay awake on the late shift.

Wale had strapped twenty thousand dollars around his body in money belts, pockets, and his underwear and stuffed another thirty thousand in his checked bag. Tinuke had carried the rest, an amount which she refused to divulge. She'd taken the risk, she said, to defraud the bank, so she would control the money. In customs, he grew nervous as a Jack Russell Terrier poked its nose into their luggage on the carousel. The customs agent took one look at their visas and slapped a bold blue sticker on their luggage: DIPLOMAT. They breezed through the lines with ease. Once outside, a limousine already waited for them in the cool winter air. He could see Table Mountain in the distance, cloud-covered and lined with rich streaks of green from the seasonal rain.

"The Nellie?" the driver asked.

"Excuse me?" Wale said.

"The Mount Nelson Hotel, sir?"

Wale had not thought to book any lodgings, expecting to stay at the fallback point. "We may not be here very long."

"The Nellie," Tinuke declared.

He was surprised at how casually his wife fit the part, as if she was used to such pampering. She had draped herself in fineries to distract herself, but there was always an accusation on her lips, a question that would cut him to his very core. Wale had downplayed apartheid to her and the coming elections, but he couldn't help feeling unsettled as the limousine motored down the N2 highway. He expected to see mustachioed policemen beating blacks to death on the side of the road, or protesters toyi-toyi'ing and hurling stones. He saw nothing other than the highway, boxy Renaults, Opels, and Volkswagens, and two cooling towers belching steam from a coal plant. South Africa may have been isolated by the international community, but you couldn't tell from the quality of the roads. He didn't see any potholes. Behind the cooling towers, he caught glimpses of shanties and black children playing cricket with highway cones for wickets.

The colonnaded entrance to the hotel was manned by a black man in full colonial garb and a pith helmet. He waved them in, even though the driver didn't stop to wait for his approval. They drove along the palm-lined drive, passing two- and three-story pink buildings with sculpted lawns. Two men ran around the car and picked up their bags from the trunk, dropping them on the curb. Then two more men shuttled the bags towards the front desk. All of them expected tips. Tinuke sauntered out of the car, leaving Wale to lead Dayo by the hand. He peeled off a few twenties.

By the time he arrived inside, Tinuke had rented the Presidential suite.

"Tinuke, what are you doing? We can't afford that."

"You can't afford it, Wale."

"That's not your money," he said. "It belongs to Femi's wife. We have to give it back to her. Our money is supposed to pay for a home in Jos. We shouldn't fritter it away in a hotel."

"I'm fed up with airport hotels, Wale. I need pampering. I want to arrive in Nigeria refreshed."

Dayo spied two children wearing floaties and took off running down the hall. "Pool! Papa. Swimma pool!"

The suite was gigantic, chamber flowing into chamber, with two bathrooms and two living rooms opening onto a private terrace graced by morning light. Fresh cut proteas and poinsettias were scattered about the room. A leopard skin lay at the foot of the bed with head intact and bared fangs. There were decanters full of sherry, a complimentary bottle of Johnnie Walker Black, and a sparkling '88 Meerlust chilled in a bucket of ice.

Diplomats must like to get smashed, he thought. There was enough alcohol in the room to kill a man several times over.

Wale sifted through his various clothes and decided to put on a fresh shirt. Tinuke put a squirming Dayo in his tiny swimsuit.

"Wear the agbada," she said.

"Out of the question. I'll stand out like a sore thumb."

"We already do," she said. "Act the part. Don't try to look local, Wale, or someone will tell you to shine their shoes."

Grumbling, he donned the agbada, sent to him from a cousin he hadn't spoken to in eight years. It was hunter green and lined with gold thread, comfortable and chilly in the winter air. He put on the matching kufi hat. Then he took the wrapped snowglobe and put it in a small backpack.

"You're not coming with me?"

"No, I'm going for a massage. Dayo's going to day care. Then the pool. Come back with Bello. I'd like to meet him."

She didn't say it. She didn't need to. Or else. Come back with Bello, or else.

The taxi driver offered to take him up to the trails of Lions Head as they climbed a steep pass that split the mountain in two. Wale was naturally drawn as a lunar geologist to the outcroppings and the misty crags that followed the shore for several miles, imagining the sand as it compressed and rose above the waves over the millennia, and the forces that had crumpled the mountain range. He knew that South Africa was a mining economy built on gold, diamonds, and platinum, yet few significant meteorites had been found here so it had never really captured his interest. He was here to see Bello.

The taxi descended into a bay littered with giant boulders that touched the shore like the spiny humps of an undersea creature. Cliff-houses lined the road with fancy sports cars behind locked gates. Here and there, he would see a domestic worker trudging up the hill to catch a minibus taxi to the townships.

"You Nigerian, sir?"

"Yes," Wale said.

"Thought so. I drive Nigerians around from time to time. Looks like we're going to beat you to it, then."

"I don't know what you're talking about."

"Looks like we're having our elections before yours. It was on the news this morning. Bloody simple idea, I think. Your President up and cancels them when things aren't going his way. Just like that. De Klerk might do well to do the same here. I like Mandela, he wouldn't be so bad, but I don't want his cronies taking over. We'll all be living in darkness. No electricity."

"You must mean Niger. Nigeria is a democracy now."

"Could be, sir," the driver deferred. "Niger, Nigeria, they sound the same to me, man. Like Guyana, ever heard of it? It's in South America. There's also Guinea, Guinea-Bissau, Equatorial Guinea, French Guiane, Papua New Guinea. I like geography, you see, but I don't know why the chaps couldn't find a new name."

The driver's name on his tag, Wale saw, was Piet de Villiers; whether it was a unique name or a common name, he couldn't tell. They wove amongst the homes for a few blocks, the taxi belching out clouds of leaded gasoline as it ascended the steep hill. The driver pointed out the homes of politicians and local movie stars.

"This is it, 251 Upper Tree." Wale stepped onto the street and declined the driver's offer to wait. "You might need your darkies."

"What's that?"

He pointed to his sunglasses. "For your eyes."

"I'm not going to the beach."

251 Upper Tree was modest compared to the luxurious cliffhouses nearby. Instead of stucco and walls of glass, it was a single-story ranch style home with a small concrete driveway for one vehicle and a one-car garage behind it. A short brick walk led to the front steps, with a large and somewhat overgrown garden that had a head-high jade plant. The home must have been one of the first in the community and you could easily miss it because of the ostentatious mansions around it. The perfect place, in many ways, for a fallback point. Bello had chosen wisely.

Wale adjusted his agbada to make himself more presentable and thought about what he would say to Bello. The taxi driver had unnerved him with that talk about the elections in Nigeria, but he had probably misread something in the tabloids. Still, it was worth asking Bello about it. He also decided it wouldn't be a good idea to attack the man but to start out politely and go through the proper greetings. He could show him the snowglobe to prove he was still committed, and Bello for all his love of innovation was something of a traditionalist with his proverbs. This could start the conversation properly, get things off on a constructive tone. Then they could devise a solution to fly to Nigeria and make sure Wale was rewarded for his troubles.

There was a security gate with a keypad and a door chime. He pressed the doorbell and could hear the chime ring softly inside the home. He waited a minute for the gate to buzz open. Nothing. After ringing a few more times, he decided Bello might have left the house—why would he wait around all day?—and entered the code from Ferguson's address slip: 41421. The gate buzzed open. He climbed the short walk and noticed a plastic toy rocket lying on its side amongst an aloe plant, almost as if a child had grown tired of it and tossed it away. He tried the knocker and then pounded his fist upon the door. Growing anxious, he circled around the back of the house, where he found rusty lawn furniture and a barbecue grill that looked like it hadn't been touched in a long time. Here again, the door was locked. The windows were barred and he could think of no way to get in.

He would have to wait, he thought dismally, for Bello or one of the other scientists to return. There was no way he would go back to the hotel empty-handed, not after the way Tinuke had spoken to him. That was out of the question. He would even spend the night here on the front steps if necessary. As he walked down the front path to the street, his eye rested on the plastic toy rocket again. Strange. Brain Gain was about going to the moon, after all. He plucked it from the bushes. He gave it a shake and could hear something rattling inside.

The key fit the top lock easily. He opened the door into a small front parlor, where a chaise longue faced the entrance with a marble-topped side table. A long hallway ran from the front parlor in both directions. To the left, he could see a few rooms branching off the hallway to the side before the house dropped two steps onto a lower level that must have led to the garage. To the right, the hallway opened into a living room with herringbone print couches and an old switch dial TV encased in a large wood cabinet. The bookshelf held a few books, all either volumes about sailing or thrillers for beach reading, the kind that tourists leave behind. There were other nautical-themed accoutrements as well: a ship's clock, a barometer, and a meter-tall hourglass that could be flipped over on a spindle. He saw no signs that anyone had used the room recently, other than the fact that there wasn't any dust on the shelves. If the home wasn't lived in, it was at least serviced along with the garden.

He found a laminated three-ringed binder on a coffee table that contained instructions about using the alarm system and avoiding baboons, several trail maps from the Mountain Club of South Africa, and some menus from various restaurants in the beach town below. The home was a vacation rental, he realized. Dayo and Tinuke could sleep comfortably here and they could stop spending their cash at the pompous colonial hotel. Once again, Bello had chosen wisely.

He moved into the kitchen. It had a small electric range and a half-dozen copper pots hung from the ceiling. On the far side by the door to the back yard, he saw a small bedroom for a domestic servant. Dayo would sleep comfortably in there. It might be nice for Wale to have some privacy with Tinuke, he thought, awaken that passion they'd shared in the Basel hotel.

The home felt a little musty but when he pulled aside a curtain, he could see a pleasant view of the bay. The first bedroom was on the smaller side and contained two twin beds. Hardly romantic. He moved towards the master bedroom. And froze.

A body lay upon the ground, face down. A black woman in a business suit. Blood had coagulated beneath the head and white powder was everywhere, covering the floor. The sheets on the bed were ruffled and torn, and a pillow had a long gash in it.

Wale dropped to his knees, his hand on his mouth.

Not again, he thought. Not again.

He approached the body slowly, avoiding the powder on the floor. The woman's hair was clean and intricately woven, as if she'd recently braided it. He mustered the courage to turn the body over. It was heavy, already stiff and unwieldy from rigor mortis. He didn't recognize the face. She had wide eyes and a forehead that sloped sharply. He could see an entry wound in the shoulder and another in the forehead—between the eyes, which lay open. He searched her pockets but couldn't find anything. Someone had been through here already. Someone had also taken the time to sprinkle lime over the body to dampen the stench.

He remembered the chocolate-skinned burglar with yellowed eyes who had attacked him in Stockholm. The man could be slinking in through the front door at this very moment, preparing to shoot Wale with the same dispassion.

A low whinny of a sound could be heard outside the house, like a soft cry coming from the waves below. He ran to the front window. He could see a car following the road that ran along the shore, its yellow siren winking in the bright midday sun. It didn't look like a police car. He watched it drive past onrushing cars, hoping it would bypass the neighborhood or head to a fire, anything but come here. The car turned and began laboring up the hill.

He searched through the closet, tossing aside clothes and old junk from the vacation cottage. He didn't so much see the doll as smell it. It was a rich scent that carried him back to his youth in Nigeria, earthy and pungent. He picked up the cloth-wrapped object and unraveled it. Inside, he found a fine statuette adorned with camwood powder and blue indigo. There were two inlaid blue glass beads along the torso, miniature breasts on the chest, and the forehead had been carved to a point. The eyes were oversized and almond shaped, with a sharp nose and full lips. He stuffed the doll into his agbada.

He hurried to the front door, then decided it would be dangerous to leave through the neighborhood and exited through the rear instead. A high stone wall protected against the crumbling bluffs behind the house. He scrambled up it and plunged through the coastal fynbos, which scraped his skin and tore at his agbada. Then he crouched low and watched as the car climbed the final distance to the home. He could barely read the sign on the vehicle: RNB Armed Response. The guard stepped out of the car and rang the doorbell a few times before keying in the security code to the front gate. He circled around the home until he saw the rear door, which Wale had stupidly left wide open. Next to the guard, Wale spied something out of the place on the ground next to the barbecue grill. His kufi.

Damn it, Wale thought. I never should have worn the thing. The hat must have fallen from his head when he fled.

But the guard didn't seem to have noticed it. He said a few words into a walkie-talkie before drawing his gun. Then he entered shouting "Armed Response!"

Wale scrambled down the rear wall to the house, afraid the guard might come out at any moment. He picked up the kufi and climbed back up the wall. As he reached the top, he heard the guard cry out from deep within the home.

He's discovered the body, he thought.

Wale climbed higher behind the house now, ducking beneath bushes until he reached a single dirt track. He pushed along it, trying to remain low. His green agbada blended well with the lush green plants that ringed the mountain and the chilly sea wind whipped through the cloth. He followed the trail for a few hundred meters, snaking above the homes as it veered towards Lion's Head. Now he climbed slowly, looking back towards the house from time to time. He could already see a trail of police cars sirening up the hill. He stayed close to the silvertrees and the thick coastal scrub, keeping out of sight.

From a cloud of fog, a lone paraglider sailed a few feet above him and began the slow drift down to the beach. The trail began to switch back until it intersected with a much wider track like a fire road. Here, a white man jogged past him with a wave of the hand and a young coloured couple high-stepped up the hill with a docile looking Rottweiler huffing on a leash. He began walking down a trail that wound around the hill towards the street as casually as he could.

His mind raced to understand what had happened. He knew it must have been the same attacker as in Stockholm. He recognized the signs: a bullet to the body followed by another between the eyes for security. The dead woman must have been a scientist, but he'd never seen her before. And the killer had left the body in the room, not even bothering to conceal anything other than the stench from the corpse. He must have been planning to come back, or worse, to wait for another victim and strike again, picking off the scientists one by one as they arrived from Nigeria to the Fallback. But where was Bello? Why hadn't he warned Wale or Femi or any of them for that matter? On the eve of his project, he had disappeared, as if abandoning them. But why? Had he been killed too?

He removed the ibeji doll from his pocket. Ibeji meant 'twin' in Yoruba. A family that gave birth to a set of twins and lost one through illness would hire a sculptor to carve a simplified likeness of the child, to placate the deceased child and protect the family. Sometimes the surviving twin would carry the doll around, or the mother might dance with it. He recalled a cousin in Lagos dressing his ibeji in simple clothes, spooning bits of gari into its wooden mouth, a ritual that he'd found wasteful. An ibeji was not something you left behind on vacation but something you treasured and carried with you for your entire life. The wood had also been recently bathed in the herbs, which meant that someone had possessed it a short time ago. It might belong to the victim or the killer. He would need to find out more about it.

He also knew it wasn't a coincidence that the armed response had arrived right when he entered the house. Either the killer had been watching or Wale had inadvertently set off the alarm. It didn't matter, because the guard had already discovered the body. At least that meant no other scientist would be callous enough to enter the Fallback when the place was surrounded by police.

The dirt road finally ended near a small ranger hut. He could see car guards wearing fluorescent pinnies and a few taxis idling on the cliffs that overlooked the smog of the City Bowl.

He found Tinuke in a bathrobe reclining by the indoor pool with cucumbers on her eyelids and her face coated in a lime green paste. An attendant was filing her toenails and massaging her calves. Dayo was splashing around in the kiddie pool, watched by a bemused, plump black woman. He would run out of the pool, giggling, and then leap into the water while flapping his floaties. There were a few toys in the pool, which he would grab and toss into the air and squirt.

The sense of loss wracked Wale's body worse than any bullets. It was over. Brain Gain was finished, even with the ibeji doll. He couldn't keep doing this to his family and he had nothing else left to give. No career, no home. If he returned to Houston he'd go to jail. Nigeria would be too dangerous without Bello's protection and anyway he'd botched the visa on his own passport and couldn't go there.

Bello shot an arrow into the sky, Tinuke had said, and covered his head with a mortar bowl.

I should have built Dayo a pool in Houston, he thought. Then none of this would have happened.

He counted out their assets in his mind. He would have about forty-five thousand dollars in cash left after they checked out of the hotel, less any extravagances. Tinuke might have fifty thousand or maybe a hundred thousand. She could return to Houston and sell the home; then, if Bello's money came through, they would have another three hundred thousand from his signing bonus. That was a hefty sum. If they lay low for a while, they could live comfortably. Buy a condo on an island somewhere. Some place cheap, where people didn't ask questions.

Tinuke was sitting erect now. The attendant had removed the cucumbers and washed the paste from her face and she looked radiant, the model of a diplomat's wife. She smiled at him expectantly. He walked over slowly as the attendant blew air upon her toenails.

"Is he outside?" she asked.

He looked away. Shook his head. His voice seemed to come from the middle of his throat, clammy and adolescent. "He wasn't there."

Tinuke stood up instantly.

"It's too early to walk on them," the attendant said.

She sat back down. "But you found the house?"

"Yes, it's there. I went inside and—Bello's not coming."

"Not coming?"

"No."

The glow in her face began to fade and for a moment, Wale saw the deepest sadness in her eyes, as if she truly knew his pain. And he thought, maybe she'll stand by me. Maybe we can do this together.

Except she set her jaw, not even angry, not even upset, just not there at all.

"You always looked good in an agbada, Wale. I wanted to see you wear it in Nigeria."

"We'll go together?"

"No, we're leaving tomorrow. Dayo and I will go back to Houston. I'll send you the papers to sign."

"What papers?"

"What other kind of papers are there?"

"You don't understand. I went to the house and—"

"—I don't want to know, Wale. What's more, I don't care. We're leaving. Pay the woman."

He slipped the attendant a twenty, then another to keep her quiet. Tinuke headed towards the changing room, shaking her head. Frowning.

He slumped into the reclining chair in the humidity of the indoor pool. He saw his boy dash around the kiddie pool one more time, ecstatic in the water. The mere sight of the child brought him joy, allowed him to breathe again.

She won't take him too, he thought. If she takes him, she takes my whole life.

He ran over to Dayo, who leapt into his arms.

"Papa!"

"Remember peekaboo, Dayo?"

Dayo covered his face with his palms, then opened them. "Peekaboo!"

"That's right, Dayo. We're going to play a big game of peekaboo now. You and I together. Want to play?"

"Peekaboo!"

Then he was running from the pool house and along the red carpet of the lobby and whistling madly for a taxi, Dayo giggling all the while at the prospect of a new adventure.

Book II

Our children play a game called leapfrog. One child leaps over the next and lands in front with a bright new perspective. It is our turn to leapfrog the North. Our dependence must evolve into independence. Oil has ruined us, smeared our Deltas with smog, poisoned our creeks and marshes, lined the pockets of the few. For us to leap, we must find another source, clean of the blood of our ancestors. It is not more oil that we need. Not gold, not diamonds. We can't swap blood for blood. What we need are minds.

*—Nurudeen Bello, Special Adjunct
to the Minister of the Environment*

The Abalone of Obz

Present Day
South Africa

Thursday Malaysius arrived in Cape Town forty minutes late. He'd hitchhiked to the Mowbray taxi rank and, not having any money, he'd had to walk a kilometer to Observatory with the cooler on his balding head. The cooler was wrapped in a garbage bag so no one knew what was inside but that didn't make it any lighter. With the abalone and the sea water, it must have weighed fifty kilos. He passed a car wash and a friendly autoelectrician pointed him towards Lower Main Road.

Rumors about the wild girls at Observatory had drifted down to Hermanus for years, so Thursday was disappointed with the paint-chipped arcades that covered the sidewalks. The stores seemed dilapidated compared to the polished tourist traps of Old Hermanus. He passed a biker bar, an internet café, and an upholstery shop with expensive polyester couches in the window. He didn't see any sex orgies or hot kinners flashing their breasts as Brother Leon had told him. The few people he saw were white-collar types wearing neckties.

Seventy-eight Lower Main should have been right next to a Chinese restaurant, but the next house was sixty-three. Across the street was forty-two. He couldn't decide whether to knock on the door of the Chinese restaurant or send Ip an SMS and sat there sweating with the cooler on his head for a minute or two. The restaurant appeared to be closed, and he was about to go across the street when there was a sound of bells. The door creaked open.

"You late."

"I ran out of taxi money."

"Where Leon?"

"He's sick."

"You bring them?"

"The work? Yeah. Are you Ip?"

"Shut up."

"No problem, my broer. Only asking."

He followed the scowling pitbull of a man through some tables with plastic table cloths set with soy and hot pepper sauces. Thursday hadn't eaten all morning so his stomach growled with the scent of oil-battered food in the air. They walked to the back of the restaurant and passed through some strips of clear plastic leading to a refrigerator about six paces deep and four wide. Shrink-wrapped egg noodles and filets of fish were stacked beside a shaker of monosodium glutamate and long red cuts of meat. A gallon-sized dispenser of duck sauce sat on the shelf. The man pulled aside a drape to reveal another door, indicating for Thursday to go in first.

Thursday hesitated because it was a much smaller room than the first dining area, but he had walked so far into the restaurant that it was too late to back out now. If something happened no one would hear him here. He had to do it. For Brother Leon.

Inside he found Timothy Ip frowning over a newspaper, which he immediately shook out and folded up. He had silky black hair and an angular Cantonese face, with sharp jaw lines that began behind his ears. There were a couple of pock marks on his cheeks but with his lavender Ralph Lauren button-down he gave off an air of cleanliness. He seemed very limber, as if he could hop out of his chair and perform push-ups at any moment.

"Please sit," he said.

Thursday set the cooler on the desk and sat. There was a Chinese restaurant in Hermanus and you ordered by number. Other than that Thursday had never talked to a man from China. The two Chinese men chattered in their language and he had no sense of the meaning. Whatever they were saying, they seemed to be direct about it. He spied a poster of the martial artist Jet Li behind Ip's head.

"Easter Island Attack," he said. "One of the best fight scenes ever, bru. The blindfolded duel was so lekker."

"Shut up," the bodyguard said.

Thursday crossed his legs. Then he uncrossed them.

"Where's Leon?" Ip asked. He didn't sound very Chinese when he spoke English.

"He's sick."

"Who are you?"

"Jones." Thursday had decided to change his name in case of trouble.

"That your first name?"

"No, it's Hampton Jones."

"Hampton, izzit?"

"Yeah."

"Smoke, Hampton?"

Ip tapped a cigarette out of a pack of Stuyvesants.

"Not around the perlies. But I'll take one."

He took two.

"So, tell me about Leon."

Ip had a nice smile and a casual way about him that made Thursday feel relaxed. He had expected it to be more difficult after all he'd heard about the Chinese Triads and smuggling. But the trip had given him time to work out a story as well.

"Leon got sick the other night. So I had to do the diving. We came up big but he's got the flu."

"And he couldn't drive you."

"No."

"Because he's got my car, you know, Hampton. It's under my name."

Thursday hadn't expected that. "What car?"

"A Mercedes. Champagne E class. Didn't he tell you about it?"

Leon had told Thursday that it was his own car, and Thursday had believed him because he felt down on his luck at the time. But Leon always told a tall tale or two, so Thursday figured there was nothing to get upset about. "I can't drive."

"Why didn't you go to one of my runners? I don't like this. I don't like people coming to me without a good reason. Do you have a good reason?"

Thursday had prepared for this question too.

"I didn't want to get cut up by a Nigerian."

Ip said some Chinese to his bodyguard, who tensed. "That incident was exaggerated, Hampton. It was a simple misunderstanding. We haven't had a problem with the Nigerians since then."

But Thursday felt emboldened by the lack of conviction in Ip's voice. "These perlies are too good to be dried. I've got a hundred, and they're all fresh."

"That's for me to decide."

"Leon said you'd pay a hundred thousand for them."

Ip laughed out loud. "He did, did he? Leon's too flashy. Much too flashy." He stabbed a finger into his folded newspaper. "It says here that there are many kinds of capital in the world. Financial capital, emotional capital, sexual capital, social capital. I'd say that Leon spends his capital before he earns it, doesn't he?"

Thursday laughed along. "He sure does. That's Leon."

"There's another problem, Hampton," Ip said.

"What's wrong? They're as healthy as perlemoen can get."

"The problem is that they need to be cool. And haven't you read the papers?"

"No."

Thursday made a point right then and there to start reading the papers more often. His troubles seemed to be coming out of them lately.

"Maybe it didn't affect you out there. Koeberg's down again."

"Koeberg?"

"That's the nuclear facility. And that's not it. The coal plant's down too. So they're load shedding in Cape Town. Four hour cycles." He pulled the string of the desk lamp. "Off." The room became so dark that Thursday couldn't see a thing. "On. Of course there are generators but with the cost of the diesel it's not worth my while to keep a few abalone alive. It's suspicious for my shop and it's too much hassle. I'm going to throw all those in the dryer."

Thursday was growing nervous. The bodyguard seemed to have moved a few inches closer when the light was off. And he couldn't believe it. It wasn't just the money, it was also that he'd grown attached to the abalone. He hated the thought of the heat shriveling them down in a dryer, their tentacles drying up into brittle matchsticks, of a slow, scorched death. At Abalone Silver he had killed them, but he was humane about it. He was sure they felt pain, he'd seen them bleed.

"I can keep them alive," he insisted.

Ip shook his head. "You're right that the flavor's better alive and there's certainly demand for them. But we ship our product by the week. It's too long for them to survive. They'll die and they can't be dried."

"No, I worked at Abalone Silver. We had blackouts all the time. I can keep them alive."

"I'll give you ten thousand rand for them dry. That's good money, Hampton. You won't find a better rate in the Cape."

Thursday was so indignant that he considered walking away with the cooler and finding another buyer. Then Ip pulled out a checkbook and scribbled out ten thousand rand. Thursday warily picked it up.

"Can't you give me cash?"

"No, I deal with banks. Next time it's direct deposit. I don't want loose cash mucking about with serial numbers on them. If you need a bank, I can get you into a credit union in Maitland."

Thursday still had about forty rand left in his Abalone Silver account back in Hermanus that he'd stowed away for hard times. He could cash the check at a branch here. He began to put the check in his pocket, but the thought of Leon leaning against the prison bars of Pollsmoor overwhelmed him.

"Leon needs the money really bad. Can't you give me more?"

Ip narrowed his eyes. "Why? It's just the flu."

Should I tell him? Thursday wondered. Should I tell him about Leon? Ip and Leon had worked together. Maybe they were friends. "Leon's been arrested."

Ip's bodyguard snorted, and Ip frowned. It was a big, upside-down half-moon of a frown. When he was happy it was not the reverse, more like he pulled his lips back and bared his teeth. The smile was a tool for survival; the frown, for feeling.

"That fool. That fucking knob!" He got up from his desk and walked to the end of the room opposite the door, behind Thursday. Thursday kept his eye on him, but it was tough with the bodyguard on the other side. He wasn't sure which one to watch.

"What happened?" Ip asked.

"It was a raid. Operation Trident or something. It was scary, broer. They caught him and I got away. He's in Pollsmoor now and I've got to bail him out."

He waited for Ip to agree, but he seemed not to have heard. "The car?"

"The car is impounded. I said that Leon's in Pollsmoor."

Ip grew furious. "I don't give a shit if Leon's in Pollsmoor! He should be in Pollsmoor! He's a fool. Too racy, too fast! Too many women! If I hadn't lost Rendell I never would have hired him. The fucking cock!" He walked up right next to Thursday, whose eyes for some reason fixed on the number of notches in his calfskin belt. Five of them. "Tell me, Hampton. One thing. Will Leon talk?"

Thursday thought about how Leon had told his girlfriend Fadanaz about the raid, but Fadanaz was not a cop. "He said he would talk about me."

"No one else?"

"No one else."

"Do you think he can make it in prison? Is he going to cry if a bloke comes and rubs butter on his arse?"

That was the one thing Thursday was sure of. Leon would run Pollsmoor by the time he got out. He wasn't afraid of anything. "No. He won't cry."

"You're sure?"

"I swear it, my broer. He's hard as nails. I swear it."

Ip paced back and forth for several minutes. He didn't sit down again at the desk.

"Alright. You can keep the money. What did you do with that cell phone he gave you?"

"It's right here."

Ip took it and removed the SIM card. He crushed it with a key, then he gave it back.

"You can keep the phone. And the check. You did the right thing by telling me, Hampton. I'll make some calls to Pollsmoor. Next time, be straight with me. I have ways of finding out the truth."

"Sure, sure, sure, no problem. Honest as my word. That's cool, man. He always said you were the best. Ip's the best, he'd say to me, heh, heh, heh." Ip shook his head and turned the door handle to leave. Thursday removed the lid of the abalone cooler. "Don't you want to look at them? They're forty years old."

Ip shook his head. "They'll be dead in an hour."

Then he left the room.

Thursday looked at the perlemoen in the water. They were hungry and packed like sardines, but still beautiful and robust. They had forty years of eking out a life in the ocean and deserved a more dignified death. He took a packet from his pocket. "I've got good fish meal for them," he said to the bodyguard. "Can you feed them until you dry them?"

The bodyguard didn't reply. Thursday reached into the cooler and let one suck its foot onto his palm. He'd gotten more abalone kisses lately, with their mollusk sensuality, than the real thing. When he looked up he was staring into the silencer of a snub-nosed pistol. "Yissus, man, what are you doing!"

"Shut up!"

"He said that I could go!"

"You shut up! You go nowhere! On the floor!"

"Ip! Ip! Come in here! He's trying to kill me!"

But the door didn't open. There was no sound at all but the slurping of the mollusk on his palm.

"On the floor!"

The bodyguard walked up and kicked Thursday forward, and he held his hand out to keep from crushing the abalone as he fell to the ground. It clattered to the floor. "Let me go!"

"No, you finished." The bodyguard removed Thursday's wallet and took the cell phone and the check.

Thursday could think of nothing to do. There was no way to kick him, not enough time to get in a punch. He covered his eyes and began to cry.

"You finished, Hampton."

The bodyguard took a step back. Then Thursday heard a low whinny. He turned to see that the thug had slipped on the abalone and discharged the pistol into the ceiling. He was flailing to keep his balance and tripped back over the cooler. The abalone spilled across the floor. Thursday spun around and tried to jump for the gun. But the man grabbed the hem of his pants and tripped him. He pulled at Thursday's heel with a crushing grip and wouldn't let go. Thursday kicked his free heel into the man's jaw and locked an arm around his head. The man was so strong he began squeezing his ribs with one arm alone. But Thursday had a firm hold and they began a slow struggle of wills. He tried to curl his bicep into the man's Adam's apple like Leon had taught him.

"Get off him!" a voice said.

It was Ip.

"Make him stop!" Thursday shouted.

Ip screamed at his guard and the man relaxed his arm around Thursday's ribs. Then Ip leveled the gun at Thursday. He swallowed. There was nothing he could do. He just sat and waited, his chest burning with pain. He felt a tiny bit of satisfaction in hearing the bodyguard cough, but it passed as Ip raised the gun.

This time Thursday didn't cry when he shut his eyes, waiting to receive the bullet in his brain. And he could have stood there for hours. He traveled down a wood-bored tunnel and back again. There were lights and dreams pushing through it like a geyser. He remembered a white crab crawling out of a hole on a beach, and running its claw back over its eye, intently. And the searing wind-blown sand of that day, whenever it was.

"You took care of these?"

He opened his eyes. Ip was looking at the mollusks drowning on the floor. They looked like furry brown saucers scattered on the ground.

"What, man?"

Ip was holding the gun up casually, not exactly in his direction. But when Thursday shifted to the side it followed him. "Don't move." He bent down to pick up an abalone, testing its weight. "These are plump." He handed the gun to his thug, who drew back the breech. Then Ip pulled out a pen knife and deftly sliced away the green foot from the abalone on the desk, the mollusk still pulsating, and drew it into thin slices. He chewed on a slice slowly. He motioned for his thug to eat some, who did so, and they exchanged some brusque words in Chinese. "Did you take care of these, Hampton?"

Thursday started adjusting to the fact that he was having a conversation again. "They were in my tub." And that words could save him.

"Did you have an aquarium? What did you give them?"

"What they need."

Ip picked up another large one. The gun was still trained on him. "Can you save them?"

"I don't know." Then: "Not if you're going to kill me."

Ip began putting the abalone in the cooler. The bodyguard, whose cheek was puffing where Thursday had gotten in a heel, looked like he was about to hurl himself at Thursday again. "Get some tap water, Chung."

"No," Thursday said. "They need sea water."

"Where can we get that?"

"The sea." He bent to pick one up, but Ip tensed. "Let me look at them." Ip grunted an assent and Thursday turned one over in his hand. "You've got about thirty minutes before they won't be able to recover. They've been under a lot of stress."

"Can you bring them back?"

Thursday nodded. "I'm the best."

"I'll pay you for them."

"You're going to kill me."

"No, I won't."

But now that he had seen the crab on the beach and the wood-boring tunnel he felt stronger. He could reckon with them. A bullet wouldn't change anything. "Put that gun down, Chinaman, and I'll think about it."

The thug lowered the pistol.

"Bail Leon out," Thursday said.

"How much is it?"

"One hundred thousand. He said these are worth it."

Ip's eyes glazed over as he did a calculation in his head.

"Leon's a fool. They're worth sixty thousand alive. That's an honest price and that's if they stay alive. We fly out the live ones and you must factor in the cost of the plane ticket. You're going to need more per-lemoen than that."

"I can take care of them."

"That won't change a thing. They're still sixty thousand alive."

"No, the ones that come in."

"No babysitter!" the bodyguard interjected.

But Ip was listening. "How much?"

Even when he had the upper hand, Thursday underestimated himself. "A hundred rand an hour."

"Can you do it without power?"

"Power has nothing to do with it."

Ip reached into the desk and counted out 10,100 rand.

"You said sixty thousand."

"That's if you keep them alive until the end of the week. Ten thousand dried. The hundred is for your first hour. I'll give you the rest if they make it through to shipment time. I pay cash. That check is worthless."

Thursday now realized how little he had understood about their prior negotiations. But he also knew that, just like the last time, he had no choice, he was negotiating for the chance to lick an ice cream cone again and do all the things he had sworn to do. If he could get out the door he could survive. If he could do that he could see how far he would have to run.

"You have twenty minutes to get to the water," Ip said. He tossed some keys to the bodyguard. "Chung will drive you. Now gather them up."

Chung was not happy about having to chauffer Thursday after their scuffle, and Thursday offered to get the sea water himself but Ip didn't trust him. Ip didn't understand anything about Thursday's kind of loyalty. It wasn't only to Leon, it was also to the abalone. Thursday would have taken the van and the bucket straight to the sea and nursed them back to health all on his own. Maybe he would have stopped for a Gatsby sandwich—chips, salad, viennas, and minced steak—but he would have returned.

They drove to the Foreshore, passing a long queue of dejected black men in front of the state warehouse. A car guard attempted to wave them into a spot, but Chung ignored him and steered towards a shipyard. They weaved through the carcasses of tugboats and passed some giant rusty propellers until they came to a ladder that hung over the side to the harbor.

"Down," Chung said. He handed Thursday a bucket.

The water was swirling with an oily film. A dead kingklip floated next to a sorry-looking trawler that probably hadn't netted a fish in a decade. "This isn't good enough," Thursday said.

"Down!"

Thursday filled the bucket, trying to lower it far down into the water to avoid taking in the oil. At the top, he said: "This will give them another hour at best. It's like poison. Take me to the sea, bru. The ocean."

"No, we go back."

"You want your boss to know that you cost him fifty thousand rand?"

Chung lit a cigarette with a butane lighter.

"Where we go?"

"Hermanus."

"Too far."

"Then False Bay, at least. They need the water they grew up in. That's the key."

They took the N2 past the water towers and the shacks with garbage bag and tarpaulin roofs and the airport, then cut out to Mitchell's Plain. Once they got to the sand dunes, Thursday started to get excited. They drove down a dirt road and Chung parked the car. Together they carried the abalone cooler down to the surf and Thursday began changing the water.

"Hurry up," Chung said.

"I don't want to shock them. They're almost dead."

A pair of Cape Bulbuls winged above the steady wash of the surf. Chung smoked a cigarette and when Thursday looked up he offered one to him, too. Looking at the crescent of the bay, he could imagine Hermanus on the other side, beyond the peaks of the barren mountains, shutting down for the evening. He wondered if anyone would miss him.

If I had a girl she would miss me, he thought. Maybe I should get a girl.

"We'll need to get a lot more water for the new ones," he said to Ip when they returned to the Chinese restaurant. "And we'll have to make a run for some gracilaria if you know what's good for them. The fish meal will bloat 'em up and it's bad for the flavor."

Ip looked at the cooler box. "Will they live?"

"Yeah," Thursday said. "They'll be fine. Now I've done my part of the bargain. Where's my money?"

"The shipment flies out on Sunday. You must keep them alive until then."

"Where? In Hermanus?"

"No, here."

"I don't have a place to stay."

"It's Observatory. There are plenty of rooms to let. Go to the supermarket and look at the notice board."

"Did you talk to Leon?"

"No, I talked to some friends of mine inside the prison. They're going to make everything right."

"Lekker."

Mrs. Niyangabo

1993
France

The sidelong glance. The whispers. The evasive walk around her by the flight attendants in the aisles. And from beneath her niqab, shadowed forms peering at her across rows of seats, saying Look! Look at her. Look at what she's wearing!, unaware or, worse yet, unconcerned that Melissa could still see them and hear them.

She was used to all these things. Even in her own home, Mlungisi Tebogo's bodyguards would avoid his daughter when left alone with her in the compound, passing along a message from her father without touching her at all. On television, girls her age were chased by boys who would give them flowers for a kiss. She'd kissed one once, a boy, until he'd seen what was beneath the veil, the white skin as lustrous as a pearl on a sienna African face.

"That's not right," he said, recoiling.

"What isn't?"

"It's just not right."

The next time he saw her, he threw a stone at her backside.

The plane had flown from Harare into Tangiers, where Melissa had switched planes for the flight to Paris. In Harare she had drawn suspicious looks because of her niqab, which covered her entire body in black silk from head to toe, and because of her gloves, which covered her hands. In Tangiers, two other girls stepped onto the plane wearing the same outfit. These girls disconcerted her. It was as if they could pierce her niqab with their eyes because they knew its folds and hidden corners. And she also noticed that the girls managed to sway their hips, to project an alluring femininity, so that instead of hiding their bodies, as Melissa tried to do, they invited others to imagine the beauty obscured by the cloth. Except the girls could remove their niqabs, while she could not. Never.

She fingered the package that her father had given her before he left on his trip with Mr. Bello.

"This is a great chance, Melissa," he'd said. "An opportunity for you to get better. In France, you can get treatment at a state-of-the-art hospital. They have the best doctors in the world, better than any you could find here. Bello told me that most of them are African anyway, transplanted from our own lands as if the marsh wasn't connected to the river. You'll get the royal treatment. We'll even have a place to stay. Doesn't that sound good?"

Anywhere was better than Zimbabwe, where she was an outcast confined to her own home. Still, she wasn't as excited as when Bello had visited, when he had made everything sound perfect, and the prospect made her nervous. "We'll go together?"

"Not this time, Melissa. This time I need you to meet me there. I want you to get started on your treatment right away. You can be a big girl and travel on your own, right? You remember what I've taught you. Mr. Bello will fetch you at the airport and I'll meet you at his home after I've finished my work."

Her father believed that the problem lay with her skin, because that's what the doctors had told him. They'd diagnosed it as vitiligo, the harmless but unsightly growth of skin cells without pigmentation. They'd never seen it spread so rapidly yet they believed that it might be possible to halt its progress. Her bleached skin covered her body so thoroughly that she looked half-albino, with irregular blots of brown skin. Her father's little coconut.

The worst that could happen, the doctors said, was a bad case of sunburn or rickets, but they didn't know about the pain. She had been through so many treatments in the hospital and from the bush doctors that her body no longer felt as if it was her own. On moonlit nights it felt as if something insidious tugged at her insides, and Melissa would toss and turn until dawn, feeling the hot blood cut through her veins until she vomited from nausea. She was afraid to tell her father because he worried about her so much. He was her one true friend after all these years and he was so often gone on his freedom missions, as he called them, that she didn't want him to fret when he was around.

She clung onto the feeling that maybe she could be cured, that she could be whole again, feel joy again, play with friends, as much for her father as for herself. France could be better than Bulawayo, she could at least start over again.

When he'd left on his trip, her father gave her a package to take to Mr. Bello and a backpack for her to carry, which he'd filled with snacks and a small wad of French money. Melissa could be trusted to deliver the package better than anyone else. Her father had taught her how to keep secrets that even his sentries didn't know. He kept the home immaculately clean and would leave signals for her: lowering the blinds meant she was to leave the home because a police raid was expected; a chalk mark behind the television meant he would be gone for a week; two chalk marks for two weeks. If he left a jar of honey in the sink, she could tell how long he had been gone by watching the trail of ants. Just a few ants meant he'd been gone an hour. A long trail of ants that wound out the door meant several hours.

Melissa liked these games. Once she began wearing the niqab, she became better at keeping secrets than anyone else. She'd seen wounded men burst into her father's compound in the middle of the night and she'd mopped up the blood and burned the soiled garments. She'd passed along coded messages from nervous dignitaries to the freedom fighters. She knew never to volunteer information unless asked and not to ask her own questions, but to listen and watch beneath her niqab. She was her father's most trusted confidant.

That was why she didn't look inside the package that he wanted her to deliver to Bello. It was sealed by layers of tape and he'd stamped it in three places in case someone tried to peel off the tape and replace it again. But there was a manilla envelope on top of the package that was, strangely, only held by a brass clasp. This she opened. It was the first sign that something was wrong.

At last the plane was descending into Charles de Gaulle Airport and banked sharply over the suburbs that ringed Paris. Her first intercontinental flight: her first landing. The flight attendant, a sweet, plain woman with a fresh spray of floral perfume, identified Melissa by the giant card around her neck that showed she was an unaccompanied minor. Melissa had briefly considered taking off the card and then abandoned the idea. She didn't know anyone in Paris.

The corridor to the flight arrivals area made her fidget, as she was taller than the flight attendant, and she could feel the stares of strange families and the limousine drivers. The other girls in their niqabs rushed towards a family holding placards with their names on it: Faisa, Fatima. There were hugs for them, but no placard for Melissa. After a few minutes, the flight attendant told her to stand next to an information desk, and went to the personal announcement system. Melissa tried to take in the multitude of faces rushing past her.

"Melissa Tebogo," a voice said behind her.

She turned to see an attractive black woman with a fine nose and excessive rouge on her cheeks. She was carrying a plain green handbag. She wore a plum-colored blouse over an ankle-length black dress. Her feet were in sandals.

"Enchantée," Melissa said.

"You don't look like your father," the woman replied, ignoring her attempt at French. She gave Melissa a stiff, mechanical hug and blew two kisses over her ear.

"Where is Mr. Bello?"

"He is indisposed," the woman said. She pulled the name card off. "You will not be needing this."

Her accent was not South African, nor did it sound like the French people on television. Beyond that Melissa hadn't a clue. Only that the woman was from elsewhere. She was pulled by the hand until they found the flight attendant negotiating to utilize the PA system.

"I am Mrs. Niyangabo," she said. "I am Melissa's aunt."

"Let me check the list," the attendant said. She nodded. "She was supposed to be fetched by Mr. Bello. Mr. Nurudeen Bello."

"He is indisposed," Mrs. Niyangabo said. "The papers are here."

"We typically require a—" Mrs. Niyangabo handed her another document. "Very good. I see you have the affidavit and the registry letter. Melissa, do you know this woman?"

Melissa didn't like Mrs. Niyangabo's stiff manner but returning to Zimbabwe seemed much worse. She had come here for a cure, not for kindness. "Yes, I know her."

"Sign here, and here, Mrs. Niyangabo. You have a very well-behaved niece." The attendant handed over a suitcase with a bright orange tag on it. "This is her luggage."

Mrs. Niyangabo gave a weak smile. They walked down a series of moving walkways laid out in a circle. The middle of the circle was open to the air with a mesh cage to keep out the birds that was covered with feathers. In the parking garage, Mrs. Niyangabo tossed Melissa's name card in the trash bin. "Did you bring the package?"

"Yes," Melissa said.

They approached a black Audi sedan. Once inside, Mrs. Niyangabo turned to her and said, severely. "Give it to me."

Melissa did as she was told and Mrs. Niyangabo turned the package over before tucking it under her seat. They drove onto a wide highway with hazy sunlight. There were old stone farmhouses with acacia trees for windbreaks, with bright green spinach plants against brown-tilled earth. Melissa did not like the speed at which Mrs. Niyangabo drove. She would zoom so close to the cars in front that they would have only a moment to switch to another lane. Not once had Mrs. Niyangabo mentioned her niqab.

"Are we going to Paris?"

"No, Bandoufle."

They drove for an hour. They exited the highway onto a frontage road then exited again into a neighborhood with a maze of roundabouts with small three-bedroom homes laid out in a housing complex. They passed the entrance to a golf course and a sports stadium that seemed much too big for the town. There weren't any people on the streets walking dogs or pushing children. Just watching the entire deserted scene made Melissa thirsty for water.

Mr. Bello's home was as lifeless as the community. A foyer with a hard bench, a kitchen, a living room, and three small bedrooms. He wasn't there. The air inside felt stale and Mrs. Niyangabo did not open the windows to let in a breeze. The living room had two burgundy couches with wooden clawfeet. There was a television, a coffee table, some still-life paintings, and plastic flowers in a vase. Melissa recognized a portrait over the fireplace of an august-looking Mr. Bello with a colorful pointed hat. Unsmiling, Mrs. Niyangabo brought water and a plate of crackers with cheese.

"Stay here." She could be heard speaking on a telephone in a language Melissa had never heard; then she returned carrying the package along with a box of matches. "You were very brave to come here, Melissa. You did the right thing. Mr. Bello is, I regret, unable to come to meet you. But first let me attend to this."

She broke the seal of the package for Bello. Inside, she flipped through some papers and paused at a bundle of airline tickets. She took out a pen and wrote down the information. She also picked up a few trinkets: a computer disk, an electronic keycard, a roll of film, and a plastic object like a pulley. She made a note of these and then placed the entire package in the fireplace. She squeezed some liquid on the cardboard and set a flame to it.

"No!" Melissa shouted.

She rushed over to put out the blaze and Mrs. Niyangabo slapped her with the back of her hand. She fell into a pile of kindling, scrambling to get up.

"Get on the couch or I'll hit you again!"

Melissa sat down and waited. She began to cry but tried not to make any noise. No one had ever hit her, ever. Mrs. Niyangabo took a poker and spread the ashes around, until some pieces poked through, added more liquid, and lit the pile again. She put on a log and burnt that, too. The smell of burning plastic filled the room.

"Take this," Mrs. Niyangabo said. She produced a clean white handkerchief. "I did not want to have to do that, Melissa. I did it for your own safety. Take a sip of water and you'll feel better."

Melissa took a sip of water. The bubbles tickled at her throat but she didn't feel any better. "I thought you were my father's friend."

"No, I am not his friend."

"Then who are you?"

"I will tell you what I believe is safe. First you must accept that you will never see your father again."

Melissa swallowed. The woman had given her no reason to trust her yet. Only to fear her. "You're lying!"

"Shut up, you insolent girl!" Mrs. Niyangabo snapped. "You don't know what you're talking about. You don't know who your father was."

"He's a freedom fighter."

"That's what he told you." She took a cracker from the table and nibbled on it daintily. "Don't look at me like that. Don't be proud. He's not a freedom fighter. He's a terrorist."

Melissa understood now that Mrs. Niyangabo was not going to help her, nor was she a friend of her father's or Mr. Bello's. Her father wasn't a terrorist! He'd spent his life helping the freedom fighters, people she had helped herself. She glanced at the door. She thought she could make a run for it and get outside. She would sort out the suburban wasteland later. There had to be a phone somewhere. In France there must be phones and there must be police.

"He will get what he deserved," Mrs. Niyangabo went on, glancing at the cinders across the room.

"Why did you burn the package?"

Mrs. Niyangabo did not seem accustomed to answering questions. Dispassionately she removed a pocket mirror from a purse, taking her time applying rouge to her cheeks, and snapped it shut. "The information in that package was dangerous. I did it to protect my people. I'm surprised, really, that your father did not find out much more than he did. His reputation was unmerited." She paused. "Are you getting sleepy?"

Melissa shook her head.

"It is called jetlag."

"I know."

"You may know it, but you haven't had it. In ten minutes you'll be asleep."

"No," Melissa pouted. "I'll stay awake. I'm not tired."

But she was tired, very much tired. It was too much. She couldn't believe what she was hearing, not after the woman had slapped her so viciously. If she believed Mrs. Niyangabo then her father would be gone forever.

"You will fall asleep. First, I need you to tell me one thing, Melissa. Answer it honestly. Entrusting you with the package was reckless, I'm afraid. I need to know so that I can protect you to the best of my ability. If you do not tell the truth, your life will be in danger." She looked Melissa in the eye. "Did you look in the package?"

"No. He told me never to look at his packages."

"You are sure."

"Yes." Then, as if it had slipped her mind: "I also found a photo of my father and me in my backpack."

"Where is it?"

She unzipped her backpack and fingered the photo, taken before her skin had begun to change. Reluctantly, she handed it to Mrs. Niyangabo. Mrs. Niyangabo glanced at it and handed it back. "You can keep it. It means nothing. You can go to sleep now, Melissa."

"I'm not tired."

"I will show you to your room." They walked down the stale hallway with more unsigned portraits of fruit and olives and flowers. At the door to the bedroom, where there was a single twin bed, Mrs. Niyangabo stopped her. "Melissa, if you are lying, I will find out. This is not a game." She clicked open Melissa's large suitcase. "Take what you need to sleep." Melissa grabbed her toothbrush and a novel about the English seaside. Mrs. Niyangabo snatched the book and leafed through it slowly, didn't notice anything, and handed it back. "Why do you wear the niqab?"

"For my skin."

"Let me see it."

Melissa peeled off her glove first on her right hand, then her left, and pulled up the sleeve. Mrs. Niyangabo wrinkled her nose but didn't touch her.

"Is it contagious?"

"No."

"You need a bath. You stink." She lugged Melissa's belongings down the hallway. "Now be a good girl and leave the door open. Good night."

Mrs. Niyangabo was correct about the jetlag, for Melissa tried very hard to stay awake, but the long flight and the suburban desert made her feel far away. Melissa knew that below the folds of her niqab, she was there, she was present, but Mrs. Niyangabo frightened her, for beneath her rouged cheeks there seemed to be nothing at all. And she was terrified of coming closer to that nothingness. Bitter and black, halfway down, in the darkness, she was falling tears, she was sadness and sleep.

She awoke at dawn having to pee but was so afraid of Mrs. Niyangabo that she didn't stir, and held it rather than go to the bathroom. She drifted into a fitful sleep and this time when she awoke she couldn't stand it and rushed to the toilet. On the way back she saw that the other bed was already made. The living room was also empty and where there had once been ashes in the fireplace there was a fresh log. Mrs. Niyangabo was nowhere to be found.

She went into the kitchen and found more crackers and cheese, laid out with a note. Back in five minutes. No signature. In the refrigerator, all the shelves were empty except for a box of long-life milk. She searched the cabinets and found dishes but no food. Cautiously, she crept through the apartment and looked at the picture frames. Mr. Bello was in several of them, smiling in the smooth way she recalled from his visit in Bulawayo, though there were no photos with her father. After she ate some crackers and drank a glass of milk, she rushed back to her bedroom and waited for Mrs. Niyangabo to arrive. At last she heard the lock—and in a flash she thought, maybe it was Mr. Bello, maybe it was her father—and she ran to the front door.

But it was a different person altogether. The woman was wearing a full-length dress with a string of large false pearls. Her face was wider than Mrs. Niyangabo's face and her skin was darker, with fuller lips. She stopped and looked at Melissa from head to toe.

"Melissa," she said. "I am Madame Kaluanda."

"Enchantée," Melissa replied.

She raised her eyebrows, impressed. "Enchantée! Quelle jolie fille! Est-ce que tu parles français?"

"Non."

"You will soon. For I am a French teacher. Would you like that, to learn français?"

"Yes."

"S'il vous plaît."

"See voo play."

"Very good. Your first lesson. Please get your things and we will go."

"Where is Mrs. Niyangabo?"

"I am sorry. This may be difficult for you, but you will not see her again. I am going to be your guardienne from now on, Mademoiselle. She gave me your luggage already. It is in the car. Dépeches-toi."

Madame Kaluanda did not hug her, but that was fine for Melissa, because she knew where she stood. They were not going to be friends. They would be acquaintances. Mrs. Niyangabo's frigidity, on the other hand, had frightened her.

"Are we going to the hospital?" she asked.

"Non, Évry."

Évry was only a fifteen minute drive from Bandoufle, and the buildings grew taller as they drove into it. She saw train tracks and a black river with some beautiful trees on the banks, and they passed through an old neighborhood with stone houses draped with dark green ivy. There were kids in some of the streets. They turned into the driveway of a large apartment complex, unloaded the bags, and got into a slow elevator with scribbles of graffiti next to the buttons that took them to the fifteenth floor. It was a long, closed hallway with a seaweed-green carpet. One of the windows, she noticed, was cracked and she could smell rich cooking oil in the air.

She was given a bedroom with two other girls. In total there were fifteen girls spread over two apartments, six in that apartment, and nine two doors down. There were two bathrooms with bathtubs and toilets without seat covers. Madame Kaluanda ran the place as a boarding house for parents who couldn't afford to move to France, or who had returned home for one reason or another and left the children to get better schooling. She was frank about this. There was none of the secrecy of Mrs. Niyangabo, none of the veiled threats. Melissa was told that there were strict rules and rent was monthly. Her rent had been paid in advance by Mrs. Niyangabo for the first year, and after that she would have to pay her own way.

"But how?" Melissa asked. "I don't have a job."

"There is money to be made in this country. You'll find a way. Classes begin in the morning."

"What about the hospital? My father said I'd be going to the hospital."

"Not unless you can afford it."

"Mr. Bello can afford it."

"Who?"

"Mr. Bello."

"I'm afraid that I have never heard of him."

"But—"

"This way, Mademoiselle. To your room."

None of the other girls spoke English. Her flatmates were from Rwanda, the Central African Republic, and Niger. The rest were from Zaire. The girl from Niger wore a hijab headscarf that showed her face. She spoke a few words to Melissa until she said, "I'm not Muslim." Then she stayed away. Madame Kaluanda's rules meant that the oldest girl was in charge, but this didn't work in practice because some were cleverer than others, and it became clear that night that a slender, gracious girl called Béatrice controlled the home. Melissa's roommates gave her some food and talked to her for an hour, asking about her niqab, and chatting warmly as if she spoke their own language, then took their beds when Béatrice ordered the lights out. Melissa refused to take off her robe.

"Papa?" one of them whispered. "Où se trouve ton Papa?" Melissa pretended not to hear her, but she kept on going: "Maman, Papa? Où se trouvent vos parents? Maman, Papa?"

She knew the girl was asking about her parents, and the girl kept on repeating, 'Maman, Papa', for a few minutes, the other chiming in with a 'maman', and at one point they said it so often they began humming 'maman, papa' to a tune, like a nursery rhyme, Melissa curling the pillow over her ears. Why did they care about her father? What did they know about such things? They knew where their parents were living; they could talk to them. Papa, Papa, Maman, Maman, Papa, Papa, Papa, the girls went on until they fell asleep.

As soon as her roommates stopped rustling, Melissa reached beneath her niqab and removed the manilla envelope that had been attached to the package for Mr. Bello. After she'd looked inside, she'd decided that her father must have wanted her to see it and she'd hidden it in her niqab. Why else would he close it with a simple clasp instead of glue like he normally did? The envelope contained a few papers. One listed names and telephone numbers:

Nurudeen Bello. 33-1-45-23-35-25
Obafemi Ferguson. 46-8-32-24-65-22
Ogun Olesegun. 33-1-56-23-74-26
Suzanne Ibibio. 49-69-24-72-83-20
Adewale George Olufunmi. 281-766-5373
Sheyi Obafemi. 81-75-93-28-12-24
Jonathan Winston Soboyoja. 416-236-2024
Mohammed Farai. 41-61-67-32-12-23

She'd never seen the names before. Her father only worked with freedom fighters in South Africa and these names did not look South African. She also didn't recognize the numbers. Then there was the money: a bundle of Francs, British pounds, and even dollars from the U.S.

The money might have been for Mr. Bello himself or for Mr. Bello to spend on Melissa. Perhaps Mr. Bello would have given it to her after she had arrived—her father seemed to trust him. Still, she was glad she had looked inside the envelope, because Mr. Bello wasn't coming to find her and she knew her father had looked after her. He would never have abandoned her the way that Mrs. Niyangabo had implied. And she felt emboldened by the money. The only question was, where had her father gone? Where could she find him?

In the morning she blamed her sleepiness on jetlag, with Mrs. Kaluanda giving her the name for the term: décalage horaires. She was forced to go with the other girls to the lycée, and struggled through classes while trying to learn French. Madame Kaluanda would occasionally stop by the apartment and offer some rudimentals of French grammar, but beyond that the girls ruled themselves. The girls taught her enough Lingala, Swahili, and French to keep up, though she realized she couldn't sustain their banter. They were afraid of her strange skin and the time she had spent alone over the past few years had left her incapable of chitter chatter.

Mostly she thought of her father and the envelope he'd left her. She was afraid of asking too much about the people on the list because she knew she couldn't talk to Madame Kaluanda. From a payphone, she dialed Mr. Bello's house phone number several times but the number had been disconnected. She decided to try the phone number of Ogun Olesegun, which she realized was also in France. The operator said he was not disponible but at least the phone number was not disconneted. And she found his name in the phonebook:

Ogun Olesegun, 14 Rue de Béarne, 3eme, Paris.

It was the best news she had heard since she arrived in France. She would finally meet someone who knew her father.

Pollsmoor Prison

Present Day
South Africa

Brother Leon held fast on his bunk when the cell door slid open, never showing, giving away little. He observed but did not focus, and heard without appearing to register the words. The guard threw in a prisoner. Leon expressed no more interest than he would in a piece of rubbish on the ground. The other cellmates, eager for excitement, began to harangue the new arrival.

The cell contained thirty men in orange jumpsuits. It was about ten meters by six meters deep, with four sets of bunk beds built to accommodate eight people. There was a single toilet and two barred windows that overlooked, through an electrified fence coated with razor wire, the golf course across the road and the taillights of the cars that would snake up the mountain pass to Nordhoek Beach. Men could go crazy watching the stream of cars continually escaping the prison of the valley. Or seeing the businessmen stroll freely to whack a golf ball into the lush green driving range. Leon had learned to gaze, to unfocus his vision until all about him at Pollsmoor prison blurred into a mass of meaningless, energetic movement. Anything else would be used against him.

The guard had pushed in a young Xhosa boy, maybe eighteen, whose wide eyes instantly betrayed a need for protection. The boy scanned the cell for other people from his neighborhood block, then his township, then his tribe. If he was lucky he would be claimed for sex. But the boy was too slight to be a fighter and his face had been scoured by malnutrition. He was so ugly that no one would want him. This meant he would be taken by several men at once.

Leon had joined the twenty-seven gang to sell drugs, unwilling to become involved with the sex trade, and he'd enlisted to stave off the rape and to buy time for Thursday to bail him out of prison. The guards had shaved the locks from his head, to prevent lice they said, but he knew it was to break him, to begin the rapid dismantling of the real Leon,

Brother Leon, and he let them cut them as if he didn't care, tucking one into his jumpsuit. At first he had vowed to beat Thursday to a pulp when he got out of prison but now he felt differently, that he might hug him nearly to death instead. The gang had ordered Leon to pick four fights, two easy targets and two equals, and he'd won each fight handily, pummeling his opponents with vicious poetry to gain respect. After lights out, Leon would remove his lock and finger it like a rosary, sometimes smell it too.

The shoving began. The cell gang leaders had ignored the boy, so their minions, used to being pushed around, slid off their sleeping mats. They insulted him in Afrikaans, slurred at him in bad Xhosa. They pushed him in the shoulder, while another circled around, preparing to trap him in the corner. The boy stumbled back over a mat as others began to hoot. A fist cracked into his jaw and he blinked stupidly. Leon, unfocused, almost turned away, but held himself from displaying any weakness. It would be cowardly to participate, more cowardly still to disapprove. The boy was so sheepish that the rape would be violent—he might not even survive it. If he fell to the floor he would be finished.

Then the boy's hand snapped out. The first man fell back, clutching at his arm. The others surged forward. The boy kicked one in the knee and slashed at another with what looked like a slice of paper. He waited for the last to charge, wound tight. Then he kicked himself out of the corner before whipping the paper down on the man's calf. There were howls of pain. His innocent face had changed to one of detached, controlled purposefulness, inviting the others to come at him. He began egging them on, holding the paper above his open mouth like a fang.

Come, he challenged with his eyes. Come.

He hadn't said a word.

Leon focused his gaze. The boy had not acted out of desperation, a feat of luck that could save you for a night or maybe a week, but a strategy that would fail as the groves of iron bars and putrid food sapped your energy. The boy had also somehow known how the men would behave. But Leon didn't recognize him. The gang members in the cell seemed equally puzzled, trying to determine his allegiance. Was he a tsotsi? A transfer from Block B? A twenty-six? If he was an insider no one seemed to know him. His arms were bare of tatoos. Leon hated allegiance and knew an opportunity to break free when he saw one.

He called to the boy in Xhosa. The boy approached slowly, muscles taut.

"Let's see that weapon, bru."

The boy scanned Leon up and down. Then he nodded. It was a thin white plastic ruler, its edge sharpened to perfection. He must have hidden it in the lining of his jumpsuit. Still, Leon was impressed that the guard hadn't caught it. Weapons usually came in through the windows or were fashioned from the frames of the beds, sometimes even a thick chip of plaster from the wall. The guards would strip you before you entered, probe your ass.

"Not bad, laatie," Leon said. "What's the name?"

"Lebo."

"I've been looking for a partner, Lebo."

"Lebo works alone."

"Izzit?" Leon said, handing the ruler back. "I do, too. But in Pollsmoor I think exceptions are in order. Don't you?" He ran his hand over his shaved head, his fingers groping blindly for his locks. Then he reached into the pocket of his jumpsuit, remembering, and gave his lock a caress. He smiled. "I'm Leon."

The boy's eyes suddenly flashed white. He took a step forward, peering down at Leon with intensity.

A pale of doubt drifted through Leon like a ghost. Maybe this was not a boy he could harness, he thought. He tried to hold his gaze, watching the boy's scarred face. The other cell mates began moving away.

"Lebo does not make exceptions, Leon," the boy said. "Lebo does what the Chinaman says." He gripped the ruler in his palm then coiled his arm to strike.

I Heard Nothing

1993
France

It took a public holiday for Melissa to get to Paris, which did not take that long, as they seemed to happen more in France than she remembered in a whole year in Zimbabwe. Madame Kaluanda arrived with an armful of baguettes and cold cuts and ordered the girls to make sandwiches. They boarded a double-level commuter train and the girls giggled the entire trip into the city. Melissa hoped they'd go to the Third Quarter but instead they went to a Congolese party at Cité Universite. The girls chatted with the boys and Madame Kaluanda found a man with whom she cuddled for hours. During a lively song, Melissa saw her chance. She excused herself to go to the bathroom of the apartment building and left through another exit.

By this time she had memorized the entire métro system and neighborhood maps of the Marais, but when she exited at the Marais she turned twice and became completely disoriented. A man at a kebab shop told her to go to La Place des Vosges, and she found her way to the cobbled square with its red brick and peaked roofs. After cutting through the line of tourists at the Maison Victor Hugo she learned that the street was not inside the plaza itself, but connected through an archway.

14 Rue de Béarne was a six-story building with nothing approaching a doorbell. There wasn't a knocker or any sign of how to get in, and she had not thought to learn an apartment number. There was also, she noticed nervously, a police gendarmerie across the street. She waited and tried to think of the next step when the door opened and a thirty-something man stepped out. She brushed past him into the foyer with a 'merci' and began walking up the worn stairs, deciding she would go straight to the top and work her way down. At the top door there was a knocker, but no one answered. Instead the apartment across the hall opened and she found herself looking at a soft-shouldered white woman

with smiling eyes and a toothy grin. She had blond eyebrows that looked odd because her hair was jet black.

"Bonjour," she said.

"Bonjour, Madame."

"Est-ce que tu cherches à Ogun?"

"Oui," Melissa said. "I'm looking for my friend, Ogun Olusegun."

The woman gave a pert nod and she let out a string of passionate words. Melissa could not follow her, and they stood there staring at each other, Melissa wondering if she'd been ordered to do something or not to do something. "I'm sorry," Melissa said in English. "Désolée. Plus lentement, s'il vous plaît."

At this the woman relaxed.

"It's about time you came. Where are you from?"

"Malawi," Melissa lied.

The woman introduced herself as Stéphanie and Melissa called herself Isabelle. The woman looked behind her into the apartment. "Please, let me get the keys."

There was no invitation to follow her, so Melissa waited at the door. Finally, the woman arrived with a key ring. She shut the door behind her and used the keys to open the apartment across the corridor. The apartment had a low roof and a couch that must have been able to turn into a bed because there was no other spot for one. It was very dark. There was a broad desk and an old-fashioned telephone, and tin pots hanging in a small antechamber over a tiny gas stove. To Melissa's relief the woman opened some glass doors that led to the terrace where there was sunlight and bunches of gladiolas and orange poppies. The sunlight silhouetted the blond hair on her arms, so Melissa guessed that her black hair was died.

"How do you know Ogun? You are young, non? Are you a niece? I am sorry but it is difficult to see beneath your niqab."

Melissa decided the easiest thing was to go right on lying. "I am seventeen."

"Seventeen? And they force you to wear that niqab like a prisoner. It's shameful. If I could talk to your father, I would give him a piece of my mind!"

"No, I wear it by choice. He wanted me to take it off."

"Ah—I see." She seemed puzzled, and frowned as if Melissa had misspoken. "Where is he?"

"In Évry. He wanted to invite Ogun to our horse party."

"Horse party? What is a horse party?"

"You see, we bought a new horse and he always has a party. We've got a hundred." She wondered if it was excessive.

Her host didn't seem surprised by it, though, and sighed: "I suppose Ogun has missed many obligations. I've tended to the flowers and kept the apartment clean. The owner wishes to throw all his things away but I received permission to wait until the end of the month. There will be new tenants then. Franchement, I expected more of his family to come." Melissa again had the feeling that something was expected of her, but stood still. "But your people are never fond of PDs, are they?"

"What is a PD?"

"Gays. Homosexuals. Did your father tell you what of Ogun's he wanted you to get?"

"No. He is a friend."

The woman explained that the furniture and practical affairs had been disposed of as she led Melissa, her back hugging the wall, to a vinyl record collection. "He was very fond of Eric Dolphy and John Coltrane. I am told many of the records would be of value."

"I can just take them?"

"Mais, bien sûr! He can do nothing more with them."

Stéphanie made it seem so obvious that Melissa was too embarrassed to ask why not. But she could never sneak in records to her bedroom in Évry because Madame Kaluanda would find out. She made an excuse.

"How about some photos for your father? Perhaps there is one of the two of them together?"

Melissa flipped through the stack of framed photos, but found none with her father in it. Ogun had a very round head, glasses, and a considered look about him, as if he was observing all of the locations with discernment—a fishing boat, a mountain chalet, a bride and a groom, a group of men wearing bright robes about the same age, a conference with formal delegates. He had a lot of friends and most of them were black. There was an attractive man that seemed to be in a lot of photos and in one of them they were holding hands. She placed one of the photos in her backpack in order to keep Stéphanie from asking questions.

"You're sure you don't want any others?"

"Yes."

They walked back towards the kitchen, and Melissa checked to see if there were any clues, any telltale signs that her father had been there. She didn't see any. The apartment felt eerily similar to Mr. Bello's; if it weren't for the flowers, the stale air would be the same. As they walked back and forth through the apartment, sifting through trinkets and things Stéphanie considered of interest, Melissa noticed she didn't once step in center of the floor. It looked like another ordinary oak floorboard.

"Why don't you step there?"

"Where?" Stéphanie said, continuing on.

"On that spot."

Stéphanie reluctantly turned. "Ah. Because that is where it happened."

"Where what happened?"

"Where he was murdered."

Melissa stiffened. Had she heard murder? Maybe she was mistaken. She became aware of the sound of car doors closing in front of the gendarmerie below.

"Such a tragédie. The police are investigating but they have made no discoveries. Ogun was a good man and a good voisin. Like a fragrance. A good neighbor."

"But what—?"

"No one knows. I was in my apartment and I heard nothing. The next day I did not hear him leave for work. I thought he had been on a trip for business affairs. He was shot twice and I heard nothing. I was here, in my apartment having some pain and café. I do it every morning."

Melissa realized that the woman was as afraid of the word 'murder' as she was, because she did not say it again. Her glance at the floorboard suggested that she was having trouble accepting what that meant, to be killed quietly while your neighbors were eating bread and drinking coffee. And the musty smell of the old apartment made murder seem inevitable. How could a man expect to live a full life in such a foreboding place?

As if in answer, a shutter burst open and the wind roared and the glass doors slammed shut. Melissa jumped.

"It is the garbage shaft," Stéphanie smiled. "He complained about it often. Do not worry." She calmly walked over and closed the shutter again.

Melissa decided she did not like this anymore, that Madame Kaluanda would be upset, that she had to leave and forget the names her father had left her. The visit was a reckless idea. She headed for the door.

"No, please," Stéphanie said, and in French began imploring her to stay. "I am sorry. I should have called your father. It is too much for a young woman to hear. But you are so tall that you look like a woman."

Melissa was in the hallway already. She was leaving this place, ready to fly, to get away. A mistake. All of it mistaken.

"Please, attends un instant," Stéphanie said. "There is one thing which you must have." Melissa watched her rummage in a desk and take some magazines. "I'd hoped to give these to his family, because it would have made them proud. But no one has come around. He gave so much to them. He was a quiet man but he made people happy and the salauds forgot him. I am not a scientist. Take these to you father. Maybe he will know what to do with them."

Melissa accepted the magazines and ran down the stairs to the street. Keeping her eyes on the police station, she paced to the Place de Vosges, where she hailed a taxi. She returned to the party, where the girls were watching the boys play soccer and Madame Kaluanda was laughing next to some japonica bushes with a different man.

She did not sleep that night. The thought that she had been so close to a murder terrified her. She had hoped to meet someone who had known her father but the man had been killed and she hadn't found anything useful. And what if the murderer came after her? He could pop the latch, sneak through the bunks in the room, and plunge a knife into her chest, all while the other girls giggled like children!

Classes were moving into examinations and her prospects were not good. Because she was so distracted, she was on the verge of failing literature and history. Her teacher arranged a conference with Madame Kaluanda where he expressed his admiration of her aptitude and disappointment at her language ability. Afterwards, Madame Kaluanda was stern.

"Melissa, I do not understand this. Haven't you been studying your grammar?"

Melissa could speak Lingala, Swahili, and some Arabic by this point but her French was atrocious. "I am trying," she said.

"I cannot keep you in the apartment if you are not going to school, Melissa. The girls can work only part-time under the law. If you fail your classes, I will have to send you out."

"Where will I go?"

She shrugged her shoulders. "I'm afraid it's up to Mrs. Niyangabo to decide."

Melissa went to her room and cried until the other girls came home. What would Mrs. Niyangabo do to her? Would she kill her? Where would she live? She had no friends in Zimbabwe, and no one to look after her in France.

To keep her mind off this horrible fate, she picked up the magazines she'd received at the man's apartment in Paris. They were all scientific journals and in English. Ogun Olusegun had written an article in every one of them. Solid State Propulsion in the New Millennium: A Comparative Discourse; Harnessing Solar Wind in a Silicon Poor World; Developing Economies and Geosynchronous Space: Towards Parity. One of the articles was a book review of a work by Dr. Olusegun and it was highly favorable, and all the other articles made some mention of the book. It seemed to have been the book that started his career. Thinking she might find some information, she visited the public library to request it.

The small librarian was small and dumpy and smelled of pastis. He said that it would take six or seven weeks to order the magazines—far too long, for Melissa knew Mrs. Niyangabo would have ruined her life by then and her father might be gone forever.

"Are these journals for you?" the librarian said quickly.

"Yes, I am a scientist."

"Ah bon? You must be a very smart girl to understand these magazines. Are there any other authors? I can make a request." He looked on the computer screen. "Here is a work by Soboyoja. The title is similar. I can have it sent in a week."

The name sounded familiar. "Can you show me?"

The librarian pivoted the computer monitor towards her and she read it again. Then she had it! It was also a name from the list that her father had given her! "Yes, please! I would love that! Thank you so much, monsieur!"

It occurred to her that perhaps the other names were scientists as well or, if they weren't, the librarian might be able to find out if they'd written any books. She scribbled out all the names.

"Can you get me these books, too?"

The librarian took the list, scanning his eyes over Melissa's niqab. "Are you Nigerian?"

"Non. I am from Malawi."

"But you like Nigerian authors?"

"Perhaps." She didn't understand what he was getting at.

"Ben Okri is géniale, don't you think?"

"Yes," she lied, unfamiliar with the name.

"Please tell me how these books are. I am not one for scientific works, but my wife is Nigerian. I will tell her. She will be happy to hear about so many Nigerian scientists. She is studying in Rennes at the moment," he added, sadly. Then, as if convincing himself: "But a happy wife on the phone is better than a sad wife at home, isn't it?"

"Yes, monsieur."

Over the next week, Melissa stopped going to school and spent the day at the library studying the journals of the authors. The librarian would sneak her spicy Nigerian dishes, perhaps to remind himself of his wife, and he seemed to think Melissa had nostalgia for the food, presenting each one with flair as if she'd been missing it. She found the rich, fishy flavors to be a pleasant escape from the bland fare the girls cooked in the apartment. All of the authors were scientists. She knew the fact that they were all from Nigeria was important, but she did not understand why. They didn't sound like Freedom Fighters. She remembered that her father had told Bello that he would never travel to Nigeria, because he had been cheated several times before. And Bello himself was Nigerian, she remembered that, too.

"Can you tell me more about Nigeria?" she asked the librarian. He directed her to several books, which seemed much too long to read.

"There isn't much to know. Before the British came, there was no Nigeria. There were different tribes living and fighting. Then they created Nigeria and controlled it. The country became independent in 1960. Then a civil war happened—that is when my wife's family left—and after that it has been controlled by the army."

"You mean they don't have a president?"

"Vous ne saviez pas? They just held elections that were canceled by President Abboud, and the new President, Rawlson Bimini, took power from him. The president before him was from the army. The army is the government and the government is the army. A pity."

He showed her a few books about the different tribes, but there were too many of them to read, so she focused on the journal articles instead. Some of the scientists were experts with fuels, others with rocks, and many were engineers. The other puzzling thing was that, although they were Nigerian, none of them lived in Nigeria. They lived in Hong Kong, Sweden, London, the United States, Japan, Australia, and Switzerland. Ogun Olusegun was the only one who lived in France. Or who had lived in France, she remembered, for he'd been murdered.

That was still enough to give her hope. If she could find the other scientists, she might be able to find her father. She could speak with them. One of them might even be his friend. But how could she get to them? She felt trapped by Madame Kaluanda and the girls, whose prying eyes seemed to know everything she did.

To make matter worse, she tossed and turned that evening, jerked awake again by her hot blood. When she looked out the window over the rooftops of Old Évry, she saw the moon rising, pulling at her insides. She felt as if her lungs were filled with light, that the white skin on her brown body would rip her apart. She peeled off her gloves and looked at her arms. Her blood shined right through her veins and she could see webs of light in her capillaries. She gasped, and covered it up. Her leg was worse, every vein exposed in a web of bluish light. She rolled over again and again in her bed.

"Qu'est-ce qu'il y a?" she heard a voice whisper. "What's the matter?"

"I'm fine," Melissa snapped.

The door creaked open. The girl's name was Béatrice, the slender girl who ruled the apartments while Madame Kaluanda was away. She was pretty and was becoming a fashion model and had everything Melissa did not. Melissa had spent her time in Évry avoiding her, afraid that she was a snitch.

"I have some pain pills."

"I don't want them."

"Is it your period?"

"No."

"Ah, well. You can wake me if you are not feeling well."

She left the medicine at the foot of the bed. Melissa swallowed one, but the pill swirled in her stomach until she was forced to vomit.

Madame Kaluanda was waiting for Melissa when she returned from the library the following afternoon, sleepy and bleary-eyed from her restless night.

"Where did you go in Paris?"

"To the party." She went to brush past, but Madame Kaluanda blocked her with an arm.

"I asked you a question, Mademoiselle. Answer it."

"I went to the party with everyone else."

Kaluanda scowled. "Tant pis. Then you can tell Mrs. Niyangabo. She is waiting for you."

Melissa shivered. Mrs. Niyangabo! Of all times! She said she would never come back! She put her hand on her chest, thinking that there was nowhere to go this time as Madame Kaluanda angrily turned to open the door.

"Non, please, Madame!"

"Are you willing to talk?"

"Yes, anything! I will tell you everything!"

"If you do not answer then I will have to send you with her. You were expelled from school yesterday morning. I know you do not want to go with her. You are a strange girl, but I will do what I can to help if you stop this insolence. The girls said that you left the party in Paris. Where did you go? Are you prostituting yourself?"

"Mais, non!"

"Tell me."

"I went to see a museum."

"If you lie then I cannot help you."

Madame Kaluanda began turning the doorknob. Melissa rushed to her and grabbed her arm. "Please, Madame! Non! Non! Ouvrez-pas! I have money. I can pay you."

Madame Kaluanda lifted an eyebrow. "How much?"

"Anything you want. Don't make me go with her."

She paused, considering the offer. "Five hundred francs per month, all in advance. And you will stay in school. But I am not sure she would agree to it. Go down to 503 and wait."

Melissa went inside the second apartment and wrung her hands. She resolved to kill herself rather than go with Mrs. Niyangabo. She would throw herself out the window, or she could grab the steering wheel of her car and kill them both. Or she could stab her, she thought desperately. She rushed into the kitchen and hid a knife in the bottom of her pack. If Mrs. Niyangabo touched her then Melissa would gore her.

At last the door opened and Madame Kaluanda returned. "You can come." Melissa read neither anger nor forgiveness in her face. And she took a sharp breath as she saw Mrs. Niyangabo sitting with an amused look on the couch.

"How is your schooling?" Mrs. Niyangabo said, patting the cushion next to her. She was wearing a blue suit with shoulder pads, and chic stilettos. Her skin had grown darker from exposure to the sun, for she was nearly the same color as Madame Kaluanda.

"Very good."

"Tsk, tsk, tsk. A lie. I know you are failing your classes. I was afraid that might happen. School is very difficult here in France. Much more difficult than in Zimbabwe. It is the First World. You were not prepared for it."

Melissa put her hand in her backpack, gripping her fingers around the knife.

"So what will we do with you? Hm? Ah, but there is no choice. You must come stay with me."

At this, Madame Kaluanda interrupted. "Perhaps that is not necessary."

"Of course it is. She is stupid. She can't survive on her own. Her father didn't leave her any money."

Melissa tightened her grip around the knife, but held her tongue.

"I will look after her," Madame Kaluanda said. "Give her a second chance. That is, of course, if you feel you can part with her company. I will remain her guardienne as before and assume all the responsibilities."

Melissa didn't like the thought of Madame Kaluanda being her guardienne, but anything was better than life with Mrs. Niyangabo, even spending her father's money.

Mrs. Niyangabo seemed to be weighing the development in her head. She asked to use the telephone. Madame Kaluanda left the apartment, throwing Melissa a stern look. Melissa squeezed the hilt of the knife in her backpack as Mrs. Niyangabo went to the telephone and dialed a number on a calling card. She didn't bother to lower her voice.

"Yes, she's here… This is his last request… I will not give him another… It is too bad… The greedy bitch won't let her get away when there is money to be made… No, no, no… The last request, remember: I do not repeat myself…"

Thinking that no harm would come to her, Melissa slid the knife under the couch cushion. When Mrs. Niyangabo sat down again, she reached into her purse and pulled out what looked like a small silver case. But when she turned the case over Melissa realized it was a gun.

"Sit down!" Mrs. Niyangabo snapped.

Warily, she sat.

"Melissa, I know you have been to Paris snooping around. I am concerned, very concerned, that you might have false hope, and false hope for a young woman is a very dangerous affair. Don't think Madame Kaluanda can protect you! She could be killed in a moment." She was shaking the gun in her face now. "This is the last time I will warn you, for I do not like to repeat myself: stop looking for your father. We have been kind to you and you are abusing our hospitality. You, too, can disappear. You are nothing to us. Do you understand, young lady?"

Melissa nodded. She knew that Mrs. Niyangabo was using the gun to scare her, and it had worked. She stared down the silver barrel, afraid to move.

"Good," Mrs. Niyangabo said. "Fetch Madame Kaluanda."

When Madame Kaluanda returned, Mrs. Niyangabo said, "It is agreed. On the condition that I—or an acquaintance—may visit at any time."

Madame Kaluanda glanced at Melissa, who was shaking her head.

"Of course, Mrs. Niyangabo. I'll send you the papers."

Melissa returned to the bedroom and picked up the photo of her next to her father. She had expected Madame Kaluanda to take the money but she had been surprised by the viciousness with which Mrs. Niyangabo had threatened her. You are nothing to us, she had said. Who was she talking about? Who was she working with? And Melissa felt that she meant what she said, that she would really shoot her if she wanted to. The photo was the last evidence that she even had a father. She couldn't remember when he had snapped the photo, in front of a marketplace of some kind, and this troubled her, as if he might disappear forever. If she could remember the day the photo was taken, then maybe she could remember him again.

"Are you busy?" someone said.

"Oui, chuis bien occupée. Don't come in!" Melissa quickly put away the photograph. It was Béatrice again, the nosy girl who had asked whether Melissa had a period. Melissa eyed her warily.

"I am sorry about what happened to you," Béatrice said. She sat beside Melissa on her bed. "Madame Kaluanda told us that we aren't allowed to talk to you about it. You miss your family, isn't that it? You were taken from them?"

Melissa said nothing.

"Your family misses you too," the girl said.

"You don't know that."

"Mais si, I do know. I have seen Madame Kaluanda collect the mail. She always takes out your letters."

"Letters? What letters?"

"I don't know who sends them, just that she gives them to that horrible woman."

Melissa felt ecstatic to know that someone had written her. Only her father or Mr. Bello could possibly know where she lived. Maybe her father had found her! But she could never get the letters back from Mrs. Niyangabo, and would be killed for even trying.

"I received a letter too," Béatrice went on, "It had my name on it but I think it is for you."

She handed Melissa a small envelope. The seal had been broken.

"You read it?"

"Yes."

Inside she found a French passport with her own photo. She had used her Zimbabwean passport when she had arrived in customs. The agent had looked at her visa without question—student—and moved her through the line. This one was different. It had the same photo and in place of a single stamped visa, there were several stamps to various countries. Her age had been changed, too, so that she was listed as 19. Then there was a letter.

> Melissa,
>
> I have done everything in my power to reach you. You are my only child and my only love in this world.
>
> I have been betrayed. There is no escape from my punishment.
>
> I regret that you are on your own now. It is time for you to leave that home. The money and passport are for your medicine. You can receive treatment as a French citizen now, finish school, live a full life. Remember the people that you love and what I taught you.
>
> Love,
> M.T.

Melissa glanced up at Béatrice. Melissa read the letter again and again, trying to make sense of it. She felt herself shaking all over, but she was afraid to move, as if she would splinter into a million pieces. How could it be? How could he write to her so plainly? Would Daddy have really said goodbye to her, just like that?

"Please don't tell anyone. I'll pay you." She handed her a bundle of the money, but the girl waved it away.

"Non, it is for you." She lowered her voice to a whisper. "Melissa, I have lived here for several years. My own parents disappeared when I was young. For all I know, they may be alive. But it does me no good to grieve for them. It brings me closer to death."

"You're an orphan, then."

"Yes, and I'm not ashamed of it. You should be happy that you are loved. You should do as your father says. Leave this awful place. Go to the hospital, live for yourself."

But Melissa couldn't bear the thought. She couldn't just abandon her father, it was her fault that she had come to France and left him alone. It was her fault that her skin was so ugly. Before she had seen the letter, she might have managed to move on, studied French like the other girls, pretended that she had a new life. Not anymore. Not after what she'd read.

"I can never leave him," she said.

Béatrice gave Melissa a hug, the first that she had felt in months.

"Then I hope you find him."

Wale's Son

In the glare of the fluorescent Monday, Dayo Olufunmi received a text message from his father that was not going to make his sale easier. Police at home. He clapped his phone shut and decided to answer the shopkeep's question to move things along:

"America," he said.

But the shopkeep was a traveler, he'd been out and about before settling in Cape Town, he said, abseiling in Patagonia and running his hand along the cartilaginous breast of a whale shark off the coast of Perth. He'd hunted and been hunted, and he had been there, to America.

"Cleveland it was," he reminisced. "Had a rock band at the time. Mind you, I'm English and those were the Dark Days, as ye call 'em. Sou Thafrica was the bloody stool of the world, wouldn't have nuffin to do with it myself. We was called the Stoppards, not after the author. Two brothers, you see, Gavin and Theo Stoppard—"

"Sir," Dayo interrupted, "can I show you my lamp? It's my own design."

"—Theo was bass, as I recall. Gavin on the guitar. Or was it the reverse? Anyway, this bloke put us up in Cleveland. And I thought they was racist here but, man. That oke sees this black guy walking down the street—they was coloured people those days, not people of color—and he says 'if that nigger touches my lawn I'll blow his bloody leg off.' I was like, 'kn 'ell!"

Dayo set the package in his hand on the countertop. Behind him the aisles were filled with lightbulbs and brackets, and chandeliers hung from the ceiling like luminous cobwebs. The shopkeeper explained that he'd shared some whiskey with his host and left with a positive impression of Cleveland.

When the man paused to take a breath, Dayo held the little lamp in his palm. There were three main sections: a black plastic conical base with an inlaid full spectrum bulb and a magnet; a water-filled globe resting upon the base containing pure silicate sand and a figurine of a cat; and a tiny array of solar cells ringing the top of the globe. When the magnet rotated in the base, the cat spun on its axis, its tail functioning as a stirrer to spread around the sand. The bulb shot light into the globe, which refracted off the sand in the water.

Dayo launched into his sales pitch. "This is the moonlight lamp. It reproduces the same clean, unfiltered illumination you get from a full moon."

The shopkeep shook his head. "I'm not in the nightlight business. You can find children's accessories at Clicks."

"This isn't a nightlight, sir. You see, not all moonlight is the same. Some moonlight is more intense than others. The moon is at its brightest during a solar flare, and the surface of the moon isn't uniform, so moonlight is affected by its geology. And some of the moonlight that we see here on Earth isn't reflected directly, but is only radiated later. My lamp reproduces this as closely as possible, at an average of about zero point seven five lux. If you look at the top, you'll see that these are next generation solar cells above the globe, here and here. The silicate is as close to the regolith on the surface as the moon as can be found here on Earth. Just like the moon, the cells store up daylight that powers the lamp all night."

The shopkeep put on his glasses and bent over it. "I reckon solar's the future but the design leaves something to be desired. Stainless is what sells these days, clean lines. Not glass. That looks like a snowglobe to me."

"It's based on a toy I had as a kid. See the cat in the bottom of the globe? A magnet in the base makes it spin so that the silicate is dispersed uniformly."

"Well, c'mon, turn it on for me."

Dayo eagerly clicked it on, and the cat began to spin until it was blanketed in a cloud of silicate.

"Where's the light? I can't see a bloody thing."

"It's on."

The shopkeep ran his hand near the globe of water. After a moment, he reached over to a small rack on the corner and plucked off a keychain, pressing a button so that the keychain LED illuminated some sales receipts on the counter. "Look how bright these are. And they're only twenty bucks."

Dayo insisted that no lamp could come closer to real moonlight, repeating the word 'real' any number of times. But the shopkeep wasn't convinced, explaining that he only bought in bulk and the customers had needs and demands.

"—and the customer is always right, ain't he, my Yankee friend?"

Dayo frantically searched the aisles of the shop looking for a lampshade, found one, frilled like a scallop shell, but it was bolted to the wall. As he scanned for a different lampshade, his cell phone began vibrating in his pocket. Another text message from his father Wale, more predictable than the first: Don't go home. Don't talk to anyone. He returned to the counter, where the shopkeep was fingering his business card.

"What kind of name is Dayo? Not American?"

"My parents are Nigerian."

The shopkeep handed the card back. "I don't work with Nigerians anymore. I had one steal my entire inventory. Too risky. No offense, of course." He donned an old-fashioned green accounting visor, and began ticking off numbers on a calculator. "Try Eskom. Cheers."

Dayo was a powerful young man of twenty, but short, with muscles that bulged in his shirt even though he'd never done a push-up in his life. His brown skin had a healthy sheen and he shaved his head twice a week with a Bic. His wide nose swelled smoothly into deep chestnut eyes and he didn't have a single hair in his eyebrows, just the suggestion that they were there. His posture was so bad that it was easy to forget about the muscles and the pretty eyes and all the things that a woman might call handsome.

Outside the shop the summer wind was beginning to rage, blowing the haze from the City Bowl and replacing it with the sweet smell of seaweed clinging to the pylons at the foreshore. It was a Wednesday afternoon, but everyone in Cape Town seemed to be leaving for the day. The intersections on Buitengracht leading to the N2 highway were gridlocked with cars and orange-pinnied newspaper sellers. Dayo had been rejected from twenty-eight lighting stores in the two years since he'd developed the moonlight lamp in a fit of inspiration. He'd visited every shop from Parow to Roeland Street without success. He'd already tried Eskom, the national power supplier, where a glum manager advised him the company only accepted inventions from its research and development wing for legal reasons.

Don't go home. Don't talk to anyone.

Dayo hopped in a minibus taxi and headed home. He was not afraid of the police, but of what the text messages on his phone might mean about his father. He stared out the window of the taxi along Main Road, where the antiques shops had covered the sidewalks with their burled furniture, guessing that his father had stopped taking his medicine. At Salt River, next to the fish and chip shops and herbalist stands, black pedestrians gesticulated and chatted over foreign newspapers. Security guards were returning home from work or heading out for the night shift. In Woodstock some coloured teens were skateboarding along a concrete escarpment by a cash machine. Finally he made it home, to the suburb called Observatory.

To his surprise, his Angolan neighbors told him that two policemen had actually been there, and for a moment panic bubbled in his chest. Had his Dad actually been right? Then the Angolan added: "They're looking for someone staying at Okeke Chikwendu's."

Dayo sighed, and took a deep breath, but he still felt a need to tell Okeke, who owned a red claptrap house down the street that he was slowly restoring. Dayo walked over and pounded on the door. "Okeke, it's Dayo."

After a few minutes, Okeke poked his head out wearing a pair of safety goggles with a paint roller in his hand. Yellow paint had splattered his denim shirt. A little man, Okeke was his father's drinking buddy and an attorney from Ibadan who had moved his family to Cape Town mistakenly thinking the Cape Bar would admit him. Now he was in real estate. "What is it, Dayo?"

"Police are looking for one of your tenants."

Okeke glanced under Dayo's arm to the street. "Thanks. It must be the coloured guy. I should have given the place to one of our own, but he paid up front." He handed Dayo some keys. "Do you think you could be bothered to—"

"You want me to take a look around, right?"

"Good man. Tell your dad I'll be at Jack's later. There's a friendly against Ghana and Taiwo's back on the wing."

The next step was to find his father. Dayo made his way past the cheery little pastel homes of Obz, with its Victorian and Edwardian homes in states of disrepair and refurbishment, its narrow left-wing streets redolent with Nag Champa incense. He joined the domestics and peddlers walking to the train station, passed over the bridge, crossed the Liesbeeck River, and padded up the grounds of the Royal Observatory. As much as he disliked confronting his father, the manicured lawns and gentle slope of the hill with its squat Cape Chestnut trees made him relax. Anyway it had to be done. At the top of the hill he couldn't hear the hoots of the minibuses zipping down the Liesbeeck Parkway. The lighting stores and their attendant failures felt far away.

The research lab consisted of three computers and a couple of analog microscopes. There was a dedicated file server that let the scientists working remotely at the Sutherland array in the Karoo transmit their data for later study. The room had two large windows facing the rear of the Observatory with sunlight that gave it a pleasant, disinfected feel. But Dayo's father had drawn the shades.

"Close the door!" Wale shouted. "Or you'll contaminate the sample."

Dayo let the door shut of its own weight. He saw that there was a can of Guinness on the table, with another in the waste bin. His father

Wale Olufunmni was an oak-skinned, skinny man who was shorter than Dayo but stood straighter so their heads were nearly the same height. Wale still had stout legs that he strengthened by playing basketball twice a week in the local community gym. His hair had begun to gray, confusing his opponents into thinking he was too slow to drive the lane.

"Dad, it's three-thirty," Dayo said, eyeing the Guinness.

His father put his hand on the can without removing his eyes from the microscope. "It's four-thirty in Istanbul. That's considered happy hour in Turkey. For those who drink."

Dayo sat down in one of the squeaking office chairs of the lab. As a volunteer at the Observatory his father enjoyed access to the research facilities. Dayo asked him to grant him access to the computer server so he could check his email. The South African patent office had written saying that Dayo had improperly filled out the forms for his application for 'Moonlight Lamp', and advised him to download Form 1216E from their website at no charge.

"The police are looking for one of Okeke's tenants," Dayo said.

Wale took his first look at son, found nothing of interest, and put his eye back on the microscope. "What for?"

"Okeke's Nigerian. That's usually enough."

"Okeke's no drug dealer," Wale declared. He scribbled some information onto a notebook beside the microscope. He beckoned for Dayo to look at the sample, and as Dayo grew closer he could smell the fumes on his father's breath. Strong, probably several more cans had been thrown out already. One of his father's skills was destroying the evidence. Through the lens of the microscope, the minerals of the lunar rock were stacked on top of each other in stratified colors of magenta, tangerine, turquoise, and alabaster. "See this spall zone?" Wale said. "The glass around it came from the impact. But the radial fractures are fairly shallow. The rest of it's untouched, so untouched that it could be from the mantle. If only I had a SET, then I could verify it. It would be a real find for this country. You're sure they were looking around at Okeke's?"

"That's what the neighbors said."

"Was there a man called Bello with them?"

"Where did you get the sample?" Dayo asked, changing the subject.

Scratching away at the meteorite, Wale complained that he had requested it from the planetarium, which had allowed kids to get their grubby hands all over it. He popped another can of Guinness. It made a sizzling sound as the widget spat nitrogen into the beer. "No sale today?"

"No." Dayo didn't want to get into that conversation, the one that began with advice and ended with his being labeled a failure. "Dad, Doctor Moodley said that drinking on your medicine will ruin your liver."

"He who is working hard, the proverb goes, should continue to do so, though he won't necessarily succeed. But if you're lucky in life you won't easily fail. I think you may be out of luck, Dayo. How many stores has it been? Twenty? Thirty? Why don't you join my bamboo business? You can try again when your luck returns."

"Are you taking your medicine? If you are then you shouldn't be drinking."

"Maybe it's your sales delivery. I sell my bamboo mash blankets by showing it to them. It's easy. I rub the blanket against their arms—the women, that is. Then I sell them. Easy. Pass me the ruler there."

Dayo passed the ruler. "You should take your medicine. There's no need to hide. Bello wasn't there. The police aren't after you. They're after Okeke."

"Sometimes a story helps," Wale said, now shining a penlight on the meteorite. "That's how I sold twenty chairs last week, and six blankets. What story do you tell them about the lamp?"

Dayo went through his routine, trying to emphasize the technical parts. He used the words 'luminosity' and 'umbra' and 'aqueous medium' with what he hoped was familiarity.

His father was shaking his head. "That's the problem, Dayo. No one cares about technicalities. They don't want to know how it works, they want to know why they should buy it. Tell them, then show them. I learned that firsthand with my full moon tours."

Even when his father was on the defensive, he managed to turn things into a lecture. And Dayo was supposed to, according to Yoruba tradition, sit there and take it. But he had been born in America and raised in South Africa. "Are you taking your medicine or not?"

"Just because I'm paranoid, it doesn't mean people aren't following me," his father intoned, taking a gulp from his Guinness. "I can't remember who said that. Okeke knows. I got it from him." He placed the meteorite back in a glass case, and, teetering through a door, shut the rock sample away in a locker in the hallway. "Come with me, Dayo. Let's go for a walk."

Wale squinted as if it was midday outside, when the sun was low in the sky, already dipping beneath the churning clouds above Table Mountain. There was a falcon circling overhead looking to dive on prey in the grass. Father and son walked along the grass until they reached an enormous manhole cover in the middle of a field. Wale squatted down and tried to lift it off, gritting his teeth. "Come, Dayo, give me a hand." Together they dragged the lid off with a hollow scraping sound, and the scent of old moss drifted from the hole. "This is where they kept the mercury. There were huge pools of it. The idea was to use the mercury as a giant focal lens to observe the stars, since science hadn't discovered how to manufacture a lens of that size. Mercury reflects like a mirror when it's still, and there were few vibrations because the scientists buried it underground. At the time it was a significant advance for the Observatory. But when they built the Liesbeeck Parkway and the N2, the vibrations from the traffic made the mirrors unworkable. Can you imagine looking into a pool of mercury? Gauging the stars in a pool of quicksilver like an alchemist? It would be like floating in space."

Dayo glanced down into the hole and all he could think about was falling into it and having his father close the lid on top of him.

"This is a popular part of my full-moon tour. It has nothing to do with selenometry anymore. No practical value. But this is where I get my repeat customers. From the story. And I let the children come up with their own reasons. You've got to come up with a story. Put some tension in it."

"I based the lamp on the snowglobe you gave me," Dayo said.

"Yeah, but what does that snowglobe mean?"

"You gave it to me when I was a child. There's nothing special about it."

His father burped and waved a finger in the air. "There is something very special about it."

Once a finger waved in the air, Dayo was certain that his father was drunk. He thought about how to get him home before he began cowering behind every bush in fear of the people he imagined to be following him.

"It's about time you knew, Dayo." He lowered his voice. "That snowglobe came from the moon."

"I'm not listening to this," Dayo said.

"Once you sell a lamp, you can stop listening. That snowglobe came from Eleven."

"Eleven what?"

"Apollo Eleven."

"It's time to go home."

"No, listen!" His father began making big gestures, pointing at the sky that was deepening into violet, and moving into black. There were a few bright stars out already that Dayo strived to name. Wale then told a rambling story about Neil Armstrong and NASA, as if he was intimate with all of them. "That's what's inside your snowglobe," he concluded. "Tell that story to your lamp shops."

"You want me to believe that the snowglobe you gave me has dust from the moon inside it."

"Yes."

"From man's first trip to the moon."

Dayo shook his head. Bello was enough. This, this would call for a whole new level of dosage. Maybe a new prescription, too.

"I don't want to hear any more. And what if someone asks me how I got the dust from Apollo Eleven?"

Wale grew quiet. He bent down and tried to drag the manhole cover back over the old pool of mercury, but careened head-over-heels into the grass. He lay on his back for a few moments, staring at the rugby ball of a gibbous moon emerging above an oak tree.

"You tell them your father gave it to you."

Seeing his father lying down like that, his hair as faintly silver as the moon, and the breath of the alcohol mixing with the moss of the manhole and the fact that Wale was both insane and correct, that Dayo hadn't made a sale and probably wouldn't anytime soon, made Dayo suddenly very angry. "You're a bamboo salesman! Why can't you just admit it? This place is bad for you. Give it up and take your medicine."

"Don't talk to me that way! I'm your father. Yoruba don't believe in medicating our problems. We deal with them. That's where your mother went wrong."

"I'm going home."

Dayo walked past two drunk bergies splayed out in front of the Yellow Rose, and some dreary men smoking a spliff right out on Lower Main Road. Inside he could see quarts of beer in plastic ice buckets and the sneer of a cricket umpire on the television. He wasn't thinking about his father's fantasies now but about his mother.

Wale refused to talk about her other than to call her names. His entire life, Dayo had heard how she had prostituted herself with strangers and become addicted to drugs in Houston. She was so desperate for drugs that she had embroiled the family in a financial scam that had been caught by the FBI. Instead of going to jail and abandoning his son to an orphanage, Wale had fled to South Africa. There, he'd started afresh by securing them refugee permits—fudging the truth a little for the papers—to allow them to remain in the country for good. Wale learned how to make bamboo furniture to pay for their home in Observatory. Everything he did in his life, Wale said, he did for the family.

Sometimes Dayo wished he had been put in an orphanage. He couldn't stand to be around his father anymore, having watched him over the years decline into this sorry state. And it was all fueled by his geology hobby; the more time he spent out at the Royal Observatory, the more unmanageable he became. For the briefest of moments Dayo would see genius, or less even—coherence—in his father's amateurish ramblings, then Wale would get drunk and launch into an incredible story like the one about Apollo Eleven, or work himself into a state with tales about the great savior Bello. His dad believed that Bello was the one person who could clear their name in America. He was a diplomat, visionary, and expediter all rolled up into one person, whose magic touch would grace his father's life with redemption. And money.

It felt like Wale's mind was on the moon, and he was beaming back signals with a three-second delay, crossing the distance through splattered debris and nonsense. The fact was that Wale sold bamboo furnishings for a living in a suburb of Cape Town that no one besides Capetonians would have missed if it disappeared. And, although Dayo didn't like it, he knew his father was right that the lamp hadn't worked. It was time for him to get a job.

The two of them lived in a comfortable home, with two bedrooms, a living room with an attached kitchen, and a carport that Wale had converted into his bamboo workshop. The workshop contained lathes, bandsaws, jointers, and cutting machines, and part of the space was reserved to experiment with new cultivars of bamboo. His father also kept a large terrarium lit by hydroponic lamps for seedlings. The latest variety, imported from Gabon, doubled in size every week but lacked the tensile strength of other varieties so Wale was trying to cross-breed them with stronger lines. The small backyard was about twenty paces across and had a garden with fastidiously weeded clusters of bamboo.

By agreement, Dayo and his father stayed out of each other's bedrooms, but after seeing Wale tonight, Dayo felt obligated to look inside to know how bad his sickness had become. He opened the door and turned on the light. The corkboard was still there. On the board, faded tea-colored newspaper clippings were connected with bright green strings. Most of the clippings were from the 1990s and from Nigeria or contained information about Nigeria. The first, way at the left of the board, bore the headline "Elections Held as Nigeria begins transition to Civilian Rule". The next read: "General Abboud Cancels Elections". And shortly to the right, another piece detailed the arrival of President Rawlson Bimini, who seized power from Abboud shortly afterwards.

Then there were several articles about a violent crackdown upon musicians and other politicians, and articles about oil in the Delta region. These Dayo had seen before.

What frightened him were the fresh new clippings about violent terrorism and interreligious strife. In the middle of these new clippings, perched in the center of the web of strings, lay a question in clipped-out capital letters, as eerie and manic as a ransom note: WHAT IS IBEJI?

Dayo had once searched for the term Ibeji online and been directed to websites of museums containing African art. They were curious little Yoruba dolls that held some importance as collectibles. The pieces were readily available on online auction sites, going for a few hundred to a few thousand dollars each, with dubious provenance, as the Western owners bent over backwards to explain how these dolls, which were supposedly so spiritually significant, had graced display cabinets in Indianapolis and Oswego and Derbyshire for decades. But that was hardly unusual for African art, and the collectors were certainly not sinister enough to conspire to ruin his father's life. The dolls meant something to the immediate family that carved them, if you believed in their spiritual power, but were otherwise harmless. And yet his father seemed to think they represented something much larger than collectible folk art, and, like Bello, were both the source of and solution to all his problems.

The clippings on the wall were a map of his father's madness that was becoming increasingly plain for the world to see. Now his father was telling him about the moon as if he'd been there and walked on it. Dayo would have to call the doctor himself, have him wire in a refill.

He shut the door quickly and retired to his room. His bedside lamp was a crude thing compared to the manufactured lamps he was selling now, the original snowglobe with his father's so-called moondust inside: basically a conventional incandescent bulb shined up into the globe, which you had to shake to get the light to refract properly, and there was a lampshade wrapped in foil that scattered the light. It had been, to his father's dismay, his Class 12 project at the Steiner Academy. The other kids had built biodiesel engines and hanging scrolls from rice paper and welded sculptures. He'd made the lamp. For his efforts he'd received a passing mark and an encouraging note from his teacher.

The snowglobe had been with him for as long as he could remember. It had a pinewood base and there was a small black housecat in the middle of the fine white flecks. And since he and Wale had moved homes all the time, the only steady pet Dayo'd had was inside the water-filled globe. He'd hold it up to a lightbulb and watch the flecks flurry inside. He imagined it shivering. So desolate was his pet in the globe, in the deserted winds.

"If one's private room gives no pleasure," his father liked to say while pinning strings to his cork board, "the town seems like a wilderness."

Dayo's room began to suffocate him so he went for a stroll, seeking the wild. His father would probably be drinking with Okeke by now and watching a soccer match, but Dayo had no money to spend. A stroll was free, and in Obz at night it could be adventurous. There was tension in the burglar bars that belied the stillness, as if the entire neighborhood thought it would be rampaged by hordes of thieves and Tsotsis at any moment, and the slinking cats on the parapets would do nothing but bear witness.

The wild soon came. Heeling past the strident top-40 music of the Stones bar, he felt someone watching him. When he looked across the street, though, the only person there was Bernard, the Congolese bouncer at Runnings, who waved and smiled beneath his puffy afro. He decided to stop into the Armchair Theatre, a live music club with torn leather furniture and candle-topped bottles, and ordered a beer from the bar, putting the drink on a tab that he declined to look at. Kesivan Naidoo was on drums with his quartet, Lee Thompson on cornet.

Dayo realized his mistake as soon as he sat down at the bar, for a guy at the end of the room, a black man with a lazy eye, got up immediately and sat next to him. When he turned around, a coloured guy had slid into the stool on the other side.

"You Dayo?" the coloured guy asked.

Dayo sized him up. A heavy man with a big chest, a man not to talk back to. He stuck out his brandy gut as if it was a source of pride. On the drums, Naidoo was swishing slowly as the quartet searched for a groove. The bassist plucked out a trim line for the others to follow.

"Yeah, I'm Dayo."

"We saw you stop into Okeke Chikeendo's earlier."

"Chikwendu."

"I'm no Nigerian. Neither is Mush, here." The guy meant his reticent partner on the other side. He flashed a badge, but closed it too quickly for Dayo to make any sense of it. He thought he saw the word 'Environmental'. "We'd like to have a word with Okeke. He seems to disappear every time we stop by."

On stage, Thompson plugged a mute in the cornet and began sending out triplets in the highest register. The notes had a strident feel, as if he was reliving an argument with a girlfriend.

"I can't help you," Dayo said.

"But you know him."

Dayo sipped his beer. "Yeah, I know him. Save yourself some trouble. We don't all sell drugs. Okeke's a family man."

Thompson had lowered his cornet and let the bearded Naidoo lean into the drums. The solo began slowly, incorporating all the contemplations that had come before on his snare and high-hats.

"We want to ask him some questions," the coloured guy went on. He proffered a business card, but there wasn't a name on it. Just a number. "Tell him to call me."

Dayo fingered the card. "He doesn't have much cell phone credit."

"He doesn't have to leave a message if he doesn't want to. Tell him to ask for Mush. We'll call him back."

"Who are you looking for, then?"

"It's none of your business, kid."

Naidoo was taking over now on the drums. His hand flicked the sticks over his kit as if he was harnessing a spreading fire, his whole body vibrating and his eyes wide. It was said that rhythm begins with the heartbeat but with Naidoo it was somewhere more fundamental. The light perhaps, the pulse of the photons shining in from the moon.

If the moon was anywhere, Dayo thought, it wasn't in the snowglobe but coursing through Naidoo's veins.

"All the tenants in Okeke's are clean," Dayo said, swallowing some beer. "If you want to arrest someone, check the hostels. The backpackers all smoke dagga."

Before he could leave, the black guy seized his arm on a pressure point. It felt like his elbow would pop out.

"You'd better tell him, Dayo," the coloured guy said. "Or we might have to swing by, what is it, Mush?"

"Wale's Bamboo Hut," the black man said. "Twenty-two Irwell."

"Wale's Bamboo Hut to find him. It'll be with a warrant, a very thorough search. Best he contacts us first."

The man let go of Dayo's arm and the blood rushed in painfully.

Fuck you, he thought, walking out. And your spineless echo of a partner.

People were clapping for the jazz quartet as Dayo stepped onto the street. He had an intense desire to convert to some far-flung religion and give up any tie to his family. His roots had given him nothing but trouble today. But at the same time, he wasn't going to turn Okeke over to a lazy cop that was strong-arming his countrymen to make a bust. If I had my lamp, he thought, this wouldn't happen. In moonlight there's no color. That bastard would actually have to protect and serve and not harass my people and our skin.

On the walk home he lingered at a patch of agapanthae blossoms spread open, and the gibbous moon was bright against the fabric of stars. A moth was tickling at the stamens of the agapanthae as they yearned for the light. In the breezy flutter of the flowers he thought he could discern the rhythms of Naidoo's drums in the jazz quartet.

As the drumbeats faded into stillness he began to feel nothing for the moon. There was no love there, just cold empty space. He unlocked the gate at his house, passed through the living room, not bothering to turn on the light, and found his bedroom in the black. Lying on his bed, he reached for his lamp and turned it on. Tomorrow his father would take his medicine. Tomorrow there would be a job.

Adrian

Present Day
South Africa

For fifteen hundred rand Thursday Malaysius got his own apartment with a separate bedroom, a closed-in balcony, a Jacuzzi bathtub, and two showers. The black owner, whose name was Okeke, mentioned casually that he was a foreigner, and when Thursday didn't react to this fact, shook his hand and agreed to the deal. The kitchen was tiny, but he wasn't there to cook. It was perfect for the abalone. With the month's deposit, a head flashlight for the blackouts, candles, food, and some extra clothes for the week, he was left with six thousand rand. He started to feel guilty and found the number for Pollsmoor prison and dialed it from a payphone. The operator transferred him from A Block to B Block to C Block until a voice said "Themba, you seen Lebo?" and the line went dead. Then he called Leon's family in Hermanus. Leon's mother was upset, but calmed down after Thursday said that he was in town trying to get Leon free.

Ip didn't trust Thursday to do anything on his own, so he ordered Chung to drive him around town to get what he needed. He picked up a basic oxygenating pump from a pet store and some PVC tubing to create a siphoning system to circulate the water during the power outages. Chung didn't talk much owing to his language problems, and he never said a word while he was eating. Over the week, though, Thursday managed to glean a lot from him.

One day they drove out to Atlantis to scrape fresh kelp from the rocks. Atlantis was a coloured community outside Cape Town that was established during apartheid to provide cheap labor to manufacturing concerns. There weren't many hills, and rows of eucalyptus trees lined the byways and sometimes there was the squawk of Cape gulls as they drifted in the chill sea wind. Atlantis was not a fishing community like Hermanus. It was a lost community. Gates were falling off hinges, creepers fissuring through paint. The only signs of renewal were televisions and automobiles and mothers pushing baby carriages. The community was lost because the industries that built the town had left it with apartheid.

The horizon was more still than Hermanus at that time of the year, too. In Hermanus the whales would be breaching and spyhopping, or slapping their fins on the water. Hermanus Bay gave you the feeling that there were larger things out there. Atlantis, on the other hand, made Thursday depressed.

"How long you been a smuggler, Chung?"

"Shut up."

Chung didn't like to get wet and cursed when his foot plunged into a tide pool.

"I've been a smuggler for two weeks. It's hard work, man. And dangerous. I've been shot at three times."

"I kill you next week."

Thursday shooed away some gulls from the protuberant rocks. "Why would you do that?"

"Ip."

"Ip said you had to do it? Well, why do you have to listen to him? Why do you have to kill me? All I want to do is help my friend. Just 'cause you're a smuggler? Is that why? That's not cricket."

"Not a smuggler. Import-export."

"Everyone knows that perlemoen is illegal. Read the papers. Operation Trident and all that." He tapped his temple. "You've got to educate your mind, my broer. I read the paper every morning now."

Chung straddled two rocks and put a kelp strand into the bucket. "Legal yesterday. Illegal today."

"That's called knowledge. It's illegal because there aren't enough to go around."

"South Africa, forty million people."

"So what?"

"China, one and a half billion people. In China it is legal. So, legal."

Thursday wasn't sure how to respond to that. One and a half billion people would kick the ass of forty million people in any fight, and there wasn't a thing you could do about it. It would be nothing like the battle between clams and abalone he used to make up in his mind, where each side had a chance.

He made his way back to the van, but Chung told him to sit down and pulled out a joint. Thursday cupped his hand against the sea breeze to get the flame going, and the dank smoke touched his nostrils. He took a few puffs and suddenly became aware of the sound of the waves and stared at the foam as the tips curled over. He had a quick flash of Leon getting arrested in the darkness and he felt sick. When he looked back, Chung had nodded off.

The first thing he noticed was that there was a big rock within reach. Without changing his position, he slowly pulled the rock towards him with his free hand. It was a gift. With it, he could knock out Chung and take the car and get away. And with the dagga in his veins this seemed a real and desirable possibility. Chung had just told him that he was going to kill him, after all.

Then he saw a shuffle in the sand before him, and a little white crab shimmied out. One claw was much larger than the other, and it rubbed the smaller claw back over its eye just like the one he'd remembered when Ip had leveled the gun at him. The wind picked up and began to cut at his bare feet. Thursday didn't know what it meant to see the same image twice. He wasn't sure if he was seeing the crab again or if he had never seen before it in the restaurant, and now his mind had projected the crab back there. Either way he let go of the rock.

When a fly tickled Chung's nose, he awoke to find the rock next to Thursday. Smiling, he threw the rock into the water and said, plain as day: "You no gangster. Let's go."

Thursday hated driving around in total silence, so he kept on asking questions as they did their tasks. He found out that Ip didn't own that Chinese restaurant. An Indian guy called Rodney owned it and Ip rented out the room when he had business. In reality, Ip owned the sushi restaurant down the street, which was flooded with Japanese tourists once a day on their way back from the tour to the Cape Point who would pay six thousand rand each for his abalone awabi sushi. He had another front, too, a scooter shop specializing in Chinese Vespa clones. His sixteen-year-old daughter ran it under her own name, and she'd made enough money to open another one. Thursday got the impression that Chung was in love with her. When Chung talked about the girl, it was possible to imagine the goon wasn't going to kill him, but if Thursday asked too many questions about her Chung would get jealous and scowl.

Once they'd collected everything he had plenty of time to himself. The siphoning system for the large bathtub kept air flowing in, and he didn't have to feed the abalone as often once they settled down. He'd read comic books and The Voice tabloid while spooning beans out of a can. His neighbors gave him privacy, and one of the wives, a petite, round-faced woman, would knock on his door and offer him a plate heaped with oily, flavorful dishes like he'd never had before. Sometimes he'd go out walking and he had a feeling that Chung was watching him, but he didn't care. He liked looking at the people pulling their dogs along the narrow streets, with their excessive apologies if the dogs stretched at the leash and yipped at him. After a while he realized that other than people with dogs and the backpackers, no white person ever walked on the same side of the street as him, and he figured out that they were crossing it so far in front of him that he wasn't aware of the change-over. It made the streets feel perpetually empty. He told himself that the last thing he needed was to be recognized. But he didn't want to be ignored, either.

Six thousand rand was more than enough money to get to Joburg or far enough away that Ip wouldn't find him, but he didn't seriously consider it, not when Leon and the abalone were dependent on him. So when Ip called him in to Rodney's after a week, he wasn't too worried. He calmly opened the cooler and showed the healthy perlemoen nibbling on the kelp.

"What are those blimey little discs?" Ip asked.

"Babies."

"What do you mean, babies? Are they sick?"

"No, they're healthy and they made some kiddies, my broer. About a thousand of them."

Ip couldn't hide his excitement. "A thousand! How long?"

"Three years before they've got good flavor. I could probably get that down to two with the right diet."

"You made good on your word, Hampton. We've got two more shipments coming in from Bettys Bay tomorrow. Look after them for me."

"Pay me first."

That was the day that Thursday began to believe in a higher power. Five hours later he had fifty thousand rand in the bank, six shooters of tequila in his stomach, and he'd won four games of foosball and two of pool. He had his own apartment and Leon was going to be freed. You could buy a car with fifty thousand rand. You could fly to Joburg fifty times. There was a job for him if he wanted it and for the first time in his life he felt he had a skill that no one else had. He was gifted with abalone.

His beatific, half-toothed smile won him a lover that evening, a cute girl named Helen with dyed black corn rows and sunburn. She peeled herself off from a group of foreigners and looked at him across from the bar. He decided to use a move that Leon had taught him.

"No woman, no cry!" he half-sang as he approached her.

"I'm sorry?" the girl said.

"No woman, no cry!"

"You mean, Bob Marley?"

"That's right!" He called the bartender over. "Two Bob Marleys!"

The bartender poured out two shots of amarula, cinnamon liqueur, and peppermint schnapps the color of a Rastafarian flag.

As he'd expected, she liked it, and he ordered two more.

"This woman won't cry," she agreed.

"What's your name, sweetie?"

"Helen."

"Where are you from?"

"Oslo."

"What part of Cape Town is that?"

"It's in Norway. Oslo is the capital."

Thursday recovered himself. "You're traveling through then, back-packing."

"No, I work at a nonprofit in Woodstock. I teach art to prisoners."

"You traveled all the way to South Africa to teach art to prisoners?"

"Yes."

"Don't you have prisoners in Norway?"

"Not like here."

"But why would you want to spend time with prisoners? We've got beaches, mountains, the karoo. You should see Hermanus. It's a lekker spot for whale watching."

Helen smiled: "I like naughty boys."

Thursday laughed with her and ordered another round of Bob Marleys. When he turned his head back to look at her, she grabbed him and pushed her tongue into his mouth. He took her back to his apartment and she took off her clothes before she left the bathroom. Whenever he was about to have sex, Thursday would remember that Leon had once told him that a real man stays in control until the moment of orgasm, and that's the only time when you can do whatever you want, but if you lose control too early and thrash around like an eel, then the girl will stop respecting you because she'll know she's got power over you. Helen didn't ask him to use a condom and he didn't have one anyway, and she guided him into her as soon as they lay down. "Oooh, yes, Hampton, do it!" She thrust her hips, bringing her face up for a kiss, and came quickly. Thursday kept Leon's advice in mind as he went on for another few minutes until they fell down together.

"You never told me, Hampton."

"What's that?"

"Why are you here in Obz? I go to Stones all the time and this is the first time I've seen you. You don't have any furniture in this apartment. You don't have any suitcases. Why are you here?"

Thursday thought about telling her everything, even his real name, but he'd be gone in a few days. He would have saved up enough money to free Leon and he'd leave as soon as he could. There was no point in getting mixed up with her when he'd only wanted to have some fun.

"I'm on vacation," he said.

When he woke she was gone. No note, just a half-empty beer bottle with an imprint of her lipstick.

Chung picked him up the next day and laughed. "You got a girl!"

"No," Thursday lied. "We just went out to weeties. All we did was talk."

"I know. You can't hide."

He was feeling guilty about it, for he realized he'd spent two hundred rand the night before that could have gone towards Leon's bail. "I didn't think living here would be so expensive."

They stopped by Ip's, or Rodney's Chinese Restaurant, on the way to another job. He walked with Chung through the dining room feeling like he was a regular at the place. The thug stopped him from going in to the back room and knocked on the door. Ip unlocked it.

There was a coloured man sitting in the chair across the table. He was plump, with a paunch and an aquamarine tee-shirt on. Thursday didn't recognize him and took up a place next to Chung. On the wall, where the Jet Li movie poster used to be, there was a double-handled broad sword with intricate filigrees on the blade. A cooler sat on the desk. The coloured man was smoking a cigarette and throwing sidelong glances at the sword.

"Hampton, this is Adrian."

"Pleased to make your acquaintance," the man said, formally. "I've heard a lot about you." Thursday went to shake the man's hand, but Chung held him back.

"Check it out, Hampton," Ip said.

Thursday opened the cooler box and saw some sickly looking abalone covered with ice. They were a good size, not as large as those he had brought from Hermanus, but respectable. "Half of them are dead,"

177

he said. "The other quarter will die no matter what. But I can save these ten here."

"You heard the man," Ip said. "Those go to the dryer. We'll weigh them when they come out. Two thousand a kilo. I'll pay you three hundred each for the live ones."

Adrian agreed. "That's good perlemoen. I know it's worth more than that but I need the money."

"Next time, keep them alive." Ip began counting out hundred rand notes.

But Thursday had noticed something else in the cooler. He whispered it into Ip's ear and Ip stopped counting. He put the cash back into his pocket.

"What?" Adrian asked, trying to act casual.

"I'm going to write you a check instead."

"Why?"

"Because these were farmed."

"I don't give a shit if they're farmed. They taste the same."

"It matters," Ip said.

"It does?" Thursday asked.

"Shut up."

"So, are you going to pay me?"

"Sure. But not in cash." Ip pulled out his checkbook. "The money will be good when they clear customs. That's about two weeks. Don't cash it until then."

Thursday swallowed. The last time Ip had offered him a check Chung had put a gun in his face. But this time what happened was even faster. As Ip handed Adrian the checkbook, Chung snatched the sword from the wall and spun around the desk. Adrian lifted up his arms to protect his head, and Chung slashed his stomach in a quick, measured movement. His intestines spilled into his lap like a bowl of egg noodles. Adrian's face recoiled in horror. He breathed in and out like he was in labour. Reaching down, he began stuffing his insides back in as a low whimper grew and grew until it became a piercing wail.

Then Ip nodded and Chung jammed the sword in the smuggler's windpipe. Adrian fell over onto the floor, his whole body spasming, until he was face down in his own mire.

Thursday hadn't moved the entire time. Ip began flicking his finger at a spot of blood that had gotten onto his shirtsleeve.

"Why the fuck did you do that, Chung!" Thursday shouted.

"Shut up."

"No," Ip said calmly. "Hampton deserves an answer to that question, Chung. The government has declared war on abalone and developed an enzyme that the farmers can insert into their tanks. When someone puts in a few drops of indicator solution, the abalone change color and the enzyme ruins the flavor. That's the danger with farmed abalone, Hampton. It can be traced. I've got a graduate student who is researching the formula of the solution, but she's not ready yet for an antidote, if you will. If we don't keep an eye out we'll end up in prison for fenced abalone. And we don't want that, do we, Hampton?"

Ip spoke as if there wasn't a gutted man bleeding on the floor.

Thursday remained furious at Chung—what would stop him from doing the same to him? And why so brutal? What good did it do anyone to kill someone like that? He could have just shot him.

Silently Thursday busied himself with sorting the live abalone from the dead ones in the ice. A few could be saved, some dignity restored. The smuggler's body jiggled madly for a moment and then stopped.

"Don't start getting judgmental, Hampton," Ip insisted. "There's no time for fools in our operation. It's business. Now if you'll please excuse us."

"We need to get these some water from the Atlantic."

"Chung will be right there. Have a seat in the restaurant and order yourself something on me."

Leaving the cooler behind, Thursday ordered a Coke from Rodney's wife and opened a fortune cookie. People are attracted to your quality leadership. He nibbled at it and the tiny piece swirled in his stomach, creating a torrent, and he ran to the bathroom to vomit. After thirty minutes of nursing the Coke, he went back and knocked on the door.

Chung opened it. The body and the blood and the grime were nowhere to be found. It was a regular dining room at a Chinese restaurant.

When they stepped out onto the sidewalk, the sun was brighter than it ought to have been. Thursday expected it to be a gray day, with rain and dogshit on the sidewalks, but the sun was there, shining onto the white plates of the people taking their breakfasts at Mimi's. Across the street an old man was leafing through a recipe book in the used bookshop. Somewhere kids were kicking a soccer ball. Maybe a girl was sunbathing. And soon a customer would be eating a bowl of prawn lo mein a room away from where a guy's neck had been skewered by a sword.

Chung was in good spirits, though, and put on some black wraparound sunglasses and said they were going for a drive. They took the N7 to Saldanha Bay, where the ericae were blooming in their showers of microcosmic colors, with blossoms so small they looked like speckles amongst the cows and the sheep going to their salt blocks in the hot sun.

"I hope Ip gets Leon out soon," Thursday said before he could help himself. He needed Leon to put those intestines in perspective.

"Forget Leon. You're Hampton. You be Hampton."

"Leon's my mate," Thursday sulked.

"Leon not your mate. Leon a fool."

"You don't know him."

"He said he turn you in. He shot dog. Stupid."

Thursday bolted up straight. He remembered that dog he'd read about in the newspaper back in Hermanus, Snoopy, the Border collie that the police had used to sniff out illegal abalone. He'd even been grateful that the dog had been shot, because it had meant the dog wouldn't sniff the abalone in his bathtub.

"What do you mean he shot a dog? He didn't shoot a dog. That wasn't Leon."

"Knowledge. You said knowledge. I read the paper and he shot dog. That's knowledge."

"But Leon said he would turn me in."

"Did you shoot dog?"

"No."

As Thursday was denying it, he was remembering the sound of gun-shots above the sound of the waves in the surf on the beach that night. Someone had fired a gun. He'd assumed it was the police.

"Did they catch abalone that night?" Chung pressed on.

"No."

"Then how Leon turn you in?"

He could recall some muffled dog barks from that night, too. Why hadn't he made the connection before? Leon had shot the dog! He had shot Snoopy! Of course, that was what Fadanaz was going on about. That was why bail was so high! He had never in his wildest imagination considered that Leon had lied to him so deeply; he thought he had learned how to sort through his kak. The Mercedes, the job: he began to wonder if Leon had actually been sick that night at all when he'd dived in to get the perlemoen. Thursday cranked down the window and stuck his head out the window. The green hills rushing past him were undulating like a serpent.

"Pull over. I've got to mamok."

He stumbled out and vomited into the weeds.

Chung gave him a joint to smoke when they were back on the road. "Forget Leon. You're Hampton. You work for us."

The power was out in Obz when he returned, and the sunsetting rays clung to the ceiling before the apartment was pulled into darkness. Unlike power outages in Hermanus, when Thursday had rushed to the generator to restart the pumps at the abalone farm, in Obz it meant you stayed inside. Being coloured, he wasn't a target for muggers, but he also wasn't stupid and could hear the rough Afrikaans of the youth gangs from Woodstock when they would walk the sidestreets looking for excitement. If they were tikked up with amphetamines the color of his skin didn't matter, they'd take him on all the same. Leon had always gotten Thursday's back in Hermanus and kept the gangbangers off him, but those days, Chung had just informed him, were over.

He began siphoning the bathtub and lit a candle. Otherwise he spent the night alone. Helen sent him a text message asking if he wanted to meet for a game of pool. He thought she was his one tie to Leon, that she could help him find Leon with the art classes she taught, but he wasn't sure what he'd say to Leon, not after Leon had lied to him and treated him like a peon. He thought of Helen and Leon and the crab on the beach and none of it made any sense. So much of his life was run by Leon; Leon was his measure of the world; Leon sifted through it for him and showed him where to go, and where not to go. He was a bully, but that was a price Thursday had been willing to pay for culling sense from the chaos. But now Leon had crossed a line. In this lie there was no friendship. No guidance.

Thursday couldn't eat a bite at Rodney's Chinese Restaurant again knowing what went on in that back room. Another shipment came in, this time with a few dozen perlies from Geoffrey's Bay, and after he gave his approval, Ip paid the man in cash and the smuggler left happy. Ip tossed five hundred rand to Thursday as a bonus and Thursday promptly handed over fifty of it to Chung for a bag of dagga.

Like most addicts, Chung was happy to get others to indulge. "It's from Thailand. Primo." He kissed his lips together like an Italian.

Thursday preferred fresh Swazi in his youth but he didn't want to press his luck by asking around in Observatory, where the armed response had begun trailing him on their bicycles. He would take the guards on the most convoluted kajalangs and in this way came to know the neighborhood: where the euphorbiae were blossoming happy and violet, where the proteas had withered into saffron cones, where the trellises stunk of rotting grapes fallen from the vines. There was an orange tabby cat here and a Jack Russell terrier behind that gate, and so on. When the armed response left him he'd head straight home, check the abalone, and roll himself a joint.

He bought himself a television for his apartment and a lime-washed chest of drawers and subscribed to The Voice newspaper under the name Hampton. He moved his mattress out onto the enclosed balcony and slept watching the steam-fitting clouds on Devil's Peak.

He decided to call Helen and they arranged to meet at Stones.

"Can I get you a Bob Marley?" he said, tapping the bar.

"No, I don't like sweet drinks."

"You liked them before."

"No, Hampton. I liked you."

She ordered two brandies and they sat together at a booth that overlooked Lower Main Road, the main thoroughfare of Obz. The streets were still quiet. The armed response officers were prowling the sidewalks but the neighborhood wouldn't become lively for a few more hours, when the undergraduates descended from the mountain.

"I need to ask you a favor, Helen."

She raised her eyebrows, but didn't say anything.

"I have a friend in prison. I'd like to visit him to make sure he's alright. You teach art classes, né? Do you think you could help me reach him?"

Helen sipped on her brandy, watching him closely.

"What's his name?"

"Leon. Leon Vermeulen."

She shook her head. "I don't know him."

"People call him Brother Leon."

"He wasn't in any of my classes. When did he go inside?"

She said 'go inside' as if she had once been locked up herself, as if moving between the inside and the outside was like passing between pockets of air.

"Three weeks ago," he said.

"He wouldn't qualify. You have to be on good behavior for at least three years to take my classes. You can't be a violent offender."

She seemed to know not to ask Thursday what Leon had done or whether he'd been violent.

"I've tried calling but I can't reach him. The line always goes dead."

She lifted her brandy as if toasting. "That's Pollsmoor. I bring cookies for the guards each time I come, and I have an official pass and a letter from my embassy. If you want to talk to him, ask for Siphiso. He's the friendliest guard. You should take money. Slip it in the cookies."

"Can't you come with me?"

"I'm afraid not, Hampton. I'm leaving tomorrow to go home."

He tried to mask his disappointment. "You're coming back?"

"No, I have to finish university."

He found himself growing annoyed. "So this was all for your studies? You're going to write about art and junkies for your professors? Are you going to write about me?"

Thursday felt bad as soon as he said it, but it bothered him that she could saunter in and out of prisons and then return back to her country and live the good life, while it would be too dangerous for him to go to Pollsmoor unaccompanied. For all he knew, Leon might point the finger at him and he'd never come out again.

Instead of arguing with him, Helen grabbed him by his cheeks and kissed him.

"I'm only going to write about us in my diary, Hampton."

They spent the night together again, sober this time, and took their time with each other. Thursday insisted on getting her email and gave her all of his personal phone numbers and the contacts of his relatives. In the morning, she gazed at the mountain, but dreamily as if already staring out the cabin window at jet streams and Nordic seas.

Helen invited him to come and visit her, but he saw no reason to go to Norway. The fjords sounded like Cape Point and he didn't like cold weather. Thursday believed that South Africa could give him whatever he needed, but when she flew away it still felt like she stole a small piece of him which would wander with her in wildernesses like a restless spirit. He wasn't sure if it was love. The thought frightened him, because he could picture himself spread out thin across the planet like a thin film, too wispy to return to Hermanus.

Thursday didn't meet anyone else like Helen, though there were plenty of girls in Obz. He met other foreigners, smiling and buying a

DEJI BRYCE OLUKOTUN

lot of drinks, and tucked a jumbo box of condoms inside his nightstand. Even in his orgasms, when he had at first felt free and gathered a sense of his own power, Leon appeared. And Leon niggled at his mind when the electricity cut off in the sleeping blackouts. The dagga smoke gave him paranoia and he'd see Leon through the burglar bars. He was paaping. He started keeping the lights off in his apartment because then he had a clear view of the street. He asked Ip about Leon several times and he was told Leon was about to get out of jail, but he couldn't bring himself to call Pollsmoor or Leon's family anymore, because he felt Leon had failed him.

After one of his walks, Thursday came home to find the stairwell dark. He reached for his keys and began searching for the lock, when he suddenly felt someone's hands on his neck. Thursday flailed out with his elbows. The person hurled him against the wall, and Thursday kicked out at his shins. He felt his nose get smashed by a round object, but he managed to leap down and put himself between his attacker and the bottom of the stairwell.

The electricity powered back on as they squared off. The man's forehead was sweating and Thursday didn't recognize him. He had darker skin than most blacks he'd met, with a youthful look and his eyes were lozenge-shaped. The man cocked his arm back and aimed a glass ball at Thursday's forehead. Only then did Thursday realize how hard he'd been hit; when he brought his hand to his nose it was drenched with blood. His head felt very light, very purple, astral.

"Get up."

It felt like someone was rubbing a towel on Thursday's nose, and he brushed it away.

"I'm taking you to the hospital."

Thursday painfully shook his head, knowing that wherever he was it was better than the emergency ward at the state hospital across the

185

street. He opened his eyes and found the young black man hunched over him, holding a checkered tea towel spotted with blood. Carefully, he brought his hand to his nose, squeezed at the nostrils. Wider than normal. Larger than normal. Stuffed.

"Take this," the man said. He handed Thursday a sack of frozen peas, which Thursday arranged delicately on his bridge. "I got them from the neighbors."

"What are you doing here?" Thursday said.

"I was sent here."

"By who? Ip?"

The young man shook his head. "No, by Okeke."

"Who is that? Is that Leomph?"

"He's the landlord."

"What kind of name is that?"

"It's Nigerian."

Thursday shuddered, grabbing at his stomach. So they'd found him! After all this time the dealers had found him. "Don't take them!"

"Take what?"

"I'll give you whatever you want, bru. Money. Anything. Just don't take them."

"What are you talking about, drugs?"

"My insides," Thursday said. "Don't cut 'em out of me."

The young man looked at him sternly. "You think I want your organs," he said evenly. "To sell."

Thursday nodded.

"Because that's what Nigerians do?"

"Ja. I'll give you whatever you want. How much, five thousand? Six? I can get it."

"Easy, man. I don't want your organs. And I don't want your drugs."

Thursday dabbed at his nose. "Then why were you breaking in?"

"I wasn't breaking in." He held up a keyring. "I have a key."

"Bullshit."

Thursday tried to get up, but felt weak.

"Take it easy, man. I can show you. It's true."

"Kak. You're a bloody poes. I'm calling the cops!"

"I wouldn't do that."

"Why not?"

"Because they were here looking for you."

"No ways, my broer. You're a liar."

"Your name's Hampton, right? They said they were looking for you. And they were asking questions."

Thursday paused. He could think of no reason why a burglar would want to learn his name.

"I didn't turn you in," the man said. "But Okeke wanted me to check it out. He's out of town and I'm supposed to collect the rent for him. Let me in and I'll explain."

"Let yourself in. You said you've got the key."

As soon as the young man looked away, Thursday inched towards the stairs, readying himself to flee. His bank card was in the apartment, but he could get a new one. He had his ID. It would be easy to skip town and leave the whole nasty business behind.

The young man's key slid in and the door opened. "There. It's the landlord's key. I haven't taken anything. I haven't been inside. You can have a look for yourself."

The young man backed far away when Thursday approached. Thursday entered and shut the door behind him and checked things out. Everything was as he left it. The T.V., his bank card, his cash, his dagga, the abalone. He flicked the water pump on and creaked the door open. The young man hadn't gone anywhere, so he passed a wad of bills through the door.

"Here's fifteen hundred rand. And extra for you to keep it quiet."

"I just need the rent. Let me in. There's more I've got to tell you."

"No ways."

"I don't have anything. You can search me."

Resting the peas on his head like a market seller, Thursday patted the young man down as he'd seen Chung do. The way he moved made Thursday believe that he wasn't South African; he didn't act guilty at all. He was uncommonly proud. The man didn't look around but went straight to Thursday's new folding chair, opened it, and sat down. He wiped his forehead with his sleeve, rolling the glass ball back and forth in his hands.

"Speak, man! I haven't got all day."

"My name's Dayo."

"Hampton."

"I don't want to know your real name. But I know it's not Hampton."

"Yeah, it is."

"You told Okeke a different name. He doesn't remember it, and I don't either. I can call you Hampton. You might want to start calling yourself something else, though. The police came looking for Hampton. They wouldn't say what it was for, so Okeke didn't tell them anything. He hates the police."

Thursday began trying to roll a joint with one hand while watching Dayo at the same time. The police! Why would the police know anything about the name Hampton? Leon couldn't have ratted on him—he'd only been using the name for a few weeks. "How much do you want?"

"You're not the only one here who's afraid of the police. None of us is a criminal but we don't like them. Are you a dealer? What do you deal, coke? Tik? Okeke doesn't want drugs. There are families in here."

"No bru, I'm no dealer!"

"What's that, then?"

Thursday saw the joint in his hand that he was in the process of burning. "No, I bought this fair and square. I don't deal."

"Okeke will find out anyway. He'll kick you out."

Thursday told him he was a professional au pair. Dayo locked eyes with him, surprisingly confident. "I don't believe you. No parent would hire you. I tried to get a job as an au pair. It's for women. So how do you make money? Is it a scam? Internet? A 419?"

Thursday blew some streams of smoke through his mouth. It quelled the pain in his nose. "No, it's no scam."

"But you carry that kind of cash."

Thursday started feeling too stoned and in too much pain to keep up the charade. He couldn't keep juggling all the variables of the lie that he had constructed, and didn't see the point. The fact that the cops were looking for him was enough reason to move on. Now that the Nigerians had found him, they could enter the apartment at any time, steal the abalone, and sell his organs. He wasn't sure if this Nigerian would do it but maybe one his mates would.

Dayo watched him smoke the joint, and nodded. He handed back the rent, peeling off two hundred rand notes. He told Thursday he'd have to move out but he would keep the two hundred for cleaning.

In a way, Thursday felt relieved. He wanted to get out anyway. The guy was just making the decision for him. He wouldn't even wait around for the deposit. He'd give the abalone back to Ip, tell him about the cops, and just clear out. He began planning his next step as the power went out again, turning the room black.

Neither of them moved. "I'll light a candle," Thursday said nervously. He made his way to the back of the room and rummaged through his chest of drawers for some tea lights.

"I've got a light," Dayo said.

There was the slosh of water. The sound of metal pieces snapping together, and suddenly a blue glow spread out next to the door. Thursday could make out Dayo holding a lamp up to his face.

"What is that?"

In the light, Dayo's teeth shone blue. "It's moonlight."

"Can I see it?"

Thursday wanted more than to see it. He wanted to hold it. To be it.

Dayo held the lamp low, stepping over a pair of jeans and some sneakers, until he was right up close. Thursday moved his hands in front of the light. "Is it a blacklight?"

"No, it's the real thing."

He stepped closer, soaking it in. The real thing of the crescent, Thursday thought, a star below it, the real thing rocking across the sky, the tidal thing, the new thing, the full thing, the werewolf thing: "The moon."

189

Dayo gave it to Thursday to hold for a minute, and he cradled it like a baby.

"If you think this is cool, Hampton, you should see it in water."

Dayo walked over to the tub in the middle of the room and ran the tap before Thursday could say anything.

"No, stop!" he screamed. He ran to shut the tap off.

"What?"

"It'll kill them!"

"Kill what?" Dayo held the lamp low over the tub and saw a few hundred black forms below. "Yissus, man. What the hell are those things?"

"I told you I'm leaving. Forget about them."

But Dayo was fascinated. He lowered the lamp until it was practically in the water. He found himself frowning from disgust, finding the hundreds of tentacles unappealing underneath the shells. "Are those oysters? What is all that shit around them? They look furry. You're the first guy I've ever met who grew oysters. And here we thought you were a tik dealer. Why didn't you tell me? Hobbies are hobbies—"

"—they're not oysters. They're perlemoen."

Dayo stood up straight. "Perlemoen?"

Thursday nodded. "That's what I babysit."

"Perlemoen? Aren't they illegal?"

"Some of them. These are."

"But they're clams."

Together they sat there and watched them. If they had been clams then maybe Thursday wouldn't have felt so despondent at having to depart from them. A tear rolled down his cheek and he stared right through the tub into a remorseful place inside himself.

"Anyway, they seem to like the lamp," Dayo added. "If only they could pay for them, then maybe I could get my business started."

Thursday watched the abalone sliding eagerly across the tank. Dayo was right: it was like they had been injected with adrenalin. He went to the refrigerator and got some kelp from a freezer bag and dropped it in. They began tearing at the kelp as quickly as he'd ever seen them move, responding to the light.

"How much is it?"

"The deposit is two hundred. But you've got to go, Hampton. I don't have a problem with this but Okeke would flip. It's weird and he hates weird things. I'm going to get going." He walked towards the door. "Take care of yourself."

"No, I mean for the lamp. I'll give you a thousand."

Dayo stopped. "You've got to be kidding."

"Okay, if that's not enough, two thousand. I've never seen anything like it, my broer. That light made them happy."

"Forget it," Dayo decided. "It's not enough. I can't survive off that. Keep your money. Go see a doctor for that nose."

"Well, how much do you need?"

"I wanted to put these up around the neighborhood, but I didn't have enough money to get the tools. I've wasted two years of my life over this thing. You're the first one who gave a shit about it. Even my friends think it's a blacklight. Besides, it's not the original. I've got more." He handed the globe to Thursday. "Consider it a going away present."

Perhaps Thursday was also grateful for the sack of peas on his nose, for he made a generous offer. "I need a week. Take a thousand. Give me a week and we'll talk."

"Forget about it. Okeke would never stand for it, Hampton."

"Give me a week. If you give me a week I can get you the money that you need."

Dayo paused. He started to leave and then stopped. Thursday went and put the thousand rand in his hand.

"I need ten thousand to grow the business."

Thursday told him, with confidence, that ten thousand was chump change for his colleagues and that he could keep the cops off, too. You scratch my back and I'll scratch yours, he said. Dayo stared at the bills in his hands as if they were burning new lines into his palm. Finally, he turned to leave. "Keep the lamp in the light during the day. That will be enough to charge it."

That was when they heard the door shut. They hadn't heard it open. And Thursday could smell the man before he saw him, the stink of dried beer stout on his jeans. They both turned, Thursday holding the lamp in one hand, and Dayo holding the bills in the other, the air reeking of dagga smoke.

"Help me during the rainy season," a deep voice said from the shadows, "and I will help you during the dry season. That's the proverb." Then the voice roared like a peel of thunder: "THAT IS THE PROVERB!"

And Dayo was yanked to the doorway by an unseen force. "DAYO! WHAT IS GOING ON HERE!"

And Thursday was running full tilt, stumbling and cursing, down the stairs, the lamp in his hand a blue streak in the stairwell.

In the Dark

1994
Basel, Switzerland

Dr. Mohammed Farai was a Ph.D. who worked for a Basel biotech firm and had published papers about analgesics, which Melissa determined had something to do with pain. He had been nearly impossible to find. The librarian in Évry had helped her yet again, tracing Farai's publication history to an editor in Basel. After some cajoling the editor had agreed to help her contact him, as long as it pertained to academic matters.

"You're interested in my work?" Farai asked over the phone, seeming surprised. "Are you a researcher?"

She'd already decided it was best to lie. "Yes, I'm a journalist for the Figaro, I would like to speak with you about your important work."

He asked her a number of questions and she fudged the answers as best she could.

"I see," he said, somewhat doubtfully. "It sounds like I may need to give you some background. It may take a while. Can you come to Basel?"

She said she could be there in a few days.

"Good. I can't meet outside, I'm afraid. I prefer not to be seen."

"That is fine," Melissa agreed. He didn't need to see the niqab, she felt, or the horror that lay beneath.

"I know just the place. There is nothing else like it in Basel."

It had rained for three days before Melissa arrived in Basel on her fake French passport and the forecast predicted three more days of rain. The glacier waters charged down the ravines at Interlaken looking like blue foamed milk. The meadows of the highlands turned a deep, rich green, sprinkled with Edelweiss, and the roads that followed the lakes were drowned in water.

Basel reminded Melissa of Paris with its balconied apartment blocks and misplaced spires, yet the city was cleaner and overrun with trams, which pounded violently down the pavement amongst the cafés and shops. The trams passed taxi stands which passed commuter lines which passed international trains, and through them all the buses wove and hooted at the passers-by. There were ornate roundabouts crowned with seasonal flowers. But even the crowded cafés and plazas seemed devoid of something, a spark of the unknown, that the surprises had either been planned away or would not be forthcoming. She felt that it was not a city where daughters found their fathers and without the weathered rolling hills there would have been no lovers.

Weaving between the camera laden tourists of the plazas, scents of attraction began teasing their way into Melissa's thoughts. She found herself eyeing certain men and desiring to speak with them. And there was another feeling, a new one growing deep within her that came and went in soft waves: that she might finally have some protection after surviving on her own. That someone might protect her again. She felt clean and excited and in pain all at once.

The dinner reservation was made for six o'clock at a restaurant across from the Münsterplatz, the old castle that loomed above the Rhine. Below the castle, the river thundered by in a wash of red and brown, having churned up sediment on its journey down from the mountains. The lights of east Basel on the opposite side glowed faintly and looked vulnerable against the force of the river. Both banks were lined with kiosks and small eateries for the summer crowds. Faint music could be heard playing in the summer breeze.

The sign outside the restaurant featured a mountain goat wearing sunglasses on top of a cobalt blue neon backdrop. Opening the tinted glass door, Melissa found the interior to be spartan, with two Scandinavian couches, a plain coffee table, and a coat rack. The colors were mismatched: a pumpkin-colored carpet, a green throw rug over the couches, ugly flower printed drapery, and a high ceiling with electric fans that were too quiet to make a noise. No effort had been made to adorn the walls with pictures, and the exposed I-beams overhead suggested that the structure may have been an old warehouse. It felt empty and practical.

There was a hostess behind the desk. "Grüezi hoi," she said.

"Je ne parle pas le suisse-allemand," Melissa replied politely. "I don't speak Swiss German."

The hostess nodded curtly and asked for her reservation. Melissa gave her a false name and the woman nodded. "Dr. Farai is not yet arrived."

"You know Dr. Farai?" Melissa asked. The woman had spoken of him with familiarity.

"Of course. He is one of our favorite customers. He was here a few days ago."

He was still alive, Melissa thought, growing excited. Even though she had spoken to him a few days ago, she hadn't expected to really meet a man who had known her father.

"Are you familiar with our restaurant?" the hostess continued.

"I have been to restaurants in Paris much nicer than this one."

It was a brash comment but the hostess did not take offense. She even seemed enthused. "Ah? Is that so? I did not think there was a restaurant such as ours in Paris."

"There are thousands of restaurants in Paris."

Now the hostess looked at her skeptically. "Perhaps you are mistaken." She indicated a velveteen couch. "Your server will be here in a few moments. Her name is Ruth. Please have a seat until Ruth arrives."

For such a poorly decorated place, Melissa found the woman's manner overly formal, as if they were in a much classier restaurant. What did she think was so special about it, anyway? She criticized the bland décor of the room on the couch until a hand squeezed her shoulder. Before her stood a young Swiss woman with shoulder length hair, wearing a plain black dress.

"I'm sorry," the girl said. "Did I scare you? I am your server. My name is Ruth."

Ruth seemed to be staring intently at a point just over Melissa's ear. She told Melissa to put her hand on her shoulder, but she didn't seem to see Melissa's hand and continued staring ahead. Then Melissa understood. The woman was blind.

They exited the large room and entered through some velvet curtains into an antechamber. "We will stay here," Ruth said, "for your eyes to adjust. When you are ready, please squeeze my shoulder. We will go into the dining room."

Melissa waited. A sliver of light peeked through the foot of the velvet curtain from the waiting room but otherwise it was dark. They remained there for a moment, with Melissa's hand on Ruth's shoulder, until she gave a squeeze. They passed through the second velvet curtain out of the antechamber and into the dining room. Even with her eyes open Melissa still couldn't see. Ruth led her through the tables, turning quickly now and again, until Melissa thought that she would never find her way out. In every direction there was blackness, and in every direction the sounds of people eating or talking, people she could not see. Whereas before she had felt pity for Ruth's blindness, the roles had reversed and she was grateful for Ruth's unassuming kindness. When Ruth announced they had reached the table, Melissa sat with relief.

"Your plate and silverware are before you," Ruth said. "Can I serve you a drink?"

Melissa ordered a glass of wine because it was offered first, in several varieties, and there was no menu. She reached out and found the fork and knife, ran her finger around the rim of the plate. Ruth returned a moment later with the wine, and guided Melissa's arm towards it.

"Your wine is here. Would you like to eat now or wait for your guest?"

"I'll wait."

She was surprised at how nervous she was to be meeting a person who had known her father. Her flesh felt alive. In the pitch dark she grasped the wine and took a sip. She usually did not drink at all, even very little water. This wine was a rich, almost syrupy red. She did not like it but she liked the distance that the feeling of the alcohol put between her and the darkness. Rolling the wine around her tongue, she tried to gauge her surroundings. She had no sense of the size of the room.

Another server seated a couple at a table not far from her, a meter perhaps. It took only a few moments to surmise they were meeting for the first time on a date, and Melissa smarted at their nervous chatter. If she could hear them so clearly it would be possible for them to hear her speak to Farai, and she wouldn't be able to talk with privacy, and she began to regret the whole thing. Her stomach began to cramp and she felt the air was being sucked from the room.

"Ruth?" Melissa said.

"Yes."

"Ruth, I would like to leave."

"You would like to use the toilet?"

"No—I would like to leave."

Instead of asking Melissa to put her hands on her shoulders again, Ruth put her hands over Melissa's eyes. There was the scent of amber. And vetiver, brief, then it seemed to fold in on itself again, and left behind citrus and cedarwood.

"Guess who?"

It was a man's voice.

Melissa tore the hands down from her face. "Ruth! Ruth, I would like to leave."

"No, it's all right, Ruth," the man continued. "Please have a seat. I'm sorry I was late."

Melissa remained standing but there was nowhere to go. She could never find her way out. And she was nervous about causing a scene. Or not being seen, being heard. Causing a row.

"The toilet?" Ruth asked again, politely.

"Oh, bloody hell," the man said. "I forgot the signal. Right, now give me your hand."

Melissa did so. Farai's hand was large and enveloped hers, dry and calloused below the fingers. He squeezed twice in the agreed upon signal. But when she let go he let his fingers softly slide along the base of her handglove. She withdrew her hand quickly.

"Thank you, Ruth. Maybe I will go later." She sat.

"Would you like a drink, Dr. Farai?"

"Some hot tea would be lovely, Ruth."

Farai could be heard pulling out a chair and sitting. Melissa remained quiet until Ruth returned a few minutes later with an herbal infusion.

"It's hibiscus tea," Farai said, "if you were wondering." His voice, which had earlier seemed confident and jovial, had now become nervous. "I'm sorry for the joke. And for being late. I—you see, I used to work here in my student days. My sister is blind, she was a waitress. I've got a feel for the place."

Melissa sensed that he was trying to impress her, and did not indulge him. She could still feel his fingers sliding along her wrist, and felt strangely distracted by it. In his touch she had sensed a promise.

"My sister is married and lives in Lucerne," Farai went on. "But they haven't changed the table arrangements. They put up sound barriers now and again to change the décor, move some flowers around, but that's it. I hope you don't mind if I ordered for us. It's the surprise dish."

"Surprise?"

"You guess the dishes."

"I am not hungry," Melissa said.

They fell into silence. With the couple on a date beside them, Melissa couldn't bring herself to ask after her father and Farai seemed at a loss for words. She wanted to act like a journalist but the charade started to feel pointless. The man at the table next to them was claiming that he spoke all kinds of languages, trying to win over his date. The girl spoke a few words of Spanish but eventually gave up and changed the subject. One of the large groups at the other end of the restaurant was growing louder. They were stealing one another's food and swapping drinks.

The food came. Melissa was not hungry and did not touch it.

"I must be going," she said, giving Farai a chance to speak.

"Wait, please," Farai said. "I shouldn't have done that earlier, putting my hands over your eyes. It was rude."

When she remained quiet, he added: "You asked me here. Didn't you want to meet me? Aren't you a reporter?"

"It was a lie."

He sounded worried, and she could hear his voice tense in the darkness. "You're not a reporter. A researcher, then? You want to know about tail flick?"

"Tail flick?"

He carried on, nervously. "It was arrogant of me, I suppose. To think that the press would be interested in tail flick. It's an important test, you know, one I developed to assess pain. That is my specialty. Rats are unique animals. They flick their tails in response to pain. There was a general range to measure the flick before, but it was hardly accurate. It was more of a binary answer: yes or no, that sort of thing. I've isolated the gene."

With difficulty, Melissa decided to indulge him.

"Tell me more about the tail flick."

He hesitated. "If that's—if that's what you want." He cleared his throat. "Now when the rat flicks its tail a specific amount, an exact dose of pain medication can be prescribed. The rat's pain has been managed when the tail stops flicking. Identifying the gene made the test a quantifiable measurement of the intensity of pain, which has been up to now a matter of speculation. In a few years we will be able to assess exactly how much pain a person is in and stop it precisely. It's a breakthrough for pharmaceuticals and, deeper, for the human experience. We can now isolate the psychological from the physiological."

"You wanted to go to Nigeria," she said, "to study this."

He released her hand. "How did you know about that?"

"By your surname. I have Nigerian friends."

She heard him suckling his tea. His voice lost its confidence again. "I've always wanted to return, but Nigeria never had the capacity to support my research. They still don't. I've been courted by my homeland, you know. I turned them down."

The couple beside them, seemingly oblivious, was searching for something to talk about:

"I would rather be deaf than blind," the girl said.

"Yes, it would be better to be deaf," her date replied.

"What do you know about a man named Bello?" Melissa whispered.

"Bello? Have you seen him?"

"No. He promised me something."

He sounded relieved. "I'm afraid you wouldn't be the first. Two years ago, Bello contacted me about developing the biotech sector. Nurudeen Bello. He claimed to be a kind of adjunct minister. I'd never heard of him."

"Go on," she said.

"He made all kinds of grand promises—that I would be the one who would steer Nigeria to a brighter future. Brain Gain, he called it. Well, I'm not afraid of Nigeria like some of my countrymen. I go home every two years. The country has changed—and it certainly has its problems—but people live their lives there like anywhere else. I told him that I wanted to see what he had in mind. Nigerians try to scam me all the time, you see. Usually it's an email scam about sending money to rescue a kidnapped dignitary. What was strange about Bello is he didn't want money—he wanted a commitment."

"Commitment?"

"He wanted me to steal something from my lab. Something that would help Brain Gain and make sure there was no turning back. Collateral, if you will. I told him I wanted to see his program in Nigeria first. That trip saved my life. It was a scam, you see. A very dangerous scam. Bello was a praise singer. He had been trained in persuasion since birth. It was a powerful combination in the hands of someone with ambition. Bello convinced me he would arrange everything. I was to get a tour of the research facilities around the country to recruit talent for my project. The only thing that worked was the plane tickets. When I got to the airport I knew something was wrong. I'm used to greasing the wheels with a bit of cash, but the customs officer gave me a devil of a time about Bello. His name was on my entry visa. Bello never showed up to escort me. The researchers seemed surprised to see me, but they were good scientists, underequipped of course and a little skeptical. None of them knew anything about Bello. The next thing I knew I was arrested. They threw me in a cell." Farai stopped abruptly. Took a drink of his tea. "I don't know what Bello had said or what he'd done, but he had a lot of enemies. Maybe he'd scammed them all, too. Thank god that I had been going back every few years. I was able to get my cousin to bribe me out of prison."

"You came home."

"Yes, I flew back to Switzerland. I haven't been back since. My cousin told me that there was a warrant for my arrest. And the rumor was that a hitman had been sent after me. A hitman! I've never even been in a fist fight, and now someone wanted to kill me. I have never been so scared. I had my address delisted. I moved. I changed my phone. I hoped I would never hear from Bello again. That's why I have to go through this absurd secrecy. And now I am thinking to myself, how do I know that it's not you?"

He said it so casually that it took her a moment to respond. "I'm here because I'm afraid of this person, too. I thought you might be able to help me find my father."

"Is that right—so I'm not alone?" She heard him fidget beneath the table, his leg accidentally brushing hers. "I should never have been put in this situation. It's my own damn fault. Bello's scam was ridiculous from the start. You need more than cash to develop a biotech sector. I'm one man! I would have been the tusk of a white elephant."

Melissa decided she could no longer resist. The thought of her father in prison rattled her. "Did you meet anyone else on your trip to Nigeria? A South African man by the name of Tebogo?"

Farai paused, thinking about it. "That's your father, is it? Bello had a man that tended to pass me messages. He arranged my flights, too. But I can't say with any certainty whether he was South African or not. I never met him. He would drop notes in my home or at the office— all very secretive. I haven't heard from him since I was arrested. A few months ago someone began contacting me and asking me questions about Nigeria. I've—I've been getting any number of calls lately."

Farai hadn't said that her father was dead, only that he didn't remember. He may have known him, perhaps received tickets from him. But she couldn't believe that her father had been part of the scam. It didn't fit. She convinced herself that she could jog his memory later.

Ruth pattered to the table and cleared the plates. Farai waited for her to leave again.

"I can see what you're thinking, that this was a conspiracy of some kind against your father, but it was just a scam. I am sorry if your father was caught up in it, too. There was only one person who could have done it—Nurudeen Bello. If you're going to Nigeria, don't ask for Bello. It will get you killed. I doubt he's even there. He's likely still roaming the earth, giving people like me a run for their money." He shifted in his chair, chuckling to himself. "You know why people always fall for these silly scams? Because they think that Africans are inferior. They think they're not capable of a sophisticated scam. I never thought I'd become like that. Never in my life. And here I am, sitting in the dark."

Melissa's craving for protection had deafened her. She could not abandon the thought that he was a man who had known her father and that Farai could be trusted. She did not sense the broken promise.

"What kind of pain do you think I'm in, Dr. Farai?"

She gave him her hand.

"You wear a glove," he said. "I cannot tell."

Reluctantly, she removed the gloves, unsure of what would be beneath. Then he slipped his hand over hers. Warm, but not clammy with nervousness like her own. She was surprised to find that his touch comforted her.

"Your palms feel healthy. You are a strong woman. I can tell that you're in good health. Yes, if you're in pain it is certainly psychological." She started to withdraw them. "Wait, I can see them." He squeezed more firmly, then turned them over. "Did you paint them? With day-glo or fluorescence?"

"No."

"Fascinating. They're almost—bioluminescent. Are you sure? You haven't been swimming in the sea? Anything like that?"

"I have been in Paris."

"It's lovely," he said. "I've never seen anything like it. Has this happened before?"

"Every month."

"What about the rest of your body?"

"The same. It's vitiligo. There is no cure."

"No, this isn't vitiligo. It's something else." He turned her hands over again in his, gently. "I don't have the facilities at my lab, but I know someone who does. I've heard of advances in this field, staining neurons with bioluminescence to map the functions of the brain, still very experimental, of course. But never in the skin. It's remarkable." And then, almost to himself, as he held her hands: "You're beautiful."

Melissa was afraid to lose the sensation of comfort. She didn't want to be studied in a lab like an exotic object. No, she could only feel this in the dark. She pulled his hand closer. She didn't want to tell him about the other scientist, the one that she had discovered murdered. Each touch of Farai's was making everything unravel. She had expected warmth. But what she felt was cool, spreading from her groin, the fluttering of a fan by the breeze. The pressure of the wind moving her along.

"There are cameras," Farai muttered.

She guided Farai's hand up her leg, thrilled by the anonymity of it, but also by the honesty of the darkness. Neither of them had seen the other's face. This was just touch. She brought her foot up to his groin. There was more sensation now, not just a breeze, but gusts, surging quickly past her, between her legs, as if swaying around a sand dune.

Melissa wanted to hold this moment. There was no finality, only branches upon branches and leaves of possibilities. Her father could be alive. This man could help her. Answers could be found. She moved her body against Farai's and felt more coolness brushing within her. A dune piling with sand, each grain moving within itself. She felt his stiffness and tried to pull his zipper down with her toes. Beyond the dune there was more. A rising and falling to the rhythm of his touch, filtered through eons of rich soil, cleaning it for her, shared by her, then hers alone, Melissa's, and she pulled down her own panties and stroked his groin with her foot while bringing her hand to her own body, cool, feeling a tug of a pure luminous satellite.

Farai groaned. Melissa couldn't stop herself and kept on moving, the wonderful unity of a release, that this man would release her, that she would release herself straight into the protection of the tides. Flow with the moon. She was being reborn, she was being released. A child of light.

A tray dropped behind them with a crash. Several glasses sounded like they were exploding at once. A small yellow light streaked out of the corner of Melissa's eye, tiny like the flame of a cigarette lighter. Then it sounded like flesh hitting someone clear to the bone. Farai kicked her hard in the knee. She pushed back her chair, clutching her leg, as two more smacks wrenched the air.

"Dr. Farai?"

All of it, the moon, the tides, was fading quickly. Melissa slid her panties up and found them moist. She fished for her shoe. At some point the couple beside them had left. She wondered if she had been the cause and decided she didn't care. For she would make them leave again to feel that release.

Farai cleared his throat. "I'm sorry," he said.

Her eyes were blinded this time not by the darkness but by the light as someone switched on the overhead lamps. As her eyesight adjusted she found everything threadbare. The room was partitioned like cubicles and above her an emergency fluorescent shined down from the ceiling. In their cubicle there were three tables, and it was impossible to see the next cubicle. As if responding to some invisible threat, people began scrambling to leave the restaurant. Farai had slumped down across from her. He seemed to have spilled wine on his chest. And the stain was spreading.

"Dr. Farai?"

For the first time she had a look at him. A small smile had fixed on his face, and he was clutching at his stomach as if enjoying a good laugh, breathing slowly. He had graying hair and was wearing a pinstriped, fitted shirt. His body was pear shaped, and his skin was pocked with scars. This was the man that had so attracted her, a man who people wouldn't look twice at on the street, who might even be found ugly. This was the man she had made love to and who had comforted her in the dark.

"Dr. Farai?"

She moved towards him. She reached to grab his hand and his smile turned into a grimace and his arms dropped to his chest. He began to slump over. Then she saw the stains for what they were. He had been shot twice in the back. She cried for help, and tried to staunch his wounds but the blood was pouring too rapidly. His body suddenly sprang awake and he threw his arms around her like a child to its mother.

In the lobby, the hostess was shouting on the phone in Swiss German. She let the phone drop to the desk and looked at Melissa in shock.

"Your skin," she said.

Melissa looked at her arm, expecting to find blood. None was there. Farai had pulled up her sleeve while he was stroking her, and the light was shimmering within her skin with a slight incandescence. Her first reaction was to brush at her arm. When nothing changed, she raised up her other sleeve. It too was capturing the light like a jewel. Never had her skin been so strong before.

"Are you alright?" the hostess asked. "You have changed."

Melissa had been released. Whatever Farai had done, he had released her.

"Did you see anyone leave here?"

"Out the rear! It opens into the Münsterplatz."

Melissa ran back through the restaurant and out the rear exit. A cool magenta light that gradually faded into a deep blue hung above the Münster castle. Listening intently, she heard the clatter of footsteps in the distance. Then she saw a cobbled path that led beneath a sandstone archway.

She walked down the path, cautiously, and found that recessed lighting had been set on a flicker setting to appear like torches. It gave the large sandstone bricks an ominous quality. A few ancient oak doors lined the passageway with large brass knockers and bronze tracery, but they were sealed shut.

The flickering light steadied towards the end of the passageway. She stepped into a wide plaza with willow trees surrounded by tall spires of the castle. Not far along, she saw a dark-skinned figure in a black overcoat pacing quickly along a wall of the plaza.

"Stop!" Melissa shouted.

The figure bolted towards the far end of the plaza. Melissa ran after him. She descended some steps to a small landing then descended again, with her hands upon a wrought iron railing. Beyond the red-brown brick of the castle she could see the Rhine River surging past in the crepuscule.

The killer fled towards an area below the castle. The steps bottomed onto a wide flat corridor that ran beside the parapets of the wall for a hundred meters. Here there were about a dozen food kiosks with umbrellas, where people were sitting on the narrow corridor eating summer sausage and drinking elderberry beer.

Melissa ran swiftly past the kiosks, clutching her niqab to her neck with the river a good ten meters below. The killer threw himself over the parapets and climbed down some iron handholds bolted into the wall of the castle. Below, there was a much smaller footpath that was nearly level with the water of the river, with a skiff rocking in the current, tethered fast by some ropes.

The killer began untying the moorings of the small boat as Melissa climbed down to cut him off. A sharp wind chopped the surface of the water.

"Stop! I want to talk to you!" she shouted, running along the bank. The high water lapped over the bank and soaked her shoes.

The figure paused for a moment, seeming unsure that he'd heard her correctly, and resumed casting off the ropes from the boat. He reached out above and, as if by magic, tugged on something invisible. The skiff began to move. Melissa looked above to see a thick-gauge wire that stretched from river bank to river bank. The boat was connected to the wire by a safety rope. It was some kind of ferry to cross the water. Hand-over-hand, the killer began pulling himself out of reach.

"Stop!" she shouted. "Please! I want to talk to you!"

This time he heard her. He stopped pulling himself along and turned his head to take in the plump woman in the niqab. His face shocked her. He looked strikingly like Mrs. Niyangabo, only less refined and even more vicious. And he had watery, yellowed eyes that glistened under the street lamps.

"Who are you?"

The killer used his free hand to draw a long black pistol from a pocket. He pointed it at Melissa's chest. There was no place for her to hide.

Then Melissa felt a tug of light quickening within her. Rising like a wild, yellow ring of fire, the moon peeked out behind the buildings across the river. The shawl of her niqab was swept upward with the wind and carried away by the water. She did not have to look at her arms this time, for she knew they were alive with the pulse of the tides. She could feel the beams moving within her, could recall the release that Farai had given her. She surged with the power of the river as the moonlight moved within her passionately.

The killer watched her, suddenly struck by her beauty, and loosed his grip on the rope.

"You're the one," he said, "that he confessed about."

The current tossed the skiff to port side and he dropped the pistol into the water. The prow swung around and he nearly fell overboard. Regaining his composure, he pulled himself up and tried to right the boat. But a small wave, full of the force of the mountains, knocked the boat sideways again. Water began to spill into the prow.

"Please, who are you?"

"I work for the Ibeji. We thought you had run away."

With the rope attached to the wire above, the water would soon capsize him. She ran to try to reel him in, but the rope was out of reach.

"Come back! Where is my father, Mlungisi Tebogo?"

"There's only one left now...Wale..."

The boat spasmed against its tether, lurching further into the water each time. Then the rope snapped and the man was swallowed by the dark river.

Melissa crumpled. She wanted to speak with him, that was all. She hadn't wanted revenge. She wanted to know the truth about her father. Instead, he had told her about someone else who knew everything, as if he hadn't heard her at all. Now he was gone, too. They all were.

She slowly began to climb back towards the castle, lost in her misery. Farai's promise had been broken. The scientist hadn't protected her at all and had been killed like the other, and her father was no closer. Nothing had changed. As she mulled over these despairing thoughts, her way up the steps was soon blocked by a small crowd.

"Look at her!"

"Her skin! Look at her skin!"

People gawked at her openly now that her niqab was gone, taken by the wind. Her face was exposed. She could still feel the moonlight moving within her veins, hotly. She tried to push through the crowd, but a hand held her back and she found herself looking into the face of a young woman.

"Are you alright?"

Melissa nodded.

"Please, tell us your name. Your skin. It's so beautiful."

"Mel—" Melissa began, then stopped. She suddenly didn't want to reveal her name. It felt like the only thing she had left in the world.

"Melle," the young woman said. "Her name is Melle."

Home Affairs

Present Day
South Africa

The bullwhip went up and snapped back in a flash, giving Wale just enough time to duck. The guard was angry, he'd been aggravated by a Tanzanian, fresh off the smuggling truck and waving a paper in his face, and finally, he'd had enough.

"THREE LINES! TWENTY-TWOS, HERE! TWENTY-THREES, HERE! TWENTY FOURS, HERE! THREE LINES!"

When Wale and Dayo didn't move, he came at them hard and fast, stepping back to stretch the full length of the bullwhip.

"Get it up, Dayo!" Wale shouted. "Raise the shield!"

Clumsily Dayo raised his basket cover, a makeshift shield, and whap!-whap!-whap! the guard rained the whip down, shooting bits of bamboo into the air. Father and son huddled together like a Roman turtle, raising their shields over their head until the guard, furious, moved on and cracked the whip at a group of Congolese men chattering in Lingala, seemingly unaware of the commotion.

"THREE LINES!"

The rest happened rapidly: the whip snapped, a pair of spectacles— glinting silver in the sun—shot into the air, one of the men fell to the ground clutching his temple, and their companion in military fatigues hurtled himself at the guard, wrestling away the whip. He had been a commander of the Ninjas in Bouenza, he shouted, and wouldn't let the guard treat him like an animal. And while more guards joined the fray to retrieve the whip that the commander had taken, Wale spied an opening in the security gate and they were running fast, fast, fast past the hundreds of others, through the turnstile and the beeping radar detector and into the gloam of the Customs House.

Inside the long, dark foyer there was a corridor that led to the elevators. A stale haze hung in the air, obscuring their vision, and they began to sweat. They put away their shields and were about to press the 'Up' button on the elevator when the guards entered dragging the military man by his shirt.

"Stay calm," Wale instructed. "Let's go to the stairs."

The elevator door opened as the guards approached with their captive. Wale pretended he had just exited the elevator, looking at his watch as if late for an important meeting. The guards pulled the man into the elevator without noticing and waited calmly for the door to close.

Dayo and his father walked briskly to the stairwell, where the steps twisted up interminably into the mottled haze.

"What will they do with him, Dad?"

"This is Home Affairs, Dayo. In here we will mind our own business. We get in and get out." He stepped over to Dayo, who was hunched over with his mouth slightly open and looking stupid, and pressed a thumb into his spine. "Stand up straight. Close your mouth."

There were no windows in the stairwell and the air felt as if it had hung there for decades.

"How far?"

"She's on fourteen."

They began to climb. These were the first words to pass between father and son for three days. What Wale had caught Dayo doing with Thursday, in that apartment, the dagga in the air, the contraband in the bathtub, was beyond reproach. A drug dealer. A drug dealer! He recalled it: Thursday barreling out the door, leaving Wale with Dayo in the dark apartment. A bag of marijuana on a chair, Dayo with a wad of hundred rand notes in his hand. He had grabbed Dayo by the nape of his neck, picking him up nearly off the ground, like a puppy. Dayo had let him take the money and toss it angrily to the floor. And when they'd gone home he'd bolted Dayo in his room for three days, slipping plates of food in, allowing him, under close watch, to use the bathroom. Wale had considered calling the cops, decided it was too much trouble; he'd contacted Narcotics Anonymous and arranged an interview for Dayo. Unable to look his own child in the eye, for the shame, for shame!, he'd given him a notepad to explain his actions in an essay with a theme of 'Justice and Responsibility'. Dayo had not written it. And, worse, Wale had realized that Dayo was perfectly happy in his confinement, as he seemed to have spent the days building new moonlight lamps. He feared that his son was lost and it was his fault, for a lack of parenting, for not having protected him from the vices. Was it time, he wondered? Time to consult religion, break down his son's mind in a house of God? And which would be most effective? Islam, perhaps, as long as he didn't get fanatical. Or maybe enroll him with the Methodists on Wesley Street.

His compromise was to take Dayo to the Refugee Reception Office. There was no better lesson in humility than waiting in line at Home Affairs. Every three months, Wale returned to the office to convince the staff that he still had a fear of persecution, and now he wanted to be the first to receive their new biometric ID. With that, provided the proper legislation went through, he might be able to secure a passport. Anything would be possible. So they had risen, grumpily, at four thirty in the morning to get to the foreshore of the bay and join the queue. But now that they had run past the guards, Wale regretted that the lesson in humility may not have been properly instilled.

Dayo had broken out in a full sweat by the mezzanine of the stairwell, and the numbered floors did not begin until they had already climbed five flights. Wale tramped up sweating, too, holding the hems of his agbada on the landings. They burst out of the fire escape into an empty corridor striped with mauve, fuchsia, and wilted sunflower paint. The fuchsia was the biggest stripe. There were exposed structural beams and air ducts from refurbishing and each door had a plastic placard with a name on it.

"Mrs. Craxton is in four-point-thirty-five-point-sixty-two-point-twenty-one," Wale said. "Or was it point-twenty-three?" He took a note from his pocket.

"I've got to go to the bathroom."

"Point-twenty-two. You ate too many yams. I told you not to eat so many yams."

They followed the hallway for a good two hundred meters until they were back at the stairwell. The only people they passed were security guards who they wished to avoid. Cautiously, they trailed a custodian and came to a window where a reception officer waited behind wrought iron bars. She claimed that Mrs. Craxton wouldn't be coming into the office until Wale, fishing in a bag of his, produced an appointment slip and a Tupperware container.

"Please send her our compliments of the season," he said. "Some dudu for you."

"Doo-doo?" she chuckled.

"Plantains. A typical food from my home country."

The receptionist smiled, now looking at the appointment slip. "I see, yes, it's for today. She'll be right here, Doctor."

They waited patiently, Wale looking agreeable but not sycophantic. Wale was wearing a honeydew-colored agbada which, slightly starched, hung out from his belly like a maternity dress. He had insisted that Dayo wear a blazer and a burgundy silk tie over a white shirt. Whereas in the queue below Wale's mannerism was humble and anonymous, his posture now conveyed a life accustomed to being treated with dignity. Mrs. Craxton arrived a half hour later with a supermarket bag in hand, spoke briefly with the receptionist, and looked suspiciously in their direction. Wale smiled warmly.

Grimy windows ran the length of Mrs. Craxton's voluminous office, and a fuzzy blob of Robben Island could be seen in Table Bay. It was a sunny day outside but there would be no way of telling in her office. Along the window ledge, a line of black crows was cackling and cawing softly, looking out at the water. For all its space, there was just a small aluminum desk and three straight-backed Shaker chairs. Then there were a few posters on the wall of the travel agency variety: washed out photos of Cinqueterre, Nepal, and Vic Falls. You could tell by the make of the vehicles and the flared jeans that the photos were several years old.

Mrs. Craxton was a fleshy, fifty-something white woman wearing a batik Mandela print dress. She had a necklace of orange plastic beads around her neck, and very full, healthy cheeks. Her watery light-gray eyes were hidden behind some plastic bifocals, and she had a slender forward-bent neck. If it wasn't for a disdainful expression one might have imagined that she had enjoyed a carefree youth. But the lines had been created from a lifetime of frowning.

Wale adopted a Nigerian accent as she entered his information, including his CTR number, into the computer. She typed laboriously with her index fingers as if it was a typewriter. Her own accent was an even mix of Afrikaner and Sou Thafrican English.

"Ah, Doctor," she said, reading at the computer monitor, "I remember now. You were one of the few Nigerians who met the criteria for persecution. The Ibeji gang, wasn't it?"

"Yes, the Ibeji. It's more of a terrorist organization, operating behind the scenes. I'm on a list of theirs for knowing too much about them. A kill list."

"You're still on it?"

"My sources tell me that my name is on top."

"I suppose we'd better extend your permit, then. You know your people can be awfully devious, with the drug syndicates and the rest."

"There are always a few bad eggs in the batch," Wale smiled.

"For Nigerians it's more than a few, isn't it? My guess is that it's the climate. People will do anything to get out of the heat. Of course, the tune's changed a bit: now it's the Delta problem. But you were one of the few who made it through, Doctor. You're a model refugee."

"By the grace of God," Wale said, quickly. Dayo was staring out the window. Normally he disliked it when Dayo didn't listen but for once he hoped he had remained in his own world. He deftly steered her towards the purpose of his appointment, applying for a biometric identification card, which Mrs. Craxton had forgotten.

"Unfortunately, the IDs aren't ready yet. The worst part of my job is managing expectations. I'm assuming this is your son, Day-Oh?"

"Die-oh. Like diology."

"What is diology?"

"That is how it is pronounced, Mrs. Craxton."

She asked a variety of questions about Wale's refugee status and his skills, all in order to get out of dealing with the biometric ID. He explained that the Ibeji organization continued to strike fear into his heart, but that he didn't have proof that it existed, except for the small wooden carving that he pulled from his sack. The carving was evidence of their heinous crimes, he said, and they would surely kill him for the doll if they found him. He handed the carving to Mrs. Craxton but she merely crossed herself against its devilry and told him that she would recommend his refugee status be continued for two more years. For good measure, he told her that he volunteered at the Royal Observatory and ran a bamboo business to put his son through private school.

"Your son is quite handsome, Doctor."

"Don't be fooled, Mrs. Craxton!" Wale laughed. "He's a trouble-maker. Children are always greener on the other side. Especially the knees."

Mrs. Craxton laughed, enjoying watching the father put the son in his place. A gust of wind began rattling the foggy window. The crows lining the ledge suddenly took flight in a black cloud, beating their wings, and then swept out into the bay. Mrs. Craxton typed away on her keyboard. Somehow, lifting her fingers made her break out in a sweat and she began eyeing the shopping bag full of chips. Wale, noticing this, reached into his bag and extracted a very large Tupperware container.

"Bloody hell," Mrs. Craxton said, opening the lid. "Not so much soup in there. More like broth with meat. Just how I like it." Then she held up a glob of yellow grain in plastic wrap. "What is this? Mealie pap? Do you eat mealie pap in Nigeria?"

"It's called gari. Made from cassava. You can dip it in the soup, or mix it together, as you like."

"I'll try both," she replied gleefully.

He did not have to mention the ID again, for, invigorated by the pepper soup, she put his name at the top of the list and gave him an appointment at the Barrack Street office where the IDs were being issued. They said goodbye, promising to get the inexplicable—but required—chest MRI. Wale rose feeling that he'd done well for Dayo.

But of course that wasn't good enough for his son, who suddenly rested his eyes on Mrs. Craxton. Dayo tugged at his tie, making it slip askance. His posture had reverted back to its usual slouching form. "There was a security guard using a whip outside," he said.

Mrs. Craxton snapped the lid on the Tupperware container and put it into a drawer in her desk. "Pardon me?"

"The security guard outside was whipping people in the line. He whipped us, too, and they beat up a man. Are you going to do anything about it?"

"We call it a queue in our country."

"Pardon?"

"We call a line a queue."

"They whipped us in the queue."

She frowned. "What did he look like?"

"Small, broad shouldered."

She waved her hand. "Oh, Themba. He's a Zulu. I suppose you don't know what that means, young man. Here, we've got tribes. Zulus, I love them to death, but they do have a history. Have you heard of Shaka?"

Dayo nodded, not seeming to think the question dignified a response.

"Themba's a Zulu who manages the queue"—she drew out the word like an elementary school teacher—"but it's not always what you think, young man. We at Home Affairs hate abuse as much as the next one. No, you can say we hate it more, because we see what it does to our clients and how it humiliates them. I was the secretary of the Sea Point Black Sash, to give you an idea."

Wale cleared his throat, attempting to salvage the bonhomie he'd garnered with the soup. "Please excuse my son, Mrs. Craxton. He's— pardon the pun—out of line. We know you're busy, we're both very grateful for your—"

"No, Doctor. He has a right to an answer. That is also something I believe in. Total transparency. It was probably the sound. Do you know the sound? Kind of like tchi, made with the tongue on the back of the teeth. Tchi, tchi, tchi, like a hummingbird. Well, that sound is a supreme insult to Xhosas and slightly less so to Zulus, but certainly enough to take offense. Many of our Francophone clients do it without thinking. I'm sure that's what happened."

"I didn't hear anything," Dayo said. "He was being whipped."

"There's no doubt it was the tchi. I've seen Themba resist all manner of insults, but that's his soft spot. For a Zulu he is like Christ. Unfortunately, tchi is a natural display of dissatisfaction for the Francophones. We've tried to post signs but you can imagine it's a very difficult message to communicate."

"They took a guy away in a military uniform," Dayo said.

She said that UNHCR had promised to task their linguists with developing good signage.

"All I want to know is if that man's alright."

"Come, Dayo!"

"Call UNHCR. Here's the number."

Mrs. Craxton scratched a number on a Post-it note and gave it to Dayo.

Wale shouted the whole ride home, feeling that Dayo had sabotaged the meeting and that Mrs. Craxton would never print a biometric ID for Dayo as well. Dayo, who had shown a momentary spark of interest during the conversation after three days of silence—of what Wale had misinterpreted as three days of penance—retreated into himself again, staring out the window along Main Road, where an advertisement for a shampoo featuring the supermodel Melle, with her lustrous skin, coated an entire building.

Dayo's silence in the passenger seat made Wale think that his point, mostly shouted and at times repeated for emphasis, was getting though, but again, he was wrong. Wale, in fact, knew little about the inner workings of his son. He didn't know his music preferences, whether he read books or played Frisbee, or had peculiar habits. That was beyond the responsibility of a father. He provided food for Dayo and Dayo ate it. He gave him water, electricity, scratched to pay his tuition at the Steiner Academy after Dayo had nearly failed public school, purchased, following a burglary, a comprehensive security package from the local armed response. Wale provided and protected, fulfilling his duty. Dayo's fascination with the snowglobe, which should have ended in primary school, was to Wale a mere hobby that should subside before his own duties. This was growing up, the acceptance of duty, of hard work without unmerited expectation of results. And Wale kept waiting for the hobby to subside.

"Give up this refugee bullshit, Dad. What kind of accent was that? Why do you sink to it? You never wear that agbada. They treat you like a dog."

Wale let go of the steering wheel. "A dog?"

"She didn't try to pronounce your name. She sits there and gobbles chips all day long. Doesn't lift a finger. Did you hear that talk about Zulus? It's disgusting. She's a remnant! Black Sash or not. She should be purged!"

"You're mistaken," Wale said, recovering the wheel. "She speaks Zulu. I have seen her do it. She grew up in KZN." It sounded unconvincing even to himself.

Dayo put his hand up on the safety handle above his window, as if steadying himself for an approaching blow. "She knows how to order people around in it. That doesn't mean she speaks it."

"Do you speak Zulu?"

"Why should I?"

"Afrikaans?"

"Who cares?"

Wale decided he would pursue this line of approach, tangling his son up in minutiae and semantics. It would buy him time to understand what was happening. Give him perspective.

"You don't speak Zulu. So how do you know what kind of Zulu she speaks?"

"I'm American! How am I supposed to tell?"

"You live here."

"The only language that matters is English. You said that yourself."

Wale braked so that a minibus taxi could cut three lanes over to pick up a pair of boys in navy blue school uniforms. "Dayo, whether a snake is large or small, it can't be used as a belt. You know what that means? That woman is powerful whether you like or not. She is the snake. We could be deported without her help. That appointment slip, I forged it myself. I cooked that food and brought the bamboo covers. I prepared my bag all last night like a—like a juju. And look: we didn't get whipped, we got what we wanted—and we would have gotten the IDs if you hadn't fouled it up. Granted, I don't like Home Affairs, but this country protects us because no other country would take us. People like Mrs. Craxton. So why are you so angry? You consort with criminals and you think you have the right to judge her. And me."

"You're missing the point."

Wale drifted into the right lane to give him more time to berate his son. He hated the term 'juju' with its colonial triteness but it had slipped into his head somehow. This was major, large; it would require a coordinated reproach. "Is it because you think you're better than them?"

"Than who?"

"Refugees."

"Than refugees? That has nothing to do with it."

"You called me a dog."

"You're twisting my words."

"You just said it. She treats me like a dog. That is not twisting words."

Dayo took a few deep breaths and closed his eyes in the passenger seat.   "Dad, fine. Fine. You're not a dog."

"Thank you."

"All I want to know is why you talk to her in that accent."

"And refugees?"

"What?"

"Do you still think they're dogs?"

"I never said that." Dayo cranked down his window. They were passing cheery pastel homes now, with narrow streets and impossible garlands of flowers draping over the wall. The flowers were always brighter in Observatory than Wale remembered them. Driving down its lanes, the color consoled father and son for a moment.

Dayo broke the quiet again. "You never tell me anything about America. You were important there. You should be proud of it."

"Don't tell me what I should be. I'm your father. I'll tell you when you're good and ready."

"I'm ready now."

Wale pulled up to the driveway, and Dayo went and unlatched the gate without being asked. He closed it when his father had pulled in and parked the bakkie. Wale didn't say much for a while. In the kitchen he began taking some pots out of the drying rack and hanging them above the range oven.

"You'll be ready when you quit consorting with criminals."

"I'm not a criminal, Dad. I went in there to help Okeke. He asked me to go. I didn't even know the guy."

"You knew him well enough to smoke his drugs and take his money. Don't try to get out of it now."

"I kept quiet because I knew you wouldn't listen to me. I don't smoke dagga and I never will. This is about you now, not me. What are you so afraid of?"

"Me?" Wale pointed a thumb at his chest. "I'm not afraid of anything. I have lived my life with dignity. I've sent you to school. I've given you a home and security. In Nigeria any honest father would have disinherited you for what I caught you doing. You're lucky to be here." He put away the last of the pots and started down the hallway. "I have to go to the Observatory. I've got a tour."

Dayo stood in front of his father, impeding his path. "Dad, I will not let you go. Let me know why you hide so much! What really happened? You made the Ibeji gang up, didn't you?"

"Ibeji is real. I've connected them to crimes all over the world. I see their hand in everything. Coincidences, moments when their name has turned up."

"But you told me that it was Mom who forced us to leave."

"Your mother was part of their syndicate. She joined them. That's why I'll always be at the top of the list. Because she'll never forgive me for walking out on her."

Dayo was shaking his head. "When will you tell me the truth, Dad? I've looked them up. Ibeji are a bunch of dolls. They're not a gang!"

Wale smacked Dayo hard across the cheek. The boy was pushing it. He was asking when he should be explaining; and to bring in his mother was to cross the line. Somehow, Wale thought, in his providing and protecting, he had spoiled the kid. "Your mother's name is not to grace your lips again."

"Why the hell not? She's gone, right? What does it matter?"

The belt slid off with ease, slipped right out of the loopholes, and into Wale's palm. He held it there, limp at his side, like a bullwhip. "Your mother was an addict and a criminal," he breathed. "She did this to us. Give me the note that Mrs. Craxton gave you. I can forge another appointment slip with the numbers on it. There are fours, sixes, and eights on it. Then I'll have all her letters."

Dayo didn't move. "No, I'm calling UNHCR about that guard."

Spoiled, spoiled, spoiled. A twenty-year-old body with the mind and posture of a child. Dayo was beyond the limits, within reproach. And, like the Zulu Christ, like the beater of the beaten and the downtrodden, Wale took a step back before snapping the leather forward, quick, into Dayo's neck, and back again, at his bottom, his palm, and when Dayo had crumpled to the floor, his flesh. Wale had transformed his wife into a malevolence of such proportions that he could never allow her true memory to be dredged up again, or he would crumble beneath it. Here she was again, her personality bubbling up in his son, inquiring, doubting, questioning his authority. His blood. My blood. Wale understood, now, why the guard had whipped the man: for their protection. For his protection.

Book III

If your own country is not in order, the global village will be a wilderness.

—Nurudeen Bello, Special Adjunct to the Minister of the Environment

Melle

And then there was one.

"Melle will not wear animal-based makeup."

One left after catwalking the world.

"Melle will not kiss another person, man or woman."

One left after learning to trace the scorches of bullets, melted carpet fibers, stains and the detergents to remove them.

"Melle will not smile. Do not ask her to eat. Do not make jokes."

How apartments are rearranged. The lengths to which people would go to believe that erecting a wall or tearing one down would hide the fact that death had occurred there.

"Melle will not flirt. If anyone flirts with Melle she will abandon the shoot, with payment in full."

It never varied: two bullets, no clues, a shadow of ignominy that cast a pall of fear over the colleagues.

"Melle, babe, can you—"

"—all questions must be directed to me, Melle's personal assistant. If the question is provocative you must write it down."

"Ma'am, could you—"

"My name is Mademoiselle Béatrice."

"Mademoiselle Béatrice, could you please ask Melle if she is ready to shoot?"

"Melle," Béatrice whispered through the flap of the tent to Melissa. "The photographer would like to know if you want to shoot."

"I need ten minutes," Melissa said. Waves were flopping near them on the beach. The moon was rising, nearly full but still soft as the light faded. The sun was a weak ring of safflower light in the spray of the surf. There were two trailers lined up along Beach Road, and Melissa in a tent to herself. Inside, there was no food, but a long table, a bottle of carbonated water, a few chairs, a phone book, and the brochure of the Royal Observatory as requested. Also some sachets of Echinacea tea. She leafed through the brochure.

"We finish at six," Melissa declared.

Béatrice pursed her lips in the French manner. "Non, non, non, Melle. There is light until seven forty-five. It is summer. You are booked until then."

"Reimburse them."

"I will speak with the photographer."

Béatrice exited the tent as Melle committed the facts of the Royal Observatory to memory. Founded in the 1800s as a southern corollary to the Observatory at Greenwich. Several second-rate discoveries, located on a site that used to be infested with snakes. Now a research facility, with the observations being carried out at the Sutherland site in the Karoo. And the most important fact, the one that she had seized on: Join us for our award-winning full-moon mystery tour. 8 o'clock. Enquiries: Contact Wale. Bookings highly encouraged.

She was close. And he was the last. The man's wife Tinuke had suspected him all along. The flight from Houston: unexplained. Their rapid transit through several countries, on the run, his fear, his guilt. The wife wouldn't have been surprised to find out he was a criminal, she said. Where do you think he is? The wife had smiled. She had asked what would happen if she revealed his location. He will be brought to justice. She had smiled again. I know exactly where he can be found, she said. Cape Town, wallowing like a dreg.

She was wearing the same costume she'd sported for years: black ankle length dress, silk sleeves, and her niqab; beneath the veil were sunglasses. Beneath those, tinted contact lenses. She was tall, over six feet, with a plump body. The body she was no longer afraid to show. But she held a monopoly on the sight of her skin.

Béatrice returned and Melissa could tell the negotiations with the photographer had not gone well. "I am sorry, Melle. But he insists that 7:06 will be magic time. It is the time when the light outside and the light inside buildings is the same."

"I know what magic time is. But we are at a beach. What building is there?"

"It is a car. An advertisement. You will be at the wheel."

"Show me the dress."

Béatrice laid the black dress on the chair beside Melissa. "I have inspected it. Twenty square centimeters of your skin will show, as agreed. It is your right breast, above the nipple."

"Good. Tell him 7:30 prompt."

Béatrice left the tent as Melissa changed. When she returned, they exited together onto the beach. There were the usual dozen assistants swarming the site. The sand had been raked so that with the giant granite boulders, the sports car sat in the middle like a fixture in a Zen rock garden. The soft boxes had been laid, the cables buried out of sight in the sand. It was a red sports car, which Melle found distasteful, but she did not complain because she was determined to leave at 7:30.

The vagaries of fashion ceased to surprise Melissa. After she had been discovered in Basel, Switzerland, by a crowd of festival goers she had been hounded by a professional photographer, first as a freak shot for the tabloids, and then, when the photos depicted the pure illumination pouring from her moonlit body, for her beauty. She had desperately contacted Béatrice at Madame Kaluanda's in Paris, asking for help.

"Take the money," Béatrice had said.

"But why?"

"To find your father."

Béatrice became her manager when the money started coming in from the photos. Melissa had no fashion experience, for she was used to hiding her body, and Béatrice taught her how to be provocative, to reveal only what excited the imagination. Melissa became Melle now in public, shedding the sickly persona of Melissa like a snake skin. Melle learned to channel the power that Farai had awakened in that dark Basel restaurant, to release herself and harness the lunar energy that charged through her naked form.

No one had ever seen a woman who exuded light from her very skin. She had never been seen fully naked. It was said that she kept several lovers who were only allowed to make love to her in the dark. There was a following of X-men fans that celebrated her, like the comic book superheroes, as an evolutionary advance. These fans suspected the military industrial-complex of conspiring to kidnap her for field camouflage. Still others suspected the military industrial-complex of having created her. She didn't complain. She didn't explain that when she had lost her pigmentation her new skin vibrated with the energy of a natural contrast agent, made visible, like a bioluminescent creature, under the light of the moon. Her niqab had inflamed her condition even further, an incubator of her own making. She took contracts that suited her in unexpected cities. She was on a mission, the tabloids surmised. On a radiant mission to bring her skin to the world. She neither denied nor acceded to this claim; she did not say anything. Melle was reclusive.

The beach had been cordoned and the paparazzi screened at police checkpoints all the way to Camps Bay and, on the other side, Bakoven. The smell of salt in the air was very strong, the Twelve Apostle Mountains behind them charred from a recent conflagration.

"Look breathtaking, Melle, stunning," the photographer said as she approached.

"Do not flatter Melle," Béatrice said. "You have an hour and forty-five minutes."

"Sure, sure, Mademoiselle Béatrice. I'm there with you. We'll treat Melle like a princess."

There was a swarthy looking black man getting made-up who Melissa recognized from her first shoot in Paris. She remained distracted the entire shoot. She felt sluggish, bloated, and at the same time viscous. The male model—his name was Charlton, she learned—was meant to be twirling a cane and eyeing her from the corner of his eye as she sat examining a map in the red sports car. The photographer explained that Charlton's motivation was an executive on a stroll on his game farm.

"Not confidence, Charlton. Ownership. You own this land, you're satisfied with this land. Good!... You just bought a rhino... And a pangolin for your kids... Think of the pangolin! Good!"

To drive the point of ownership home, Charlton was supposed to hold a tamed fish eagle on a gloved hand, but the eagle kept screeching and the handler had to rush in and feed it scraps of dead mouse. The bird would raise its black wings and twist its white head from side to side, so that Charlton complained that his arm was getting tired. It did not seem to like the agitation of the flashes from the soft-box. Tame or not, there was something uncontained in the eagle's nature, and Charlton began having trouble maintaining his sense of ownership.

"It scratched my arm!"

Click.

Click. Click.

"Nonsense, Charles, you're its master!"

Click. Click.

"Ow! It bit me!"

"Where's the handler? Get him to feed it."

The handler ran up with more mouse scraps. Then they were shooting again.

"Alright, Charlton, ownership! Possession! Good! Melle, you're ravishing!"

"No flattery!" Béatrice interjected.

Click.

Click.

The bird began making a hacking sound.

"What is it doing?" Charlton asked. "Is it sick?"

More hacking.

"What is that? 'Kn 'ell it stinks!"

The eagle had coughed up a mousehead onto Charlton's sleeve and just as soon began pecking it back up.

Click.

"Roll with it, Charlton! You're the Possessor!"

Click.

Click.

In the midst of Charlton's groans, Melissa examined the clock in the car and saw there were twenty-five minutes to go.

"Magic time," the photographer announced. "Charlton, pick your arm up!"

"The bloke is heavy!"

More flashes.

Click.

Click.

Click.

The clouds were now dripping down the parched mountains, then pouring along the ravines, and flowing out onto the sea. The sun disappeared so quickly it became hard to believe that its rays had ever touched down upon the beach. The photographer was not from Cape Town and had not prepared for the instant changes in weather, in a peninsula where there was always obscurity, the mountains hiding a storm until it was already there. In response, he made a mistake. He called a break. Because while switching films and hauling in more soft boxes; while Charlton was ordering wardrobe to give him a clean shirt; while the fish eagle had been permitted by its handler to frolic in the tuffeted wind, Melissa walked off at 7:30 precisely, where a cab, called by Béatrice, was waiting.

"Where to ma'am?"

"The Royal Observatory."

Constable Viljoen

Present Day
South Africa

In a moment of carelessness, Thursday brushed within striking distance of a white and chestnut patchwork beagle on Arnold Street. He was close enough for the dog to tear a hole in his trousers and it jammed its wet nose through the fence.

Too late, he thought, it has me.

But it didn't yip at him. Instead it panted a few times and sniffed at the blue orb on the lamp in his palm. Then it cocked its head back and howled the call of canines past and to come, of wolves and strays and jackals it had never met, but whose presence the beagle could feel quickening in the glow of lamp. The other dogs of Obz gave a few barks before curling back down to sleep.

It had been a strange evening. Returning to find a young man breaking into Thursday's apartment, making what he thought, or hoped, might have been an ally and then seeing him yanked across the room. In the light of the lamp, the form that had attacked had seemed spectral and malevolent. And that voice. That roaring baritone: "Dayo! Dayo! What are you doing here!"

Thursday had run. He'd run from fear and then slowed on Irwell Street, trying not to attract attention from the bicycle patrols that followed him as a matter of course. He was not successful. The patrol pedaled behind him all the way to Lower Main.

He paced to Rodney's Chinese Restaurant feeling lucky to be unbitten and alive. After consideration, he tucked the lamp into the pocket of his tracksuit, hesitating at the door to tousle his hair. He'd gotten a mop cut the other day, with his receding black bangs hovering over his flared nostrils, that the stylist had insisted showed off his eyes. It had to be ruffled, like an unmade but inviting bed, but not sloppy. Just the bed, the stylist said, no jeans or socks splayed all over it. That was the look.

In Rodney's restaurant there was a silver-haired couple, a family, and then two men, a black and a coloured guy, greedily enjoying a plate of fried rice, egg rolls, and flash-fried julienned vegetables. Music trickled through on the stereo, the same pentatonic tune of Chinese music that Rodney always played. Rodney's wife was speaking to the two men and she let out a laugh that reminded Thursday of her husband.

When she saw Thursday, she stopped laughing to approach his table. "He's not here," she hissed, somewhat rudely.

"Rodney?"

She shook her head. He pursed his lips to say "Ip?" but she interrupted him. "He's not here."

He hadn't quite expected Ip to be there, but he knew that showing up would send the signal that he wanted to meet.

"What can I get you, sir?" she asked, again he thought loudly. Formally, too.

"A Coke."

She scratched some letters on her order sheet. "Chicken lo mein and a Coke."

"No," Thursday said. "Just a—"

"Be right out."

She disappeared into the kitchen.

Thursday had resolved never to eat food in Rodney's restaurant after the sword incident but he was slightly afraid of Rodney's wife, so he leafed through a copy of The Tatler. There was an article entitled Melle Brightens the Heart of Darkness. It explained that this year's fashion season would be eclipsed by a visit from the sensation Melle, who would be introducing her new line of niqab-inspired clothing called Antumbra. Melle had never before come to the continent and she was rumored to be visiting several charities. A local man quipped that they should wire her to the grid, so that she could stop the rolling blackouts.

Rodney's wife dropped the noodles in front of him in record time. There was a fortune cookie plain in the middle of the noodles. He picked up a fork and twirled on some noodles but when he brought them to his lips they were stone cold. When he raised his hand to call

Rodney's wife back, she scowled at him. Sipping his drink, he broke the fortune cookie. Inside it read: Convention is therefore a reason. On the reverse, a handwritten note: Get out of here. Cops. Swallow.

Thursday scanned the room. There, the table with the two men scooping up noodles by the packet full. Not talking to each other, but eating. The ones that Rodney's wife was doting over.

Look normal, he thought. Act normal. Drink your Coke. Eat your fortune cookie. Then get out. Get out and go.

He ate the cookie whole and the paper got lodged in the back of his throat. He swallowed some Coke and it went down the wrong hole, so he coughed violently. He dropped the lamp, and the globe of water dislodged from the base and rolled across the floor. Right under the table of the cops.

The coloured guy picked up the globe and inspected it curiously, leaving Thursday no choice but to walk over.

"A cat?" the cop said. "Never seen a cat before."

"It's new," Thursday said. He reached to grab it back.

The man was turning it over. "There a light inside?" Then he was shaking it.

"Sure."

"How does it work?"

The snow was eddying over the cat's ears.

"I don't know. I just bought it."

"How much was it?"

"Seventy bucks," Thursday said.

"That's it?"

"I mean a hundred. A hundred and seventy."

"A hundred or a hundred and seventy?"

Take it, Thursday thought. Take it and run.

The man showed the water-filled globe to his black colleague, who put his egg roll down and examined it with intensity, turning it over and over again before handing it back. Then Thursday was headed back to the table. He put a fifty rand note on his plate, picked up his coat, and walked out the door.

They arrested him at the corner. He heard the ring of the bells on the door and turned around. The coloured guy began calling for him. Thursday pretended not to hear him and kept going, but the black cop had gone around the block and cut him off.

"Come with us, Hampton," the coloured guy said.

Thursday didn't think to ask for his rights. He didn't think to do anything.

The Woodstock police station had a tiny red stone entrance, with a couple of steps and a sign the size of a shoe box. There weren't any police cars out front and the only person Thursday saw come out was an old woman carrying a satchel of tea towels. Inside it was equally calm. No one screaming, no bergies or wounded men, a long desk with four uniformed clerks answering phone calls. He was taken to a small room with an ash desk, a lamp, and three chairs. They hadn't cuffed him.

"Please have a seat while we get our papers together," the coloured guy said, almost apologetically.

One of the clerks brought him some tea with too much sugar, and a biscuit with a dollop of crystallized jelly in the middle. It was all very civilized.

The two cops were still wearing plain clothes when they entered the room. He had, for some reason, expected them to change into uniforms. The black man had thick blue plastic glasses and a shaved head, with a lazy eye and a birthmark on his temple and a conciliatory manner that seemed to want to make up for these deficiencies. The coloured man was bigger, with a barrel chest and a goatee that was blending into his five o'clock shadow. He moved like a man who in his home would sneeze loudly, laugh loudly, and tear down the walls to get his way.

"Hampton," the coloured guy began. "I'm Constable Viljoen, Senior Detective for the Environmental Crimes Division of Operation Trident. Have you enjoyed your tea?"

"My name's Thursday."

"Our witnesses say it's Hampton."

"Check my ID."

"I did. But the pass-laws are over. We know that what's printed in there doesn't have anything to do with who you really are. That's what we learned in the Struggle."

"My name's Thursday Malaysius."

At this Constable Viljoen glanced over at his partner. "What do you think, Mush?"

Mush shrugged. He got up and walked around the ash desk to Thursday's side. He pulled open a drawer, and to Thursday's surprise, pulled the globe from his moonlight lamp out of it. He began tossing it back and forth from hand to hand. His grip didn't look very steady. Not a cricketer: soccer.

"I don't believe," Constable Viljoen continued, "in beating about the bush, Hampton. Save yourself some trouble. We know more about you than you do at the end of the day. All I need you to do is one simple thing. Identify Timothy Ip in court. That's it. Will you do that for us? Then you can walk free and forget the whole thing. It's on the twenty-third of this month. An expedited hearing. We'll give you full witness protection and then you're out. If you don't do it, you're going to prison." He leaned his heavy frame back as his partner, Mush, began tossing the snowglobe higher up into the air.

Thursday was feeling meek, but he wasn't going to agree until he knew what they had. If he was going down, he wanted the fall to be informed.

"I don't know what you're talking about."

Viljoen grunted. "Is that right? You don't know? You've never heard of Timothy Ip?"

"No."

"How about Leon Vermeulen?"

It was all Thursday could do to cough. If his eyes hadn't been focused on the snowglobe then he would have given himself away at Ip's name too. Ip he could deny, Leon never.

"Leon and I went to school together."

"Where was that, Hampton?"

"Hermanus."

"Would it be fair to say you were mates?"

Blindly: "We were bras."

"But you're not anymore?"

"No."

"What happened, would you say, Hampton? Did Leon take your girl? He had that reputation, we know. We've done our homework. Which girl was it? Fadanaz?"

Fuck, Thursday thought. Fuck it all.

And the globe was being tossed high now. Up. Down. Sloshing and snowy. It occurred to him that snowmen were conceived of their own blood. That a snowman was blood peeking back at itself. What did that make him? What were criminals?

"I agree with you, Hampton. You're no longer bras. He's dead."

"Kak."

"Oh, no, not kak. He's dead. He's been dead for weeks."

"But he's in Pollsmoor."

"He was in Pollsmoor. Just like Mandela was in Pollsmoor. But we needed Mandela at the end of the day, didn't we, Mush?"

Mush didn't toss the snowglobe up this time. He blinked. Maybe an old argument. Maybe a new one.

"The strange thing is, Hampton, we wanted Leon, too. But we didn't need him to take down Ip. Because we've got you."

Thursday tried to soak it in. Viljoen had to be bluffing. Because if Leon ever died, God would be bluffing. He would pop out of his grave without a care for the hierarchy of things.

"What happened to Leon?" he said skeptically.

"What do you think?"

"AIDS?"

Viljoen leaned back his head and let out a rolling laugh from his barrel chest. "AIDS!" He nudged Mush in the arm. "He says AIDS! In three weeks!" He nudged his partner again, this time while the globe was in mid-throw and the globe flew back over Mush's shoulder and smashed in a shower of glass and water on the floor. Mush looked even more disappointed than Thursday. The little black cat had survived the fall intact with its whiskers aimed at the door.

"Sorry about that, Hampton. I know that was, what, Mush, seventy bucks?"

"One hundred and seventy," Mush replied angrily.

"We'll get you a new one." He let out another chuckle. "AIDS. Mush, we'll have to get Hampton one of our outreach pamphlets about HIV. Must not have reached Hermanus."

"Tell me what happened," Thursday snapped.

Viljoen described, in detail, the weapon that had killed Leon, a thin plastic blade that was a signature for hits arranged by the smuggler Ip. Ip had contacts inside and was known, crudely, as the Swordmaster. It was that word—sword—that rattled Thursday. Viljoen might have been a bully but he wasn't creative enough to have invented the story. He remembered how deftly Chung had chopped at that guy's belly, how routinized the entire slaughter had been. Dead! Here he'd been living his life in Observatory, getting dragged through Leon's garbage and he'd been dead all along. He could have skipped town. He could be back in Joburg, or in Norway with his backpacker, free as a bird.

But beyond that it was worse. Beyond that was the fact that he missed Leon and wanted someone to take his place. Leon had bullied him into blindness and he didn't know which way to go.

Viljoen was saying that Leon had been found dead, as all victims in prison are found, in the morning, with everyone looking innocent.

"But why?" Thursday breathed. "What did Leon do?"

Viljoen glanced at his partner. "Sounds pretty concerned for an old bra, don't you think? I thought they weren't friends anymore. Did I hear him say that, Mush?"

"He did. He said 'we were friends.'"

"Thanks, Mush." To Thursday: "Doesn't say much, Mush. But he remembers. He remembers everything. Down to the letter. It's a matter of time before he takes my job. Let's end this, Hampton. Have you heard enough? Will you appear in court? It's free. I'll throw in a new lamp. No? Is that a no? That's your decision, Hampton. Then I'll keep talking. When you say 'yes' I stop."

He cracked his knuckles. Leon had been arrested for shooting the dog, as Chung had said, and had been implicated in a large shipment of fresh abalone to Ip. The abalone had been stolen from a farm and had been traced back to Observatory from Hong Kong. Viljoen gave no indication he'd made the connection that Thursday was with Leon on the day Leon was arrested. Mush was harder to read, impassable. He could have been lamenting about the lamp; he could have been replaying a soccer game in his head.

"I can't help you," Thursday said.

Thursday nearly missed it, but Mush gave the tiniest squint in Viljoen's direction. Viljoen stood up instantly. "Your tea's getting cold. Want a refill?"

Thursday hadn't had a sip. Viljoen picked up the cup and saucer and could be heard telling a clerk to microwave it. Mush's fist shot out across the desk and clocked Thursday in the jaw. Another jab came out of nowhere and Thursday fell over the chair to the ground.

"You're lying," Mush said, straightening his collar.

Viljoen returned, seemingly unaware, and bent down to help Thursday off the floor. "Lose your balance, Hampton? Must be thirsty. Not to worry, your tea will be right along."

Thursday rubbed his jaw, feeling it swell up. Now Mush, who was as reserved as ever, circled around the desk. Thursday flinched in anticipation of another punch, but Mush pulled open a drawer and took out a packet of paperclips. Viljoen eagerly snatched the packet, emptying it onto the desk. "You've got to understand that about the Triads. We've had a devil of a time trying to break up these smugglers because they're not organized. Being a Triad is usually nothing more than saying you're a fruit seller at the market." He started moving the paperclips around to demonstrate his point. "You're selling fruit and the guy next to you's selling fruit. Every once in a while you get together to make a big purchase of bananas"—he piled some paperclips together—"to lower costs. But once that's over you're back on your own. The advantage is that if the stall next to you runs out of fruit, you're fine. Take one out and there are three more where they came from. These guys are not Godfathers. They're more like entrepreneurs in the gray and black markets. Sometimes above the line."

The clerk arrived with the tea. There was another cookie on the saucer. Chocolate, which Thursday could never bite through after that shot to his jaw. He couldn't imagine chewing. There was the scent of bergamot.

"Earl Grey," Viljoen observed. "Froofy for my tastes, but one shouldn't complain." He shoved the paperclips together. "When Ip came along, everything changed. All the bananas in a bunch. We don't need much. A witness against him, a witness for just about anything. Could be murder, could be petty theft, and we'll let you go, Hampton. Simple."

A witness. Thursday thought of the smuggler Ip had butchered. The memory of the man clutching his stomach, hands full of his own insides, was more real than any other he had. It was why he couldn't eat Chinese anymore. It was why he was starting to think, with Mush about to launch another punch at him, that he might turn Ip in. Still, he needed time to think it through and denied it, causing Mush to squint, and they went through the whole routine again, this time with a crippling punch to his abdomen.

"Sit up straight, Hampton, it helps," Viljoen said, tossing him a handkerchief when he returned. "We've got two guys who say they gave you a ride to Observatory with a cooler full of abalone. We know you have a connection with Leon and, now, with Ip," he added. "We're going to put you away for—how much is it Mush at the end of the day?"

At the end of what day, Thursday thought. My day? Why did Viljoen make it sound like the day was always in danger of ending?

"Five."

"Five," Viljoen repeated, somewhat disappointed. "I thought it was ten."

"Five under the terms of the statute."

"You heard him, Hampton. Five. If we get DNA from the perlies, that doubles, right, Mush?"

"Right."

"Kak," Thursday groaned.

"Not very creative is he, Mush? Kak, this. Kak, that. All we need is one, Hampton. One chip of shell and you're in for ten. Any shell in that apartment of yours? Any sand get stuck between your toes? I'll tell you what. We won't look for those shells if you work with us. You're small, Hampton. You're not even a fruit seller. We want Ip, not you. Let's help each other. As far as I can tell, these men have used you. You're nothing to them. Why are they anything to you?"

Two other men were in the holding cell and they had both been beaten badly. They were sitting in the corner, facing the wall, staring at a crack where a rat poked its head out when one of them snored. Upon close inspection, Thursday realized they were the Rastas who had given him a ride from Observatory all those months back. One of them suddenly turned to face him when he approached. His lip was swollen and he had a shiner with dried blood at the rim of his eye socket.

"How was that clam suppa, Hampton?" he asked. Thursday found himself backing away. "Don't be 'fraid, Hampton. Georgie miss you."

So these were the witnesses Viljoen had against him, the ones who had turned him in. Strange that Viljoen would put him in a cell with them. However irrational it was, Thursday was also bothered that he had looked after their stinky dog Georgie at the beach and now they were going to testify against him. It seemed ungrateful. But that might have been the pain in his jaw doing the thinking.

Deciding he could offer a deal to the Rastas, Thursday mustered the courage to approach them until Mush appeared at the cell gate with a key. The Rastas immediately protected their heads with their arms. Mush drew a black sjambok and hit one in the side a few times. Then he kicked the other one until he began to cough blood on the floor and shout in Xhosa. When Mush finished with them he took a long, blank look at Thursday before exiting the cell, and blinked both eyes. He'd had no expression when he was beating the men, nor had he said anything. There'd been nothing at all, and that was what terrified Thursday the most, for what if that nothingness came after him? He didn't sleep a wink that night and his jaw hurt so much he couldn't put any food down.

Viljoen was appealing to his reason and self-interest, to the fact that the people Thursday trusted had betrayed him again and again. There was every reason to turn Ip in. The police were probably finding the abalone in his apartment as he sat there in the cell. If Leon hadn't survived Pollsmoor, there was no way Thursday could survive it. Leon was a man who drove things, who made things happen. If Pollsmoor could chop Leon up then it would do much worse to Thursday. He didn't know what that death would be, but he had the feeling that someone inside the mang would have the patience to think of it.

For a fleeting moment he thought that Ip would protect him if he kept quiet. But then he remembered that Ip had killed Leon. And even though Leon had ratted on Thursday and threatened him and manipulated him, he knew that if he went under Ip's wing any longer he would be through and through a coward. If he came out of Pollsmoor he'd have nothing. He needed other people—he understood that—but he would be no good to anyone if he was owned. Leon was gone. It was only him now. Only him.

The rat skittered back into its crack when a guard came and called his name. His real name.

"Thursday Malaysius."

"Yeah." Thursday walked over to the gate, expecting to see Mush with his sleeves rolled up, ready to swing. Maybe this was beating time. Maybe it was his time to moan in the corner.

"Sign here."

The officer passed a sheet towards Thursday covered with fine print. He was too tired to read it. "What is it?"

"Release form. Just sign it."

Thursday signed and the officer unlocked the bars of the cell while Thursday composed his answer to Viljoen in his head. He would turn Ip in with conditions. Protections and such, and money to survive. He wanted those things.

He was marched out of the cell block, past the front desk, and right onto the bright morning street bustling with traffic. There were no cops there. Viljoen was nowhere to be seen. Instead, he saw an assured young black woman wearing a suit. She had finely braided black hair and a nose as wide as Thursdays with a stud in it. Her lashes were very long, very curled.

"I'd like to see the release form," she said.

The cop produced it. She read through it and crossed out two lines with a pen. "This is old language. It shouldn't be on here. Initial, please, Thursday." Thursday initialed next to the crossed-out lines. "Thank you."

Then she heeled across Main Road, Thursday keeping up, and stopped in front of a gunmetal hatchback. "Get in. I'll explain on the way." The doors locked on their own once he was inside. His eyes were still adjusting to the brightness of the day and he half-expected that rat from the cell to peer out of the air vents and gnaw on him. "I'm Constance Makeka. I'm an advocate and I paid your bail. I was hired by someone you will meet shortly. It's best to keep quiet until we get there."

By this, Thursday understood he shouldn't ask if Ip had paid for her.

"You're not free at the moment, so don't think about running away. That'll make things worse. I rifled a habeas corpus demand through while Mush was gone, but once he gets in he'll be sorting through the paperwork and he'll try to call you in on a twenty-four-three." Anticipating his next question, she added: "That'll be in about a week."

They got onto the M5 and exited at the Kenilworth race track, then they drove until they arrived at a small shopping center near a railway line. There was a stationery store, an art shop, and a bar called Pineapple Jam. They went inside and there was the smell of stale beer and sour tequila. On top of this scent a deep fryer was sending out the aroma of fries. The tables were brightly painted and there were fake vines and birds, with a crude cabana thatch over the bar. They were the only ones in the bar besides the mopey waiter, which was probably for the best at eight-thirty in the morning. If you were drinking at that time, the rest of the day would be nothing but a struggle.

"We're early," the lawyer said. "My client will be here in fifteen minutes." She got up and ordered some things from the waiter. Thursday was so ravenous that he hoped she had ordered for him, too. With freedom the pain in his jaw was already melting away.

It dawned on him that he was about to see Ip, so he began reformulating the demands he had intended for Constable Viljoen so that he could use them on Ip. It was easier because he could use out-and-out blackmail. If Ip touched him, he'd tell Viljoen about the sword killing. Simple.

Ip wasn't the next person that opened the door, though. It was a teenage girl. He heard the growl of a motorcycle as it downshifted and the engine cut. She was about Thursday's height, wearing takkies and a pair of stretch jeans that showed long legs, and a flat, small bottom. Her chest was pert, not big but blessed, would likely remain that way her whole life. Her face confused him. He wanted her to be Chinese but she was not; her hair was thick and smooth like Ip's, but her skin was darker, her lips fuller, and her eyes were either gold or brown. In the sunlight maybe he could see them better. In the sunlight he would understand why he was breathing so fast.

"I ordered you some flatbread and a coffee," Constance said to the girl, suddenly matronly. "Did you want sour cream?"

"Extra."

The lawyer called the waiter over and ordered the extra sour cream. Finally the girl turned to look at Thursday. Gold in the eyes, he was sure of it. "My dad told me about you, Thursday. That you were good."

This was the girl, he thought, the girl that Chung was in love with! Never had he considered that she might be half-coloured or half-black, that she'd be like him. He felt a rush of flirtation, and he made his posture more confident. Her accent wasn't coloured, though. She used the word mos so many times that he had to filter them out as he listened.

"Go ahead, Constance," the girl said to her attorney.

The coffee arrived and all three of them sipped at it. The lawyer asked Thursday if he'd been abused in any way, psychologically or physically. Then she asked about Viljoen's line of questioning and the Rastas. He summarized what he could remember, but left out the part about Leon's death. He made it sound as if he was just a clueless man who didn't have the power to do anything. Neither of the women reacted to any of the charges, seemingly having heard them before. Rather, Constance grilled him again and again about the exact words he'd used.

"I can get the Rastas tossed out as witnesses on credibility alone— they're drug dealers. I'm guessing that's how they were brought in. But knowing Viljoen I also suspect that's not his line. Be precise, Thursday. In court these words will make a difference. Trident is as discretionary as can be. Any tidbit will be used. You told him you knew Leon but you never admitted to working with him?"

"Right."

"And Mr. Ip? You're sure you never said his name."

"I don't remember."

"What do you mean you don't remember?"

"I may have repeated his name after they asked me. Or something."

"That's it?" she asked. Thursday nodded. "I must be prepared for that. The conversation was probably taped. We must request the tapes to make sure they're not spliced. They're a vicious team. I'm lucky I got to you when I did. Mush has more complaints at the ICD than any other cop. Most of the guys don't survive the night."

So that was why Viljoen kept saying the day was in danger of ending, Thursday thought.

"That's all I said," he insisted.

"Okay. I'm finished, Seneca."

Ip's daughter smiled. Flat teeth with an odd metallic glint to them. "Thank you, Constance. We'll be right out."

The attorney downed her coffee and left the restaurant. Then it was Thursday and a girl in a room with paintings of waves on a beach on the walls. In her presence, he wouldn't have been surprised if one of the waves had lapped off the wall around their ankles. He could see why the goon Chung had fallen in love with the girl.

"Thursday, I'm running things now. Dad's out of the picture for the moment. Constance thinks she can get him out in two, maybe three years. So I'm running things."

"But you're only sixteen!"

"I'm nineteen. Like, I just look young. And I don't share his name. As far as we know, Viljoen doesn't know I exist. He knows you exist." She sipped her coffee, keeping her eyes on him as she lifted the rim to her lips. "I've had your apartment cleared out and cleaned."

"The perlies?"

"Dried." That meant the Rastas couldn't turn him in for smuggling. And that made Thursday feel free and, oddly, even more hungry. Seneca said Ip wanted him to go with him inside Pollsmoor unless Thursday convinced her. Rodney and his wife had also agreed to keep quiet. "They've got nothing hard to connect you to Dad now. Tell me why I should keep you. Dad said he'd rather have you go inside with him, but he said if you can convince me then he'll let you stay out."

Thursday tried to keep his wits about him. He made an effort to think of her lips as speaking words and not as blowing kisses. As he gathered himself, with two sips of coffee and a generous tear of the flat bread—which she glowered at—he remembered that he had more information than she did. She didn't know about Adrian. He would hold this close to himself. She was a geitjie, a girl who was bad news, and he would treat her like a geitjie. He fixed an image of the shriveling perlies in his mind to stoke his anger.

He thought of how Leon would handle a girl like this, how he'd trip up her words and make her doubt. Leon would make her unsure whether she could see him again, and in so doing make her want to.

"You're saying he'll drag me in?"

She nodded.

"Okay. I reckon I'll go inside with your Dad."

She hesitated. "You want to go to jail?"

"Yeah," he said. "I don't want to run. We'll spend a few years together and then we can work outside again."

"Are you mad?"

"What?" he said, really acting now, getting into the role. "You said he could protect me!"

"But it's prison! There's violence. There's rape!"

"Your dad's not afraid, is he?"

"No! But Dad's not afraid of anything. He's powerful. You're not."

"First you said he could protect me. Now you say—"

Her lips swelled in her frustration and her eyes widened. She ordered more coffee, realizing that she'd given away the bluff. "Listen, Thursday. Let's not argue. All I want to know is what you can do for us." She looked like she was going to add more, and stopped.

"I can increase your profits."

"By inspecting a few shells?" she laughed. "I don't think so."

"No, not with shells. I found something that can make them grow faster."

"We're not farmers. We're distributors."

"Your dad liked the idea. You can ask him. We can take the small wild ones and grow them larger in a matter of a month. I found a special lamp that works like the moon. I think it will work."

She skeptically asked for a demonstration, and he explained that he couldn't because the cops had broken it while he was in custody.

She looked towards the door, where her attorney was presumably waiting. "Did they know what it was for?"

"No, they thought the lamp was a toy. I need to get more. And for that I need ten thousand rand."

"Nooitie. No ways."

"And," he added, "I need a share of the profits. That's full service I'm talking about. I check them out. I keep them alive. And I grow them bigger." He stuck his finger in the sour cream and licked it. "Mmm, this is good. Me and your dad partners."

She was laughing now. "He doesn't need you, Thursday. That's the whole point. He's not going to make you a partner. Bloody hell, you don't own a thing. You don't know any of the routes."

"You're right," Thursday agreed. "I don't have much. I'm a—" he tried to remember Constable Viljoen's metaphor—"a fruit guy. Might as well go inside with your dad. We'll be two peas in a pod." He paused. "That is, unless I don't go in."

She glared at him suspiciously. "What do you mean?"

"Maybe I know something. Maybe I know something about a guy called Adrian." He leaned back and looked at his empty plate. "I'm still hungry. What is this, Mexican food?"

"Cuban."

"Can you get the waitron to come over here? I love this stuff. I love Cuban food." She stared at him in disbelief, so he went to the bar to order some more flat bread and a steak assado. When he sat down, he said: "Why don't you ask your dad about Adrian? Why don't you tell him that this fellow called Adrian is enough to put him away for his life? Oh, yeah. And Chung, too. Do you know Chung?"

"Leave Chung alone!"

"Well, I know Chung. It'll put Chung away too. Ask your dad."

She folded her arms. "Blackmail."

"Colouredmail," he smiled.

"You're cruel!"

No, Thursday thought, cruel is what your dad did to Leon. Cruel is what you did to the perlies.

"All I want is ten thousand rand to buy some lamps and some profits. That's it."

"No ways," Seneca huffed. She slid out her chair and dropped a hundred rand note on the table.

"Wait," Thursday added. "Tell your dad that I've got friends who also know this broer Adrian. Anything happens to me, you know what friends do. They gossip. Plenty of gossip all around town about Adrian."

He watched her go. He hadn't wanted to bully her, but he wasn't going to take orders from a nineteen-year-old geitjie either. He'd had enough. And part of him felt weak for picking on a girl and not saying the same thing to Ip's face when he'd had the chance, but if Ip was using her as a messenger then he'd use her right back. She may have been smart, but she wasn't smart enough—or cruel enough—to run things. Ip would pull the strings from the inside the mang just like he had in Observatory. Not a very considerate father.

The food arrived and Thursday requested a full steak knife. He felt serene for a moment, until he remembered Mush blinking at him back in the cell. It was as if Mush's blinking and squinting had crossed the natural distance that separates normal people. He could have walked out from the bathroom right then, opened a drawer behind the bar, and pulled out a moonlight lamp. Then Thursday would have covered his hands with his head like the Rastas.

Rubbing his jaw, Thursday cut at his assado and speared some rice on the fork. Then he stuffed his cheeks with the flatbread. The food warmed him and restored him, temporarily, to peace. How amazing, he thought, not to have tried the flatbread before. On the wall there was a photo of Che Guevarra, whom he'd seen a movie about on a motorcycle, and, munching on flatbread in a Cuban restaurant, he felt solidarity with the man, for he was charging into the face of power, liberating the abalone with dignity, keeping them out of the dryer. Flatbread like Che: unleavened, miraculous.

In the McClean

Present Day
South Africa

When Wale had first started giving tours at the Royal Observatory he'd kept them dry and cited formulas in the interest of objectivity. That had garnered him a loyal following of one hack scientist. Now his full moon tour was more popular than the crowd-puller 'The Sky Tonight', which revealed the constellations of the season and celebrated the planets. Nothing in the sky had changed to make the tour more sought after: the moon sailed in its usual place, there'd been no celestial events of note, and he was drinking more than ever, having incorporated tots of sherry into his routine. It was what came out of Wale's mouth that was different, spiced by the sherry, or a new feel for his audience in the suburb of Obz, and the penchant for mysticism in people that had lost it. He'd learned to speak at length about the city of Harran and its moongod Sin.

"Harran thrived a long time ago," Wale was saying outside the Mc-Clean telescope, "about twenty-five hundred years ago. What kind of animal do you think the Harranians called the crescent moon?" He used his finger and thumb to make a crescent and then set his hand on his forehead, wiggling his finger. There was laughter.

"Oh, it's a cow!" a young woman chuckled.

"That's right, a bull. The Harranians called the moon Lord Wild Bull."

"Wild bull!" a kid said, and began pawing the ground.

"Now we will enter the temple of the moon god. Please go quietly."

Moving from mirth to solemnity: good for the tension, good for the tour.

"Wild bull!"

The temple was the highlight of the show, the reason why the spiritual channelers and the yoga instructors kept coming back. It set them at ease, sliced open the fabric of the night sky to that realm where one escapes, is escaping—where Wale was comfortable. The temple of the

McClean telescope was old and classical, with a white dome and a long refracting telescope. It had a wooden floor powered by a hydraulic lift. When the tour entered the dome, a ladder stood uselessly in the middle of the room, but once everyone was safely inside, Wale switched a lever and the pulleys silently raised the floor five meters until the ladder was right beneath the viewfinder of the telescope. There were about twenty tourists in all, mostly white, with a few coloured or Indian or both and one black couple. Then a tall, plump Muslim woman wearing a niqab. Wale had a glance of her lips, which were sparkling seductively with that glitter goo the girls put on nowadays, but mistrusted his eyes.

The airy chamber of the telescope instilled respect in the tour, and the people kept as quiet as a real temple might have demanded. Votive candles had been arranged in the shape of an octagon. Wale lit them and burned pine rods in a censer, with the smoke curling up, and pulled out an ironwood bowl. The mixture he passed around for the tour to sniff.

"Pine rods in Mesopotamia were symbols of eternal life. This is called turmus, a mixture of flour, terebinth, olives, raisins, hackberry, and shelled walnuts, all delicacies of the ancient world."

He walked over to a crate by the wall and picked up a stuffed toy lamb. He instructed a little girl to make bleating sounds, taking the turmus powder and sprinkling it over the toy. "O seven deities, accept our sacrifice!" The girl kept on bleating. "Very good, young maiden, the lambs are prepared. You have performed excellently." She hid beneath her mother's legs.

Normally, Wale stopped the mysticism there and moved to the telescope. But the girl hiding behind her mother's legs, peering out, made him continue. He remembered when his son Dayo had peered out like that once, long ago, historically. The archaeologists were thankfully unaware of the carbon dated exploits of Wale's crumbling family. He kept talking about Mesopotamia. The Temple of the Moongod, his mouth was saying, had been destroyed many times, to be built again, and the discoveries were bizarre and exotic.

"There was a chamber where an enormous cauldron of wrought iron was discovered. The cuneiform inscriptions suggested that it had once held the Head of Harran." He lowered his voice, and used a candle to illuminate his visage from below. "This was a fate so sinister that the rumor of it alone provoked enemies of the Harranians to destroy the temple." He identified the small kid in the group who had shouted out earlier. "A young boy—yes, a young boy much like you, little Wild Bull— was seized from his family in the middle of the night and brought to the temple. There they boiled borax in the giant cauldron and cast the child in, where he would suffer the most unimaginable pain. For hours and hours he would boil in the cauldron. Hours and hours." Now Wale went up to the boy, placing a hand under his jaw. "After supplicating the seven deities, the high priest would approach the human sacrifice and lift his head." He pretended to lift the boy's head, knowing not to touch him to avoid angering the parents. "The tendons would be as soft as chickens in a stew. The priest would pull the head above the cauldron, and ask the child to reveal the prophecies of the moon." He allowed the silence to gather. Then: "IN THE NAME OF RAB EL-BAHT," he boomed, "TELL US WHAT YOU SEE ON THE DISC OF THE MOON!"

There was quiet. A woman coughed. Wale cocked his ear, ready to channel the spirits.

"Wild Bull!" the boy shouted, and began running about the room.

"And there you have it," Wale concluded. "The words of the prophetic Head of Harran."

The tour laughed with relief as Wale waved his hand towards the ladder. "Enough of this hocus-pocus. Come on, come on, step right up. One at a time. Look into the telescope and see your future."

He was greeted with applause as the members of the tour took their turns peering through the telescope, nodding their heads at his informed comments. He helped children mount the ladder, one father, an aloe farmer from the Karoo, asking questions with the patience of a man who spent his days surrounded by succulents.

"And what do you think of water on the Moon?... What, if anything, do unmanned missions do?... A supernova is, correct me if I'm wrong, an explosion?"

Wale dispensed the answers with ease, feeling confident, feeling valued, until the woman in the niqab, who had remained quiet, said: "I have a few questions, Doctor Olufunmi."

Startled, Wale said: "Doctor? I'm hardly a doctor. I'm only a volunteer. And a sometimes priest."

"Yes, of course," the woman agreed quickly. "But I have been advised you are very knowledgeable in astronomical matters. Specifically the geology of lunar rocks."

Forcing a laugh: "I am an amateur."

"Are you familiar with Jonathan Shoboyoja's work? Or perhaps that of Suzanne Ibibio?"

Wale looked at her more closely. Who was this woman asking after Nigerian scientists? Not Nigerian, for she had mispronounced the names. He noticed that the other members of the group were as unsettled by her as he was. But their fear seemed more awe-inspired than suspicious, since they trotted around her with respect. He denied any knowledge of the names with humor, prompting a chuckle. It was enough. The woman may have smiled beneath the niqab, may have frowned, but either way, she relented and the rest of the tour relaxed. They continued peering through the telescope. Then the room suddenly grew dark.

"Why did you turn off the lights?" someone asked.

"I did nothing of the sort. The power must have gone out."

The mother nervously inquired if they were stuck in the dome.

"No, the floor is hydraulic." Wale pulled out a pocket flashlight and walked over to a pulley. "Nothing to fret over. We have them in my home country every day."

"I suppose we should be grateful here," someone muttered.

He asked his acolytes to blow out the candles. Next, he lowered the hydraulic floor, and escorted the group under the scratchy oak trees and across the manicured lawns to the gift shop, where the attendant was waiting with a flashlight. The town of Observatory was half a kilometer away, but the grounds of the complex felt very removed on the hill.

Wale was thanked and offered tips, which he refused, and made his way to the lab. There he downed a few pints of Guinness and scratched at a rock sample. The woman in the veil had startled him with those questions about the other Nigerians. Two names, unrelated to the tour. He had avoided answering her questions well enough, he thought, but then that might also be a problem. Maybe he shouldn't have answered at all.

Rather than steadying his nerves, the beer made him restless. His legs walked him outside of their own drunken motion, the grass slippery in the evening dew. Like a dowsing stick they pulled him to the man-hole cover, his hands wrenched it off, and he was staring down into the pool of mercury with the moon shining through some receding clouds.

For some reason he had skipped showing the pool to the tour, when he normally lingered at it; the story about the cauldron and the borax had been extemporaneous, but true, gleaned from a text he read when he was a boy looking away to the stars. It was back now: why? Because even at that age he'd wondered at the parents of Harran, their responsibility, their inability to protect the sacrificial child, all for a few words of prophetic gibberish. It was a tale of failed protection. Or of communal protection, the boy seized to protect the community.

He got it now: his legs had drawn him to the well because it was where he had last shared a moment with Dayo, advised him dutifully about selling the lamp and tried to help him avoid repeating his own mistakes. Beaten him too hard after Home Affairs? Not enough? But what could he, as a father, have done? He'd caught Dayo smoking drugs and consorting with a criminal. It was his duty to set him right. Either him, or the police, and Dayo, when he got older, would thank him for not turning him over to the police.

The part that troubled Wale was that Dayo didn't cry when he beat him with the belt and sat there and took it, even when the belt snapped up and drew blood from his lip. Then, as the blood ran down his shirt, Dayo had held up his hand and said: "Enough." Dayo said enough, as if the decision to beat him had been mutual. Dayo hadn't been mad. He'd been impassive, as if he had gone to an unreachable space. And for a Yoruba the greatest sin was to recede, to deny your participation in the game.

"What are you looking at?" a voice asked.

Wale struggled to his feet, realizing he'd left his flashlight in the lab. He turned to see the girl in the niqab from the tour.

"How did you find me here?" He found himself protecting the manhole.

"I saw you walking over here," the woman said. "I hoped you might answer a few more questions."

"The tour is over. Please come back next month."

"Is there someone down there?" the girl said, suddenly anxious. She dropped her composure for a moment.

Wale retreated to the manhole and started dragging the lid over. He had to pause to recover his balance. The girl moved beside him; wrapped in black, smelling of sweet tobacco. "I never considered that—" Then she said desperately: "Daddy?"

Here he was looking for his son out in the field and the girl had called for her daddy. This odd conflation of desires confused him, and he let her pass. She produced a flashlight from somewhere and shined it down into the manhole. Again: "Hello?"

Recover your wits, breathe in, Wale, breathe in the damp air.

"They used the pools of mercury," he said quickly, "as giant lenses for stargazing. Quicksilver is a metal that has been utilized through the ages to take the pulse of the Earth. Bridging the states of liquid and solid, such a strange element must be seen as a gift from the cosmos. In my opinion."

She shined the beam all over the manhole, getting down on her knees.

"And you like to look at it," she said, calm again, standing up and straightening her skirt. "You see something in there, is that it, Doctor? One of those prophecies?"

"Please, come back later, Miss. I'll be happy to show you another time. As my people say, if night does not fall in your presence, it will be difficult to walk in the darkness. You won't know where to step. Look: The moon is behind the clouds." He closed the lid shut and began heading back to the lab. Daddy? Doctor? Had she said 'Doctor' again? Too much drink, too much boiling in his belly. With her long legs the woman did not have difficulty keeping pace. But alas, he understood: the mental hospital was just over the hill. Valkenberg loony bin. He should have suspected, what with the veil and the questions. The patients scrambled over the fence all the time, jabbering non sequiturs when they slipped into the tour; he'd had crayons thrown at him, green, and a fried samoosa, mince, on one of the tours. Who in her right mind would think that her father was living under a manhole?

"But Doctor—"

"Miss, you will be expected back at the hospital. It's policy. You're not meant to leave the grounds at night."

"Please excuse me, Dr. Olufunmi, I've been rude."

"—it's nothing to be ashamed of. I've been there myself. I don't take my medicine, but it's nothing to be ashamed of, really. I'll call Dr. Moodley. He'll be understanding."

She was close to him now, uncomfortably so. He moved away. With maniacs one never knew when a limb would strike out; there were nerves involved, impulses.

"I'm a journalist and was hoping to ask a few questions about your tour. They're very popular."

"A journalist who asks for her daddy in the ground," Wale declared, "will not receive answers to her questions. Good night."

He was nearly at the lab now and his shoes were wet from the dew and he was thinking that another Guinness might, in the end, clarify the situation for him. He had no intention of calling Dr. Moodley at the mental hospital for fear of being reprimanded himself for not taking his own medicine, but he kept repeating the threat to the woman until he was at the door.

"Please, Doctor. It's a mistake. I was shaken, you might say, by the setting. I didn't really think my Daddy was in the ground, the word is Kinyarwanda for—for 'cat'. Would you look at me? I'm a journalist. Look at me."

"You're a bad liar. Night, miss. Please give Dr. Moodley my regards."

"At least look at me," the girl said. "Then you will know."

The key was not working and became stuck to the grooves in the lock. He fiddled with it, shaking it about, until it bent. Then he turned back, angry at her.

The clouds had retreated with Cape Town rapidity behind the mountain and had streamed out over the ocean, Devil's Peak robust and starkly present. When Wale wheeled on her, the girl was clothed in a band of pale blue light and her sleeves were up. The light was trembling within her skin. Within her.

Something is at play here, Wale thought. Something is afoot. Light does not behave in such a manner.

"Just a few questions, Doctor," the girl said.

She beckoned him to follow her and he followed, her scintillating arms searing into his mind like a photostat, as they made their way across the grass towards the McClean. He could not keep his eyes from her bare arms. He wanted to see more, to know what the light would do with her body, sensed that in such light there would be possibilities.

They arrived at the telescope.

"Take me up," she said.

"Why?"

"Do it, Doctor."

"Are you sure? What do you want to see? The McClean can't catch much now. It's preferable to use the Dell."

"Do what I said."

That was her first mistake, for the electricity was still off. When they stepped inside the atrium to the telescope it was dark. Wale began questioning himself. He felt disoriented and angry that he was being forced to give a tour after hours. And he was beginning to feel menaced by her, that beneath her veil loomed a sinister intent.

Impulsively his fist shot out into her gut. She crumpled. He opened the door and ran.

Don't look back, he thought, if you do she will have you. She will luminesce. Call Dr. Moodley, as much for you as for her, he will put the guts of pills in your blood. The capsule will dissolve naturally, you will feel better.

But he had scarcely run a few paces when the woman was ahead of him.

"Stop!"

There was a pistol in her hand. When he balked, she fired a shot into the air, saying "non, stope, stope" and he backstepped towards the Mc-Clean, where, when he turned, she was before him again, holding her stomach. The woman was as fast as the light and clothed in black. Now she was nudging him forward with the gun until he realized there were two women in niqabs, the same height, one with sleeves up, the other sleeves down, one smelling of vanilla tobacco, the other of rosewater. It was not double vision but two distinct entities working together.

"Open the door," the first woman said, coughing. She was still bending over slightly from the blow. The other pushed him into the room.

The two women spoke to each other in French and the gun passed from the second woman to the first. The second woman was pleading about something, in a tender way, to have the other rebuke her sharply. A name slipped out: Béatrice. Béatrice handed the other one a small cloth bag. Then the one with the bag ordered Wale to take her up to the voluminous dome of the McClean. Béatrice was left behind.

"I told you," Wale said, "the Dell is better. The McClean can't view much with the light pollution."

"Do what I said."

Wale had lived in Cape Town for more than ten years, so he had been mugged before and learned not to question the motive. But who was this woman? She was finely dressed, tall, elegant, seductive. She had the skin of jewels and sequins. He had the sense that he could overpower her except the frigidity of her voice, and the fact that the other woman would surely be waiting, made him reluctant. She also hadn't demanded anything.

But an opening was an opening. Her second mistake. When Wale saw that she had given him room to move, he swiftly pulled the lever to raise the hydraulic floor of the telescope. The floor lurched. He heard the woman tumble to the ground and he ran to the wall to open the door before the floor ascended above it. He turned the knob, shoving it open. There was just enough time to crawl through before the floor was too high. A light trained on his face. The girl pulled the trigger of the gun and a bullet sparked over his hand, ricocheting up and out of the dome. He froze as the hydraulics readjusted. The floor began rising up steadily.

"I missed on purpose. Next time I will not. Now move."

The woman used the flashlight to point him towards the telescope in the center of the room. He noticed the ladder to the viewfinder had fallen over, but he couldn't think of how to use that fact to his advantage.

"Sit down on the floor," the woman said. "Away from the wall."

He did as ordered, bringing his knees to his chest, with the smell of the pine rods from his earlier tour still lingering in the air.

"I do not wish to be violent. But since you are dangerous I have no choice. Answer my questions and you will be free to go." She produced a photo of a little black girl and a man in a colorful urban neighborhood. It was old, faded, with the corners weathered by thumb prints, and anyway he didn't recognize the man. "I am looking for this man."

"I've never seen him."

He tried to give the photo back to her.

"Never is a strong word. Hold onto that and I will help you refresh your memory. The photo was taken in 1993. There were certain events that transpired in that year of which I'm sure you're aware."

The photo did not jog any memories, but the year could not have been forgotten. It was the year of the theft, the year he had left Houston. Of the end of his family.

"1993. Yes. The Hubble telescope needed servicing in December," he said, neutrally. "The Bulls won the title for the third time. I'm sure there's more."

"Don't play stupid."

"Who are you?"

"I think you know, Doctor," the woman said.

"You're wearing a veil. I can't see what you look like."

The woman grew silent again. They sat there in the quiet, Wale racing through all means of escape. There was only the emergency ladder at the edge of the floor and he couldn't imagine descending it without an injury. He couldn't compel his body to hurl down it, even with a gun in his face.

"I'll ask you again. Have you met this man?"

He examined the photo again, pretended to look at it. He snapped his finger. "That's right. I met him once at the Rotary Club in Pinelands. We had some discussions, nothing conclusive. More of a social encounter."

"You lie."

"I'm telling you what you want to hear. You must understand my situation."

"Too well. It's the truth that will save you."

"Ah, but you see, interrogations have little to do with the truth. If you want truth, let me go. Let it come of my own volition."

The light wavered down onto his belt, then picked back up, as if she'd been considering something. "It's too late for that. Have you seen my father?"

So that was who it was. He took another look at the photo. Father and daughter, though he saw little resemblance. "No. Please, I'm a bamboo peddler, not a Doctor. I don't even get paid to work here."

The woman stomped over and whacked him across his face with the butt of her gun. His front teeth grew numb, and he waited for the pain to come. When it did, he spat blood.

"Stop it! Stop pretending! You're not a bamboo seller. I know your history."

"But—what history? I've lived here for twenty years."

"You were lead scientist of lunar geology at the Johnson Space Laboratory in Houston. In May 1993, you disappeared with no explanation."

When he looked at her blankly, she told him about Onur and the other scientists from his lab at the JSL. The shock of hearing these names distracted Wale as he tried to recall their faces. He could remember Onur gobbling donut holes. Rilker swaggering down a hallway to the water cooler. But it conjured the same feeling as seeing someone through the rear view mirror of a car and driving away.

"Pay attention!" She shot the gun into the ceiling. The sound reverberated in the dome like a cannon. "There were eight of you in Brain Gain. They're all dead now. You're the last one. It's only you, Doctor!"

It wasn't the gunshot but that name, Brain Gain, that set the flames of his memory ablaze. The air in the room began to move, as if it was being heated from below. As if the entire dome was a great cauldron with flames underneath and he was boiling in the borax. They were in the temple of the moongod and the cauldron of memories had been lit. The priestess was approaching, reaching to yank up his head. And what words were slithering in his throat, whose would they be?

A voice, distended and rich as marrow, said: "It was Bello."

There was silence. He could see a pinpoint of light poking through the dome where the bullet went out, faintly, for the clouds had swept back over. He thought he could hear the girl breathing oddly, wheezing even. But in the cauldron he didn't trust his words or his hearing.

"Say it again," the girl said.

"It was Bello," the Doctor continued. "Bello who ordered me to steal the twenty-three. He said I needed to show commitment. I was doing what I was told. It was a harmless contingency sample. Of course, there was historical significance, but it was worthless geologically. I took it."

He had not imagined that in the boiling borax there might be a kind of release. That the words channeling through his head might be soothing, that prophecies could coat his voice box like eucalyptus oil. He told her about Bello, the failed drop point and his flight to Cape Town.

"I hid. I did, I'll admit it. I hid, but only because Bello didn't show. People were being killed. I wanted something better for my family." The woman raised the gun as if to smack him again. "Okay, it wasn't only my family. I wanted to go to the moon! But that's all I ever wanted to do! To go up!"

There was a longer pause now. She was giving him time, he realized. He could keep talking. Either that or dive down the emergency ladder.

"All I wanted to do was go to the moon. You're going to shoot me for that? For wanting to be an astronaut? Then fine, do it. Shoot me. But know that you're robbing a son of his father!"

Dive now for the ladder, he thought. Dive now or die.

His body didn't budge. There was the sound of a switch, of metal sliding. And he was staring into a halo of bright light.

"Tell me about Nurudeen Bello."

"You've seen him?" he said, suddenly hopeful.

"He was with my father when he disappeared."

"I see."

He found himself repeating Bello's words from way back in Houston, the ones he'd used to convince Wale to defect. That he was the great mind returning home to steer Nigeria to a brighter future, that there were innumerable benefits from a space program: communications satellites, trickle-down technology, accurate population censuses, extraction of valuable minerals from the lunar surface. Somehow it all came out sounding shallow, when Bello had assured him they'd be gallivanting about the moon in a few years. What else was there to say? Yes, Wale had believed it. Yes, he would probably believe it again.

"You think it was a scam."

"No, no, no. It was no scam. Bello was in the government in Abuja, he was an adjunct minister. He was a dreamer. A dreamer who was very good with words."

"Where is he now?"

"He disappeared. No one knows what happened and I can't go to Nigeria anymore." He swallowed. "Because I'm a refugee."

He was considering how to better justify himself when his cell phone began to ring.

"Don't answer that," the woman said. "Hand it to me."

He begrudgingly handed it to her. If it hadn't been a clamshell phone then he could have answered it, or used the voice recorder, done a hundred things better. The woman looked at the screen.

"Who is Dayo?"

"A drinking mate."

He heard the woman rustle in her bag and turn quickly, hiding her face, to light a cigarette. Vanilla, as he had guessed. The scent did not mix agreeably with the pine smoke already in the air. Vanilla smelled of home; pine of mountain escapes.

"Where is the sample you spoke of? The sample you stole."

"I can't tell you that."

The light was back on his face. "Why not?"

Because it is with Dayo, he thought. It is with my son, and you will not seize him, too.

"Because if I am the last one," he declared, "the killing will stop with me."

For a second he thought she was going to let him go, but she crossed her legs. Her voice hardened. "I don't believe you."

"Why not?"

"My father was a freedom fighter. Bello convinced him to help with Brain Gain. He was the one that arranged your flights—he was the one that was supposed to move you to Nigeria."

Wale recalled the notes that had been dropped in his locker, the tickets, all those years back. "Look at this," he said. "I'll prove it to you."

"Don't move."

"I'm merely going to the wall." He turned his back on her, daring her to shoot him. He picked up a doll that lay at the rim of the dome which he had included in his ceremony about Harran. To the tourists, it was just a bizarre totem.

"This is proof," he said.

She snorted. "It's a statue."

"No, it's not a statue. It's an ibeji doll. In my tribe, a doll is carved when twin children are born. I found this hidden in the home that Bello had rented in Cape Town. I know that the killer was there. It's proof that the Ibeji exist. I've kept it for years to help me find out what happened. Maybe you can help me."

He handed it to her.

"What did you call it?"

"Ibeji. People do not lose these dolls lightly. There are spiritual consequences. If a twin dies, he must be reinvigorated or the twin can torment the family. Whoever left the doll in the house must have been planning to come back to collect it. It might lead you to your father."

She nodded cruelly. "Then it is you. After all this time. My father wrote me that he had been betrayed. He wrote of a traitor. The killer in Basel told me that he worked for the Ibeji, and that there was only one left who knew everything. You. Bello is gone. You said so, yourself. I've seen your medical report, your history of paranoid delusions. I think you're the killer. And this doll of yours proves it." She raised the gun. "Your wife suspected you all along."

He tried to steady his voice. "My wife? Tinuke? Where is she?"

"Austin."

"Is she married?"

"Happily," the woman snapped. "With three children."

More, than anything else the woman had said tonight, this thought crushed him. A family! Children!

"What does her husband do?"

"What does it matter?"

It's the only thing that matters, Wale thought. The nature of the family. He feared that this priestess had come to tear his apart.

"I came for an answer," the woman continued. "Tell me where my father is."

"Ask my wife what happened to my money, because I never received it or I wouldn't be living in Observatory. All this killing is beyond me. I would never kill anyone. I'm only a scientist. I ran away. That's it."

Tears were falling out behind her veil, and Wale was so mired in his own shame at hearing about his wife that he felt no desire to comfort her.

"Enough!" the woman snapped. "I suppose you were passive in all this, too. That all these things were happening to you. All of these people were just dying around you. If what you're saying is true, then show me the sample that you say you stole from NASA."

The moonlight flickered through the dome, and the woman lifted up her veil. The light frolicked upon her skin except where she had obscured it with makeup. But like irridescent minnows swirling in the sea, when she lowered the veil, the glimmer dissipated into the darkness. He finally recognized her.

"You're that model from the magazines," he said.

"I'm the daughter of Mlungisi Tebogo. This is the last time: where is he?"

"I don't know. He was probably killed with the others."

"He's alive."

Something told Wale that what he was going to say next should be handled with sensitivity, but this was not his voice, but the boiled voice, the voice of the Wild Bull. It came through him again: "You're a famous model." He paused. "Forgive me if your name escapes me. Mole, is it? Molly? If all of my colleagues, as you admit, are dead, then these are dangerous people. We have a proverb: if a man does not hold the hilt of the sword firmly in his hands, he does not ask why his father was killed. Don't go searching for revenge unless you're on firm ground. Right now, you are not on firm ground. Your father could have told you where he was, and he didn't. As a father, he did it to protect you. You'd best leave it alone. Enjoy the life you've been given."

His thoughts turned to Dayo again. His son had stomped out of the house that morning, ignoring Wale as usual. Okeke had told him that Dayo had swung by his place, asking for power tools, and that he was preparing some kind of special demonstration for his lamps. Wale had laughed at the thought; his son could never give a sales pitch, and power tools wouldn't help his cause. Dayo was probably calling to borrow more money. But Wale would give it to him, readily, anything to speak with him again.

"Show me the sample."

"You can't have it."

"Then I will talk to this mate of yours." She pulled the phone out. "Dayo. I'm going to talk to Dayo. Maybe he knows where I can find it."

Wale lunged for the gun, but she was quicker. The bullet tore through his chest and the impact spun him into the electronic panel on the telescope. There was no numbness this time, only pain. The roof of the dome began to retract as his tongue screamed for water. His left hand was on his torso, but he couldn't feel the resistance of his own flesh on his fingertips. They were fumbling in a burning fire. He limped to the emergency ladder smelling pine smoke, cauterized flesh, the solvent on the yellowwood floor.

"I didn't want to shoot you! Tell me where he is!"

My son or your father, he thought, as the clouds shifted in the sky of the open dome behind the girl's head. But the answer was the same. He shook his head.

Then he was wrenched off the ground by his head, hands cupped around his jaw. Tell me, the woman was pleading. Tell me.

He could feel the end. The running was over. One less thief of the world. And then the flood of blue light on the white clouds, the light of the regolith, of the mare and all the lab-dead breccias, running through the girl's numinous silhouette. The light pouring through the priestess' skin as he began his ascent. I am going home. I'm going up now. I want to go there.

Load-shedding

Present Day
South Africa

"Dayo, Dayo, come in. Did you see him?"

Dayo strived in vain to remember the code name. It had something to do with coffee and clouds. "No, I haven't seen him—man."

"Dayo, how about Mush? You seen Mush?"

"Forget about them. You've got to focus, Thursday."

"Call me Mocha Thunder. You tell me if you see Mush. Or Viljoen." Then, thoughtfully, he added: "Tell me if you see anything."

Thursday did not want to be mentioned on the air because Constable Viljoen was bitterly monitoring his every move like a bull that had just backed down from a charge, and was reconsidering, but Dayo had needed the walkie-talkies to coordinate. Thursday had paid for the cables and silicon wafers, for the glass blower in Salt River, for the giant disco ball, for the hydroponic foils, for the distilled water, for the imported silicate from Tonga, for the gold-plated wiring: for everything. They were R2,500 over budget, with the extra coming from Thursday's pocket.

The power company had indicated that the second reactor at the Koeberg facility would be down again, but also that the load-shedding schedule, to conserve energy and help businesses, would be accurately published down to the minute. First Khayelitsha, Camps Bay, Table View, Parow, and Langa would be shut off. Then Mowbray, Newlands, Gugs, Nyanga, and Sea Point at 21:27. Mowbray included Observatory.

Dayo had called in a favor to a friend at an advertising company who had done a thorough below-the-line job. He'd invited every lighting man in the business, postered all the bars, dropped cards in mailboxes, and phoned local politicians, telling them to come out at 21:30 to the Obz Community Centre for, depending on the recipient, an acoustic musical tribute to Steve Biko, a psychedelic trance spin-off, a braii featuring surprise members of the Springbok rugby team, a gay pride parade, and the catch-all, a tribute to the visiting fashion phenomenon Melle. Mothers boiled kettles, girls showered, and men ran any power tool they could find in anticipation of the blackout. At 21:25, people began dribbling out of their homes to attend the fictional events. A couple walked their dogs to the park off Station Road. A few families ambled on the streets with their children, who threw tennis balls against garage doors or footraced down the street. The bergies and drunks pestered Dayo for change as he fastened the lamps to the streetposts. It was a warm evening with a light breeze carrying the scent of the game animals on the Rhodes Reserve above the state hospital. Sheets of cloud hung low over the town, sliding by rapidly, with pockets of black sky between the sheets.

Maybe it was the money at stake that was giving Thursday the paranoia; or perhaps it was the dagga he'd smoked, to help him relax, and it'd had the opposite effect. He had the paris, he was paaping. Thursday continued pestering Dayo about whether Mush was in sight, seeming more terrified of that silent cop than his gregarious partner Viljoen.

At 21:27 the power was still on. More people were now perambulating the streets, trying to determine how bikers and cross-dressers fit into whatever rally they had come for. Dayo picked up his cell phone. This was the time, he thought, this time or never, for his father's moonlight tour should be ending at the Royal Observatory. He cycled through the menu on the screen. Dad Cell. Then he dialed his father and waited for an answer. The phone rang ten times and went to the spartan voicemail. This is Wale. I'll call you back. Dayo had not considered that his father would be unavailable, tried it again, and put it down, vowing to try again later.

Twenty minutes later the load-shedding of the power began and the neighborhood was dark. The moonlamps were arranged. The solar grids aligned. Forty lamps were spread wide across the suburb. Dayo dialed his father three more times and left two messages. He was about to put the walkie-talkie to his lips when Thursday interrupted him.

"Dayo, he's here! They're both here! I've got to go!"

"No, Thursday, please, not now! I need you now!"

"Don't use my name! Mush saw me, my broer! I've got to go!"

"Thursday, no, give me the power switch! I need the switch!"

"I've got to go."

And despite Dayo's pleading and reasoning, the line went dead. He thought he heard a car screech in the tumult, but couldn't have been sure. As good as the lamps were there were certain technicalities involved in illuminating them at the same time. He had switched in stronger bulbs, which meant they would run out of power faster, and he used the hydroponic foils to amplify the light. The lamps would in theory beam their light towards a disco ball, which would shower it throughout the neighborhood. He needed the beams to converge precisely, and he'd carelessly given Thursday the main switch to hold, which he'd promptly walked off with, twitching with paranoia.

The bikers and school kids were by now angrily clamoring for the Springboks to make their promised appearance. Parents shepherded their children inside with candles; there were nursery rhymes. Sleep. Then the school boys were taunting the trancehounds with their glow-sticks and fire batons, and the gangbangers were profiting in the darkness by stealing from everyone, and the armed response arrived with their yellow lights, and the cops with their red and blue ones and their sirens.

Without the power switch Dayo would have to rewire all the lamps. By that time the evening would be over. Rage, pure and Nigerian, purely present, purely there, began surging through Dayo's hunched form. He was angry at this failure. His spine straightened and he stomped towards a pile of rubble. He picked up a brick. Gauging its heft, he threw it with all of his ecstatic strength into the nearest lamp.

The projectile missed its target and instead hit the lamp's aluminum collar. The lamp dropped down, halted by the width of the post at the base. He moved forward to smash it, but an enterprising bergie swiftly plucked the lamp from its collar.

"Fifty rand," the drunk said.

Dayo tackled the man full-on with a running start, feeling his shoulder drive into the drunk's chest and smelling his fetid sweat. They rolled on the ground, the bergie scratching at his neck, until a flash of light blinded him. The bergie sensed an opening and sunk his toothless gums into Dayo's forearm. Dayo stumbled off, blinking his eyes. When he looked back he saw that the lamp had come alive. It was illuminating the tarmac around them. The drunk began a slow, stumbling march down the street with the lamp in his hand hurling insults in Dayo's direction.

But that was it! The bergie had done it! Free of the lamp post, which had grounded the charge, the light was working. Dayo began running from lamp post to lamp post, snipping wires, pleading with people to hold up the lamps in their hands. He offered out sums of money he did not have. He promised chocolates and pints of cane spirit. Within a short while, he had assembled an army of drunks, passers-by, and hippies bonded by a chain of shimmering blue light.

The forty lamps sent the moonlight shooting into the disco ball, scattering it throughout Obz. A chorus of barking dogs struck up at once. The police, who had earlier torn after the gang-bangers, lost their sense of color in the light, and lowered their sjamboks, unable to tell black from white, rich from poor. The bikers put down their rebel flags and the hippies doused their flaming batons. And the parents, who had locked their security gates and their burglar bars as they put the children to sleep, set down the braii-forks and butcher knives they had held ready against intruders, and peered, cautiously, outside at the suburban moonscape.

Dayo dialed his father again on the cell phone. "Come on, Dad, pick up!" He left a message—"Dad, the lamp worked! The lamps worked! Tell the tour to look up!" He was feeling present, he was feeing there and his father was gone.

Slowly the denizens of Obz came out to see Dayo's lamps: car guards in fluorescent pinnies, painters, sculptors, goths, teachers, Malikis, Anglicans, Catholics, Jews, pagans perfumed with Nag Champa, booksellers, dagga dealers, capoeiristas, live-in domestics, cash-in-transit men, waitrons scooping up their tips, woodworkers, plumbers, conveyancers, sound engineers, publicans, photographers with flashes and, then, confused by the light, without them, PAs, actors and actresses, doctors, guitarists, graphic designers, beauticians, trinket peddlers, nurses, cobblers, pan-African dancers, ballet dancers, modern dancers, students and professors, overland tour operators, slam poets, and jacks of all trades. They came out.

Dayo tried his father one last time, and this time the call went through. He heard belabored breathing and static. "Dad, Dad, that you?" He cupped his hand over his free ear to drown out the noise of the crowds. "Dad?"

"Your father needs help." It was a woman's voice, husky; garbled.

"Dad? Dad? Who is this?"

"Your father needs help. Call an ambulance."

"Who is this? Where's my father?"

"He's in the McClean."

And their cohabitants: the dogs, the chittering rats, the mice, the feral cats, the stick-bugs, the rose beetles, mosquitoes pursing their probosci, moths, crickets, geckos, and ants. They came out. Watching the moon emerge not from the sky but from the streets, hands waving in the light, shadow puppeting, and Okeke toting his dundun talking drum with his Nigerian tenants. Squeezing out rhythms into the blackness between the stars. They came out. For it had begun.

A Hundred and Seventy

Present Day
South Africa

As in a dream, Thursday Malaysius is running and Mush only walking but somehow narrowing the distance between them. Thursday hurls himself over a garden wall, cutting his palms on the shards of glass. Someone close by shouts at him and he flees over the opposite wall onto another street. This street is clear but the walls are too low to hide. He realizes this is a mistake, that it would have been safer to stay in the crowd, and tries to think of a way back to the main thoroughfare. But on the other side of the road there is the long brick wall of a factory that stretches on forever and he can't think of how to traverse it. His hands are hurting now and when he looks his palms are dripping black blood in the shadows.

The narrow streets with their double-parked cars shrink his sense of space. The clouds above, which usually brighten the neighborhood from the tangerine reflection of the street lamps, coat the streets in stillness. Far down the street he sees the spark of static electricity as two lovers embrace in neoprene jerseys. There are no silhouettes, only forms. Constable Viljoen has circled around to head him off, and Thursday is unable to scale the brick wall of the factory. He can only watch one of them, either Mush or Viljoen; this is their genius, two spiders attacking from both sides of the web. He decides that if he is going to be punched, he will want to see the fist. He turns towards Mush to deprive him of the satisfaction, his own fists smarting as he clenches them. Each step of Mush's closes off his escape like a boxer.

"Where you going, Hampton?" Viljoen taunts him. "Hey, Hampton! We want to talk with you!"

There is the deep scream of an engine. Thursday looks up into the black sky expecting to see a jet plane. The sound comes closer and he ducks, feeling the wind of the turbine. Still he cannot see it.

"Thursday!" the girl shouts right behind him. "Get on!"

It is Ip's daughter Seneca on her motorcycle, with the headlight off. But Thursday trusts no one and refuses to fly from one web into another.

"It's okay," she says. "Dad made you a partner."

He does not move. He is not accustomed to making these kinds of decisions. He is used to having Leon decide for him, but Leon never told him how to handle the cops or a girl on a motorcycle. Viljoen is running towards him and offering to buy him another lamp.

"A hundred and seventy, right, Hampton? I've got it right here in my pocket."

"Thursday," Seneca insists, "Don't listen to him. It's a trap. Get on!"

Where are you, Leon? Thursday wants to know. What would you do?

The moonlight erupts above the Community Centre from Dayo's lamps and shoots off the mirrored ball into the neighborhood. Thursday becomes suddenly aware, looking into the pattern of the bricks of the factory wall, of the scent of Seneca's perfume in the exhaust. Maybe it is this smell that makes him commit. Maybe he is afraid of what Mush will do with his fists. Either way he climbs onto the bike as Seneca peels out in a roar of two-cycle pistons and gears. She mounts the curb behind some parked cars and Viljoen draws his pistol.

Viljoen fires twice, shattering the windshields as Mush, mesmerized by the moonlight, slowly joins him. Seneca clears the sidewalk and screeches along the road towards Salt River. Looking back, Thursday sees Mush coaxing his partner's gun down in the moonshine, pointing at the sky.

"No," Mush's lips say, "look."

They race ahead. Thursday closes his eyes, smelling the leather of the girl's racing jacket. He thinks of Dayo's moonlight and all the proud perlemoen he will nurture, and how he's never held a girl like this before, and how, with his unmade mop streaming in the wind, roaring through the moonscape with all this fragile potential, Leon has finally let him be.

Abuja

Present Day
Nigeria

A short flight, but a long drive in the evening, as the yellow danfo mini-buses careened across the dirt-smattered lanes in a city of dim lights. Lagos: dampened, soft under the rain, moss on the walls, a landscape under a special gravity, heavy with people. Those were Melissa's impressions in the ride from the airport to Victoria Island, and then back again the following morning, the sun brighter but the feel much the same: only more people. The President had been able to offer the private jet of a friend to the capital of Abuja, but solely one-way. On the return trip the President could offer her a guest-of-state visa and a chauffer who could accompany her to Lagos if she paid the bill.

Béatrice had insisted upon accompanying Melle to Lagos, and had arranged the clothing and, with the help of the President's aide, the visa and the suite at the Hilton. The President had promised to ensure the rest ran smoothly after the brief stop over in Lagos. And it had. Melissa made the mistake of purchasing a Hausa headdress at the dutyfree shop, because the baggage handler pestered her to provide certification from a museum that it was not a stolen artifact, hoping for a bribe, until the President's aide had intervened. In Abuja there were none of the potholes of Lagos and much fewer people. They drove past kilometers of planted cashuarina trees, where parishioners were gathering after an all-night event in the soccer stadium, and circular huts could be seen through the foliage lining the dirt frontage roads. Mountains erupted out of the fertile landscape, with green trees clinging to their sides. The mountains had a red-kneed dynamism and seemed to be continuously pushing themselves from the earth.

Not for the first time Melle was glad for the niqab. Her tears flowed freely beneath it until she caught the aide watching in the rear view mirror, and stopped. She had not wanted to shoot the scientist and had called an ambulance. She was not a religious woman but the sight of the

271

moonlight rising from the neighborhood beyond the Royal Observatory portended something—what it was she was not sure—only that she knew she could not kill Wale in cold blood. In the pandemonium of the multitudes and the cops in the suburb, Béatrice had escorted Melissa from the Observatory, knowing not to ask questions.

The hotel suite in Abuja had been designed in the early Eighties, with a king-sized bed in the middle of the floor and drapes that could be pulled around the bed to partition it from the room. There was a full dining set and Jacuzzi bath, and satellite television. The view was of a pentagonal pool, some tennis courts, and the mountains behind it. On her bed in the hotel suite the President's aide had provided an international SIM card for her cell phone, with enough credit to dial internationally. Melissa inserted the new card into her phone and dialed the aide, who explained he would pick her up in the early evening. Although they normally shared the same bed, Béatrice had been allocated a much smaller room and Melissa did not want to visit her.

"You are crazy to go to Abuja," Béatrice said. "The moon is waning and you will not have the same influence. No one knows what happens there."

But it was the last place that Bello had been seen. He had disappeared in the capital city and if anyone knew where he was it would be the President. Béatrice made Melissa promise that if her father was not in Abuja then she would never look for him again.

For the first time in years, Melissa turned on the television and scanned for news reports about herself. There was nothing, no mention of the moon that had fallen into Cape Town or the fate of the wounded scientist. She drifted off to sleep.

The President's aide fetched them as dusk set in. As Melissa had requested, he did not use her real name. They passed through the lobby where there was a flagship Skoda sedan on display and a multicultural queue at the cash machines. The hotel bar was packed with guests enjoying peanuts and green bottles of Star beer and black bottles of

Guinness, with a jazz pianist tickling the ivories. Some eyebrows lifted as she walked by, for Melissa and Béatrice were a striking pair in their matching niqabs and could not stifle their graceful gaits.

Melissa felt the humidity rolling off the car park and took refuge in the air conditioning of the aide's car. "How far is it to see the President?" she asked.

"Not far," the aide replied. "We are going to a function first, where the President has declared you the guest of honor."

Béatrice immediately began to protest, but the aide shrugged his shoulders, stating that it was out of his hands, and the driver continued forward. They passed a giant golden mosque with minarets, then further along the central church, which the aide explained had taken fifteen years to build. The shingles on the roof were made from a copper that wouldn't tarnish; no expense had been spared. By six-thirty the myriad streets were dark. Compared to what Melissa had seen of Lagos there was less poverty in Abuja, but she had a feeling the people were simply hidden. For a city of seven million she had seen enough homes for maybe a hundred thousand.

They arrived at an enormous, columned convention center, where a troupe of photographers was taking instant photographs of the guests alighting from their vehicles. Here Béatrice refused to open the door until the photographers were cleared, and further demanded that they be given their own table at the banquet.

Although many of the guests were smiling in their suits and agbadas and glinting headwraps, all of them seemed tired of each other. Waiters scurried about with hors d'oevres, malt sodas, electric red Chapmans sodas, and fresh juices. Flags of African countries draped the walls. There was the smell of fish, delicate colognes and perfume, of polished shoe leather. Béatrice helped herself to some nuts on the table.

A recorded announcement blared: "Presenting the Honorable Speaker of the Federal Territory, Rahim Odonkor."

A side door opened and a stout, elegantly dressed man entered wearing a mauve three piece suit with a matching hat.

"It's him!" She raised herself from her seat.

Béatrice coaxed her back down. "He said his name was Odonkor."

"It's Bello! I know it."

He had put on weight. He was lighter skinned than Melissa remembered and sported wire-rimmed glasses. Bello's hands were large for his body, and he was now using them to shake the hands of the guests seated at the tables nearest the microphone. Here was the man who was supposed to have disappeared, standing right before her, looking healthy as could be. His voice was buttery, his tongue moving over words with comfort. He had an infectious laugh. Every time he chuckled everyone else did too.

"We are in the difficult position," he joked to the audience, "of having a guest of honor whom I can neither name nor of whom you may take a photograph. Nonetheless she is well-known to all in this room of having glorified our God-given African beauty, elevated us from the exotic to the sublime. Let us raise our glasses, then, to our flag, and to all the flags of our continent, the wardrobe of our guest, the most celebrated ambassador of all our peoples." He raised his glass to an imaginary point in the air. "Cheers."

Melissa had grown used to having eyes upon her and could ignore them. She did it now. It was Béatrice who disliked the attention.

Bello then apologized that the President would be unable to attend the function, owing to reasons of political expediency. Like the guest of honor, the President rarely made public appearances. He nevertheless encouraged the guests to make merry and enjoy the President's generosity. Most of the guests remained, although a few rose from their tables and left, evidently upset at the slight.

"I do not like him," Béatrice whispered. "Let us go."

How many lives had Bello crushed? Yet here he was, safe and commanding a room of dignitaries with ease. There was a dance show, with strong rhythms and wiry dancers and a man who could flex his shoulders like a bird, and songs about Abuja, and a comedian called Meatchops who made raucous jokes about the differences between Hausas, Igbos, and Yorubas that Melissa neither understood nor cared for. A large video screen was lowered at the rear wall beneath the flags that began, Abuja, its pristine drinking water, sophisticated highways, glorious pillars of religion, and towering convention halls that have hosted the world's leaders, showing the Queen of England hobbling up a red carpet, a gallant horse show of hooded sultans from Sokoto. Mid-way through the ceremony the power went out and, whereas there had been nervousness in Cape Town, Meatchops the comedian joked about praying to electric generators, and when the power returned, ten minutes later, people served themselves at a buffet dinner as if the evening had been uninterrupted. They were hurried, eating fast, passing business cards, disappointed that they could not curry favor with the President, and in an hour the banquet was declared finished.

Béatrice was becoming increasingly uncomfortable. She frowned at the guests and remained suspicious of Bello. "Melissa, please, let's go. I do not like this. We should leave."

"I am not leaving until I find my father."

"I don't trust him," she continued. "The moon is too soft. You won't have influence."

"It's too late."

"Your father will be different. You were just a girl then, Melle. You are a woman now. Things will not be the same."

Not after these years of searching, Melissa thought, not after what she'd done to Wale. She also knew she couldn't search for her father and fight Béatrice too.

"You're right, Béatrice. I must do this alone." She ordered Béatrice to take a flight to France that evening. She refused to discuss the matter further as Bello came to take her arm.

They took separate cars, with Bello riding ahead in a cream-colored limousine and some motorcycles flanking his vehicle on each side. The caravan stopped after twenty minutes at a gate where ten men were sitting around chatting. There was a loud discussion and eventually the gate opened and they motored along a paved driveway with a number of large structures lit in the distance across well-kempt lawns. They stopped at a building that was indistinguishable from the others in the darkness. It was Bello who opened her door, smiling and agreeable. He enfolded her hand in his giant paws.

"Welcome, Melle, welcome to Abuja!" he said, shaking all the while. "It is an honor to be visited by such a world-renowned guest."

Melissa did not lift her veil. "Thank you, Honorable Speaker, but I do not enjoy flattery."

"Please, call me Rahim. There is a difference, Melle, between flattery and reflecting the truth, or, in your condition, the light."

She was a whole hand taller than him. She also noticed, as she assured him that the arrangements had been fine, that he had changed his shirt in the car ride. It was now of bright red silk.

"Excellent," Bello said. "If you'd allow me to indulge, I'd much prefer walking the grounds than sitting again after all that pomp and circumstance."

He was providing her with an opportunity to thank him for being the guest of honor, but, not having wanted to attend the party in the first place, she did not. Bello attempted to grab her arm, causing her to tense, and smoothly slid his hand into his pocket as if that had been his intention all along. Small spotlights had been ensconced in the bushes and trees, giving the grounds the air of a sculpture garden, with elaborate topiaries carved into the hedgerows and shrubs. Now and again, a worker would pass with a gardening tool in his hand, bowing slightly in deference to Bello, who explained that the President paid a nighttime crew to cultivate certain plants, thereby increasing employment. But many of the passersby paid him no particular attention or even seemed to recognize him.

"You live here?" she asked.

"At the request of the President," he said. "If I had my way, I would live in a much smaller compound, but the military men knew how to take good care of themselves. This is all borne of the oil boom in the Eighties. I am not, you will find, a typical politician. I detest largesse. What I desire is harnessing the potential of our country. We have enormous resources in Nigeria—natural and human—and that is what gets me up in the morning."

For all his high-minded talk, Bello didn't walk with the ease of a person who had earned his success. And Melissa was starting to recognize that he could bend even the worst news into lilting ribbons of uplifting phrases.

"Your facsimile," he prompted casually, "indicated that you wish to organize a charitable fashion show to benefit the people of Abuja."

"I regret that I have come with ulterior motives."

"That's nothing to worry about, Melle. May I call you Melle? We all have ulterior motives," he smiled. "Charity, provided there is an element of sustainability, is always welcome in Abuja."

Each of the buildings they were passing could have served as a church. There were wings jutting into the shadows, high plaster walls, small square windows with tinted glass. There was no way of telling which was a domicile and which an office. The palm trees, shrubs, and terraformed lawns were much more appealing. Bello would bend over now and again to sniff a flower, or tear off a dead leaf. He maintained a constant chatter while speaking with apparent sincerity and passion.

They passed a security guard in military uniform with an automatic rifle on his shoulder and Bello uttered a few words to him. The guard left guffawing. Bello took Melle to a greenhouse and showed her the President's prize vegetables, before escorting her to an array of solar panels, which the President used to power the compound during blackouts instead of a diesel generator. He went into excessive detail about the small medical clinic, where he assured her they had the best midwives in the country. They paused again before one of the giant structures.

"I have always found it unfair," Bello said seriously, "what happened to you, Melle."

Melissa stopped to look him in the eye, wondering if he knew more than he'd let on. Did he know why she had come?

"You were orphaned at a young age, wasn't it? Fashion models in the global North, in the Western global North," he clarified, "are in an unfortunate position. It is a question of the homely and the comely. Northerners don't know what to do with people who are comely, so they tell them to become models. As if it's too painful to admit that people can be more physically attractive and have the same passions and desires. The same needs."

So he wasn't talking about her father, Melissa thought. But his words were still lulling her into listening. Never had she been in the presence of such an orator. It was as if he was watching each quiver of her lips and choosing his words accordingly.

"Because Northerners think," Bello was saying, "that it would be too easy for beautiful people, charmed with physical gifts, to live the same lives as them. And it would not be fair." He pinched a dead petal from an African violet. "And then society's jewels—its orphans—are mocked when they fall into the addiction of self-doubt. Yet the homely would all deep down want to be as beautiful as the comely. As you, Melle."

Caught up in his empathic monologue, Melle thought she could, in her weakness, in his understanding, find some direction. That had happened to her: she had been abandoned by her friends because of her skin, she had failed at school in France, and she was now in the vicious gaze of the paparazzi. Her addiction? What was her addiction?

Bello added that no such thing would happen in Nigeria, that she would be celebrated and valued as an intelligent woman of means.

Then he proposed that she accept his hand in marriage. This bold step, which might have beguiled a less determined woman, startled her from his spell.

"I am sorry but you are mistaken, Rahim."

Unphased, he quickly pointed how he had been shortlisted to become the next Minister of the Federal Territories, based on his unorthodox thinking and integrity, his principled stance against corruption, and would like nothing more than to share the demands and benefits of his office with her, a fellow Muslim.

"I'm not Muslim."

"But you wear a niqab."

"It is for fashion."

"I see, then, it is for adornment. You could convert—I would have the sultan arrange a ceremony suitable to your tastes. I am a progressive Muslim, not one of these women's-work types. You would be encouraged to grow, to explore. I am a firm believer in independence, pragmatism, self-actualization—"

"—I am looking for my father, Mlungisi Tebogo."

Bello was suddenly and uncharacteristically at a loss for words. "What are you talking about? You're from France. Your passport is from France. Your name is Melle. I signed your visa myself."

"I changed my name, something you are familiar with." Bello began walking wide paths around the security guards, shushing her to lower her voice. She ignored him. "I would like you to tell me where he is," she added. "I met you in Bulawayo in 1993, Mr. Bello. You came to my father's house and asked for his help. His name is Mlungisi Tebogo."

"My name is Rahim Odonkor. You heard it announced this evening."

She removed Wale's ibeji doll from her purse. Then she passed him the statuette, watching his face closely. Bello held it in his palm, puzzled. But as he examined the figurine, his furrowed brow slowly relaxed. Wrinkles spread across his face and soon he was all smiles.

"Do you know what this is?" he said.

"An ibeji doll."

"That's right. But it's not just any ibeji doll. It was made by a very special carver. All of the dolls were. This hasn't been seen since—" He paused, pulling the statuette close to his chest.

"Since when?"

"I suppose the cat's out of the bag, isn't it?" He took a deep breath. "Since it disappeared in Cape Town. She will be so thrilled! It's superstition, of course. A token of memory, crenellated into wood. My people, you must understand, have numerous traditions, ancient and modern, that we adopt in syncretic harmony with the demands of modern life—"

"You were there. Your name is Nurudeen Bello and you worked with my father."

The joy began to fade from Bello's face. In response, Melle removed the veil from her niqab now, and stood in the open air, where faint moonlight struggled through the humid air.

"That was a long time ago," he said quietly. "You should forget about it."

"My father told me you would help me get treatment for my skin."

Bello smiled. "Ah, but then you wouldn't be who you are today, would you? I have fond memories of your father."

She felt relieved that Bello wouldn't deny that he'd known her father. That was at least a start. She removed a strap of her dress from her shoulder, forcing him to remain in place. "You haven't answered my question, Mr. Bello. Where is he?"

Bello chuckled, tilting back his head. For he now knew that he had information she desired, information he would guard more closely since she had just rejected his marriage proposal. Melissa regretted having turned him down so quickly.

"We are wracked by possibilities, aren't we, Melle? There are parallel constructions, complementary influences. Hypotheticals. You must understand it was a critical time in our nation's history. We shook out the corrupt and separated the wheat from the chaff. Your father was riding on the crest of this wave of change, in which sacrifices, pivotal and plenary, had to be made—"

He had taken on that tone again, the one he used to win over politicians and funders—and nearly herself—and she knew he was simply going to evade the question. She decided to try another tack: "What about the Brain Gain program?"

"I don't know what—"

"I've seen the names," she said. "I know all about the scientists you lured here. I know about the space program. They're all dead now."

Bello opened his mouth, changed his mind, and, with determination, began pacing towards the parking area.

"Melle, there are some stones that are better left unturned. For your own safety, I will have a driver escort you to the hotel. You are Melle now, and I am Rahim Odonkor. I will forget we spoke about this."

She ran before him. In Observatory, all she had needed was a sleeve to captivate Wale, but in the humid half-light in Abuja, she was forced to reveal much more of herself than she normally allowed. Both shoulders now. It was enough to keep him talking, but not to stop moving forward.

To her surprise he began smiling. "Those were halcyon days of paradigm-shifting visions. Wale and his colleagues were the most capable scientists Nigeria would have ever seen. We would have harnessed the potential of our most accomplished expatriates. We were going to leapfrog the global North..."

This time Bello interrupted himself, and, in so doing, revealed one of the secrets to his power, that he had the uncommon ability to string together persiflage and flattering words while thinking about something entirely different. For he pointed his finger in the air: "Fish, yes, fish! The President's aide told me that you didn't eat a morsel at dinner. Why don't we grab some fresh fish? Would you like that, some fresh fish? The chef keeps a pond."

"I am hardly in the mood—"

"Ah, but moods are unpredictable. You will not know your mood until the fish is in front of you, steaming and seasoned with our local spices, a hodgepodge of flavors from our peoples..." and on he went until they were at the front door of a building. He rang the doorbell and a butler opened the door, tucking in his shirttails after evidently awaking from sleep. He bowed slightly and Bello said a few words to him. He seemed almost piqued by Bello's presence, as if he was a guest who had overstayed his welcome.

"Please excuse the formality," Bello said.

The butler performed a thorough search of Melissa's purse until Bello intervened, and they walked to a capacious dining room with a table that could seat fifty people comfortably. Hundreds of carvings lined the walls, with a Nigerian flagged draped in each corner. After some time, the butler opened a rear door and hissed some words. The chef, also looking sleepy, came carrying a basin with four or five whiskered catfish sloshing about, vying for water.

"May we take this one?" Bello asked, pointing at a fat one.

The chef nodded disparagingly. Like the butler, he didn't seem happy to be doting on Bello, and Melle had the unusual sense that Bello was a guest in his own compound. Bello continued talking in his hyperbole, looking not at her but at the table, sipping at a malt soda and flicking a speck from the pristine tablecloth. She told him everything that Wale had advised her, watching him for reactions, for any clue about whether she could expect him to tell the truth. His manner changed from expecting to wed a world-renowned model to a man cringing in expectation of a blow.

"I never made it back to Cape Town," he said, mildly interested. "It was tit-for-tat during those pivotal times, a zero sum purge, the intractability of an illegitimate regime, the conflation of interests and needs, power absolutely corrupted…"

"But Wale killed them all."

"No, it wasn't Wale. He wouldn't hurt a fly. He was a basketball fan, if I recall. A bureaucrat and a skilled scientist."

I would never kill anyone, he'd said to her. I'm only a scientist. And she shot him. She killed an innocent man. She robbed the son of his father.

Her throat felt as if it was filling with gauze.

"Are you feeling alright?" Bello asked.

"Water, please. One squeeze of lime."

The butler scurried from the room and they were silent until he returned. She sipped and the bite of the lime juice made her feel that Wale might have survived. Perhaps the ambulance had saved him.

Then she thought: forget Wale. Forget him anyway. This is about Daddy. Focus on Daddy or you'll be alone forever.

"Why did you contact my father in Zimbabwe?"

"I needed his services. You might say that your father and I shared the same ideals. You might say that we were too idealistic, treading, like the freedom fighters of yore, against the rip tides of the status quo."

The room suddenly went dark. Melissa could hear footsteps and the rear door to the kitchen swing open. She heard the butler hiss some more orders and a few moments later he returned with a flashlight.

"It's normal," Bello said. "We have an enormous problem of illegal tapping that drains the grid. The President is trying to clean it up. In a moment they'll switch over to the solar generator."

She cared only about using light, or darkness, to her advantage. Bello had told her nothing so far, confirmed only that he knew Wale. She wanted to corner him, to pin his lofty words down to a reality. "My father told me to meet you in Paris. But when I arrived you weren't there. I had no money and no one to look after me. I didn't even speak French. You'd promised us that you would help me get treatment, but Mrs. Niyangabo put me in an orphanage. How could you do that to us?"

He seemed to cower, slightly, at hearing the name. He beckoned Melissa towards him with her finger, throwing a suspicious glance at the butler. "I was," he whispered, "I was in prison."

The lights flickered for a moment and remained off. Finally, the power switched on. Diesel, not solar, as he had said. The weak light did not help her.

"But you've been here for years."

"Yes," he agreed, matter-of-factly. He went on to talk about various things but Melissa had learned by now to sift through his words and knew that he wasn't saying anything at all. His pose, staid and falsely noble, took her to France all those years back, for it reminded her of the august portrait of Bello that had hung in the living room in the suburb of Bandoufle.

"Wale told me that you wanted to change the way things were done in Nigeria. But now," she added, "you work for the government. Quite comfortably, it seems to me."

Bello was tapping his fingers on the table, not really listening. He seemed to be waiting for something, glancing at the front door, then from the door to the kitchen. When it wasn't coming he began whispering again.

"I was tortured there." As if taking a cue from Melissa, he unbuttoned his collar and pulled up his undershirt. He showed her various scars on his torso, legs and ankles, some of them quite deep, and in doing so became less and less confident, practically ducking beneath the table as he described the beatings. The pain of these memories seemed to be the first sincere gesture he'd made the entire evening.

"What do you mean?" she asked.

He shrugged. "In prison. I was caught in the crackdown before I could warn the others. There was a groundswell of democratic energy and elections had been held. I thought the nation was changing. No one even knew the Ibeji existed. Not even your father."

"What is the Ibeji?"

"Look around you."

She looked more closely now at the carvings on the wall. There were ornamental masks, and headdresses, but now she realized that the entire room was ringed with ibeji dolls like the one Wale had given her.

He spread his hands wide: "This compound is Ibeji. It's the counterterrorism and intelligence unit, unofficial, unannounced, but very much alive. Ibeji was created by the late President Rawlson Bimini in 1993 to purge the country of all its enemies, at home and abroad, before he seized power. We were the enemies abroad. Of course, at the time I thought President Bimini's response was heavy-handed. But now"— and now he began speaking much more loudly, pumping his fist in the air—"I realize that sometimes leadership requires rash decisions. There is perspective that is gained in steering the ship of state, wisdom cultivated. And while the keel beneath might swing from the left or the right, it must be there, keeping the ship afloat. Brain Gain—your father and I, Wale and his team—would have smashed the keel. We were going to tap Nigeria's minds and not its oil. Our project would have taken the ship into uncharted waters, waters combed by industrial pirates and mercenaries."

Bello truly seemed to believe his own words. She could tell that he had really wanted Brain Gain to work. Wale was right: it had not been a scam.

"What about the others?"

"They—they were soon caught by Ibeji, too."

Melissa suddenly remembered what her father had written her, that he had been betrayed. Bello had said it himself, that he had joined the administration. And he'd been caught before the others.

"It was you! You sold them all out, Bello! You betrayed your own program and then changed your name!"

She tore off her gloves and threw herself upon him. His chair fell over backwards. He knocked his head against the ground as she scratched at him with her nails. The butler ran over with two kitchen attendants to pull her off. They tied her down, kicking and scratching, to a chair, so tight that the twine dug into her wrists.

Bello searched the tiles for his eyeglasses. Eventually he picked them up. One of the lenses had popped out and the wires had bent, so they slipped off his nose, and he set them on the table. "I didn't betray anyone," he whispered, squinting. "Brain Gain was accused of being a coup d'état of the intelligentsia. And President Bimini was right. It was a coup—a coup of the mind. That's why the Ibeji eliminated them. I'd planned for Nigeria to be ruled by its acumen and not by the wallet or the family. After President Bimini seized power, Ibeji began the worst crackdown the country has ever seen. Our luminaries were hanged, our leaders jailed, all while the rest of the world watched. When I confessed our intentions under torture, I revealed nothing but the truth. Our program was not traitorous, not perfidious, but bold—"

"Where is he?" she interrupted. "Where is my father?"

He ignored her as he gained momentum: "—and since then—since then, yes, bold!—I have spent every waking day trying to make good on the sacrifices that were made. President Bimini died fifteen years ago, from a heart attack, and new Presidents have come and gone—yet Ibeji lives on. There are hundreds of operatives. Each of these dolls represents a living, breathing member. There are no nations which are transparent, Melle. While I have been here, I can say with pride that I have cracked the opacity of our country and moved it, however modestly, towards translucency. We have legions of hungry young entrepreneurs lending their minds to our development. Our mobile networks are coursing through Nigeria, eradicating poverty by linking the marsh to the river. Nigeria just launched our fifth satellite into space. Our fifth! It's not Brain Gain—the satellites are built by the Chinese—but I am proud of my contribution to the future of Nigeria."

She spat at him. "Sacrifices? You could have sacrificed yourself! You sold them out to live like a king!"

"No, my appointment as Speaker of the Federal Territory was contingent upon stringent conditions." He glanced again at the door.

"Why do you keep looking at the door?"

"I am under house arrest," he confessed. "My every move is watched. But it's the price that I paid for my country."

"Your country," she sneered, trying to dislodge the twine on her arm. The butler disappeared into the kitchen and reported that the power had come back on. He inquired if they should switch back over to the grid.

"Let it go for a few minutes," Bello said, seeming to give it real thought. "Then we'll see. You can untie her now. You'll behave, won't you?"

Melissa didn't reply as the butler begrudgingly snipped her bonds with scissors. As if none of the conversation had happened, as if Melissa was still interested, Bello tried to engage her in small talk about Abuja and suggested the convention center as a possible venue for her charity event. She watched Bello in disbelief. Servants brought bowls of jolof rice and the catfish as long as her forearm, with the eyes cloudy from grilling. He pushed the plate in front of Melissa in a paternal gesture. Then he took a knife and began cutting the fish, glancing at the front door from time to time.

"Who are you waiting for?"

"Who you wanted. I am not the one who can tell you about your father. The head of Ibeji is coming to join us." He tugged at his collar. She pressed him for more, but he said that he'd already revealed too much and waxed about the succulent flesh of the fish that was imported from the Yangtze in China for its flavor. A kitchen attendant brought fresh lime water. Disgusted, Melissa pushed back her chair and headed to the front door.

"I'm afraid you can't leave," Bello said. But he remained in his seat. She opened the front door to find two uniformed soldiers with rifles. They raised them until she backed away and returned to the table.

"What will happen to me?"

"I suggest you eat while you can. She will be here shortly."

He himself ate ravenously, salting the fish at times, squeezing lemon here and there, all as if he might never eat catfish again.

Then they heard voices at the front door. No one knocked, but the butler quick-stepped to open it.

Melissa watched the woman heel into the room. She felt bonded to her chair as if the twine had never been cut from her wrists. The woman glanced briefly at Bello and then trained her eyes on Melissa. She had aged slightly, the rouge on her cheeks giving a caked, matted look, covering up what the years had done to her. Her hair was blacker than Melissa remembered it, perhaps dyed. But her gaze had lost none of its clinical frigidity. It was a gaze that was assessing tendons, tissues, valves, and ventricles, and considering how to sever the life flowing through them.

I am not afraid of you anymore, Melissa thought.

"Please, be lenient!" Bello whined. "Look! Look what she found!"

He handed her the ibeji doll. For the first time, Mrs. Niyangabo softened in Melissa's presence. She reached out her hand and stroked the doll's hair as if it was a real person. "This was Remi's," she said. "He was one of our first. Now we can honor his commitment. We'll hold a full ceremony for him."

She held the statuette for the butler to take. He approached her, bowed, and shuttled the doll into the kitchen.

"What will you do with her?" Bello asked.

"What she deserves!"

Melissa rose from her chair to remove her shoes. She peeled down her stockings, unzipped her niqab, shaking her shoulders until it fell to the ground. Then she unfastened her bra, the diesel-powered light illuminating her form. It was the body that had turned lovers against themselves, taken her from Paris to Cape Town, and brought her here, naked before them. The comely standing before the homely.

"You will not touch me," she said.

But Mrs. Niyangabo only wrinkled her nose in disgust as Bello rushed to Melissa's side.

"Please, let her go."

"Ah, but she knows too much now. I gave her a chance to get away. I gave her a chance to live. And she abused our hospitality."

She shouted for the guards. Four soldiers burst into the room, but halted at seeing the naked woman before them.

"Don't stop! Take her out of here! It's time she joined her father."

"No!" Bello said. "Leave her be!"

"You impudent little weasel! How dare you question me! I've had enough of you. Go on, then, take him too."

One of the guards stepped forward and seized Melissa's elbow in a painful grip, forcing her towards the door. She looked over her shoulder and Bello was being cornered, too, and he was speaking quickly, thrusting the dolls in their faces, imploring the guards to end the reign of darkness by seizing this sacred moment for the bright future of their children and their country.

Transplant

Present Day
South Africa

Dayo's lamp demonstration did not make the international press, but the neighborhood of Observatory appeared in the headlines, for it was the last place that fashion sensation Melle had been seen in South Africa. A photographer leaked that Melle had stormed off the set at a beachside photoshoot in Cape Town, and a taxi driver admitted that he had given her a lift to Obz. A policeman had then confused her with Dayo's lamp demonstration, drawing upon several unreliable drunken witnesses, and the popular theory was that Melle had channeled the light of the moon by stripping off her clothes, blinding the neighborhood in her radiance. Dayo didn't mind that the article hadn't mentioned him—his lamps weren't ready and he'd narrowly avoided a burn-out as it was. There would be plenty of time to make another demonstration.

He had since kept vigil at his father's bedside and would walk the wide, sanitized corridors of the hospital while waiting for an improvement in his condition. The Groote Schuur building was a white leviathan of concrete and glass that dominated the upper half of Observatory, with Devil's Peak being washed by the clouds above it.

Thursday Malaysius seemed less afraid of the cops, and had offered to help watch over Wale so Dayo could get some rest. Sometimes he'd arrive with his girl Seneca, but he usually came alone, asking innumerable questions of the doctors and nurses about the intravenous needles and titration techniques, looking for new ways to keep his abalone healthy. His abalone had its own street name now—Obz—and was setting a new standard for flavor and quality. Dayo appreciated the help and Thursday promised to fetch him if anything happened.

Once, after Thursday had replaced him at the bedside, Dayo had wandered down an old wing of the hospital and found the tiny Heart Transplant Museum. The attendant had been so starved for visitors that she'd waived the entrance fee and showed Dayo a video about Dr.

Christiaan Barnard, the first doctor in the world to conduct a successful heart transplant. Barnard had experimented on forty-nine dogs before moving on to people. The first human donor had been hit by a car a few blocks from Dayo's house, and Barnard had transplanted her heart into a burly man, where it had thumped for two weeks before the man's body ultimately rejected the tissue and he died. The dashing Barnard had immediately gone on to tour the world, missing his patient's funeral, and Groote Schuur hospital began swapping dozens of hearts a year to people of all creeds and classes. Like Melle, Dr. Barnard had once been on the cover of every magazine.

Dayo wouldn't have cared about any of this before his father's attack, but now he visited the museum everyday with one of his lamps. The museum had meticulously recreated the original operating theatre with wax mannequins, rosy-cheeked nurses and doctors in their scrubs. There had once been a stench of formaline and ether, of the medicines that anaesthetists in those days had administered equally to children and elephants, but now there was only a damp mildewy smell.

Dayo liked to sit in the operating theatre in the dark. If there was a blackout, he'd walk right in; if the power was on, he'd switch off the light. He still needed to design a proper mounting piece for the lamp, so he'd begun working with cuttings from his father's bamboo patch, trying out different configurations in the theatre. He'd illuminate the lamp and watch the shadows breathe life into the wax nurses, almost hearing the squeeze of the metal clamps on the arteries and tissues of the patient. It was possible to imagine Dr. Barnard moving confidently about the theatre in his stoical manner, uttering a stern word of reproach to his orderlies as he guided the heart into place.

Sometimes he'd watch the wax figure of Dr. Barnard, who was conducting his fifty-year-old procedure in perpetuity, and wonder what he would transplant for his father, if he could. A feeling? A dream? Just like Barnard's patient, something might be swapped but there was always the danger of rejection, that the old life would turn against its new blood.

Wale had confessed to Dayo during one of his drunken rants that all he had ever wanted to do was to go into space, which had embarrassed and frightened Dayo at the time. Maybe that was the dream his father needed again. A dissident who had escaped house arrest in Nigeria was now claiming on television that he could prove that officials at the highest levels of government had perpetrated shocking human rights abuses in the name of counterterrorism. He was calling for nothing less than to mark a new era of transparency with the launch of the country's first home-grown rocket, one that could take a manned mission to the moon and plunge a Nigerian flag into the dusty regolith.

Dr. Barnard would continue operating on his patient forever, but Dayo knew that his own visits to the museum wouldn't last. His father was too strong-willed to allow it. One day he would hear shouting in the corridor. He would turn to see the tufts of Wale's hair in the lamplight as he hobbled towards him. And then he would tell his father that it's happening. You can go there now. You can go up.

Notes on the Story

The bulk of this novel was written while I was living in South Africa. As such, there are certain assumptions about a reader's knowledge of South African and Nigerian culture. Rather than use footnotes, which change the nature of the format, I decided to add this section to make it easier to understand the story.

South Africa contains a variety of ethnic groups and the constitution endorses eleven official languages. The Coloured community that lives around Cape Town, on the Western Coast of South Africa, is descended from a mix of Malaysian slaves, indigenous groups such as the Khoi Khoi, Khoi San, and Xhosa, and Europeans. They speak a rich dialect of Afrikaans—a language which is itself comprised of eighty percent Dutch and twenty percent indigenous and other languages. Today most youth also speak English, mixing the two languages in clever ways as the conversation demands. Apartheid, the national legislated program of minority white domination, officially began in 1948 and ended in 1994 with the election of the African National Congress. The anti-apartheid struggle included surrounding—or 'frontline'—nations and involved everything from peaceful protest, to economic boycotts, to violent sabotage. The suburb of Observatory may be found in Cape Town.

Nigeria is situated in the bend of West Africa. The country has over two hundred and fifty ethnic groups and many distinct languages. The main character of this book is from the Yoruba tribe, which is primarily situated in the Lagos region, but historically extended deep into the country and thrived across colonial boundaries into French-speaking Benin. The Yoruba religion contains many gods and spirits, but some Yoruba people are also Christian or Muslim. The variety of proverbs in this novel are generally Yoruba with certain proverbs borrowed from other ethnic groups. Nigeria was once a British colony like South Africa. The majority of the population speaks English or pidgin, a fiery hodgepodge of indigenous languages and English. Part of this story is set between 1992 and 1993, when Nigeria experimented with democracy after decades of military rule. The country experienced a democratic election in 1998 and held its third election in 2011. At the time of this writing, ninety-eight percent of Nigeria's economy is fueled by exports of high-quality crude oil.

The last manned trip to the moon was the American National Aeronautics and Space Administration's Apollo 17 mission in 1975. Nigeria launched its first satellite, NigeriaSat-1, in 2003. A seventeen-year-old girl from Ebonyi state participated in Nigeria's first parabolic weightlessness flight in 2006 in a jetplane. She was called an astronaut.

The phrase "Bitter and black, halfway down, in the darkness" comes from Virginia Woolf in her stunningly beautiful 1927 novel To the Lighthouse. I had written a chapter around this passage, but it got cut because it wasn't any good. But the line lives on.

This is a work of fiction. It reflects reality inasmuch as it has to. Everything else is made up.

Acknowledgments

This text previously appeared in part in: World Literature Today (2009); Crime Beat South Africa (2011); Molossus (2009, 2012)

The book was created with the help of many skillful and talented people. Andre Wiesner was the original editor of the text, and gave a random bunch of scribbles some shape and direction.

I would also like to thank my literary agent Gary Heidt at Signature Literary.

Thank you to Mike Nicol, who inspired the noir elements of the book, and Marla Johnson, who has believed in me from the beginning. Malcom Cumming provided his insights into South African modeling and his short story "The Destination" prompted me to visit the Royal Observatory in Cape Town, without which the plot would have made no sense whatsoever.

Thank you as well to the following experts: Prosecutor P.J. Snijman, Abagold, University of Cape Town Law Clinic, and the Hermanus Library.

Nigerian proverbs were derived in part from Oyekan Owomoyela, University of Nebraska, Lincoln, The Good Person (website); Isaac O. Delano, Yoruba Proverbs—Their Meaning and Usage (Oxford University Press, 1966); Gerd de Ley,African Proverbs, (Hippocrene, 1999). General Yoruba lore came from: Allen Wardwell, ed. Yoruba: Nine Centuries of African Art and Thought (Center for African Art, 1989); Robert Farris Thompson, Black Gods and Kings (University of California, 1971) …and growing up part Yoruba.

Information about lunar rocks and the sample collection taken from: Grant Heiken, David Vaniman, and Bevan M. French, Lunar Sourcebook: a user's guide to the moon (Cambridge University Press, 1991). For the myths and legends of Harran, I relied upon Tamara M. Green, The City of the Moon God: Religious Traditions of Harran (E.J. Brill, 1992).

Thank you to my friends and family for your enduring support and love.

About the Author

DEJI BRYCE OLUKOTUN graduated with an MA in Creative Writing from the University of Cape Town, and also holds degrees from Yale College and Stanford Law School. He became the inaugural Ford Foundation Freedom to Write Fellow at PEN American Center, a human rights organization that promotes literature and defends free expression. His work has been published in Guernica, Joyland, Words Without Borders, World Literature Today, Molossus, The London Magazine, Men's Health, Litnet, and international law journals. A passionate soccer fan, he grew up in Hopewell, New Jersey.